Time Will Tell

Time Will Tell

A NOVEL BY

SUZANNE BUSH
&
DEB TAKES

PUBLISHED BY
Imagining
POSSIBILITIES, LLC

timeandtimeagainandagain.com

GWYNEDD VALLEY, PA

This book is a work of fiction, mixed with history.
The names, characters, organizations, institutions and events
depicted in modern-day New York are fictitious.
Any resemblance to actual people or institutions or organizations
is unintentional. Historical figures mentioned in the book are not fictitious.

Jacket design "From Shakespeare to New York City"
copyright by Stephanie Takes-Desbiens. Reproduced
with permission.
Photo of authors by Mary Loewenstein Anderson.

PUBLISHED BY

Imagining
POSSIBILITIES, LLC

timeandtimeagainandagain.com

GWYNEDD VALLEY, PA

ISBN 0-9747426-0-0

Acknowledgements

This book would not have been possible without the encouragement, help and support of several important people:

Walter Bender, who told us to follow our dream;

Guy Bush, a voracious reader whose questions, comments and suggestions made the book so much better;

Faith and Molly, who believed in what we had to say;

Mae McMichael, whose enthusiasm and support were sources of energy--especially when she asked for a new chapter because she couldn't wait to see what happened next;

Stephanie Takes-Desbiens, Deb's sister, for her beautiful cover artwork and for that wonderful telephone call to tell us how good the book was;

Mary Loewenstein Anderson, Suzanne's sister, for her beautiful photos and a memorable afternoon along the creek;

Delores Takes, who did all the wonderful things moms do;

Phil Freedman, an extraordinary editor who showed us how to tell a better story;

Friends and relatives who always believed that we would eventually finish this book and who didn't laugh when we sat down at the computer.

DEDICATED TO MOLLY M.,
NORA E., MOLLY E. AND LILY E.--
THE GIRLS WHO INSPIRED THIS BOOK.

*"Only dead fish
swim with the stream."
Anonymous*

It happened again today. Lily, Corky and I went to Becks after school, looking for the lip gloss we saw in XC. "Smooches & Cream" is so cool that even Mackenzie hasn't tried it yet. We wanted to get it before everyone else had it. The lady at the cosmetic counter heard about "Smooches & Cream," but she said it wasn't in stock yet. It must have been a slow day at Becks, because the lady decided to talk to us and even offered to let us try some other make-up. She was going on about stuff like bronzing gels "very in this year, what with the bad news about too much sun..." Then she looked at me. Like she just noticed me for the first time. "You certainly don't need any bronzing gel, with your complexion, honey" she said. Lily and Corky were turning bronze and not paying attention. Then the cosmetic lady told me she didn't think she had anything "appropriate" for my skin type. Why couldn't I look more like Lily or Corky? Why am I always too big or too dark or too everything? I wanted to die. It seemed like forever before Lily and Corky were ready to leave. They found eye shadow and lip gloss to go with their bronzing gels, and when we got out of the store they both looked like the girls on the cover of last month's XC. But I still looked like me...

Chapter 1

Late March in Manhattan isn't the happiest time of the year. The calendar says spring, but there's not much evidence that spring is even a possibility. The rain is not cold enough to be snow, but it's too cold to walk around in capris, a fuzzy top, and the season's must-have fashion accessory: strappy sandals. And if you are 12 years old and hoping to get invited to the Spring Dance (but pretty sure you won't get an invitation because Tyler doesn't even look at you when you pass him in the hall), spring can be downright sad.

Katie Farrell had a lot on her mind, besides Tyler. It wasn't that she wanted to be someone else, because, frankly, her life was pretty good. Who could ask for more than her wonderful parents, who were loving and happy and who wanted the best for her? She had Tuffy, the best dog in the world, even if he had a little attitude problem that made him impatient with people who didn't realize that his stature might be small but his impact on his world was huge.

When Katie's dad was trying to sound like he knew how kids talk, he would say that "Tuffy rules."

Katie didn't want to trade her life for anyone else's, but she would have been happy to trade her looks with almost anyone she knew. One lady who was visiting her mother said that Katie's face was "exotic," which Katie took to mean strange and difficult to classify. She never heard her friends, Lily or Corky, described that way.

Her friend Lily Hanover, for instance, was often referred to as "cute." Her dark brown hair was silky and long, falling to the middle of her back. Slight and wispy, like you might picture a ballerina, with big blue eyes and a small, pert nose, Lily could be Alice in Wonderland. That is if you put her in a blue dress with a white smock and threw her down a rabbit hole.

One of Katie's favorite characters was Alice in Wonderland, whose sense of wonder always enthralled Katie. She admired the way Alice dealt with some very confusing encounters. Often, Katie felt like Alice. Although she didn't fall down a rabbit hole, she did drop out of one life into another, and she often felt terribly out of place and out of step.

It was hard for anyone to talk about Corky without mentioning her startling green eyes, which were the same color as the leaves on the oak tree growing right in the middle of the yard at Katie's family's weekend home near Hyde Park. As assertive and outgoing as Lily was shy and reserved, Corky sported a "don't mess with me" attitude and a temper as fiery as her red hair. The package was oddly charming.

Corky was born in Ireland, but had very few memories of living there. She hadn't seen her dad in almost eight years. It had been a rainy, cold day and Corky watched her mother, Chloe, frantically grab clothes out of closets and dressers and stuff them into several large suitcases. Her father was out of the house somewhere. Corky and her mother left before he came back. She remembered riding on a train and then getting on a boat, and hearing her mother cry at night.

When they first arrived in the United States, Corky often asked her mother why her father wasn't with them. But she never got any answers, and it seemed to upset her mother to even think about it. So she stopped asking. But she never stopped wondering.

For Corky and Katie, spending time with Lily and her family was always fun. Mrs. Hanover loved baking, and was famous among Katie and her friends for her chocolate chip cookies. Saturdays with the Hanovers meant long walks in the park, or matinees, or bike rides or sledding—and sometimes helping Dr. Hanover at his veterinary office.

The girls would clean cages or walk dogs or feed the animals. At the end of the day, Mrs. Hanover always had warm cookies and hot cocoa ready for the girls. She called the ritual "high tea," but they called it "love at first bite," and they had great fun pretending they were members of some uppity royal family. The air was thick with nonsensical chatter in exaggerated English accents. Corky's accent was the most authentic, spiced with the Irish brogue she could never fully disguise. "Do tell, ladies," she would say, "d'ya think the prince will be havin' a spot of tea with us when he returns from the hunt?"

When the three friends were together away from school, Katie felt less like an outsider. But inevitably, something would happen that would awaken her self doubt and sense of being alone.

Once, the girls discovered a trunk full of Mrs. Hanover's old clothes. They were having great fun mocking the "disco fever" look of the dresses, and decided to try them on. Lily and Corky slipped easily into the clothes. Katie couldn't even get the most shapeless dress zipped. She grabbed a fringed shawl and wrapped it around herself, pretending that she was cold.

"Let's go see if your father needs help with the dogs," Corky said when she noticed that Katie seemed withdrawn. "I'll bet some of them need a good walkin'."

Corky always looked out for Katie, ever since they met at Manhattan Prep, the school the girls attended. One day, when Corky and

Katie were in third grade, stuck-up Brittany Morgan pushed Katie into a coat closet and locked the door.

She had turned to the gaggle of friends that always swarmed around her, and winked. They were laughing, enjoying the prank, despite Katie's terrified cries.

"And who d'ya think you are, Blondie?" Corky screamed at Brittany. "Are ya bold when you're not with your gang of thugs, then?"

"I'm only joking with her," Brittany said sarcastically. "Honestly, she's such a baby!"

Just as Brittany said the word "baby," Corky shoved her into her friends and unlocked the closet, freeing Katie. She turned around to face Brittany then.

"If you're lookin' for someone to pick on, Blondie, why not find someone deservin' of your stupid pranks."

A teacher coming into the room just then only saw Corky shove Brittany, and assumed that the tough Irish girl who was frequently in trouble for minor infractions had instigated a quarrel. Off to the head-master's office went Corky, with the teacher escorting her.

Corky lost her recess privileges for two weeks, but she gained a lifelong friend in Katie. The two girls were surprised when they realized that their mothers not only knew each other, but worked together! Corky's mother, Chloe, was a hairdresser and make-up artist, and Katie's mother, Charlotte, was an actress in a soap opera.

When she looked at herself in the mirror, Katie didn't see anything that even resembled her two best friends. She saw hair that was curly and black and impossible to tame. She saw skin that was neither white nor brown. It was an in-between color that refused to be pinned down to a name. Her eyes were so dark brown that she could barely see her own pupils. She saw a body that was round where it should have been nar-row. It was not a look that got on the cover of *XC*. Ever. And that sim-ple fact made all the difference to Katie these days.

Katie thought it a safe bet that her mother never worried about how she looked. She was the star of daytime TV's most successful soap opera, "Love's Labours." Her face could be summed up in one word: gorgeous. She got letters by the truckload from fans who told her how beautiful and smart and courageous and kind she was. They adored her.

Of course, those fans didn't realize that the Charlotte Farrell they saw on TV was only half as good as the Charlotte Farrell that Katie saw at home. On TV, Charlotte played a woman named Julia Devereaux, a crusading newspaper publisher in the suburbs of New York who struggled against the forces of evil and greed and jealousy. Julia Devereaux was the show's most beloved character.

Katie and her parents lived in a three bedroom apartment that took up a whole floor in the Shelbourne, a beautiful old building overlooking Central Park.

When Katie and her parents went out to dinner or even out for walks in Central Park, people stared at them. Some people waved and called out "Hey, Julia, don't back down to those creepy Montaines." Her parents were amused by the way people behaved, and the way people rooted for the feisty Julia Devereaux in her endless conflicts between the evil, blue-blooded, old money Montaine family and the hardworking, newly wealthy Capullanos.

Katie's father, John, was an English professor at Vassar College in Poughkeepsie, New York, and an author of several biographies of play-wrights. But once upon a time he was a graduate student at Columbia, looking for part-time work. He wanted to do freelance writing for a newspaper or a magazine, but wound up taking the first job offer that came his way. He became a script writer for "Love's Labours."

It was 1987, and he was supposed to write a sequence about a young reporter for a business magazine who was interviewing the patri-arch of the Montaine family. It was supposed to be a one or two-episode sequence that would highlight the Montaine family's vast empire of fac-tories, banks and other businesses.

The reporter, Julia Devereaux, was supposed to be beautiful and smart and was to be cast in the show for two episodes at most. Maybe it was John's spectacular writing.

Maybe it was Charlotte's incredible beauty and acting skill. But "Love's Labours'" fans didn't want to say goodbye to Julia. Thirteen years later, they still couldn't get enough of her. Even though John stopped writing for the show, Julia's character continued to enthrall view-ers and excite the show's advertisers.

When they told the story, Charlotte and John impatiently finished each other's sentences. How John asked to meet the actress who was to play Julia Devereaux. How Charlotte thought that was an insult to her acting. How John was worried that writing for a soap opera would become an embarrassment to him when he achieved writing success.

How Charlotte wanted the soap opera to be her springboard to a serious acting career. How they both were prepared to hate each other. And how, instead, they fell in love.

Their courtship, although exciting, couldn't compare to the way Katie came into their lives.

Chapter 2

In 1990, Charlotte spent three weeks visiting orphanages in Romania, as part of a United Nations mission to focus the world's attention on children orphaned by war and disease.

In 1989 the Romanian people had had enough of the poverty and misery caused by the despot who ran the country. They revolted, and overthrew the Communist government and Nicolae Ceausescu, one of the vilest and most corrupt people in the country's history.

The orphanages were bursting with children of all ages, some abandoned by parents who could not care for them, others orphaned by the country's bloody conflict.

It was a trip that would change Charlotte and John, and it would also change their future. It had started as a public relations effort. It almost ended prematurely.

The trip quickly drained Charlotte of her optimism and cheerfulness. She was on the phone several times a day with John, crying about the babies that would surely die of neglect and disease.

"John, I can't do this. It hurts too much to see these babies…to know what's going to happen to them." She was choking on her tears. The pain she felt was in her soul and in her heart and it gnawed at her even when she wasn't face to face with the orphans.

"I love you, and I'm so proud of you. I wish I were there to help you get through this," he said over and over. But her pain was also his. And he knew that his words were not enough to provide real comfort for either one of them.

At night, alone in her hotel room, Charlotte cried. She had nightmares about motherless children growing up without love or safety or the knowledge that they were not alone in the world.

In their New York apartment, John was miserable too. Nightmares and guilt and fear for Charlotte's safety made his nights seem endless and his days pointless. He had been storming around the empty apartment, cursing himself for not going along with Charlotte for the whole trip. He hadn't slept well in days and had become obsessed with the fear that something horrible was going to happen. *What was I thinking, letting her go there alone? What if something happens to her? What if we never see each other again?*

In the middle of the second week, he called the United Nations liaison who had arranged the trip.

"You've got to help me get to Romania," he said, without giving her a chance to argue. "Just tell me how to get the paperwork done and I'll arrange the flight. You'll need to give me an itinerary, so I can catch up with Charlotte's group."

"But, Mr. Farrell," she protested. "I can not make this for you..."

"You don't understand. I'm not asking you to help me. I'm telling you that you need to help me."

"Sir, it is complicated," she said, "but, they have...ah...how do you say it?...security. Your wife and the others, they are perfectly safe."

John was silent, and he thought about his days as a reporter in San Francisco, his first job out of college. There were lots of times when he had to bluff his way into meetings. *But this is different,* he thought to himself. *Those days I knew what I had to do. I knew what I was looking for. All I know now is that I have to get to Charlotte!*

"Look, I'm sorry. I know this sounds stupid. But, to be honest with you, I'm frightened and worried about my wife. She's having a hard time dealing with all the...the..." He struggled for the right word— one that would accurately describe his situation without offending this Romanian woman who had orchestrated the trip. *If it's so safe,* he thought to himself, *why is she still in New York while they're in some cold, dingy hotel hoping that they'll at least get a hot meal?*

"Please! I talked to her this morning. She needs me...I need to be with her." He was nearly overcome with the emotion and fatigue and the need to be with his wife. He felt as if he were on the verge of losing his temper, and that fact made him recognize just how desperate he was. He was hoarse and exhausted and the woman must have heard it all in his voice.

"Mr. Farrell. Listen. I will do as you ask. Please, you will give me the call in one hour and I make the information you need." She hesitated for a minute. "And…I happen to know that a plane to Bucharest goes this night at six. It goes out from JFK…you must know also that the trains not good in Romania today. I…I can make the ticket for you and help you."

"Thank you. Thank you." John whispered. "I can't thank you enough."

Charlotte had called him that morning, before leaving Bucharest for the city of Timisoara. There was a school that had been turned into a makeshift orphanage. The situation in Timisoara was apparently even worse than what they had seen thus far, and everyone was edgy about what would confront them the next day.

It was in this city, in the Banat region of Romania, where the revolution had begun in December, 1989. Timisoara is almost close enough to touch the borders of Hungary and what used to be Yugoslavia but is now known as Serbia. The revolution started with an act of resistance in the Metropolitan Cathedral.

A Hungarian Protestant priest, Father Laszlo Tokes, had denounced the regime of Nicolae Ceausescu, and was facing arrest for his defiance. He refused to leave the Cathedral, and suddenly the National Salvation Front, an underground movement opposing the government, emerged to unify the numerous protest groups that Father Tokes' actions had energized.

Even though they toppled the government, the revolutionaries could do little to help the children and other victims of Ceausescu's corrupt regime. Hunger, poverty and despair are not problems that can be solved overnight, as the children Charlotte met could tell you.

John put everything he needed in a backpack. The United Nations woman had given him several papers that would help him get from Bucharest to Charlotte, without any red tape. His flight seemed to take forever. It gave him too much time to think and to worry. He wanted to be with his wife, but he was worried about how he himself would respond, once he was face to face with the misery Charlotte had been describing.

He caught up with the United Nations group on their second day in Timisoara. They were having breakfast at the hotel. Charlotte was talking to one of the United Nations representatives who had been living in Timisoara for several months. She was telling Charlotte about Ceausescu's edicts about families. He believed that the ultimate success of his government would require large numbers of workers, and so his government policies strongly encouraged families to have lots of children.

Unfortunately, his economic policies were so ill-conceived that the country suffered from high unemployment, low wages, and rising rates of malnutrition, disease and other side effects of poverty.

Charlotte wanted to prolong breakfast and postpone the visit to the school-turned-orphanage for as long as possible, but she knew that she could not delay the group much longer.

"Charlotte!" John was about 10 feet from the table where she was sitting, and he couldn't stop himself from calling her name. She was momentarily confused by the sound of a voice she loved and missed desperately. When she turned toward the voice, she was almost overcome with joy.

"How did you get here? Why? I've missed you so much..." She practically cried as he kissed her and began to describe his journey. His train ride from Bucharest to Timisoara seemed to take longer than the flight from New York to Bucharest. But all that mattered now was the fact that John and Charlotte would face the rest of the United Nations trip together.

John gulped some coffee and grabbed a piece of toast. Then they went to visit a school that had been turned into an orphanage. There was a classroom that was filled with cribs, some with two and three babies. One of the United Nations people introduced the group to Sophia, a woman who had come to Timisoara in search of her husband. He had been one of the protesters who protected Father Tokes from the government's Securitate—the police force, and in the violence that marked the beginning of the revolution, he had vanished.

Sophia later learned that he had been killed near the Cathedral a few days before Christmas. She believed that she had nothing left to live for, and she stayed in Timisoara, to be closer to the place her husband died. She had no place to live, and no food. She went to the school where the United Nations relief group had set up a shelter for refugees. Grieving and in shock, Sophia wandered around Timisoara in the daytime, and returned to the shelter of the school at night. She was hungry, but could not eat. Eventually, she began to see that there were many other victims of Romania's tragedy. She recognized that the fates of the orphans she saw in the school were even more tragic than her own.

She had known love and companionship. Her husband was a hero. These children might never experience the things that Sophia had. To ease her grief, she volunteered to care for some of the children in the orphanage.

John had picked up a crying baby, and tried to calm her by humming and rocking her. "She's not even one years old," Sophia said, sadly. "Her mother dies one month before. No papa."

Charlotte looked at John, holding the baby who had grown quiet in his arms. Charlotte's eyes filled with tears at the sight of her husband and the baby. Her tears were not quite tears of sorrow. They were a mixture of joy, determination and sadness. As she watched him, she thought about what had been most upsetting to her throughout her stay in Romania. She was devastated by a sense of powerlessness, and overwhelmed by the tragedy of so many children with so many needs. She needed to be able to do something—just one thing—to give herself a sense of purpose and to start a process that could help these children.

Charlotte and John had often talked about children. Both agreed that their ultimate goal was to adopt children.

"There are so many children who need loving parents, and we have the love, the resources and the kind of commitment that can actually make a difference for these children," John had said.

Charlotte felt the same way, and had always yearned to adopt children, even when she was growing up. One of her mother's friends had adopted several children, and Charlotte loved the stories this woman told about how she and her husband had traveled to China and South America and Russia, each time for the purpose of bringing home a child to love.

That family was a loving band of several distinct cultures bound together by love. The family's image had stayed with Charlotte all her life.

"John!" she whispered as she knelt next to him.

"The baby has no one. Isn't this what we've talked about forever?

We're here together, there's so much we could do for this baby, so much we could give her." She had one hand resting on John's arm and the other gently caressed the baby's forehead. "I think this is our moment to actually do what we've always talked about."

The United Nations representatives and Charlotte had been talking about using this trip to encourage Americans to consider adopting Romanian orphans. Charlotte had been too overwhelmed by the endless stream of babies to think about what this might mean to her personally, but suddenly it struck her that she and John were meant to be here at this moment for this baby.

"Our moment?" John was looking at the baby, and he knew what Charlotte was thinking, but he wanted her to make the first move. Holding this baby felt so right to him.

"We could adopt her, she would be our daughter, we've talked about adopting a child…" Charlotte was talking so fast that she was breathless.

"Are we prepared to do this now?" John asked. "Yes, we've talked about it. But are we ready now?"

"If we're not ready now, seeing what we're seeing," Charlotte said, "we may never be ready. We don't always get to pick the time to fulfill a dream. Sometimes the time picks us."

They looked at each other, silently. Each imagined the way life would change for them, and they quickly realized that it was true. Time had picked them. Their lives were already changing because of what they were seeing and experiencing together.

"I love you," John said.

"I love you, too. I know this is the right thing for us."

At that precise moment, while John and Charlotte were staring at the tiny person in John's arms, the baby hiccupped, opened her dark eyes, and smiled at the two of them as if she knew what they were talking about.

They would come home from Romania as expectant parents—having begun the process that would bring this baby into their lives permanently. Because of her work on behalf of the Romanian orphans, Charlotte was given special consideration when she and John applied to bring the baby home. Katie wasn't even a year old when she became an American citizen.

They wanted the baby to grow up understanding her own heritage, as well as adopting the heritage Charlotte and John would bring to her life. They had been touched by Sophia's situation, and talked to her about possibly joining them in America. They believed Sophia could be a living connection to the baby's past, and that America would be an avenue for Sophia to build a new, hopeful future.

So that's how the Farrell party of two became a family of four—changed forever by the dark eyes of a baby in a city called Timisoara.

Sophia was grateful for the chance to escape the poverty and the darkness that had overtaken her. Thirty years old, and alone in the world, she had come to believe that she could never go back home. But there was really nothing for her in Timisoara, either. Her grief seemed to have no boundaries. The days and nights and weeks she had spent in Timisoara had proved to her that she would survive—that she could survive.

As she looked around at the rubble that was her country, and thought about what the next several years would bring to Romania, she thought that her life would get a better start in a place where there was stability and safety. She liked Charlotte and John, and thought that the opportunity they offered her would be a good way to start a new life.

They agreed to a one-year trial, after which they would decide if the relationship should continue. That was in 1990. For 12 years, Sophia, Charlotte, John and Katie had been a team. And Sophia had been working with the foundation the Farrells had created to provide medical care and support to the thousands of orphans they left behind in Romania. She arrived in America with nothing but a small valise containing the few things she still possessed. Although she never thought she would see Romania again, she never gave up her memories of the days in her homeland before things turned chaotic and tragic.

At first, Sophia was scared and timid at the enormity that was New York City. She couldn't believe the wealth she saw…shiny, fresh vegetables and fruits piled high on sidewalk displays alongside dozens and dozens of kinds of breads, cakes, cookies, and pies. The grocery stores were bright and clean, packed with beautifully labeled cans of foods she had never even heard of. Sophia loved the rich aromas of coffees and teas.

On the streets, cars stretched in noisy congestion as far as she could see. And the stores! Some sold only produce. Some sold shoes. Some sold luggage. *Whatever things you wants, you find here!* She thought to herself, marveling at the variety. *What for you needs same things in many colors? Who knows this? I can buy same shoes in red or white or black or green. Is amazing!*

Sometimes, she closed her eyes, scared that it was all a dream and that she would wake up and find herself back in Romania. She spent hours pushing Katie's carriage around the neighborhood. Occasionally, she would sit on a park bench and sing to Katie. The Romanian songs always calmed Katie, but they often made Sophia cry. She never thought she would get over the loss of her husband and her country. The gleaming stores and the masses of people and the neon lights were distractions, but in her heart, Sophia ached for the sound of her own language.

Sophia took care of Katie when her parents were working. Charlotte's rehearsal and shooting schedules on "Love's Labours," were not as regular as Charlotte would have liked, and John commuted to Vassar College four days a week to teach his classes.

Sophia soon got used to the energy of the city and, little by little, ventured a few blocks further than the day before when she took Katie out for a walk in her carriage.

"Today I tell you about your home," Sophia would say as she pushed Katie's carriage along the paths in the park. She would chatter to Katie about Romania—what it looked like, its history, the culture, the language. Soon Katie was learning Romanian words and phrases, which thrilled Sophia.

"Caine!" she would say, pointing at a dog.

"Politist!" she would shout, pointing at a policeman.

But the word that Katie loved best was "harta." She loved the "harta," the map of Romania her parents had framed and hung in her bedroom. It showed the historical boundaries of the country, and detailed the proud history of Katie's ancestors.

She would point at the map and plead with Sophia to help her learn the names of the cities and districts. To Katie, the Romanian map was a door into a world where she fit perfectly. It was a memento that always reminded her that she was special and cherished.

The time they shared forged a bond between Katie and Sophia. The bond stretched across continents and time and cultures and connected them both to their common history.

Despite the first harsh months of her life, Katie thrived in school. It's where she and Lily and Corky became inseparable.

It wasn't until she was nine that Katie began to realize how different she looked from her parents and the other kids at Manhattan Prep, where the most coveted look was slender and long. She was neither.

The "in" look for hair was shiny and smooth. Hers was curly and often impossible to tame. With her slightly rounded body, black curly hair that refused to be smoothed by brush and comb, olive skin and dark almond-shaped eyes, she stood out as different from the other kids at school.

Just like Alice in Wonderland.

The only thing the girls at school are talking about is the Spring Dance.
Who's going to ask who. Lily and Corky really want to go with someone,
and I think I do, too, but what if they get asked and I don't?
How embarrassing. And they'd feel badly,
going with dates if I wound up sitting with all the other losers
who couldn't get a date. Sophia says that boys in America are very
immature compared with the boys in Romania. That American boys
"don't know any good things when they see one," meaning me, of course.
But geez, when Sophia was in Romania, there was a war going on. I bet
no one there was worried about a Spring Dance.
They were probably trying to keep from getting shot. Maybe I'll get to
work with Tyler on the cell cycle project in science lab and we'll start
talking and he'll see how nice I am and HE'LL ASK ME TO THE
DANCE! Maybe not...

Chapter 3

Tuesday started dark and gloomy. Rain. And rain in New York
makes it look much darker than it really is. All those towering buildings
block the sky, so what little sunlight there might be gets stuck behind
skyscrapers.

Charlotte had to be at work by 6 o'clock that morning on the set
of "Love's Labours," and John had caught an early train to Poughkeepsie

for his classes, so the apartment was quiet except for Sophia singing some Romanian love song to herself and clanging around the kitchen making tea. Katie had eaten a bowl of yogurt with some berries. She finished half a glass of orange juice and went to her room to finish getting ready for school. She took one last look in the mirror, and she watched the humidity attack her hair, battling her for control.

She thought the gray and red plaid skirt of her school uniform and the gray blazer were the worst possible colors for her. In her imagination, the whole outfit was a conspiracy against her, to make her look like a cartoon character stuffed into a disguise. And this morning, her hair was making the uniform issue even more frustrating. She was thinking about different things she could do to harness what was quickly becoming a wild-looking mass of curls.

Why can't my hair be sleek and straight like Lily's? Or cute like Corky's? she thought, as she gathered all the curls up and twisted the nest into a sort of bun-ponytail on top of her head to see if it made her face any less round. It didn't. *I look like a pumpkin!* she wailed to herself. She agonized over her hair, even when there was very little humidity.

"Katie, your hair is beautiful," her mom always said. "You can't imagine how much people pay to get hair that's as curly and thick as yours."

"But I want your hair. I want my hair to be sleek," she protested. Sleek hair was a concept she and her friends had discovered reading *XC*. Like the lip gloss everyone wanted and the fuzzy tops, sleek hair—and the many ways to achieve sleek hair—got promoted heavily in *XC*.

"Honey, my hair is different from yours. It's not better. Your hair is perfect for you. It's natural and beautiful, just like you."

These hair conversations, like the "why-can't-I-be-taller?" conversations always ended the same way. Charlotte would tell Katie how much she loved her, just the way she was, and that she wouldn't want even one hair on Katie's head to be different.

Today, however, Charlotte wasn't there to reassure Katie. There was just the rain and the humidity and the fact that the Spring Dance was just a few weeks away and another issue of *XC* with even more examples of why Katie and her rounded body and curly hair and olive complexion would never, ever fit in.

Okay, maybe the Spring Dance was not actually what most people would consider a dance. True, there was dancing, but the event was designed more as a lesson in social skills for the seventh and eighth grade students. It was Giles Needham, the headmaster, who dreamed of turning out cultivated ladies and gentlemen as well as scholars. And so, the Spring Dance was created.

"We are pleased to announce the creation of a brand new program for the young ladies and gentlemen of Manhattan Preparatory School," Giles Needham's letter to parents began.

"We believe this program will become one of the most beloved of the many traditions of this school." Mr. Needham had approached the parents who were most active in the school's activities to get their ideas and their support for his idea. Katie's parents had been very involved in fund-raising for the school's scholarship program, and had personally donated thousands of dollars on behalf of that program. They jumped at the idea of a combination social event and fund-raiser, and even suggested a new program that could benefit from the fund-raising.

"We like the dance idea, Mr. Needham," John had said at their first meeting, "and we have a couple of ideas that might make it a successful fund-raiser, too." He and Charlotte had talked to Katie and her friends about Mr. Needham's vision of a new social event for the school.

"Mrs. Farrell, would you be startin' another party for the cool kids to turn their noses up at us again?" Corky was not thrilled by the idea of giving the snotty cool kids another reason to strut their expensive clothes and creepy attitudes.

"Corky, there are other kids in school besides Brittany and Jordan and their gang," Lily said. "Maybe a dance would be a good idea. The rest of us would get a chance to get together. Would we get to wear prom dresses, Mrs. Farrell?"

"All that is still in the planning stages. What do you think, Lily? Would you like to have a dressy kind of dance? I think you kids are way too young for prom dresses, but how about nice party dresses?"

"That sounds nice, I guess. Would we get dates?"

"Well, that might be a little too serious, since all the parents are expected to go, too. That would make the dates seem…I don't know, Charlotte…what do you think?" At this, all three girls gawked at Katie's parents, wondering if they were joking about the whole thing.

"How would this work, Mom? You and Dad and all the parents would go with us? *To…a…dance?*" Katie's questions sort of tumbled out before she had a chance to dial down the *how-could-that-be-any-fun* tone in her voice.

"We would be there, but not right in the room where you will be dancing. You kids would have a nice catered dinner and there would be a DJ so you could dance. The parents would be having the same dinner in another room, and we would be doing something different for the evening...we...your father and I...we weren't always this old. Believe me, we do remember what it is like to be your age."

"What's a catered dinner? Is that the stuff you and Dad get at your parties?"

"Maybe this would be a good time for you girls to learn about that old cliché that there's no such thing as a free lunch," Katie's father said, laughing. "You see, honey, Mr. Needham thinks you kids would have too much fun if he just had a dance and pizza party for you. So he's going to make you work for your dance by feeding you stuff you probably would never eat if you had the choice."

"John, don't scare them. It's not that bad, girls. Mr. Needham just wants you to experience different kinds of food, so that...help me here, John...so that..."

"So that someday when you and your clueless parents are eating at a fancy restaurant and someone puts a plate of snails in front of you..."

"Snails? We have to eat snails? No way! I'm not going to any dance if we have to eat snails!" Katie was practically gagging just thinking about it.

"Go on, then, Mr. Farrell. They wouldn't be makin' us eat bugs would they? Are you havin' fun with us, or something?" Corky could usually tell when Katie's father was teasing them, and enjoyed teasing him back. But she couldn't imagine why he would bring up something as unappetizing as a dinner of snails—unless there really was a plan to make the kids eat weird stuff like that.

"Thanks, John. That really helped. Maybe you'd like to tell them about Mr. Needham's plan for them to wash the dishes, too."

"Would that be after they mop up the dance floor, Charlotte? I'm trying to remember the sequence here."

"Mom! What kind of fun is this supposed to be? We're going to have to wash dishes?"

"Okay, girls. Here's the real story. Mr. Needham had an idea that the dance could be something educational, where you kids could learn about different countries and the foods that the people in other countries eat. Not snails, John! Corky, do you remember any of the foods you used to eat when you lived in Ireland? Things that you don't really get to eat here in the states?"

"Sure I do. My grandma was a fine cook, and was always treatin' us to these little meat pies—you don't get them here—we called them pasties. And in the morning, she made us boxty pancakes with bacon. Do ya think Mr. Needham will be servin' us pasties, then, Mrs. Farrell?"

"I'm not sure, honey. But Mr. Farrell will probably be calling your mother later to get her recipes. He always believed that he was meant to be born in Ireland. It was an accident that he was born in San Francisco instead. Anyway, don't you girls think it would be fun to try foods from other countries?"

"Mrs. Farrell, would our parents eat dinner with us, and then leave so we could dance?"

"Well, what do you think about that, Lily? Is that how you'd like it to be?"

"I don't know. I was just thinking that it might be fun if we could pretend that we were all at a fancy restaurant, eating. I mean, just our friends…I'm sorry…that didn't come out the way I wanted. I meant that we…"

"No need to explain, Lily. Mrs. Farrell and I know when we're not wanted. We're okay with that. We're used to people not wanting us around. Honest." Katie's father was pretending to be very hurt.

"I'm sorry, Mr. Farrell! I didn't mean…"

"Honey, Mr. Farrell is teasing you. Really! We want you kids to be straight with us, so we can help Mr. Needham turn this into something you and your friends will really enjoy. Actually, what we were thinking is that the parents could have the same dinner, but that we would have a silent auction to raise money for the international exchange program. We would bring you kids to the school, and you wouldn't see us again until the evening is over and we take you home."

"The international what, Mom?"

"We want to bring students from other countries to Manhattan Prep, and send some students to schools in other countries. A lot of public schools do that, but since we're a private school, we'd need to fund the program ourselves. What do you think? Would you girls be interested in going to another country for a year when you're in high school?"

"Just think, Corky, you could go to France, where they eat snails and frogs' legs and all sorts of things that I'm sure you'd love!"

"Mr. Farrell, don't be teasing me, now. They truly eat the legs off frogs, then? Are ya serious, or what?"

"I can see that you girls need to get out more. People say frogs' legs taste like chicken."

"Well, then, Mr. Farrell, why would they be wastin' their time pickin' away on those little froggy legs when they could be doin' less work for chicken?"

"As usual, Corky, you've made an excellent point. It does seem kind of silly, doesn't it?"

"So, girls, what do you think? A dinner and dance for you and your friends; a silent auction and dinner for the parents? And dressy clothes?"

"But no bugs or frogs, please."

"Right, then, Corky. No bugs or frogs on the menu."

"I think it sounds like fun, Mrs. Farrell." Lily was already imagining what her dressy dress would look like.

Mr. Needham was thrilled at the response, and the first Spring Dance was scheduled. Although dating, per se, was discouraged, the students immediately outmaneuvered every attempt by teachers, parents, school officials and other adults to keep the affair a family-oriented social gathering.

They managed to pre-arrange their dates, and planned to pair off once the parents delivered them to the school's cafeteria, which would be transformed for the event into a trendy bistro, or a South Sea Island, or whatever theme the students had decided they wanted to experience. Mr. Needham had agreed to let the students vote for which country would be the theme for the event. The overwhelming choice for this first Spring Dance was China.

After the dinner, there would be dancing. This was when all the girls would get to show off their fancy dresses and the "dates" they had managed to snag for the occasion. While many of the students actually would go to the dance without specific dates, it was clear that only the least cool students would arrive without plans to spend the evening dining and dancing with one specific partner.

"Katie! You are ready soon?" Sophia's voice brought Katie back to her out-of-control hair. Tuffy sat on the bed waiting for Katie to notice him and give him a hug and kiss. In his Staffordshire Terrier mind, the universe was built with him at the center. It dismayed and irritated him when anything disrupted that world. Katie was so intent on studying her reflection in the mirror that Tuffy yelped and quivered for attention.

"Tuffy, I haven't forgotten you. I'm having a hair crisis. You wouldn't know anything about that, though. Your hair is always perfect." He was on the floor now, leaping all around her feet. *Attention! At last!* It was what he craved from her. Since Tuffy couldn't have cared less about Katie's hair, he rolled over on the floor so Katie could rub his brown and white belly.

"You are such a spoiled dog," she teased. He sat up and looked at her with his little head tilted. His forehead was furrowed slightly, giving his eyes an expectant look. She laughed at the expression on his face. His left ear was brown, and the brown continued all around his left eye. The spot was shaped like a fried egg, with his eye being the yolk. His right ear was brown and white and the rest of his face was white, except for a couple of brown dots near his nose. When he looked at her that way, it almost seemed as if they were having a conversation.

"Why aren't you worried about the Spring Dance?" she asked. He dragged a sock out from under her bed and demonstrated how fast he could shake it. She tried to rescue the sock and he started running in circles, leaping onto the bed, off the bed, over Katie's backpack and books and other obstacles scattered on the floor of her room.

"Katie, come! You will be late to school. Everything outside goes slow in the rain." Sophia was referring to the traffic problems that were everyday occurrences, but became even more difficult whenever it rained. Usually, Sophia walked Katie to school, using the time to tell her about life in Romania, and the people who lived in Timisoara, where Katie was born.

"You know about the people called the gypsy?" She asked Katie one day.

"I've heard about gypsies," Katie said. "They're bad people aren't they? They steal from people."

"The gypsy is not all a bad people, Katie. They like to say 'Roma' instead of gypsy. Do you know they all are slaves before?"

"You mean like the people were slaves here in the United States?"

"Yes, Katie. The Roma was not treated good, but in 1864, was no more slaves. Still, though, people don't like them too much. I think because they have mysteries. They move from place to place all the time, and don't care about houses and cars and money. Some Roma play wonderful music, though. In big cities in Romania, Roma peoples play music on violins and some people thinks they are…what is the word…I think they say 'mystic.'"

Katie was fascinated by these stories, and it always seemed the 20-minute walk to school went by too quickly. But on rainy days, there were no walks with Sophia.

Sophia, the worrier, always took her in a cab when it rained to protect her from the wet weather, convinced that dampness caused colds. The cab rides left very little time for talk, and Katie always felt the day started too quickly when she was deprived of Sophia's history lessons.

Katie gave Tuffy a kiss on his left ear and one on his right. She pretended she was in one of those countries where people kissed that way. "I luff you, dahling," she said in her foreign accent. "Ta ta!"

Tuffy followed her out of her bedroom and down the hall, and ran into the closet to help Katie find her raincoat. *Out, out, out!* he thought. *I'm going out!!!!* Tuffy always assumed that anyone who was leaving the apartment was planning to take him, and it was hard to persuade him that was not always the case.

"No, Tuffy, I'm going to school. Sophia will take you to the park later."

"Cab will be here in minutes," Sophia said as she stuffed some tissues into the front of Katie's backpack. "You make your homework good?" she asked.

"I finished all of it. Even the math," Katie said.

"You found your train answer?" Sophia asked. It was a math problem that had confused Katie. She and her dad had worked on it last night, and Sophia was fascinated by the way the problem was presented. Two trains leaving one station, at different times and different speeds. She was amused by all the diagrams John had done to help Katie understand the problem. "In Romania," she said, "almost never one train leaves station. Two trains leaving same times is never." They all laughed at how Sophia solved the train problem.

Chapter 4

Dr. Hanover had dropped Lily off at school on his way into his office. Corky lived the furthest from school and she rode the bus every day. The three girls met at Corky's locker.

"Did you guys figure out the big math problem?" Lily asked.

"It was like the ones Mrs. Cannon put on the board during class yesterday" Corky said. "I think I got it right."

"I had trouble, too, but my dad helped me with it. We asked Sophia if one train left track A at 5 pm going 55 and another left track B at 5:30 pm going 65, which one would get to the station first. She said that in Romania they rarely had one train leaving, let alone two trains leaving for the same place," Katie said. Her friends loved Sophia almost as much as Katie did, and they enjoyed her take on life in America and the social issues that Katie and her friends obsessed about. When they talked to Sophia about how the cool kids treated them, Sophia was sympathetic but realistic.

"These kids, they don't know what is all about in life, so they thinks that being this *kooul* business is everything. They are very foolish, I think. Some days they will be very sorry they don't know anything but this *kooul*."

As the girls were laughing about Sophia's train story, Mackenzie, Brittany, and Jordan came around the corner. They were whispering to each other and laughing, seemingly engaged in the top secret goings on of the 7th grade. Mackenzie noticed Katie, Lily, and Corky and motioned for her two friends to stop talking. Without so much as an acknowledgement that Katie and her friends even existed, the cool ones silently passed the trio before resuming their secret chatter. They moved like a flock of birds, constantly signaling one another to turn this way or that, to stop chattering, to laugh. There were three of them, but often it seemed as if there were only one mind occupying three bodies.

"Wonder if they've been asked to the Spring Dance," Katie said.

"I'm sure of it, and they'll surely be gettin' their dresses from Paris or *Heaves Saint Larant.*" Corky said in an exaggerated and extremely nasal attempt to sound French. She could be so sarcastic at times, but it was almost always funny.

The girls were laughing at Corky's French accent, and didn't notice Henry Rathbone walking toward them. He was a computer geek, and was often the target of nasty jokes and harassment by some of the cool kids. Henry's dad had started a software company a few years ago. People called Mr. Rathbone a genius, and Katie thought that's probably where Henry got his love for computers. Henry could do anything with a computer.

Katie could only imagine what Henry's dad could do. Probably start World War III with the push of a button. Henry was really a nice guy. He was smart, but not in a show off way – he was genuinely very bright. Katie's mom said that Henry reminded her of Steven Jobs...whoever that was.

"Hey Henry," Katie said.

"Hi guys. How's it going?" Henry looked as though he wanted to say more. He stood near the three girls, but not quite in their group. For a minute, he seemed suspended there, like a puppet, uncomfortable and embarrassed by the shy silence that arrived with him. Then he muttered something that sounded like "gotta go," and walked off toward class.

"Katie," Lily said, "I think Henry might want to ask you to the Spring Dance."

"You're kidding," Katie looked surprised. "Why do you think that? Did someone say something to you?"

"I've noticed him sort of staring at you every once in a while during class," Lily said. Corky jumped right on the bandwagon. "Katie, what'll you be doing if he asks you?"

"I don't know. I still don't know why you think he will." Katie tried to imagine herself dancing with Henry. It just didn't compute, no pun intended.

"Do you guys think you're going to get asked?" Katie said trying to change the subject quickly before she became any more embarrassed than she already was. Lily got a little red-faced and started stammering. It became clear to Katie and Corky that she was keeping something from them.

"Okay, let it out," insisted Corky, narrowing her green eyes in mock suspicion. Lily looked as though she wanted the ground to open up and swallow her. She lowered her eyes and whispered softly, "Tyler called me last night and asked me."

Katie's heart sank with disappointment. Tyler, her Tyler, wanted Lily. *Well of course he did,* Katie reasoned. *Who wouldn't want Lily? She's cute and sweet and everything else that XC says girls should be.* But it still hurt. Katie knew Lily wasn't aware of her secret crush on Tyler. It wasn't Lily's fault that Tyler preferred her over Katie. She tried to be happy for her friend. She forced herself to smile and said, "Well, what did you say? Yes, I hope."

"Oh, I don't even know what I want to do." Lily was obviously conflicted, and it seemed that she wanted her friends to make the decision for her. "I told him I'd have to let him know. I felt somehow as if I would be betraying you guys if I got asked and you didn't."

Mercifully, Corky jumped in. "Of course you'll go with him, Lily. He's a cute one, he is, and the topper is it'll probably murder Mackenzie and her crowd that he asked you and not one of them. Ooh! I'd surely love to see their faces when they hear the news!"

"Corky's right," Katie agreed. "You say yes. Don't worry about Corky and me. The Dance is still three weeks away…" Corky elbowed Katie gently, saying "Katie and I'll be goin' together, just like ma always goes everywhere with Mrs. Farrell." They had said exactly what Lily had hoped to hear.

"You two are the best friends I've ever had! Are you sure you're not mad at me? Are you sure you're okay with this?" Lily put her arms around Katie and Corky. The bell rang and the three girls walked into their homeroom to begin another day at Manhattan Prep.

Chapter 5

Katie was looking forward to Social Studies later in the day, and the beginning of the class study of the United States justice system. She loved the idea of courts and juries and attorneys fighting over who was right and who was wrong. Who could have known on this rainy Tuesday in March, just how real the class project on justice would become?

The system of courts and all the laws seemed very logical and not at all like courts on television. Every year or so there was a trial story line in "Love's Labours," and Charlotte—as Julia Devereaux—was always somehow involved in the case, if for no other reason than to oversee coverage of it in the fictional newspaper serving the fictional town of Bishop's Pointe. Television was the closest Katie had ever gotten to the justice system, so she wasn't sure how much was true.

"The question today," Mr. Murwata announced solemnly, "is what constitutes justice." Katie loved listening to Mr. Murwata talk. When he said "constitutes," it sounded like "consti-tyeuts." His accent was so interesting, and he always told such vivid stories to explain how the system of government in the United States almost always succeeded in giving people the opportunity to do the right thing, and punishing them when they didn't take that opportunity. He was from Africa, and through the experiences of his early life, he learned a lot about justice and how many people in the world never find it.

Brittany Morgan spoke up since her father was a fairly famous attorney in New York. Mr. Morgan usually defended gigantic corporations in lawsuits.

"My father told me that our justice system is imperfect at best," Brittany said, trying to strike a serious tone. Katie wondered if Mr. Morgan had that opinion because he had defended guilty clients and gotten them off.

"Why did your father make that comment, Brittany?" Mr. Murwata asked. "Can you explain his reasoning?"

"I think it's because many times my dad wins because he's a better lawyer than his opponent. He did go to Harvard Law School, you know. It's not hard to win when your opponent graduated from a state school," Brittany explained as if the rest of them were dummies for not knowing this important fact.

"So your father believes that the guilt or innocence of those on trial has nothing to do with the truth?" Mr. Murwata asked.

"My father says that truth is relative," Brittany explained, not really understanding what she was saying.

"Well, class. Brittany has made some interesting points. What do you think about what she has said?" Mr. Murwata wanted to involve more of the class in the discussion.

"And what d'ya have to say about the statue of justice, the one with the blindfold? Isn't that supposed to mean that justice is blind?" Corky asked.

Katie admired Corky for taking on Brittany in this rather spirited debate. Brittany was definitely one of the cool kids and, if crossed, could become a powerful social enemy.

"Wonderful in theory, he always says," said Brittany smugly.

"What do you, yourself, think, Brittany? What is your opinion?" Mr. Murwata asked, gently.

"I think my father is right," she said.

"So, d'ya truly think that only people with the money to hire Harvard lawyers can get justice?" Corky practically screamed. "That's not right. How could that be right?" Corky's face was getting red, her anger a mix of resentment for the way Brittany and her crowd treated others, and her sense of loss for having no relationship or knowledge of her own father.

"Why is justice portrayed as being blind?" Mr. Murwata asked.

"What is that supposed to say to us?"

"I think it means that justice can't see how much your lawyer paid for his suit," Henry said. He was smiling, but Katie could see that he was actually pretty serious. Many of the students laughed. But Brittany and her crowd scowled at Henry.

"Does everyone agree with Brittany's father?" Mr. Murwata asked. "Or are any of you still a little bit idealistic about our system of justice?"

"I'll bet my father could arrange it so our whole class could visit a real live courtroom during a case he was trying," offered Brittany. She glowed as everyone in the class focused their attention on her.

She's used to being at the center of everyone's life, starting with her father, thought Katie. Her long blond hair was swept into a neat updo with curling tendrils framing her face. *She really is beautiful,* thought Katie, despondently. *Just like one of the models from XC.*

Katie also knew from her mom that Brittany's mother designed fabulously expensive jewelry. She was so famous for her designs that she only used her first name, Lydia. The kids knew her as Mrs. Morgan, but the movie stars who wore her jewelry creations (to the Oscars for gosh sakes!) referred to her as "Lydia."

"This necklace? Lydia designed it for me," an actress would explain to those reporters who swarmed all over celebrities making their ways into restaurants or airports or big ceremonies like the Oscars. The name said it all. "I'm rich, famous and dressed to kill, so of course I've got a necklace by Lydia."

"Well, class. How do you feel about Brittany's offer to take us all to court?" Mr. Murwata asked.

Mackenzie and Jordan both nodded and mumbled words of support for Brittany's suggestion. Katie had never been in a real live courtroom. Well, actually she had, when her mom and dad formally adopted her, but she didn't remember any of it since she had been just a baby during her citizenship ceremony. Rodney Sabol, a quiet, studious, intense young man, raised his hand.

"Yes, Rodney?" Mr. Murwata said.

"Wouldn't it be neat if Brittany's father was trying a case in front of my father?" Rodney casually mentioned, as if no one in class knew that Judge Sabol was one of the highest ranking judges in New York City.

"Oh Rodney," gushed Brittany, "wouldn't that be just delicious fun? Everyone knows that your dad is one of the most pro-business judges around."

Katie looked at Corky, who was sitting in the row beside her. She wondered if Corky knew what a pro-business judge was. As if reading her mind, Corky just shrugged her shoulders. Katie made a mental note to ask her father about it.

"Brittany, why don't you have your father give me a call or e-mail me, and I'll see to the arrangements. I think there would be no better lesson in justice than for all of us to see the law in action with Mr. Morgan trying a case, possibly in front of Judge Sabol," Mr. Murwata said.

"In the meantime, I think each of you should think about the questions raised in our discussion today, particularly Corky's questions about why justice is portrayed as being blind, and whether it's true that justice is something to be purchased by the wealthy."

Corky's face was now red with embarrassment, and it was clear that Brittany was not happy with the fact that Mr. Murwata chose Corky's questions as being important.

With the end of class rapidly approaching, Mr. Murwata jotted the class' homework assignment on the board. "Tomorrow, we'll discuss some famous American courtroom cases in history," he said. The bell rang and the class scrambled to gather their belongings and move on to fifth period.

Chapter 6

Fifth period was lunchtime for Katie, Lily, and Corky. They strolled to the cafeteria chatting about how much Brittany lorded it over everyone that her father was a famous attorney.

"But Corky," Lily said softly, "It was great that you made people think about the other side of things in class today."

"It was so cool, to see Brittany get cranky," Katie said.

"D'ya know what I can't see?" Corky said, her voice still angry. "Why does everyone think Blondie's father is so grand? Katie's ma is a real TV star. Don't ya think that's better than a lawyer?"

Lily nodded in agreement. "On a TV show that is one of the most popular in America."

"But Mom told me once that some people think people like her aren't really actors. They think that soap opera actors aren't good enough to make it in the theater."

"But your mom did work in theater, didn't she?" asked Lily.

"I don't remember it, but she was in some plays on Broadway and off Broadway when she started out acting She took the job on 'Love's Labours' to fill some time between acting roles on stage. Then she just stayed there; but that was before I was born," Katie explained.

"Well, I think your mother is great. Plus she's a lot nicer than Brittany's mom. Remember that time Mrs. Morgan came to the school play and made a big stink because Brittany wasn't the star?"

"Ooh, but do ya recall how she screamed at Blondie outside, tellin' her she would not have even come to the play if she knew the part was so meager. Sometimes, I think the girl is nasty just because her parents are that way."

"That was awful. My parents saw the whole thing and said they felt so sorry for Brittany. Katie, didn't your mother see it too?"

"I think so. She was pretty upset about it. She tried to say something, but Mrs. Morgan told her it wasn't any of her business. I can't imagine what it would be like if my parents talked to me like that."

"Ah, Katie, your ma would never say a harsh word to anyone. My ma says she's as sweet as jam, and treats everyone kindly. She says she's lucky to be workin' with her."

"Well, I think we're all lucky to have such nice parents," Lily said. Then she realized that only she and Katie had two parents. Corky's father was somewhere in Ireland, and nobody ever talked about him. She tried to change the subject quickly.

"How do Mackenzie, Brittany, and Jordan all manage to look like models even in these uniforms?"

Katie and Corky groaned. Frankly, it was depressing to always be comparing themselves to "the cool ones" and the less they talked about it, the better.

It seemed that when she tried to look like someone out of *XC*, Katie just ended up looking goofy. She decided that she was tired of thinking about it. She had ice cream for lunch.

But the three of them continued talking about the justice issue during lunch, and Katie noticed Henry sitting alone a couple of tables away from them. There was something spilled all over his books, and Katie realized that whatever it was had also gotten all over Henry. He looked so sad and lonely, and Katie felt guilty about not wanting him to ask her to the dance.

"And what do you suppose happened there?" Corky asked, gesturing toward Henry.

"Henry looks wet. Something is all over his books and…him!" Lily said. "I wonder how that happened?"

"Did ya see Blondie's face when Henry mocked her about the lawyers' suits? I thought he was bold to do it, and maybe he's payin' the price now."

32

Henry looked over at Katie's table, realized they were talking about him, and he gathered his wet books and ran out of the cafeteria. He came right by their table, but didn't acknowledge them.

"We think we've got it bad," Lily said. "They just ignore us, but those kids really are mean to Henry."

"Why do they pick on him?" Katie asked. "He never did anything to them."

"They live for the pleasure of makin' others feel inferior," Corky said. "They're creeps. Sure, they're cool creeps, but creeps, just the same."

Katie was confused. She couldn't understand why anyone would want to hurt other peoples' feelings. She thought about how she felt when Lily said Henry wanted to ask her to the dance. She wanted to be pretty and cool and look just like the girls in *XC*. She wondered what Brittany would do if Henry asked her to the dance? In a tiny corner of her brain, she wondered if she would be any more kind than Brittany would be.

*I wish I knew what really happened to Henry today, and
who keeps doing all those mean things to him. He looked so sad.
I want to be his friend, but I don't want to go to the dance with him. If I
try to help him, he might think I want him to ask me. Am I as mean as
the people who dumped stuff all over him? What if they did that to me?
I want them to like me, but I hate the way they treat people who aren't
cool. What if they did something to Corky or Lily? What would I do?
Why don't they like us? They all look so perfect all the time. They're all
thin and pretty, just like the girls in XC. Maybe they think I'm too ugly to
be their friend. I wonder what it's like to be that pretty and perfect. I
wish I could explain it to Mom, but I don't know what to say. It's all so
confusing. But Mom seems sad, too. Last night she was crying when she
got home. Someone was mean to her at work. I need to ask her about
Henry and the kids who are mean to him, and why they hate him. I need
to ask her why I'm so afraid that he'll ask me to go to the dance with
him. Sometimes I think I was caught in some kind of time warp, like I
belong in another century before anyone ever knew about XC or sleek
hair or perfect bodies...*

Chapter 7

"Actors, actors, where are my actors?" The director was getting
impatient and angry. For several weeks now, the taping of "Love's

Labours" was an unlovely labor, because one of the stars of the show, Stewart Mason, kept disappearing. Or forgetting his lines. Or throwing tantrums that would make the world's most spoiled three-year-old look like an angel. Stewart's character, Randolph Montaine, was a rich, arrogant, greedy businessman. Lately, it seemed, Stewart the actor was acting too much like Randolph the rich guy. "Someone find Randolph, PUHLEEZE," he pleaded. "Time is money and we're not getting any richer here." His voice grew louder by the second, and those who actually were on the set, in their places, were getting cranky, too. "Tick tock!" he boomed, finally. His assistants scattered, anticipating major fireworks if Randolph didn't materialize quickly. "I swear that Randolph is looking to get fired," the director muttered to himself.

Charlotte was ready, waiting, and one of the most frustrated people on the set. Stewart had been having a difficult time remembering his lines lately. While it might have usually taken two or three takes to capture a scene on tape, recently it had been taking a dozen before the director was satisfied. Rumors were flying around the studio, some claiming Stewart had a drinking or a drug problem. Others said that he was trying to cope with serious personal problems. Whatever the reason for the actor's problems, all the extra takes were causing the days to run from early in the morning until 7 or 8 at night.

Charlotte didn't like missing Katie at both ends of her days, and she especially didn't like the fact that she was now on the verge of missing dinner with her family for the fifth night in a row.

She was angry for another reason, too. When Stewart's problems first began to affect the show, she tried to take him aside to find out what was bothering him. Although Charlotte and Stewart weren't good friends, they had always respected each other.

"My dear," he said in a voice that sounded more like the character he played than the actor Charlotte had known for years. "You need to check the calendar, and get ready for that inevitable day when the people who run this stupid network decide that you no longer cut it with the 'target demos.' Time is not on your side."

Charlotte and everyone else in this business understood the basic relationship between the show and its advertisers. Advertisers paid a lot of money to reach specific consumers. Young married women, for instance, or teens—people with lots of money to spend on their products. While the storyline itself was important, it always seemed that the most important ingredient was the quality of the audience. Quality being defined by the advertisers, not the audience.

Occasionally, representatives from the advertising agencies would sit in on script sessions, and they would comment on the story. Lately, it seemed, they were there almost every day. "This seems to skew a little downscale," they would say in the jargon that seemed to make sense only to them and their counterparts at the network. "This'll move the meter in the teen target!" they might exclaim about episodes that featured the youngest actors in the show.

Charlotte ignored Stewart's comment that day, but it began to bother her a few weeks later when she had questioned some ideas that were discussed in a script meeting.

"It seems as if we're changing several of the characters and what motivates them," she said. "Victor and Roberto don't have any history of involvement with hoodlums and drug dealers. Why are they suddenly getting mixed up in something like this?"

There was silence in the room. Charlotte felt as if she had asked a question that everyone had already discussed without her. One of the advertising agency representatives smiled at her and winked at the others sitting around the table. "Charlotte…uh, may I call you Charlotte? We've done some audience research, and it seems that viewers are getting a little tired of the…let's call it 'high mindedness' of all the people in the show. They want a little *excitement*, a little something to shock them, if you will." He emphasized the word "excitement," and hesitated momentarily after saying it.

"Shock?" Charlotte didn't like the agency guy, and felt as if he were talking down to her. "Where are we going with this?"

"Don't worry, love, the audience still worships you. They still see you as young and 'with it.' But we want to push some buttons with a key demographic group. They respond to a little more *action*." There was that inflection again. And Charlotte was no longer a person with a name. Now she was some nameless creature called "love," and she could feel herself losing her temper.

She clenched her teeth, and tried to sound polite, but several of the actors sitting around the table seemed startled by what she said. "I'm sorry. Actually, even my husband doesn't call me 'love,' and I would appreciate your not calling me that either. I asked about the script, and why we're turning these two young men into thugs. Frankly I don't care about your key demographics or the buttons you want to push. What I do care about is this show, and how the changes you're—are you demanding them, or asking for them, or suggesting them—looking for will affect the quality of the *product* we've been delivering customers for several years." She emphasized the word "product," to mimic his arrogance.

"Oops! My bad. Didn't mean to offend you, *Charlotte*," the agency guy said, adding an extra syllable to her name. "Of course, you don't need to take our suggestions. We're just here because we're interested in the show vis-à-vis moving product for our advertisers." His tone of voice was more like that of a parent explaining life to a child. Along with all the clichés he used, he had somehow managed to expose one of Charlotte's biggest fears about her future with the show—and with her career in general—as she grew older. That meeting had ended rather quickly, because they had a full day of rehearsing and shooting ahead of them. But it bothered Charlotte all day. By the time she got home that night, at 8:30, she had missed dinner and helping Katie with her homework, and the family time that meant so much to her. Tired, frustrated and feeling insecure about her career, Charlotte had gone to her room and cried. She was not looking forward to the next day of shooting, and the possibility of more meetings with the agency people.

"What's wrong with Mom?" Katie was worried. Her mother was always so cheerful and happy. It was unusual to see her crying.

"Someone was mean to her at work today, honey. But she's all right. Honest." John wanted to reassure Katie, but he was worried, too.

"How could anyone be mean to Mom? She's so…beautiful and wonderful."

"Honey, it doesn't have anything to do with the way your mother looks or acts. It's just that there are some people who are mean."

Katie tried to match her mother's troubles at work with her own conflicts with the cool, popular kids at school. The more she thought about it, the more confused she got. She had always believed that the cool kids didn't like her because she wasn't thin and pretty, because her hair was curly and her skin was that in-between color that nobody knew exactly how to describe.

"Why, Dad? Why are they mean?"

"I don't know, honey. Sometimes it has more to do with things that happen to people before we ever meet them. Sometimes people just don't know how to deal with things that frighten them or worry them."

"Grownups are afraid of things? What are they afraid of?" Katie felt as if some kind of window was opening. She wanted to look at what was beyond the window, but she was a little scared about it.

"Honey, everyone is afraid of something. Your mother and I worry about you, about making sure you're healthy and safe and happy. We want to protect you from every possible bad thing that could happen. The point is that we all have to take positive steps to deal with our fears."

"What steps?"

"For one thing, we take you to the doctor and the dentist for regular check-ups." Katie's dad didn't want to create new things for Katie to worry about, but he wanted to assure her that he and Charlotte and Sophia were always there to protect and care for her.

"But what about the people who were mean to Mom? What are they afraid of?" Katie hoped that her father's insights could help her figure out why some of her classmates behaved so badly.

"I don't know what they're afraid of, honey. Maybe they're afraid of losing their jobs. Maybe they're afraid that people won't respect them. Maybe they're afraid that what they're doing with their lives isn't important enough."

"Are people mean to you at work?"

"No, honey…well, sometimes people where I work get jealous of each other, and that makes them do mean things. But it's usually pretty obvious why they do them. People where your mother works have a lot of different things to worry about. I'll bet most of them don't even know they're being mean—or if they do know, they don't know why they're being mean."

He started wondering if there was something else on Katie's mind. *Is she feeling insecure? Is it starting to bother her that she's adopted? Does she think she won't fit in because of that?* He was starting to think the discussion was heading toward a larger issue that might be a little too difficult for Katie to handle. While he knew that he and Charlotte would eventually have to talk to Katie about Romania and the more grisly realities that children Katie's age still faced there, he didn't want to talk about it yet.

"Are you afraid of things, honey?" He hoped he could change the direction of the discussion.

Katie wanted to talk about her problems at school. But she was afraid that her father wouldn't understand. Her silence concerned her father.

"Katie? Honey, are you afraid of something?" He had pulled her close to him on the sofa, and was patting her shoulder reassuringly. Tuffy was sitting next to her, and seemed to be waiting for her to answer.

"Something happened at school today. Some kids were mean to Henry. I guess I just don't know why they don't like him."

"What did they do to him? Did they hurt him?" John tried to temper his concern, and control his tone so Katie would tell him what happened.

"I don't think they hurt him. But they made him sad. I think they poured soda on him, but I didn't see it happen. It just seems like every day, something happens to Henry. One day he tripped on the steps and cracked his glasses. Then someone stole his clothes while he was in the shower after gym class...I don't know, maybe it's nothing, but..." Now that she had said these things out loud to her father, she worried that she had started something worse than what had already happened.

"Are you sure these things—the tripping and spilling—weren't accidents?"

Katie realized that she didn't have any actual evidence. She and her friends believed that the things they had been seeing were mean-spirited pranks. But now, she wasn't sure.

"I don't know. It's just that they're so mean to people that aren't cool like them." Katie wanted the discussion to end, but she couldn't find the right words to make her father stop asking her questions.

"How are they mean? Are they mean to you?"

Katie thought about it for a minute. Tuffy had moved onto her lap, and was distressed that she wasn't paying enough attention to him. He pushed her arm with his nose, made a couple of whimpering sounds and then jumped to the floor and started running circles around the coffee table.

"They don't do anything, Dad. They just ignore people who aren't cool."

"What does it mean to be cool?" John asked. He wanted to believe that there wasn't any real bullying, and he thought the topic of what's cool would be easier to discuss with Katie at 9:30 at night. Her bedtime was approaching, and he wanted to make sure she was not feeling stressed. Charlotte had begun to feel better—actually she was feeling a little embarrassed about crying in her room about the stupid problems at work. She found Katie and John in the living room and joined them on the sofa.

"What are we talking about? Can I join the conversation?" she asked cheerfully.

"We're talking about cool," John said. "How do people get cool?"

"Dad, it's not that simple." Katie said. "You can't just say you want to be cool. It's something else. I think you've got to be born with it." She said it so seriously. She had one of Tuffy's toys in her hands, and she was absently waving it at the dog. But it struck John funny and he had to stifle the impulse to laugh.

Charlotte smiled at him and then made a face at him to get him to take this more seriously. "Honey, why is it important to be cool?"

"Because the cool kids are so pretty. They look like the girls in *XC*." Although Katie was getting sleepy, she didn't want to leave the sofa. Having her parents close to her made her feel safe and happy. Charlotte thought for a minute about the magazine and the way it seemed to give Katie and her friends all the wrong ideas about what's important.

"Katie, honey...matching someone's ideas of what's pretty seems like the most important thing right now. But there are more ways of being pretty than you see in that magazine. You're a beautiful little girl. But more important than that, you're a kind, sweet, compassionate girl, and you are good to your friends. You care about people, and about animals. Those are the things that will last forever." Charlotte kissed Katie and hugged her. "Your Dad and I love you more than anything in the world. Don't ever forget that."

The three of them walked down the hall to Katie's bedroom, with Tuffy leading the way. He leapt onto Katie's bed and burrowed under the covers. *This is the best,* Tuffy thought. *Everyone's watching me!* The sight of the moving lump under the covers made them all laugh. Katie pulled the covers back, exposing Tuffy and the stash of toys he had near the foot of the bed. She grabbed the dog, and curled up in bed with him.

"Lights out!" John said, as he kissed Katie goodnight. "Sweet dreams, my love." Charlotte stroked Katie's cheek. "And as for you, Mr. Tuffy, don't keep Katie awake all night with your toys."

Katie's parents left her room and returned to the living room, where Charlotte described the horrible day she had.

"Have you talked to Sylvie? She might have some ideas about

how you could put some pressure on the producers to back off a little."

Sylvie Campion was Charlotte's agent. Flamboyant and often cranky, Sylvie had been representing Charlotte for years. She had become part of the Farrell's extended family, and was fiercely protective of everyone in the family, from Charlotte, to John, to Katie and to Sophia. She even adored Tuffy ("And who wouldn't?" she would ask if anyone wondered why). Sylvie carried a cavernous brief case-purse-lunch bag-gym bag. When she visited the Farrell home, this sack was one of Tuffy's favorite places to relax. It had an additional charm for Tuffy: Sylvie often brought little treats for him, which she usually "forgot" to give him. He understood her forgetfulness, and thoughtfully extracted them for himself. They were always in the same place, a small pouch on one side of the bag.

"I've got about a two-hour break tomorrow when I don't have to be on the set. We're planning to have coffee and talk about this."

"Char, you know that you don't have to keep doing this. You've had so many offers from other producers. And there are other projects you've talked about, too. Maybe this is a good time to step back and think about what you really want to do."

They were sitting together on the sofa, so close that they were whispering to one another.

"Can you imagine Sylvie taking on that marketing guy? I'd pay just for the privilege of watching her explain the concept of good writing to him."

"I know," Charlotte laughed. "Sylvie would start by tossing that sack of hers onto the table, crushing everything. Then she'd start drumming her fingers on the table, flashing that huge diamond ring—and then she'd probably ask him how old he is."

"Seriously, though, Char. She could probably give you a lot of support on this."

"I know, honey. I hope we can get something resolved tomorrow—maybe come up with some kind of plan."

Chapter 8

The alarm clock jolted Charlotte awake, and she felt as if she had hardly slept at all. John had tried to reassure her and bolster her self-confidence. In her heart, she knew he was right, but at the same time, she saw signs everywhere at work that things were changing dramatically.

The day had gone pretty well, with rehearsals and pre-planning for some location shots that would be needed for an upcoming sequence. Charlotte and Sylvie had met and talked about what Charlotte saw as storm clouds gathering on the horizon.

"It's not going to affect things immediately, Sylvie. But I can see that these people are insinuating themselves into every aspect of the show. It really scares me."

"What are you scared of? That they'll replace you, or that they'll ruin the show?" As usual, Sylvie approached the problem in a no-non-sense manner. It was her way of making people focus, she said, when people told her how undiplomatic she was.

"I guess I'm scared of losing the sense of control I have always had. It used to be that the network respected us and the show. That always made me feel as if our ideas meant something to them. It gave us all the...I don't know what to call it...inspiration, maybe?...to give our best every day, every shot."

"Empowerment. I think that's what you're losing." Sylvie had taken a notebook out of her bag and was writing feverishly. "The whole universe has changed, Charlotte. It doesn't matter anymore what they throw onto TV, as long as it brings the network more money. The perspective is changed. When your underlying strategy is to provide quality programming, then that becomes the driving force. When your underlying strategy is to make as much money as possible to impress Wall Street or Madison Avenue or whoever, then there's really no room for thinking about quality, is there?"

"That's a pretty depressing thought."

"But true, don't you think? Think about it, Charlotte. Look at what's happening to all the media. Remember the story you told me about that newspaper where John worked? The company that bought the newspaper didn't care that reporters like John and those guys who won that Pulitzer Prize really cared about what they were doing. What was the first thing they did? They dumped about 30 people onto the street— people who had invested their lives in that newspaper. And the second thing? They cut out about half of the coverage of local news. When was the last time you heard about media honchos investing in things that raise standards of quality and excellence? I swear, in my next life I'm coming back as a billionaire, and I'm going to use my money to make life miserable for these idiots who can't see anything past the next quarterly earnings report."

Sylvie was getting up a full head of steam on what was rapidly becoming one of her favorite issues to rant about. She pounded her fist on the table so loudly that everyone in the coffee shop turned to see what all the fuss was about.

"Just look at that pile of garbage the kids are all reading, *XC*. What is that all about? You would think that anorexic blonds with pierced bellies and iridescent eyelids are actually role models!" Sylvie had very little patience with superficiality. And, unfortunately, she was finding more and more of it everywhere she looked.

"You know, there are some good things in the magazine. I just wish they wouldn't focus so much on purely physical things. Last month they had a very good article about the Hollywood actresses who are starving themselves so they can wear size zero clothes. But they ruined the message by showing a model who had 'recovered' from anorexia. She couldn't have weighed more than 95 pounds—and the magazine portrayed her as healthy! Naturally the photo spread showed her in those low-cut jeans and a top that barely covered her breasts. The girls take it so seriously. John and I try to read every issue and then talk to Katie about the articles. But the images—of those girls with such perfect bodies and perfect skin and perfect teeth—are so powerful. They really overwhelm kids."

"Well, honey, I know we've gotten off the topic of what is happening to your show, but the point is that there are a lot of issues that are causing the people at the network to behave this way. I'm going to make some calls today and see if there is something else driving the people who are interfering with production of 'Love's Labours.' Maybe we can at least get them to back off."

Even though Charlotte and Sylvie didn't solve any of the problems that were bothering Charlotte, she did feel better after their meeting, and her mood definitely improved.

Everyone had returned from lunch anticipating a relatively smooth afternoon of shooting.

But here they were again, the agency guy and the network marketing director, calling another meeting. Same agenda—different day. Charlotte and the other actors were anxious to start shooting. The director was anxious to start shooting. The crew was anxious to start shooting. The writers were anxious to start shooting. But all their collective energy was put on hold again, as the two marketing experts laid out more ammunition to back up their script ideas.

They dragged the group through a seemingly endless presentation of graphs and pie charts and summaries of focus group interviews. They talked about everything but creativity and quality and integrity.

"All we're looking for is a little more action-oriented story, which this particular demographic group responds to. It's the sort of story lines your competitors are running quite successfully." The agency guy tapped his pen lightly on the edge of his laptop computer, almost daring Charlotte to challenge his research and his participation in the script session.

"Action-oriented?" Charlotte said. "They're saturated with violence and racial stereotypes. They're written as if young people have no brains and no aspirations higher than getting drunk and wearing ridiculous clothes. And as for the demographic groups you're hoping to impress by turning two characters into thugs, maybe you should think a little harder about what you're saying about those groups."

"I know you theater types don't like outsiders getting too involved, but you shouldn't think of us as outsiders. We're part of the team here. When you win, we all win."

"But you can't burn these two characters, just to 'push some buttons,' because then what do you have after there are no more buttons and you've ruined these guys?" Charlotte could feel herself getting emotional, and she looked around the room to see if anyone else was as upset as she. It was almost 4:30, and the other actors, the director and a few of the people on the crew were getting restless. They agreed with Charlotte, but knew that nothing would actually change. At least not that day.

The director seized the moment of silence to end the meeting. He stood up, poured himself some coffee and moved toward the door. "Everyone ready to shoot? We start in five minutes."

Charlotte left the room, angry and filled with a sense of dread. She went back to the area where the show's hairdressers and make-up artists worked. Corky's mother, Chloe, had been Charlotte's make-up artist for 10 years, and the two of them enjoyed an easy and close relationship. As Charlotte was finding out more and more lately, the TV world could be cutthroat, but she trusted Chloe implicitly.

"What in the name of all that's holy happened there?" Chloe asked Charlotte. She was pointing a hairbrush in the direction of the room where the script meeting was breaking up. Charlotte slumped in the chair with a sigh of sadness and frustration. The script meeting had disturbed her, and added to the tension she was feeling about the show.

"I'm not sure, exactly," Charlotte said. "But it seems as if they're trying to take the show in a different direction. I guess they think that if they add some violence and more sex, they can attract more viewers to the show."

Chloe put the finishing touches on Charlotte's lipstick and patted her hair lightly. "I don't know about the rest of this sad-lookin' crew, but you're all ready to go. Now just get that frown line off your lovely face," she said cheerfully. Her Irish accent almost made it sound as if she were singing. "It'll all work out. The devil always loses in the end."

Charlotte made an exaggerated expression of happiness and good cheer—like a happy jack-o-lantern on Halloween—which made Chloe laugh. "That's the ticket, my girl!"

The director was stomping around the set, yelling for his actors to take their marks. "Let's see how many takes we're going to need today,"

45

Charlotte whispered to Chloe as she headed toward the set. "I still don't see Stewart, though."

The scene they were shooting involved Randolph Montaine, along with Charlotte's character, Julia Devereaux, and two of the Capullano brothers, Victor and Roberto. As usual, the Montaines and the Capullanos were engaged in a bitter rivalry over something both families wanted. Although the story line had, in the past, had them fighting over companies, inventions, political candidates, land, and even artwork, their current feud was over Julia Devereaux's newspaper. The Montaines wanted the newspaper because they wanted to silence Julia's unrelenting criticism of the Montaine empire. The Capullanos wanted it because the Montaines wanted it.

Sam Harris, the director's assistant was nervously pacing near the dressing rooms. Every time the director screamed for the actors, Sam cringed. Although he was in charge of the thousands of details that went into producing each day's episode of "Love's Labours," Sam was easily unnerved by the things he could not control. Like actors who vanished.

The actors playing Victor and Roberto were on their marks. Charlotte was where she was supposed to be. But the patriarch of the Montaine family was nowhere to be found.

After a half hour of searching the dressing rooms and the sound-stage, and all of Stewart's known hiding places in the studio, the director called all the actors together. "We can't do this without Randolph. Let's call it a day and pick up tomorrow morning." There was loud grumbling from the actors, the stagehands, the technicians and everyone else who was inconvenienced by one actor's failure to appear. "People! People!" The director shouted above the grumbling. "Let's make it a 7 a.m. call. That's it. Go!" He waved his arms to emphasize that everyone was dismissed. Then turned to his assistant. "Sam, get me Stewart's agent on the phone, NOW," he shouted as he stormed off the set.

Charlotte hurried to change and remove her stage makeup. "What a waste of an hour," she said to Chloe. "All that work for nothing! At least Stewart's lack of consideration has one benefit, though. I'll actually get to have dinner with John and Katie tonight. We've been working so late that I've hardly seen them during the daylight hours!"

"I know what you mean, Charlotte," said Chloe. "My ma's been staying with Corky after school until I'm home. Our building is nice, but the girl shouldn't be alone. She's only 12, you know. Ma says I'm too much the worrier, but…"

"No, Chloe, you're right. I don't know what I'd do without Sophia. Do you want to share a cab home?"

The two left together and caught a cab. It was a quick ride uptown for Charlotte, and she gave Chloe a quick hug in the cab as she got out in front her apartment building. "See you tomorrow, as the drama of the missing Stewart continues," she laughed.

Chapter 9

"Surprise! Guess who's actually coming to dinner!" Charlotte was so happy to be home early that her concerns about the show melted away. "Charlotte? You're home on time. Better day today?" John asked as he gave her a hug.

"Stewart took off during the middle of shooting. He was nowhere to be found so the director called it a night with one scene left to shoot for the next episode. I have a feeling Randolph is about to have plastic surgery," explained Charlotte.

"Plastic surgery" was what happened when soap opera producers decided to replace an actor. The character would be involved in a terrible accident, like a car crash, and need extensive plastic surgery. When the bandages were removed, voila! A new actor was introduced.

"Mom?" Katie bounded down the hallway in her socks, sliding along the hardwood floors with Tuffy barking and running after her.

"You're home!" Katie cried, as she slid into Charlotte's open arms. "Guess what! Yesterday Lily got asked to the Spring Dance. By Tyler. She wasn't going to go because she felt bad that she got asked and Corky and I didn't, but we talked her into going, and then Corky got into an argument in Social Studies with Brittany and Mr. Murwata said Corky was right..."

Katie blurted all this news out so quickly that she was suddenly out of breath. She hadn't been able to talk to her mother about all these things the day they happened, because Charlotte had been so upset when she came home from work.

"Well, that's a lot of breaking news. Julia Devereaux would stop the presses," Charlotte said smiling at Katie, and tousling her hair. "Sophia, something smells absolutely heavenly," Charlotte continued as she put her arm around Katie and began walking towards the dining room. "Is that Shrimp Scampi?"

"I make Shrimp Scampi like was on the TV today with 'In the Kitchen with Mama,' and Mama says this is a good dish for the season. The fish market, it have beautiful shrimps today," Sophia explained. "So I try something new. You sit down and relax. Was the day good?"

"Oh, Sophia, it was a day that was filled with the usual drama of 'Love's Labours,'" Charlotte said with an exaggerated sigh. "We temporarily lost our Randolph, so we called it quits early. I'm so happy to be home on time."

"Mom, and guess what else? Mr. Murwata is going to take us to a real live courtroom. Brittany said her father could get us in to see a trial. And Rodney Sabol was going to see if his father, who's a judge, could talk to us."

"A field trip to court. To hear Kyle Morgan defend one of his clients. Sounds like you're in for some drama of your own, honey. Mr. Morgan is supposed to be a brilliant lawyer," Charlotte mused.

"That's exactly what Brittany said about him," Katie said.

"The teacher in me suspects a day in court will prove very enlightening, Katie. Do you have any idea what kind of case you'll be seeing?" Katie's father was thinking about the issues he had been discussing with Katie the previous night.

"We're studying the American justice system, but we don't know what kind of trial we're going to see."

"What was the argument about? Between Corky and Brittany?" John asked.

"Brittany said that her father was the best because he went to Harvard, and Corky said that that justice lady with the blindfold meant that it didn't matter what school he went to and it wasn't fair if that's all that mattered."

"Sounds like a pretty deep discussion for the 7th grade," said John winking at Charlotte.

"Dinner. Please come now. Shrimp gets cold," Sophia was anxious for everyone to try the new dish she discovered. Discussion about the justice system was temporarily delayed as everyone took a place around the table.

"In a trial, how does the judge know who to believe?" Katie asked.

"That is a huge question, honey," John said. "Sometimes the judge doesn't decide. A jury does."

"I don't get it." Katie thought her parents would have a clear answer, and she was confused when they didn't. "Isn't it either justice or not?" she questioned.

"Let me give you an example of what a complicated issue justice can be," John said. "Before the Civil War in the United States, it was legal for white people to own black slaves. The laws of our country allowed some human beings to own others. It was considered perfectly just. But can a country have true justice when one group can enslave others?" John asked Katie.

"So grownups sometimes make mistakes about what justice is?"

"The entire American justice system is based upon the fact that justice is not always obvious," John said. "In fact, you could say that the question of justice in *any* country is always an ongoing quest," he added. Katie was quiet while she digested this piece of information.

"Like in Romania. They had slaves, too, didn't they, Sophia?"

"That's right, Katie. The Roma was slaves until 1864."

"Sophia," John said. "That's almost the exact time when America's slaves were set free. I never knew that about Romania."

It's not just adults who can't figure justice out, Katie thought to herself, while the adults talked about the things that made Romania and America similar. The memory of Henry sitting in the cafeteria with soda poured over him and his books came back to her.

Katie had always been a thoughtful child and Charlotte and John knew that the more she learned, the more she would continue to struggle with questions about justice. Sensing a need to lighten the conversation up a bit, John changed the subject.

"You are never going to guess who called me today."

"Who?" Charlotte, Katie and Sophia asked in unison.

"Jim Gargan from The Hudson Players."

The Hudson Players' theatre was located about a mile from the Farrell's summer home in Hyde Park. Charlotte, John, Katie, and Sophia saw most of the productions. The first year John and Charlotte took

Sophia, she was in awe of the production. She had never seen live the-atre before. She hadn't understood much of the play since she hardly knew any English, but the costumes, the lights, and the sets had mesmer-ized her. Through the years, John and Charlotte had become quite friend-ly with the group and had often helped the Players out with monetary contributions or advice. One year the Players did "Steel Magnolias" and Charlotte helped them get all the hair salon props for the main set of the show. Charlotte loved the little troupe because they reminded her of her early days as an actress.

Charlotte's "Love's Labours" production schedule changed during the summer. The producers generally doubled up taping throughout May, shooting twice as many episodes per week as they usually did. In this way, the cast and crew would be able to have most of the summer off, with only a day or two of studio work every couple of weeks from June to September.

"Are they already working on the summer show?" Charlotte asked.

"Well, yes and no," John answered. "They're kind of stuck. They've cast the July show and the director had a heart attack last week, so she can't continue. They've asked me to take over as director. Char, they're doing 'The Merchant of Venice!'"

"Oh, John! What fun! Katie and I can help you with costumes and sets. Wouldn't that be a wonderful adventure, Katie?" Charlotte turned to her daughter.

"Is that Shakespeare?" Katie asked.

"It is indeed," answered her father. "It's one of Shakespeare's most controversial plays, and it's not done that much these days. I'm surprised the Hudson Valley Players chose this one."

"Why is it controversial?"

"Well, honey, it's because of the way Shakespeare portrayed Jewish people in the play."

"Did he say bad things about them?"

"You have to understand the context of the play and Shakespeare's time. There was very little tolerance for any religion other than the one dictated by the monarchy. In England in Shakespeare's time, there was only one religion permitted. It was called the Church of England. Being a Catholic priest was illegal. And people were punished for practicing any religion other than the Church of England."

"But how could they make people give up their religion?"

"The monarchy had more power than you can imagine. Catholics were persecuted, but Jews were treated like animals. The government made it impossible for them to have most jobs. It was a kind of discrimination that the government sanctioned and even encouraged. People believed that Jews were evil, and it was fairly common for playwrights to make Jews the villains in their plays."

"How could they be so mean to people just because of their religion?"

"For one thing, people were probably afraid to speak out—the fear of persecution was very real. Do you understand what that means?"

"Does it mean that someone would hurt them?"

"Not just someone, honey. The government. They had the ultimate power over peoples' lives—they could tell people what to believe, how to worship, what they were allowed to say. Shakespeare was a lot like other writers. He wanted to make sure the government didn't start censoring or controlling what he wrote. He may not have been anti-Semitic, but he didn't really challenge those who were."

"How can everyone think he was so great then? Shouldn't people stand up for what they believe, even if it's dangerous?" Katie's imagination was rapidly spinning through issues ranging from her class discussions about the justice system, to the horrible things she knew about her native country.

"Actually honey, a lot of people believe Shakespeare did make a difference. Most writers made Jews the villains, with no redeeming qualities whatsoever. In 'The Merchant of Venice', Shylock was a Jew, and somewhat the villain. But Shakespeare made him a little more complex, different from what people were used to seeing in the theatre. And he gave him a daughter, Jessica, who was not evil or mean. By today's standards, it doesn't seem like a very courageous gesture. But in his time, it was something extraordinary. Do you understand?"

Katie thought for a minute. She tried to imagine what it would be like if the government had that much power over what people thought and did. "But why didn't he do more? If he was so great, why didn't he try harder?"

"Maybe he thought he was doing everything he could do. We'll never really know what he was thinking. We can only judge him by what he wrote, and how his writing differed from the things others were writing at the same time. That's the frustration of trying to understand people who have been dead for hundreds of years."

"What if those people who talk to dead people could ask him what he meant?" Katie asked. "There was this lady on television last week and she said she could talk to any dead person."

Katie's parents looked at each other and stifled the impulse to laugh.

"Honey, those people don't really do that," Charlotte said. "They may believe that they're doing it, and they may be really good at acting like they're doing it, but they're not talking to dead people."

Katie pursed her lips, thinking about the woman she had seen on television. "But what if someone could? Talk to dead people, I mean?"

"Imagine what it would be like if we could actually ask Shakespeare what he meant to do when he created this character." Katie's father said. "Maybe it wouldn't be the lady who says she talks to dead people. But let's imagine that somehow it was possible."

"What would you ask him, Dad? I mean, if you could."

"What do you think would be a good question, honey?"

Katie thought about it. She was intrigued by the idea of talking to someone from the past and asking him what he meant to do or say or write.

"Maybe I would ask him if he ever met any Jewish people, or why he didn't like them. Or maybe I would ask him what he would write about if he didn't have to be afraid of the government."

"Those are some very good questions. I wonder what Mr. Shakespeare would have to say about them." Katie's father looked across the table. Charlotte and Sophia were smiling at Katie, imagining what a conversation between Shakespeare and Katie would be like.

"Well, sweetie, it sounds like you'll have a lot to think about this summer when your Dad directs the show. You said 'yes,' didn't you?" Charlotte reached across the table for John's hand.

"Well, it's a big commitment, and I wanted to talk to you about it first. What do you think?"

"Yes! It would be wonderful! It's Shakespeare, your great passion. How could we...you...not do it? What do you think, Katie?"

"I think it would be fun, Dad. Can Corky and Lily help when they come up?"

"We'll need all the help we can get, honey. It will be a Farrell family project."

Lily and Corky always came to Hyde Park for two or three weeks at a time, thus making the summers even more wonderful for Katie. Together the girls picked wild blueberries near the cottage and went to the local fire company's summer carnival.

Sophia loved the cottage, too, because it reminded her of Romania when she was a little girl. Before the government had been taken over by the madman. Sophia walked to farm stands and bought fresh fruits and vegetables. The family cooked out and had picnics along the river. Even Tuffy loved the country, where he could feel like a real dog and chase rabbits and birds. And Tuffy loved having Katie home all the time instead of losing her to school every day. He rarely left her side during that magical time in the summer.

I had such a weird dream last night! It seemed so real. Too real. I dreamed that I was in Romania again, and someone had sold me as a slave. Mom and Dad weren't there. The people who bought me made me clean their floors and wash their clothes and take care of their babies. They were mean and called me 'the stupid gypsy.' But they weren't Romanian. It was Brittany and her friends! They were so stuck up that they didn't want to speak the language, so they needed Sophia and me to translate everything for them. All they wanted to do was shop for clothes and makeup. Sophia said that we could tell them whatever we wanted, because they were so clueless. So when they wanted us to ask for something for them, Sophia told the shopkeepers that Brittany and her friends were idiots, but that they were really sensitive about being stupid, so they should not laugh out loud. Everyone wore strange glittery clothes, with funny hats. But Sophia and I had to wear sheets, because we were slaves, and we were not allowed to wear makeup or jewelry. Brittany even made us wear our price tags on our sheets so everyone would know that we were the most expensive slaves in town. Even Tuffy was a slave, and he had to wear a little sheet and couldn't play with any toys. Dad finally woke me up because he said I was making funny noises and Tuffy was barking.

Chapter 10

"I wish we didn't have to wear these stupid uniforms. We're going to go see a real trial today. I wonder if it will be a murder or something. I wonder if a real murderer looks like one from TV," Katie was talking to no one in particular, but Tuffy seemed an attentive audience. He was sitting on Katie's bed, quivering with excitement. His beloved Katie was talking, but he had not heard his name mentioned. He suspected that she had just forgotten to include him personally in her conversation. She seemed so intense.

Hey, what about me? he thought and wondered if he should break the spell of this moment by diving for one of his toys. He could see it from where he was sitting. His favorite. A squeaky toy shaped like a sheep and covered in white wooly stuff.

"Katie, come on honey! You'll be late!" Katie's father was taking her to school today, since he had some work to do at the library before going to Poughkeepsie. She was looking forward to hearing more about the story of "The Merchant of Venice."

"Tuffy, you're squashing my hat!" Tuffy had found the perfect spot on Katie's bed, right on top of her beret. It was one of her favorite things to wear because Sophia had found it for her and had told her that it made her look "very continental," whatever that meant. Katie thought it sounded great. And the beret actually hid a lot of her hair, and for that reason she appreciated it even more.

Tuffy was so thrilled to hear his name mentioned that he leapt for the squeaky toy and pranced around the room with it, squeaking it over and over. Katie chased him, scolding him in her "continental" accent for his crime against her hat. "You leetle devile, you have ruined my fashion sheew. You must be ze spy who tries to make my beeutivul model look zilly!"

"Ekaterina!" Katie's father rarely used her real name. It always got her attention when she heard it. "We've got to get going! Now, please!" Katie had trapped Tuffy near her closet. "You are now my slave, you leetle devile. But do not vorry. I vill be kind to you!" She kissed him on his left ear, then his right. "Ta ta, my leetle slave doggie. I vill zee you later!"

Katie and Tuffy raced down the hall. Katie laughing. Tuffy barking. The commotion brought Sophia out of the kitchen.

"Katie! You don't eat all your breakfast yet and now you are running like a crazy person. What goes on in your head?"

Katie's father laughed at the sight of Katie and Tuffy skidding down the hallway, but he tried to act serious for Sophia's benefit.

"You're not finished your breakfast yet, young lady? Do you know what time it is?"

"Dad, we've got plenty of time. Will you finish telling me about the 'Merchant?' Does he get to slice some meat off that guy he loaned money to?"

"What is to slice meat off a guy?" Sophia asked. "What for a play is this?"

"It's Shakespeare, Sophia. I think you'll enjoy the play once you see all the action. I promise, nobody slices anybody. At least not in any production that I would direct," John replied.

"But Dad, doesn't the Merchant slice off a pound of flesh?" Her father had briefly summarized the play for her when he first talked about directing it. She was fascinated by the story of the merchant who extracted a terrible bargain from a man desperate for a loan, of the trial in which the merchant was accused of attempting murder, of the woman who disguised herself as a man to save the merchant's life. But, without question, the part that stuck in Katie's imagination was the villain's demand for a pound of flesh from the man who couldn't pay his debt on time.

"Honey, you seem to be stuck on one part of the play, not the larger theme Shakespeare was working on. It's obvious we need to talk about this some more." He put his arm around her and picked a few strands of dog hair off the top of her beret.

"Now, let's get going, okay? I've got some work to do at the library, and you've got a court date, today, don't you?"

As they walked up the street, they could hear Tuffy still racing around the apartment, barking excitedly.

"Do you think we'll see a murderer in court today, Dad? Or something like that?"

"Katie, where is this obsession with violence coming from? If you're going to see Kyle Morgan, I can guarantee it won't be a murder trial. He does corporate law, not criminal law."

"Corporate law? What's that?"

"It means Mr. Morgan represents big companies. For instance, remember when we read all those news stories about people who were hurt when their cars flipped over? A lot of those people might sue the company that made the cars, because it turned out there was something wrong with the cars. The car company would need legal representation, and that's the kind of law Mr. Morgan practices."

Katie was thinking back on the day Brittany had suggested the court visit. She remembered that she wanted to ask her father about something else Brittany had said in class.

"What does it mean that a judge is prone-business?"

"Prone-business?" Katie's father was confused.

"Brittany said that Rodney's father was prone-business, or something like that."

Her father thought for a minute, and tried to imagine the context in which Brittany had talked about Judge Sabol.

"Oh, honey. I think the word is 'pro-business,' not 'prone,' although there's a certain logic to the way you said it. Pro-business means that he is more inclined to agree with the business side of an issue."

"You mean Judge Sabol would say that the car company didn't do anything wrong?"

"Well, honey, I don't think I would ever say that Judge Sabol is pro-business, or that he's not pro-business. He has a reputation as a fair-minded judge. But maybe there are some judges who do let their personal preferences interfere with their judgments."

"But what about the justice lady with the blindfold? Aren't judges supposed to be like her?"

Katie's father stopped walking for a minute, and thought about how to answer her question. It was one of those things that might generate a two-hour discussion with Katie, or it might end with a simple "Oh, okay," from Katie. Either way, her father knew that Katie would not just let go of an issue that struck so close to the core of her developing sense of right and wrong. He knew that this would be only the beginning of many discussions about justice—especially as the family got more involved with the Hudson Valley Players' production of "The Merchant of Venice."

"Honey, the statue represents an ideal—something that the justice system tries to achieve. But the fact is that people are not perfect. Everyone has his own way of seeing things; that perspective comes from the experiences they've had in their lives. That doesn't mean they're not being fair or just. It means that they're human beings."

They had begun walking again, and were across the street from

Katie's school. She was quiet, absorbing what her father had told her, and changing her imaginary scenario of what the class trip would be like. He gave her a hug, kissed her on the cheek and whispered in her ear.

"Do well, my sweet. I love you."

"Bye, Dad!" Katie bounded up the school steps, one hand on her beret. Her father watched her disappear into the school. He wished for a moment that he could go to court with the class, to see his daughter's first encounter with justice. As it turned out, he missed quite an adventure.

Chapter 11

The court visit turned into much more than a class trip. Brittany had regretted her suggestion almost as soon as she made it that day in class. At her first break after the Social Studies class, she had gone to her locker, retrieved her cell phone and called her father's office.

"Hi, this is Brittany. Is my father there?" Her voice on the phone lacked the confidence that so intimidated her peers at Manhattan Prep.

"Oh, hi, dear! Your father is just getting ready to take a deposition. Can I help you with something?" Mr. Morgan's secretary, Annie, had always taken an interest in Brittany's activities, and truly enjoyed talking with her.

"Well...I sort of wanted to talk to him, but...I can, I guess, I can wait until I see him, if he's too busy," Brittany stammered.

"No, no, honey. He's never too busy for you," Annie tried to reassure Brittany. "Let me just catch him. You hold on, okay?"

Brittany waited nervously, trying to figure out how to explain to her father the commitment she had made. She was worried that he would be mad, or get impatient with her if she took up too much of his time.

"Brit, make it fast, hon, what do you need?" Her father's voice had that edge that said, *I don't have time for you, so this better be important.* Brittany could feel her shoulders tensing, and she completely forgot the little script she had memorized to make this conversation go well.

"Dad...today in Social Studies...we...um...we were talking about court cases and I said that maybe...I...I didn't promise anything....but maybe...you could get us in..."

"Brit, what are you trying to say? C'mon, what do you want?" The impatience in his voice only made her stammer more.

"Well...I said maybe...maybe you could...if you could...you could get us in to see an actual trial that you were doing. It would be a class field trip, or something. You don't have to say yes or anything...we...we can talk about it later or if you're going to be home early tonight and then we can talk about it, sort of..."

"Brit, you're rambling. You want me to arrange a court visit for your class, is that it?"

"Yes, Dad. That's it. Can you do it? Will you do it?"

"I think we can do something. Actually, I'm about ready for jury selection for a trial that might work out okay. I'll let Annie handle it. I'm putting her back on the phone now. Just tell her what you need."

"Um. Well, Mr. Murwata said you or someone should just talk to him for the arrangements, if that's okay?"

"Brit, I said Annie can handle it. I'm sure your teacher will trust her. I really have to go, now Brit. Love ya." With that, Mr. Morgan was off on an important mission, and Annie was back on the line with Brittany. Annie listened to Brittany's explanation, asking a few questions, and praising her for thinking of the idea. Brittany felt relieved after talking to Annie, and was once again excited by the prospect of going with her classmates to watch her father work.

Chapter 12

Just two weeks later, Katie and her 7th grade class were hurrying down to the front of the school where a bus was waiting. Mackenzie, Brittany, and Jordan huddled so closely that it looked as though they had been braided together. As usual, they were whispering and giggling. Katie, Lily and Corky hung back and waited until the crush of kids trying to get on the bus subsided.

"This seat is saved," Rodney said coldly as Henry started to sit beside him on the bus. Katie heard the contempt in Rodney's voice and she turned to see Henry's face turn red in embarrassment. *Why do they treat Henry that way?* she wondered to herself.

The bus seats were four across with an aisle separating them in the middle. Katie spied four seats across in the second to the last row and she gently nudged Lily and Corky to take two of the seats. She tapped Henry on the shoulder. "Can you sit with us and give me some help with our math homework? I'm confused about one of the problems. You're really good at understanding these word problems."

Lily and Corky looked at Katie quizzically. They obviously hadn't heard Rodney's cruel remark. Katie mouthed the words "I'll explain later" to her friends.

"Okay, sure, be glad to see if I could help you," Henry said gratefully.

From where she sat, Katie could see Tyler looking back from his seat in the front. He was obviously trying to see where Lily was sitting. The Spring Dance was only a week away and still no one had asked either Katie or Corky to go. Lily was downplaying the whole event, but Katie knew in her heart that Lily was thrilled to be going with Tyler. Lily's mom had taken her shopping and Lily had gotten the coolest dress.

Katie knew Lily would look really beautiful and for just a moment, she felt a pang of jealousy. *This is not Lily's fault,* Katie reprimanded herself. *She doesn't know how I feel about Tyler.* Lily had noticed Tyler and she smiled back at him.

"How can they call anything that moves this slowly 'rush hour'?" Katie asked. "Actually," Henry said, "only people who aren't going anywhere call it that." Katie smiled at Henry's attempt at humor, and wondered again what made people hurt others thoughtlessly.

In preparation for the visit to court, Mr. Murwata had broken the class into four teams. Each team was assigned a famous court case to research and present to the class. Katie and Corky had been on a team with Jordan and Ashley Sinclair. Ashley had recently transferred to Manhattan Prep, and her mother had immediately become very active in the scholarship program that Katie's parents had started. Their case had been a famous trial in history called the Scopes trial. Another team had been assigned to research the play, The Crucible, which was about the Salem, Massachusetts witch trials. The third team studied *Brown vs. The Board of Education*, a famous Supreme Court case from 1954. Mr. Murwata said that case was important in the 1960s.

"Do you understand about the civil rights movement in America?" he had asked the class. "This case was as important to that movement as The Declaration of Independence was to America's beginning."

The fourth team studied the trial of two immigrants, Sacco and Vanzetti, who had been tried and convicted of treason in the 1920s.

Katie thought the witch trial sounded the most interesting. Jordan complained to Mr. Murwata that she had been separated from Mackenzie and Brittany, but Mr. Murwata would not budge.

"Often, Jordan, people who spend a lot of time together tend to think alike. That's not a bad thing, necessarily. But this is an opportunity for everyone to get a fresh perspective. It's particularly important as we look at this issue of justice." He pronounced the words so formally, opportunity sounding like "oppor-**teune**-ity" and particularly sounding like "par-**tick**-you-larly". He had asked each team to give the rest of the class a presentation outlining the case, explaining who the defendants were, and what was happening in America when the trial took place, and the outcome of the trial.

Katie found the research and the discussion about the Scopes trial fascinating. She wondered if she had the makings of a great lawyer. She dove into the research enthusiastically. The Scopes Trial (also known as The Monkey Trial) had taken place early in the 20th century and involved a teacher who taught his class Darwin's Theory of Evolution – the theory that mankind had descended from monkeys. John Scopes, the teacher, was arrested and put on trial for daring to teach something other than the Biblical interpretation of Creation. Katie couldn't believe that there had been a time in history when teachers couldn't present new ideas to students. The only possible advantage of this antiquated system of education would have been the possible elimination of word problems.

The famous trials the class studied highlighted the fact that the definition of justice was constant but its interpretation didn't always match the definition. At certain times in history, even recent history like the Civil Rights movement, justice had a different outcome.

Mr. Murwata continued to challenge Katie and her classmates about the concept of justice. Just when Katie thought she understood what was going on, Mr. Murwata would bring up another question.

"Was justice served?" Mr. Murwata would ask as each group presented their findings.

"Is justice something that remains the same from one century to the next?" Mr. Murwata's pronunciation of "century" made it sound like three words.

"Justice has different meanings for different people," Brittany said, as the class discussed the Scopes trial. "I mean, who would even think of such a thing today?"

"It might surprise all of you that a school district in Kansas just last year declared that teaching evolution was wrong," Mr. Murwata waited for a reaction from the class.

Katie thought about the discussion she had with her parents about slavery, and Sophia's story about the Roma.

"Does justice mean that people who have been hurt are all better?" she asked. Mr. Murwata was a little surprised to hear Katie's question. He was intrigued by the direction he thought she was taking.

"What do you think, class? Is that what justice means?" Katie was slightly embarrassed by the silence that met her question, and Mr. Murwata's follow-up questions. But she pressed on. The idea had been rumbling around in her thoughts for a couple of days, and had even invaded her dreams. It was finally forming itself into a real question.

"In the beginning of this country, everyone thought it was right to own slaves. Then the slaves were freed, but they weren't all better. But people say that justice was done and I wonder how it ever could get done. I mean, all the slaves who died without justice and all the families that were never brought back together, they never felt justice. Maybe justice is only a way for people to feel better about the bad things they've done," Katie finished.

Mr. Murwata was smiling, but his eyes were very sad. He seemed to be lost in her thought, temporarily unable to think of a way to make the discussion go forward.

"What do you think might be better, Katie?" he asked gently. Rodney jumped into the discussion before Katie could answer.

"Maybe they should all sue for millions of dollars. Like my dad says, 'everyone thinks they deserve a fortune just because something bad happened to them.'" There was laughter as the students considered Rodney's solution.

"What I meant was that sometimes it's impossible to fix what's broken. Calling some things justice doesn't mean that's what they are." Katie felt her face getting hot. She sensed that her hair was slipping into her face, and she wondered if her classmates thought she was stupid.

Jordan spoke up. "When we were doing our research, we found that the whole trial started out as a way for the town to get publicity and attract tourists. It turned into something else, but Mr. Scopes helped organize the whole thing. One of the questions we asked ourselves was how could this case become something so important when it started out as a way for this hick town to get money?"

"And what did you conclude, Jordan?" Mr. Murwata was clearly amused by this turn of events.

Jordan thought for a moment. She was torn. Suddenly she had to say things in public that she had only thought about and discussed in the privacy of her team of researchers on the Scopes Monkey Trial. She looked over at Mackenzie and Brittany, who had their heads cocked at exactly the same angle, and they were looking at her as if they couldn't believe she was saying something they hadn't already heard.

"We wondered about Mr. Scopes, and about all the things that happened at the trial. It seemed silly that these people would deliberately create such a horrible situation for the students, just to get more tourists to come to their town. But..." she hesitated again.

"But what, Jordan?" Mr. Murwata's voice betrayed no emotion. It was quiet, non-threatening, gentle.

"But," she started hesitatingly. "But the case was about teaching ideas from science that some people thought were against God. Even though the whole thing started out as something else. You could see that the people who were leading both sides were surprised by what happened."

"Surprised?" Mr. Murwata asked.

"I mean, they weren't expecting what happened. And all that stuff about Creation and evolution—that stuff was supposed to be the point, but the people who started all the trouble didn't care about it, and the people who came to town to argue about it didn't care about the students. It was a show. Everyone was using the students for stuff that didn't really have anything to do with justice...and...and we, I mean...we wondered, like Katie said, what was the point of it?"

"So, now, students. We have a famous court case that turns out to be something much more complicated than a court case. I must ask, now. Was justice done? And, perhaps even more importantly, what did this case have to do with justice after all?"

Mr. Murwata was enjoying his students' sense of discovery. During the remaining 20 minutes of class that day, the debate about justice was vigorous, occasionally outrageous, and, in Mr. Murwata's eyes, at least, a successful attempt to force some of the students to look at the world a little differently. It was a perfect set-up for the students' day in court.

Chapter 13

The bus arrived at the courthouse and an armed guard escorted Mr. Murwata and the class through the security checkpoints into an anteroom where Mr. Morgan and several of his assistants and junior associates awaited them. Mr. Morgan was meeting the class prior to the start of the trial to explain what was going on so that the students would be better able to follow the proceedings.

With a booming "Welcome!" Mr. Morgan motioned for the class to sit down, and then he launched into an explanation of what they were going to see over the next few hours.

"My client, the Greater New York City Zoo, is defending its right to keep one of the animal's records private. The plaintiff, that's the party suing the Zoo, is the Association to Free Zoo Animals. They claim that animals don't belong in zoos and therefore caging animals actually imprisons them. The whole case is complicated by the fact that a monkey at the zoo died and the Association to Free Zoo Animals claims that the monkey's death was a result of the zoo's negligence. The zoo is claiming that making the dead monkey's medical records public is an invasion of privacy. Now," Mr. Morgan paused dramatically, "My defense is that even zoo animals have a right to privacy. Does anyone have any questions?"

Katie was astounded. Mr. Morgan was actually going to court to keep a monkey's medical records private? She had been hoping for more drama. Katie looked over at Lily and Corky. They seemed equally surprised. "This is stupid," Corky whispered. "Amazing," Lily added.

"Mr. Morgan," Henry piped up. "Are you defending the monkey or the zoo?" A few students snickered.

"I am defending the zoo's right to keep their records from public scrutiny," Mr. Morgan said importantly. "The charge is absolutely ridiculous," he added.

"Who owns the zoo? I mean, does a person own it?" Henry's curiosity had overcome the embarrassment he had experienced on the bus on the way to court.

"This particular zoo is a municipal entity created and maintained for the benefit of the citizens of this city," Mr. Morgan answered.

"So, the City owns it? Does the City own all the animals? I mean, I heard that lots of zoos loan animals to other zoos. Like tigers and Panda bears? Does this zoo have any animals they borrowed from other zoos?" Henry was oblivious to the cold stares of some of his classmates. For that matter, he didn't seem to notice anything other than Mr. Morgan's answers.

"Well, young man. Perhaps later you'll have the opportunity to ask someone from the zoo that very interesting question." Mr. Morgan had the sense that Henry was an animal lover who visited the zoo frequently. *The kid seems awfully interested in how the zoo works,* he thought to himself.

Henry raised his hand again, another question already forming on his lips. But Mr. Morgan glanced at his watch, just as one of his assistants tapped him on the shoulder.

"We might be able to get to more questions later. But unfortunately we're out of time right now," Mr. Morgan said.

With that, Mr. Morgan nodded to one of his assistants and the group immediately fell into line as if marching in a school band formation. Several of them carried briefcases and boxes of files.

The class followed Mr. Morgan's entourage into the courtroom—a beautiful, stately old room, with gleaming wooden railings and seats. A United States flag hung on a pole on one side of the judge's bench and the flag of New York State on the other side.

"All rise," intoned a young man in a uniform, announcing the arrival of Rodney's father. As if lifted by a sudden wind, everyone in the courtroom rose as Judge Sabol, robe cascading from his neck to his heels, strode to his chair high above the court. The Judge cleared his throat, adjusted the glasses on his nose, and rapped his gavel. "The court will come to order," the Judge said. "Before we begin, I want to welcome the 7th grade class of Manhattan Prep, and I'd like to remind everyone that— as always, we need to be on our best behavior. Especially in the presence of these youngsters, many of whom will take with them today lifelong impressions of our nation's justice system. Enough said?" The judge smiled briefly, then ordered everyone to be seated.

With a rustle, everyone in the courtroom took their seats. Brittany could hardly contain her excitement. Her father was the star of the show. Forget about the monkey. Privately, Mr. Morgan had explained to Brittany that any kind of publicity that led to questions about the zoo's records would seriously jeopardize the zoo's fundraising efforts.

The zoo was in the middle of a big drive to encourage people to name the zoo's animals in exchange for a donation. For example, for $1000, someone could name an elephant. For $100, someone could name a bird. The concept had been extremely successful in years past, netting the zoo hundreds of thousands of dollars. Brittany thought the idea was weird because who would keep track of all the names and how would the animals learn what their names were? What would happen if an animal died and the contributor wanted their money back? But then again, how would they know if the giraffe they paid $500 to name Claude had died? They could just get another giraffe. In fact, Brittany thought, they could sell 100 different people the right to name the same giraffe and no one would even know. It's not like the people contributing the money would come to the zoo to engage in conversations with the animals.

Brittany's opinion of the zoo's marketing department went up several notches as she considered the possibilities of this fund-raising scheme. She'd have to remember it when she joined a sorority and needed to raise money for parties. You could really clean up!

"Is the plaintiff ready?" the judge asked the young attorney seated in front of him. His name was Mr. Dillon, and he was clearly nervous in the presence of an attorney as famous as Brittany's father. But he swallowed hard and responded to the judge with a firm, confident voice.

"We are, Your Honor."

"Is the defense ready?"

"We are!" Mr. Morgan boomed in his "I'm going to win this one" voice that sent shivers through Mr. Dillon.

"Proceed, Mr. Dillon," the judge said.

"Your Honor, members of the jury, it is the contention of my client, the Association to Free Zoo Animals, that animals do not belong in cages, that zoos should not be supported by public money, and that the enslavement of animals in zoos constitutes cruel and unusual punishment. We believe that, either as a result of his being held as a slave, or his deliberate and wanton mistreatment by the zoo's staff, the monkey died. We demand the zoo's records to help show that the deceased monkey in question was mistreated by being caged and therefore his death was caused by the zoo's negligence." Mr. Dillon almost ran out of breath.

He rambled on for several minutes about enslavement and natural habitat. Out of the corner of her eye, Katie saw Tyler sneaking peeks at Lily, Corky, and her. Katie was momentarily lost in thoughts about the Spring Dance, and she missed what Mr. Dillon was saying.

Pay attention, this is important! she said to herself.

Mr. Dillon called a series of witnesses, which both he and Mr. Morgan questioned—for what seemed an eternity. Mr. Morgan's questions seemed very complicated and his sentences were *very* long. It was no wonder that some of the witnesses became severely tongue-tied upon cross examination.

"The plaintiff rests, Your Honor." Mr. Dillon finally said. He seemed relieved and exhausted, but slightly nervous about his opponents' case and their track record.

"Very well. We'll take a 10 minute recess before we begin with the defense," the judge intoned. He rose grandly.

"All rise," the man in the uniform bellowed. Everyone in the courtroom stood while Rodney's father swept out of the courtroom. Judge Sabol was a very impressive man, and Katie thought he would be wonderful on "Love's Labours."

Mr. Murwata motioned for the students to congregate on one side of the courtroom. The class then followed their teacher to an empty conference room that Mr. Morgan had reserved for them. "Well," Mr. Murwata began, "what are your impressions thus far?"

Mackenzie's hand shot up. "Yes, Mackenzie," Mr. Murwata said.

"Now I know why my parents want me to get a good education and get into an Ivy League school," Mackenzie said.

"Why is that, Mackenzie and what has it to do with the case?" Mr. Murwata asked.

"Well, it's obvious to me that the animal lawyer has no idea what he's doing. It's obvious that Mr. Morgan is so much smarter than him and the animal people are going to lose," Mackenzie said solemnly.

"What would you be talkin' about?" Corky nearly screamed her question, but managed to control her voice so it betrayed only exasperation.

"Did ya not hear Mr. Dillon? What he was sayin' was important, even if ya can't see his point. Besides, are we not here to watch as the wheels of justice turn?" Corky smiled sweetly, disguising her sarcasm.

Mr. Murwata quickly spoke up. "What are the issues in this case?"

Rodney spoke without raising his hand, as though everyone was at his house and he was in charge. "The issue is whether or not the public has the right to private records of an organization partly supported by public funds."

Katie raised her hand, and started asking her question almost before Mr. Murwata called on her.

"What about the animals? Who stands up for them? Do animals really belong in cages, being raised in captivity? Don't all living creatures deserve some sort of justice?"

"Katie, you are *so* naïve," Brittany said with an air of superiority. "Animals have no rights. Everyone knows that. Only humans have rights. Haven't you ever heard about the law of the jungle? Where do you think that law came from?" She wasn't even looking at Katie, but was focused intently on Mr. Murwata, hoping to hear her own ideas thrown back to the class as interesting, worthy of further thought and comment.

"Brittany, the law of the jungle isn't a real law. What do you think? Congress passed the law of the jungle?" Henry asked incredulously.

"Ah, Brittany, but what about corporations, or entities such as the zoo? Do they have rights?" Mr. Murwata asked. Brittany's attention was still on Henry's comment, and she didn't understand exactly what Mr. Murwata meant by his question. "Corporations?" She asked. "What about them?"

"Do they have rights?" Mr. Murwata's voice was kind, and he

was trying to tone down some of the high emotions of the students.

"Of course corporations have rights. They pay taxes don't they?" Brittany said angrily. It was clear she was interpreting all the questions as personal attacks on her and her father.

The door opened and the class was startled at the interruption, so intent were they on the comments flying back and forth between Brittany, Henry and Katie. Mr. Morgan was ushering another guest into the conference room.

"Class, I'd like to introduce Mr. Gary Riverdale, Sr. Mr. Riverdale is the CEO of Anpro Incorporated and Chairman of the Board of Directors of the Greater New York City Zoo. We go back a long way, don't we Gary?" Mr. Morgan asked, clearly eager to please his important client.

"We do, indeed," Mr. Riverdale replied in a voice that seemed rather soft and high-pitched.

"Brittany, Rodney, nice to see you again," he continued. It was obvious that the Riverdales and the Morgans were friends with Judge Sabol and his family.

Mr. Riverdale had the look of a man who didn't enjoy smiling, small talk or interactions with anyone who wasn't rich and important. His lips were so thin and tightly clenched that it almost seemed he didn't have lips at all. Katie was surprised at his coldness, and wondered why he agreed to even visit with the students.

"Mr. Riverdale wanted to meet all of you and give you the opportunity to ask some questions about the trial. Do any of you have any questions?" Mr. Morgan asked.

Mackenzie raised her hand and was actually a little surprised that she was first. "Mr. Riverdale, how do the zoo workers know what the animals like to eat?"

Frankly, Katie thought, *what do the animals' diets have to do with the case?*

"Well young lady, I'm afraid I can't answer your question. That's a day-to-day operational question and I don't get involved in details such as the animals' diets," Mr. Riverdale said.

Henry raised his hand.

"Yes, young man?" Mr. Riverdale asked, assuming control of the question and answer period.

"How long do monkeys live?"

Mr. Riverdale's tight little mouth smiled again, and he relaxed slightly.

"Are you referring to the type of monkey we're discussing in this trial? Or another type of monkey? As you may know, there are many, many different kinds of monkeys."

"Rhesus monkeys. How old do they get?" Henry was unaware of the reactions his questions were causing among Brittany and her friends. Although Brittany's crowd remained silent, they were communicating their contempt for Henry through very clear body language.

"Well, young man, I'm told they can live as long as 50 years." Mr. Riverdale said.

"And the babies. What happens to them?" Henry seemed to be on a mission, although where that mission was taking him was known only to him.

Mr. Riverdale cleared his throat and became noticeably tense.

"My parents always take my sisters and me to the zoo, and we even paid to name one of the monkeys. We named him Barney. And we always recognized Barney because he had a big scar on his face. The last few times we went to the zoo, Barney wasn't there, but there were other babies and younger monkeys but no monkeys Barney's age. It seems that, in all the years we've been going to the zoo, there have only been six monkeys. There are new babies every year, but still only six monkeys. Where do they go?"

Henry was so focused on Barney and getting some answers that he didn't notice how agitated Brittany and her friends had become.

It figures, Brittany said to herself. *Henry the geek would be one of the idiots who would actually try to find the monkey he named.*

Mr. Riverdale blushed, red splotches appearing on his pasty white neck and face. He shuffled his feet briefly, then stood as if he were a general leading his troops into battle. His hands were clasped tightly behind his back and his face looked like it had been carved out of cold stone. Splotchy stone, but stone nonetheless.

"Just what do you think happened to…what did you call him, Barney?…" Mr. Riverdale's voice was even higher-pitched than before. He coughed, then cleared his throat and coughed again.

Henry hesitated for a minute. "I don't know, sir. I thought you might know. Someone told me that zoos like to keep baby animals because they're cute. But once they get older they get more expensive to feed, and so the zoos, they…"

Mr. Morgan interrupted, and pointed out that they needed to give someone else a chance to ask questions.

Katie thought Mr. Riverdale was going to explode. His face was now blood red and the veins in his neck visibly vibrated.

"I don't care what you've heard, young man," Mr. Morgan said. "The Greater New York City Zoo does not mistreat their animals, do they Gary?" Mr. Morgan asked, turning toward Mr. Riverdale.

Mr. Riverdale cleared his throat and took a deep breath. "You cannot believe everything you hear," he said, so softly that some of the students couldn't even hear him.

But Henry's questions had cracked open a dam, and soon Mr. Riverdale was flooded with questions from other kids. Everyone wanted to know where the baby tigers go when they grow up, or where the baby elephants go, or where the baby giraffes go.

Mr. Morgan glared at Brittany, as if silently blaming her for the embarrassing questions her classmate was asking.

Chapter 14

One of Mr. Morgan's harried assistants poked her head in the door and told Mr. Morgan that the judge was about to resume the trial. Mr. Riverdale looked relieved to be escaping this unexpected line of questions, and Mr. Morgan just looked mad. He nodded to Mr. Murwata and said they had better get seated, so the debate stopped and the class filed quietly into the courtroom.

Katie noticed Brittany shooting disgusted looks at Henry. You could almost see the steam coming out of her head, she was so angry at Henry's questions. She thought he was trying to make her dad and Mr. Riverdale look as if they were defending monsters. No sooner had they gotten seated than the court officer ordered everyone to rise again for the judge. Judge Sabol swept back into the courtroom and assumed his position above all the people.

"Proceed, Mr. Morgan," he said.

"The defense calls Mr. Gary Riverdale," Mr. Morgan said tapping his papers into even corners. Katie stole a look at Henry. She wondered if what Henry had revealed was really true. She also wondered at the possible repercussions that would follow since Henry had so angered Brittany. She was lost in thought when the day's real excitement started. There was a huge commotion near the judge. Everyone was huddled around the witness stand, and Mr. Riverdale had vanished into the sea of people.

Voices from all over the room were whispering "What happened?" and "Who is that?" and "Is he dead?"

Katie looked at Corky and Lily. "Mr. Riverdale fell down," Corky said. "Katie, remember that time we were at the taping of your mother's show and that Mr. Montaine was pretending to be sick? That's exactly what Mr. Riverdale did."

All of sudden, three men burst through the courtroom doors and quickly rolled a stretcher down the center aisle. They began to gently ease Mr. Riverdale onto the gurney and take his vital signs, yelling out numbers and orders. It happened so fast that it all seemed like a scene from a movie. Katie, Lily, and Corky just clung to each other, holding each other's hands.

Brittany was sobbing hysterically, her grand moment in the sun ruined first by Henry and now by Mr. Riverdale's collapse. Mr. Morgan was torn between tending to his star witness and quieting his daughter. Judge Sabol was speechless. He tried rapping his gavel to regain control of his courtroom, but the hysteria over Mr. Riverdale's collapse overwhelmed the power of justice.

Mr. Murwata raised his hand and gestured for the class to gather at one side of the room. He wanted to get the students out of the way. He wasn't sure what was going to happen, so he stood there helplessly as chaos erupted.

Judge Sabol's insistent rapping finally got everyone's attention and the room quieted down. "Counsel, why don't we recess indefinitely until we find out how Mr. Riverdale is?" he asked the two lawyers.

"Your Honor, we hate wasting the court's time. Why can't Mr. Morgan call his next witness?" Mr. Dillon asked.

"Your Honor," Mr. Morgan said, in an exasperated tone. "Resuming after such a shock would be a terrible injustice to my client. Mr. Riverdale is the Chairman of the Zoo Board. Wouldn't it be more seemly if we recessed until his condition can be determined?" Mr. Morgan asked, his eyebrows raised so high over his eyes that Katie thought they were going to shoot right off his face.

"I concur," Judge Sabol said, staring sternly at Mr. Dillon. "Let's show a little respect, Mr. Dillon." And with that, he rose and practically raced out of the courtroom before anyone could rise.

"Class, get in line and let's proceed quietly to our bus," Mr.

Murwata said as he turned toward Brittany's father. "Mr. Morgan, we thank you for your hospitality and for spending so much time with our students. I hope we didn't make the terrible events of today any more confusing. Please let us know how Mr. Riverdale is once he arrives at the hospital."

"Of course, Mr. Murwata," Mr. Morgan said. "Brit, honey, pull yourself together. Do you want to go back to school? Or do you want to come back to the office with me. I've got a couple of things to wrap up and then I'll take you home."

Brittany's tears were turning to rage. And the focus of her rage was Henry, whom she believed caused this entire fiasco. *That geek*, she thought. *How could he do this to me?* "I...I think I'll go with you, if that's okay, Dad," Brittany sniffed.

Mr. Murwata reached out to shake Mr. Morgan's hand. "Thank you for all your courtesies," he said. "And please do keep us up to date on your case."

"Sure thing," Mr. Morgan said, looking past the teacher.

The trip back to Manhattan Prep was quiet. Students whispered quietly to their seatmates, but Katie didn't know what to say to Henry. So, rather than make a bad situation any worse, she kept her mouth shut. But Katie had to admit to herself that she was intensely curious about Mr. Riverdale's attack on the stand. Perhaps she was a bad person for thinking the thoughts that were racing through her head on the ride back.

But she seriously wondered if Mr. Riverdale had really suffered an attack or if the whole scene had been staged to avoid his testifying. She'd ask her family what they thought at dinner tonight. At this moment, Katie had had enough of the American justice system.

*The Spring Dance is tomorrow night, and Corky and I will be
sitting with the other losers who couldn't get dates. I'm going to feel so
dumb. Mom said I shouldn't worry so much.
She said I'm still really young and she didn't go on her first date
until she was 17. It's hard to imagine no one asking Mom to a big dance.
She's so totally gorgeous. But that was ages and ages ago, and maybe
times have changed. Mom said we can leave the dance right after the
parents hear about the scholarship program. Then we're going to
Gelato's with Corky and her mother. Corky and Lily and I love Gelato's,
but of course Lily will be all dressed up and having a wonderful time
with Tyler. I'm trying not to let it bother me, but it really does. First I
was afraid that Henry was going to ask me to the Dance and I didn't
think I wanted to go with him, but in a way I'm disappointed
that he didn't ask. I wonder if I'll ever understand all these things...*

Chapter 15

Most of the students in Mr. Murwata's class wondered what had
happened with Mr. Morgan's defense of the Greater New York City Zoo.
By the time Mr. Riverdale had been treated at the hospital and released,
Judge Sabol had begun another trial and was too involved to reschedule
Mr. Morgan's case. Brittany told the class that she didn't know what had
been wrong with Mr. Riverdale, but Katie suspected that he hadn't been
ill at all.

When she told her parents about what had happened, they were shocked. But they didn't think that Mr. Riverdale was faking an illness.

"Katie, sometimes people react to extreme pressure with physical symptoms, just like the ones Mr. Riverdale had. Sometimes people actually do have heart attacks, when they're under a lot of stress." Katie's father explained during dinner that night.

"But Dad, you didn't see him. It looked just like Mr. Montaine on Mom's show. Corky thought so, too."

"Honey, maybe the guy who plays Mr. Montaine—what's his real name, Char?—maybe he's a better actor than he gets credit for."

"Stewart Mason. I'm sure he would agree with you that he's one of the finest actors in New York," Charlotte said, laughing. "But your father is right, Katie. Mr. Riverdale was probably very nervous about having to testify in court—that alone is a very unnerving situation. But Henry's questions may have actually uncovered something that made Mr. Riverdale even more uncomfortable."

"Do you think they kill the animals?" Katie asked, incredulously.

"I've never actually thought about what they do at the zoo," Katie's father said. "But, now that I think about what Henry said, it's certainly an intriguing question. I wonder what happens when the babies get older."

"In Romania, the madman's soldiers just killed animals to show what good skill they are with guns," Sophia said. "Those people, they do everything to make people frightened. What is the word, 'crawl?'"

"Do you mean cruel? You're right, Sophia, they were cruel. Maybe the people here are doing something else with the animals. I can't believe they would do anything to hurt them, though. Besides being horribly immoral, it would be a public relations disaster if anyone ever found out."

Even as he said it, he realized how incredible it would be— incredible on so many levels—if the people at the zoo actually were doing something illicit with the animals. Yes, he was growing very curious about the zoo. He took out the small notebook that always bulged from the pocket of his shirt, and wrote something down. Katie, Sophia and Charlotte continued exploring the topic, which was growing more gruesome by the minute, while John made his notes.

Even though he had given up a career in journalism to become a college professor, he could never give up what got him into journalism in the first place: insatiable curiosity. He loved doing research about things, from the commonplace to the truly unusual. Once he had spent several hours in the library doing research on the best way to train dogs. When he and Charlotte first talked about getting a dog for Katie, John wanted to make sure they knew everything possible about training and caring for a dog. He came home with an armload of books on dog breeds, dog feeds and dog needs.

"Can't you just get a dog from the Humane Society?" Charlotte had asked him, as she thumbed through a 600-page book about the care and training of sport dogs.

"Honey, it doesn't matter where you get the dog. What matters is that you don't get surprised by how much time and patience puppies need." He rummaged through a stack of papers that had been stuffed into the books. "One of the articles I read today said that most of the dogs that need to be rescued would have very different lives if their owners knew how to train them and take care of them. Ah, here it is. Do you want to read it?"

"Maybe I'll read it later," Charlotte had said, giving John a kiss on the cheek. "I love the way you dive into these things. It doesn't matter whether it's about a dog or about foreign policy. You just love finding out about everything, don't you?"

"It's the old reporter in me. I can't help myself."

As he made notes about the zoo that evening, John could feel the reporter instinct awakening again. Charlotte, Katie and Sophia continued talking about the zoo, and all the possible explanations for Mr. Riverdale's behavior, and the fact that Henry had noticed that many of the animals he and his family had visited over the years had simply disappeared.

"Hey! How did we get off the subject of what a great actor Stewart Mason is, though?" He said, looking up from his notebook. The conversation stopped for a moment, as everyone considered his question. They all laughed and returned to the topic of Mr. Riverdale's "condition." But in his heart, Katie's father wondered if there really was something else going on at the zoo.

Katie was curious, too. In school, Brittany had told the class that the case would probably be rescheduled for later in the year.

"My father said that it might not get to court again until sometime in the fall. Anyway, we're just glad that Mr. Riverdale is okay. He's one of my father's most important clients, as you know." She glared at Henry.

Katie was sure that Brittany would never forgive Henry for his persistent questions on the day of the trial. But, try as she might, Brittany just wasn't clever enough with words to humiliate Henry. Her lack of creativity didn't stop her, Jordan, and Mackenzie from pointedly ignoring Henry whenever possible, though.

In a way, it was more hurtful to be treated as if you didn't exist. Katie was glad she had Lily and Corky. Except for the three of them, hardly anyone talked to Henry at all. Katie had gone from being bewildered about this turn of events to angry and confused. She and Lily and Corky talked about how unfair their classmates were to Henry. None of them could figure out how to help Henry, or why he had become such an outcast.

Katie wanted to ask Mr. Murwata about it, but she wasn't sure what to say. Instead, she kept quiet and made it a point to include Henry in more conversations so he wouldn't feel so alone. One day when Katie was walking home from school with Sophia, she brought the subject up. Katie wasn't sure she'd be able to explain all of this to Sophia. The whole situation seemed so far away from Sophia's world, but much to Katie's surprise, Sophia seemed to understand the strange social situation at Manhattan Prep.

"These girls are," Sophia struggled to come up with the English word she was looking for. "How you say it, not safe?"

"Not safe?" Katie said. "What do you mean?"

"These girls see this boy, Henry, and he has not the look like other boys, so it goes better for them to just not pay attention. They get afraid because this boy isn't so easy to understand. They don't see the boy. They see something different, more hard to think about. You see?" Sophia asked Katie. "That way, they no have to try and figure out. Make senses to me," she added helpfully.

The explanation was not helping Katie understand, and really, it was draining her emotions to continually worry about it, so Katie nodded and changed the subject. Besides, she had the whole Spring Dance issue to wrestle with. Sometimes Katie thought that growing up was too hard.

Chapter 16

On Friday, the day of the Spring Dance, Katie woke up with a sense of dread. Even Tuffy trying to lure her into a game of tug-of-war couldn't raise her spirits. As if to mock her, the sky was a beautiful, bright, New York blue. A light breeze blew and the new leaves on the trees across the street swayed back and forth as if curtsying to Katie. "Katie, the Princess of New York," as her dad often said.

"Well, Tuffy, this Princess is feeling more like a troll today. Oh yuck!" Katie exclaimed as she glimpsed herself in the mirror. "My hair is a disaster!" she said to no one in particular. Her hair was a mess of tangled curls. "My hair looks like it got caught in Sophia's vacuum cleaner," she said to the mirror.

It was such a beautiful day, there was no question that Katie and Sophia would walk to school together, after which Sophia would stop at the market to pick fresh produce. If she lived in America a thousand years, Sophia would never get tired of the wonderful fruits and vegetables available on every block of New York.

"Katie, you almost ready for school?" Sophia shouted down the hallway.

"Coming, Sophia," Katie answered.

"No breakfast today? No good. Should eat something or brain will not run," Sophia admonished. "How about I fix you a nice piece of cinnamon toast? I can tempt you with that?"

"That'll be good, Sophia. Would you feed Tuffy while I try and do something civilized with my hair?" Katie asked.

"Tuffy, the most spoiled dog in all of America, come and get your breakfast. We feed you some nice liver and bacon flavored doggie food. In Romania, this is big treat for people. Come, Tuffy," Sophia said.

Tuffy raced down the hallway, stopping halfway to see if Katie was following him. When it became clear that she was not, Tuffy cloaked himself in dignity and trotted down the hall to a waiting Sophia. At least someone was paying attention to him this morning!

On the way to school, Sophia told Katie about the day the two of them arrived in New York. How Katie slept for much of the flight from Bucharest, but woke up about an hour before the plane landed in New York. How the passengers on the plane helped Sophia with her carry-on bags and Katie. And how Sophia turned their passage through Customs into a hilarious comedy.

"When I arrive, I carry you off plane and into airport. You was tiny baby, but wiggling all over. Man at Custom looks at my passport and your papers, and say to me, 'where you coming from?' How he doesn't know this? I say 'I come from plane, outside.' He looks like giant bear, and makes nasty sound at me. Then he say, 'I know from plane, but where comes plane from?' I think he tries to play tricks on me, so I say 'plane comes from sky.' He don't laugh, but peoples behind me laughing very loud. Then he say 'how long you will stay here?' I don't know how long it take to get out of airport, so I say to him 'maybe one hour, if baby's mama and papa helps us find baggages.' Now peoples laughing even louder, and you now crying. What for an adventure we have, little one!"

"We're lucky he didn't send us back!" Katie said, laughing.

"We lucky peoples behind help me know what the big bear wants to know. Now, little one, have a good day in school."

At the corner across the street from the school, Katie gave Sophia a quick kiss on the cheek and ran to catch up with Corky, who was just getting off the bus. Corky waved to Sophia and, as soon as Katie reached her, they gave each other a quick hug.

"Ready for the night of the living dread?" Corky asked Katie. Her ability to turn even the most depressing facts into comedy always made Katie laugh.

But she didn't understand why no one had asked Corky to the dance. Corky was cute, and everyone—every grownup who met her—remarked that her features were startling and lovely. But Katie suspected that Corky intimidated some boys because she was so outspoken. One thing about Corky: You always knew where you stood with her. She didn't conceal her emotions or her feelings very well.

Often on Saturday afternoons, the girls would walk dogs for Lily's father, a veterinarian. One Saturday afternoon, they saw something none of them would ever forget. They were near Central Park, waiting for a light to change so they could cross the street into the park. A woman on the other side of the street was having trouble controlling the small dog she was walking.

"Sit!" She screamed at the dog.

"I said 'sit!'" She screamed again, yanking violently at the dog's collar.

The little dog started barking, panicked by the woman's screaming. The more he barked, the louder she screamed and the more violently she yanked at the dog. Finally, as the light changed, the woman kicked the dog, cursed at it and then hit it.

Lily and Katie were stunned by the woman's cruelty, and stood in shocked silence, but Corky flew into the intersection, shrieking at the woman. She had given Lily the leash of the dog she was walking, and had both hands free.

"What do you think you're doin', you hag? Leave the dog alone!"

"Get out of my way!" The woman screamed at Corky, pushing her off the curb. Corky tripped, and fell into the street, but grabbed the dog and held onto him as the woman tugged on the leash. "Let go of the damn dog!"

"I'll not let go of him, you don't deserve to have him." Corky unclipped the leash from the dog's collar, and stood facing the woman. Her knees were scraped and bleeding from her fall, but she was clearly not going to give up the dog. "Go ahead, call a cop and I'll be glad to tell him how you've been treatin' this poor dog."

A crowd had gathered around the scene. Lily and Katie were trying to keep the dogs they were walking calm, even as they tried to protect Corky from the angry woman.

"Get away from her!" Katie shouted as the woman lurched toward Corky, demanding that she give the dog back. Lily was on her cell phone, calling her father.

The adults in the crowd had gotten between Corky and the now enraged dog owner.

"My dad is on his way here," Lily said. "I think he called the police, too."

The dog owner was cursing and screaming, and some of the people in the crowd were telling her to keep it down.

Lily's father and the two police officers arrived within a few minutes. "Corky, honey, are you okay? You're bleeding. Let me take a look at you."

"I'm fine, Dr. Hanover. This dog is cryin', though. I think he's been hurt. She kicked him pretty hard."

One of the police officers took the dog owner aside, while the other spoke to Corky.

"Can you tell me what happened here?"

"That hag was cursin' and kickin' the poor little dog. I couldn't stand to see it and I tried to stop her. She pushed me and I tripped."

"Did you touch the woman? Push her?"

"I should have kicked her the way she was kickin' her dog," Corky said. "But I didn't, I'm ashamed to say."

"Officer, my daughter here was a witness. She said the woman was pretty violent with the dog." Dr. Hanover now had the dog in his arms. "The dog is bleeding. It looks like he's got a couple of broken teeth."

The whole incident ended with the police charging the dog owner with animal abuse. They took the dog away from her, pending a hearing; and gave Dr. Hanover temporary custody until the matter was settled. Lily and Katie were deeply saddened by the episode, but Corky seemed unable to let go of her anger. "I'd do it again in a second," she told her friends. "I just can't let a thing like that pass. D'ya think I'm crazy as a loon, for going after that witch?"

Katie and Lily thought Corky was brave, not crazy. It was so typical of her, to leap into action without giving her own safety a thought. They always wondered if Corky's "take me as I am or get out of my way" attitude was her own way of coping with the mysterious absence of her father.

Chapter 17

The day seemed to drag on, probably because Katie was so depressed about the Spring Dance.

This is ridiculous, she thought to herself. *How can I let this one night make me feel this awful?* Still, she couldn't stifle the feeling that she was left out of an important social event. The bell rang and the halls emptied as students raced to make it to the next class. Katie realized she had forgotten a book she needed for her Social Studies class so she made a quick detour to her locker to retrieve it. There was hardly anyone left in the hall as she approached her locker.

She thought she heard a scratching sound. It sounded like Tuffy when he was trying to get through a closed door. She strained to hear and she heard the scratching again, followed by someone whispering, "Help, help me, please."

What's going on? She was growing uneasy, but she went toward where she thought the sound was coming from. It was Henry's locker! Katie looked around the empty hallway.

"Help!"

The voice was so soft, Katie almost didn't think it was real.

"Henry?" Katie said in a soft voice.

"Katie? Is that you, Katie? Please, get me out of here!" Katie could hear panic and fear in Henry's voice. "I can't open the door! Please help me!"

Katie lifted up the padlock, and noticed gratefully that it had not been closed. Her heart was pounding as she removed it and swung open the door. There was Henry! His face was white and he looked as if he might throw up.

"Henry, what's going on? Who did this to you?" Katie was shocked and frightened for Henry.

"I...nothing...please! Don't tell anyone..." Henry stammered, and brushed past her. He darted down the hall almost stumbling. Katie thought he was crying. At that moment, she wished it had been Corky that found Henry. She thought Corky would know exactly how to handle the situation.

Katie closed Henry's locker, locked it and left, upset and scared. Already late, she hurried into class.

"Sorry, Mr. Murwata. I had to go to my locker to get a book for class. Um, sorry," Katie said in attempt to explain. Mr. Murwata nodded, but noticed that Katie looked upset and distracted. Although Katie was always one of the most reliable students when it came to class participation, this day she was withdrawn. Even when he asked her a question, she had nothing to say.

"I'm sorry. I guess I wasn't ready for class today…um…I don't know the answer." Katie mumbled her excuse with hardly a glance at the teacher.

Finally the bell rang and Mr. Murwata dismissed the class, but asked Katie to wait a moment. Katie noticed that Mackenzie and Brittany were staring at her, probably thinking she was going to get into trouble for being late for class. Jordan seemed different, though. She looked sad, and although she was watching Katie along with Brittany and Mackenzie, for the first time in months, Katie got the feeling that something had changed among the threesome that Corky always referred to as the "Queen beasts."

The three of them whispered something in their Cool Kid Code, and immediately balance was restored. They laughed in unison and sauntered out of the classroom, no doubt on their way to the spa to get pampered for their big night at the Spring Dance.

"Katie, is everything all right?" Mr. Murwata asked.

"Sure, Mr. Murwata…why do you ask?"

"When you arrived for class you seemed awfully upset. Has something happened? Is there anything I can do to help you?" Mr. Murwata said, truly wanting to help Katie. Mr. Murwata knew what it felt like to be an outsider and he suspected that Katie often felt the same way.

Katie hesitated. She seemed to want to tell him something but couldn't make up her mind whether to confide in him or not. She was worried about what had happened to Henry. She felt she needed to tell someone because she suspected Henry would be scared to do anything. She was confused about what, exactly, was the right thing to do. What if she told Mr. Murwata what she had found and he told the principal and then everyone knew and Henry was humiliated?

"Perhaps I can help. If you need my confidence, I pledge that I will keep whatever you tell me to myself," Mr. Murwata said.

Katie decided that she could trust Mr. Murwata. She didn't know why she felt that way, she just knew that she had to tell a grownup what had happened and Mr. Murwata was so dignified and proper, he'd know the right thing to do.

"I forgot my book and I was hurrying to my locker to get it when I heard an awful scratching sound coming from one of the lockers," Katie said as she began to tell Mr. Murwata what had happened. "Then I thought I heard a voice. As I got closer, I realized the voice was coming from Henry's locker. His padlock was looped through the latch, but it wasn't locked. Henry was stuck in there. He didn't tell me anything, he just ran down the hall. I don't even know where he went," Katie was getting more upset as she retold the story.

The pieces fell into place for Mr. Murwata. Katie arriving late for class. Henry not coming at all.

"Kids can be very mean to one another, Katie," Mr. Murwata explained. "Do you have any idea who would do this to Henry? You know, if Henry won't tell his parents or teachers, we can't really do anything." Mr. Murwata was hoping to get more details from Katie.

"I don't think Henry has many friends, Mr. Murwata," Katie said. "Some kids are mean to him sometimes. I don't understand what's going on. Henry's a really nice, smart boy. But it seems that if Lily, Corky, and I didn't talk to him, no one at all would talk to him," Katie said, her voice trailing off. "I don't know what to do. Should I tell my parents?" Katie asked her teacher.

"Katie, why not let me handle this?" Mr. Murwata replied. "I think I can quietly delve into what went on here this afternoon without violating your confidence. It's clear Henry is embarrassed about what has happened so I suspect that someone did this to him as a cruel joke. And it must stop, Katie. What happened this afternoon could be dangerous. What if you hadn't heard him and he had been stuck for several hours? Just think about him not showing up at home after school. How frantic his parents would have been. No, this must stop," Mr. Murwata said thoughtfully.

"Do you have to tell someone else?" Katie asked, now worried that somehow she had set some awful machine in motion.

"I promised you that I would not violate your confidence, but I must tell you that we cannot help Henry until we speak to others about this, Katie. I'm asking you to trust me to do what is best for Henry in this situation."

Mr. Murwata's voice was firm, yet extraordinarily polite and gentle. Katie thought for a minute. Her emotions seemed so jumbled. The dance, the fact that she and Corky felt like outcasts, and now this thing with Henry. She couldn't find the right words to say to Mr. Murwata. Instead, she fell back on what they were talking about in class.

"How can we all spend so much time talking about justice and then be so mean to each other?" Katie asked.

"Ah, Katie, that's the dilemma we spoke about, isn't it? Everyone wants justice for themselves, but not everyone knows how to give justice to others. Even if they cannot find justice in their hearts, they should at least discover mercy, yes?" Mr. Murwata was trying to reassure Katie, but even he was distressed about this situation.

"I'm going to talk to Mr. Needham, Katie, if you agree—and only if you agree. Let's see if we can't straighten this whole thing out without causing any more upset than has already been caused." Mr. Murwata waited for Katie to agree. She was torn about getting the Headmaster involved. Once he knew about what had happened, there would be consequences for everyone. She was uncomfortable about taking the problem to a much higher level, but she also had a sick feeling in her stomach, and wanted to make it go away.

"You will let me take care of this? You've had a terrible fright today. I can't imagine how I'd feel if I discovered someone locked in a locker," Mr. Murwata smiled gently at Katie, obviously trying to make her feel better.

"Okay, I guess that'll be all right," Katie responded. She gathered her things and walked out of the classroom to find Lily and Corky waiting outside in the hall for her.

"What happened in there? Are you sick or somethin'? What did Mr. Murwata want with you?" Corky was curious but also concerned about her friend's sad face.

"You are not going to believe what happened to make me late for class," Katie whispered, and as they walked out of school, she told her two friends what she had found.

"This has gone too far," Corky said raising her voice. "I know who did this to Henry, and who's been doing him wrong for weeks now. You can see the connection between Blondie and her crowd. To be sure, they wouldn't get their own hands dirty, now would they? I'm betting they had someone else do their dirty work for them...to get back at Henry for his questions to that creepy zoo guy." Corky was getting so riled up that her face was starting to turn red.

"Poor Henry," Lily said. "Can you imagine what it must feel like, locked inside one of these lockers?" Lily shivered at the thought.

It remained unsaid between Katie, Lily, and Corky, but all three had come to the same conclusion. Things had gotten out of hand and someone was going to get hurt. They could just feel it.

By the time they reached the front door of the school, the girls could see Lily's mom waiting for her. She was talking to Sophia, who was waiting for Katie.

Corky was going home with Katie to get ready for the Dance, since Charlotte and Chloe were scheduled to be shooting "Love's Labours" until 5:30 in the evening. Lily's mom caught sight of the girls and waved.

"We'll see you tonight," Corky said as she and Katie hugged Lily goodbye. They both waved at Mrs. Hanover.

"My parents and I are coming around 6:30. I'm going to meet Tyler here with his parents," Lily said. She felt the sadness about

Henry's situation covering her like a web, and wondered if she would even enjoy this evening with Tyler.

"Our moms will have just enough time to change and meet us here at 7," Katie told Lily. "My dad is bringing Corky and me," she added. "We'll see you later, okay?"

"See ya," Lily said, as she and her mom walked toward their car.

"Well, girls, how was school? What did you learn today?" Sophia asked.

"Oh, Sophia, something strange happened," Katie said. "But you've got to swear not to tell Mom and Dad about it, okay?"

"Swear to keep secrets? Katie, you must not tell me things what I cannot discuss with your parents. Is not correct."

Sophia looked at Katie and noticed how sad she looked. "Is a bad thing? Is dangerous? You must not keep secret what is dangerous, Katie."

"I talked to Mr. Murwata, Sophia. He's taking care of it, and it was not something dangerous," Katie said, again worrying about making too much of a fuss about what had happened. She changed the subject to detour Sophia's train of thought.

"Are Corky's clothes in my room? Did her mom drop off everything this morning?"

"Yes, clothes are beautiful. Corky will be belle of ball," Sophia said. "Your mama says you must be careful with dress, Corky, because it makes stain easy. And she say to you remember not to put lips on until after dress is on."

"What am I, then, a total dork?" Corky said, rolling her eyes.

"Sophia, do you think we can do something with my hair? I can't exactly wear my beret to the Dance." Katie was hoping Sophia had some ideas about how to tame her curls for the occasion. They had talked earlier about braiding her hair and Sophia promised to think about it while Katie was at school.

"I think we make beautiful braid—not old lady braid but French braid, yes?"

"Will it make my hair look normal?"

"Katie, your hair is beautiful! What you say about normal? Why you girls always want to look like all the other girls? In Europe is good to be different. Boys like girls who are not same, you know that?"

"But, Sophia, we're not in Europe, you know. It seems that here, the boys seem to like everything but girls like Katie and me," Corky protested.

"Girls what try to be something else don't do good. People must be what is real, not phony-baloney. You girls, I tell you, are beautiful. If boys don't know that, they are stupid. No more talk about this." Sophia made a slashing gesture with her arm, to emphasize that she would not discuss the issue with them further.

"Your father probably home by now," Sophia said as they arrived at the apartment.

As soon as Sophia put the key in the lock of the front door, Katie could hear Tuffy barking. *He's been waiting all day for us,* she thought.

"Tuffy! Come, my leetle prinze!" Katie cried and she gathered the little dog up in her arms. "Look who I brought home with me," she said. "Your other favorite Princess, Corky!" Tuffy licked Katie's face in reply. Katie could have sworn that Tuffy knew exactly what she was saying.

"Hey, Tuffy, you sweet darlin'! How's the grandest dog in all the land?" Corky patted Tuffy on the head. "Tuffy want kisses? Ummm. Smooch," she said as she kissed him behind his velvety ears.

Yes! Tuffy thought to himself. *This is my destiny! To be the center of attention, cuddled, kissed, adored.*

Corky would have loved to have had a dog, but the apartment she and her mom rented didn't allow pets, so Corky was destined to a life with only goldfish, and a part-time relationship with Tuffy.

The girls went to Katie's room, Tuffy hot on their trail. Sophia went into the kitchen to make them a snack.

"What do you think will happen with Henry?" The girls had dropped their backpacks in a heap on the floor and flopped onto Katie's bed. Katie couldn't get Henry off her mind.

"What I'm lookin' to find out is who did it," Corky said. "There's no way they'll stop at something like this. But, you know I don't get it. Why are they so nasty to him?"

"Remember that day in court, Corky, when Henry was asking all those questions about the zoo? I think Mr. Morgan thought Henry was a smart mouth and Mr. Morgan probably said something to Brittany. Somehow I think she's behind this," Katie said thoughtfully.

"Then they'll all be at the Dance, looking gorgeous and sooo sophisticated. Don't you think they have any conscience at all? How can they hurt him like that, and then just go on having fun? What kind of people are they?"

"It just makes this whole thing even more depressing. Going to this dance tonight was bad enough. Now with this thing about Henry, it's even worse." Katie was staring at the ceiling. "Are you dreading tonight as much as I am?" Katie asked Corky.

"Dread isn't the word. It's like knowing you have a really bad dentist appointment, and you know you've a cavity the size of an eyeball, and you have to go back to school with your mouth all numb, so everyone can see you drooling and looking stupid."

The girls laughed at the eyeball-sized cavity and the amount of numbness it would require.

"Who's drooling?" Katie's father appeared at the door. The girls stopped laughing and stared at each other, briefly wondering if he had heard any of their conversation about Henry.

"Hi, Mr. Farrell. How are you?"

"Hey, Corky. I guess you girls will be my dates tonight. I hope you weren't worried that I was so old that I would embarrass you by drooling all over my shirt."

"Dad, we were thinking that this stupid dance would be more like going to the dentist, and then you'd have this big cavity and then your face would be numb..." Katie was stumbling through an abbreviated explanation of how the two girls had found themselves laughing instead of dreading the dance.

"Hey, aren't you girls looking forward to this? Remember, your moms agreed we can all sneak out as soon as we've fulfilled our obligations. Then it's off to Gelato's and ice cream sundaes."

"Girls! Come get your snacks!" Sophia had made little sandwiches for the girls, and had developed a timeline for getting everyone ready to leave the apartment on time. It was critical that everyone stick to Sophia's schedule for the remainder of the afternoon. The girls brought the latest copy of *XC* to the table with them. As usual, they were chattering excitedly about every nuance of fashion extolled by the magazine. This time, there was something else, though.

"Oh, no! Katie! You've got to see this! It's Brittany's ma, smothered in her jewels!" Corky was gawking at a full-page picture of Lydia Morgan, dressed like a prom queen and covered in expensive-looking jewelry.

"What's she doing in *XC*?"

"Lydia Morgan, whose designs have graced the wrists of royalty and celebrities all over the world, has created what she calls her 'legacy to her daughter'—a fabulous collection of jewelry made just for young girls." Corky was reading from an article that went on for several pages. "They're making her out to be the patron saint of pearls," she said incredulously. "And look at this! Ads for the stuff. They're all over the place."

The girls were transfixed by the lush settings where the jewelry models were photographed.

"And would you look at the lass with the red hair! Her dress is missin' the whole front!" Corky was amazed. "I can see ma now, letting me actually leave the house dressed like that—with or without that choker thing around my neck."

"Corky, look at that pin! It's gorgeous, isn't it?"

"What are you girls looking at?" Katie's father had come into the kitchen, lured by the girls' oohing and aahing.

"Dad, look at these pictures of Brittany's mom in *XC*! Isn't she gorgeous?"

"Well, honey, she has her charms. But don't you think all that jewelry is a little much?" He looked closer at the picture, then flipped the pages to look at some of the ads. "How come all those little girls are wearing all that stuff? Whoa! Where's the rest of that dress?"

"Dad! Mrs. Morgan is famous. The models are showing stuff

that Mrs. Morgan designed as a…a…what's that word, Corky?"

"Legacy, for cryin' out loud. She's gone and made a legacy to Blondie!"

"Dad they're a legacy to Brittany Morgan! Can you imagine how much cooler she's going to be after everyone sees this?" Katie was dismayed. As if Brittany needed more reasons to be stuck up and to treat Katie and her friends like garbage. " I'll bet she'll be dripping with it tonight."

"Do you girls really believe that something you wear will make you more important, or prettier?"

"Dad, you don't understand. It's…it's…"

"It's just that Blondie doesn't even have to work a minute at bein' cool. People keep pourin' cool all over her!" Corky was half-amused, half-confused. "How does this stuff happen? We're nice to people, we work hard, we get good grades…how come we don't get legacies and magazine articles in *XC* and such?"

"Girls, you've got to stop looking at all the stuff everyone else says and does and has. Like Corky said, you're nice to people, you work hard at school and get good grades. Those things are important and good whether any magazine notices or not."

Katie's father was worried that he was losing ground in this argument. The momentum of the hugely popular *XC* magazine was against him. "Besides, I think you're both beautiful. Someday you'll have a better perspective on this, and understand that what a bunch of kids do in school is not nearly as important as what they do with their lives."

The two girls looked at him, unconvinced. Frustrated, he left the kitchen to return to the den where he had been working.

"Girls, you must not keep talking. Time to get ready for dance." Sophia was waving the schedule at the girls, to remind them that the clock was ticking. "Now, Corky, your mama says you must have nice shower, and I says I take care of your hair. Towels and everything ready for you in Katie's bathroom. And Katie, you make your shower first, so I can make your braid. Dresses all ready crisp and clean and hanging in Katie's closet. I even get something special for you ladies, a surprise!"

Sophia had one of the royal blue Becks Department Store bags in her hand. It was a tiny bag, with the distinctive Becks logo in gleaming gold script. The girls were overcome with curiosity.

"C'mon Sophia, what did you get? What's in the bag? When did you go to Becks?" They were as excited as if it were Christmas morning and Santa Claus was there in person with one last gift.

After teasing the girls with suggestions about what might be in the bag, Sophia dramatically reached into it and produced two slender tubes of one of the most elusive products ever to be touted in the bible of adolescent cool, *XC*.

"It's Smooches & Cream!" The two girls erupted in simultaneous squeals of excitement. "How did you find it? When did you get it?

We've been looking everywhere for it!" The girls swarmed Sophia with hugs and kisses.

"Go! Now go! You girls must make you showers and be ready to go!" Sophia shooed the girls out of the kitchen, blowing kisses at them as they went.

The girls raced toward Katie's room, still clutching the latest issue of *XC*.

"This is all everyone will be talking about tonight, Corky. We're going to look even more like losers."

"Yeah, but losers wearin' Smooches & Cream! I give up. Your father is right, Katie. We've got to be who we are, and let the world take us or leave us." The girls were sitting on Katie's bed, still unable to tear themselves away from the magazine.

"It isn't a wonder that she's been acting so snooty lately, even for her. She knew that she'd be a real celebrity just in time for tonight," Corky said.

"Look at these bracelets. Can you imagine buying a bracelet that cost $900? My dad would have a fit!"

"Look at those earrings! Geez, they're as big as saucers. What are those, diamonds hanging off them?"

The girls decided that the jewelry was not for them, although the clothes on the models were really cool.

"This stuff will be hangin' all over Blondie tonight. She'll have bracelets up to her elbows and sparkling things that'll surely blind you if you look straight at her. Do ya think she'll be surrounded by those pop-perrazies, then?" Corky said, laughing.

"Popper-whats?"

"You know, those people who chase movie stars and famous people all over the place, snapping their pictures."

The girls thought the word "paparazzi" was so funny that they began to make up all sorts of words to rhyme with it.

"Katie, you must hurry or your braid goes away." Sophia was serious, but Katie and Corky fell onto the bed again, laughing at the thought of Katie's hair leaving for the dance without her.

"Hey, what was all the commotion here?" Katie's father had heard the girls screaming about Sophia's gift, and returned to the kitchen. "What are smooches and cream?" He was confused and bewildered by the girls' roller coaster of emotions.

"It's for the lips. I don't know why they think it so hard to find. It only takes me three weeks to get it," Sophia explained.

"Oh, that stuff Katie has been obsessed about? You must be a better detective than Sherlock Holmes," he said.

"Not detective, just good shopper. Now, you need something to eat before you go? I can make you sandwich, yes?"

"No, thanks, Sophia. I had a big lunch today. Besides, I've still got some work to finish up before we leave this evening." He turned to leave the kitchen, hesitated for a minute and then went back to the kitchen.

"It was really sweet of you to go out of your way to find that lipstick for the girls. Katie has been talking to Charlotte about that stuff for weeks. I don't know how you find all these things that nobody else seems able to locate."

"I love being here. I love helping my American family. How I can not do everything is possible to makes Katie happy girl?"

Tuffy sensed that there was an opportunity for him in all the commotion. He deftly leaped onto Corky's chair at the kitchen table, where he could get a better view of what was left of the girls' snack.

Hmmm. Butter! He thought to himself. *And half a sandwich! Mine!* He licked a dab of butter off the edge of Corky's plate and grabbed the rest of her sandwich before he suddenly became the center of attention again.

"Tuffy!" Sophia was using her "get off that table now or else" voice, which always motivated Tuffy to do whatever she said. "Bad dog. You know you not allowed on table. Why you can't wait for me to give you what is left over?"

Tuffy was back on the floor, looking apologetic and chastised. He knew that Sophia's heart would melt at the sight of his downcast eyes. Just in case she was really angry, he added the gesture he knew she could never resist. He raised his right paw slightly, as if offering to shake her hand. She caved in instantly, and scooped him up in her arms.

"Come, doggie, I make you an egg, yes? Then you get your own plate." She put him down on the kitchen floor while she fried an egg for him. He decided to have some water while she cooked. The sound of the egg frying, and its delicious aroma, combined with the distant sounds of Katie and Corky doing whatever it was that was making them laugh and chatter like a couple of squirrels and the voice of Katie's father on the phone in the den...in Tuffy's mind, it was a snapshot of wonder and happiness and peace.

Life is good, Tuffy thought to himself. *I wonder if other dogs could possibly be this happy...*

Chapter 18

In Katie's room, the air was thick with the aroma of perfume and shampoo and crème rinse. The girls were working hard on getting ready for the dance, and although their hearts were not necessarily in the effort, their moods were brightened by Sophia's gift and the realization that they wouldn't have to suffer through much more than an hour or so.

"Truly, Katie, if not for you and Lily, I wouldn't be going at all," Corky said through a mouth full of toothpaste. "I'm just happy our moms said we don't have to stay for the whole thing."

"My mom said that it shouldn't take more than an hour to get through the report on the scholarship program, so we can practically count the minutes," Katie said. She was trying to get her mass of curls semi-dry for Sophia to work her magic.

Tuffy had returned to help the girls get ready. But he was suddenly overwhelmed with the desire to nap. He walked past Katie, brushing against her leg slightly, just to let her know he was there, and jumped onto her bed, snuggling up in the pillows at the top of the bed. It was the perfect place to keep an eye on what was happening with Katie, and to remain absolutely comfortable, in case he fell asleep.

"Katie, don't make hair all the way dry! I need some damp to work with," Sophia called out.

"Okay, Sophia. I think it's ready."

Katie was excited about Sophia's ideas for her hair, and thrilled that she would be wearing "Smooches & Cream" on her lips. In her imagination, her hair would be a stunning triumph. The kids at school would not be able to take their eyes off her. And the boys in her class would be kicking themselves all over Manhattan for not having the good sense to ask her to the dance. Then, almost as soon as she arrived, she would be gone, like Cinderella. But in their minds, she would be an unforgettable presence. She looked at her dress, hanging in the closet. It was a beautiful shade of yellow, enhanced by a delicate dotted swiss overlay on the skirt. Sophia, in one of her excursions to out-of-the-way boutiques, had discovered a seamstress who, like Sophia, had come from Romania.

"I find woman from Romania who makes beautiful girl dresses. She works in shop on 40th Street. You come with me someday and we see what she has if you like it, yes?"

When Sophia first started inviting Katie to go with her to the boutiques, Katie worried that she would wind up in clothes that would make her look dumpy and totally out of touch, setting her even further apart from the kids at her school. But Sophia was so insistent, and Katie didn't want to hurt her feelings. Soon Katie was as enthusiastic as Sophia. It wasn't just the clothes she found. It was the sound of all the different languages and the way the people in the tiny shops loved talking with Sophia and Katie.

Katie was intrigued by the people in the shops, and their stories about how they came to America, and the families and lives they left behind in Italy or Greece or Ireland or Serbia. She felt a kinship with them, and a sense of belonging. She realized that shopping was not the purpose of these trips; they were Sophia's way to expose Katie to other people who were immigrants, and who retained a deep sense of pride about their homelands—even as they grew to love America.

But these trips also gave Sophia a connection to her other world—a world that she could never forget. It didn't matter how many years separated her from Romania. In her dreams, and in her heart, she knew that part of her would always be there.

The pale yellow dress came from Mimi's, a shop that didn't even have dresses in the front window. The display space was taken up by fabrics draped gracefully over an old sewing machine. Mimi was about 50 years old, and her store was jammed floor to ceiling with bolts of fabric. She made everything, from slipcovers to fancy ball gowns.

"You look for a dress to go dancing?" She asked Katie.

"Well, it's a dress to wear to a school dance. But I probably won't be dancing," Katie said despondently.

"Close your eyes, little one. I think I have a beautiful fabric for you to look at." Katie put her hands over her eyes, while Mimi practically dove into shelf of fabric bolts. She heard Sophia gasp in awe as Mimi returned with her prize.

"Open now!"

Mimi was holding two pieces of fabric, one the beautiful pale yellow material that reminded Katie of a ribbon, and the other a transparent fabric with tiny ivory dots.

"Is called organza," Mimi said as she pressed the yellow fabric against Katie's cheek. "Is beautiful color for you."

"You can make this into a dress?" Katie asked.

"I'm thinking a dress with pretty top and flare skirt. I cover skirt with dots," she said.

"What do you think, Katie?" Sophia asked. "I love this fabric. It is lovely color for you, and nobody else will have dress this beautiful."

Katie couldn't take her eyes off the fabrics. The combination of crisp organza and the soft transparent fabric reminded Katie of something Cinderella would wear. She imagined what she might look like arriving at the Dance in this lovely combination of textures.

"I only take measurement now, and next week you come back for fitting, okay?" Mimi said, tapping Katie on the shoulder.

The thought of having to get measured for the dress snapped Katie back to the cold reality that she was not Cinderella, but something rounder and darker. Mimi gently cupped Katie's chin in her hand and looked deep into her eyes. It was almost as though Mimi could read her mind.

"You know what is most beautiful in a person?" she asked Katie. "Here, and here," she said pointing to Katie's head and heart.

Sophia's hands were resting on Katie's shoulders.

"I tell her all the time that beauty is not a skinny body but a kind heart," Sophia said. "But you know girls today, they thinks everyone must look like they are cookies in a cutter."

Katie turned to face Sophia and hugged her. She loved the way Sophia could mix up language but make her points very clearly.

"I think it's a cookie cutter," she said, laughing.

"Yes, a cookie cutter, whatever. These girls they don't care about anything but a mirror. You, my little one, are more beautiful than you know."

Chapter 19

It had taken Mimi a week to finish the dress, and it was as beautiful as Katie had imagined. She took the dress out of the closet, and hung it on a hook on the door, next to Corky's dress, which was an emerald green color as outspoken as Corky herself.

"If we stand too close to each other, we're going to look like a daffodil." Corky said. "Brittany and Jordan and Mackenzie will look like lilies, of course. And we'll be a giant daffodil."

Katie laughed at the image of a giant daffodil among the slender, graceful lilies.

"I love your dress, Corky. It's the color of your eyes. What do you think Brittany will be wearing?"

"Maybe monkey fur," Corky said sarcastically. Katie looked at Corky, startled by the image her comment evoked. Then she thought of some alternatives.

"No, I think it will be baby tiger fur."

"No, it will be baby polar bear fur."

By now, the girls were again dissolved in laughter, imagining all sorts of animal skins draped over Brittany, along with enough jewelry to sink a battleship. But the clock was ticking and Sophia's schedule was starting to crack. She heard the laughter as she tapped on Katie's bedroom door, and poked her head into the room.

"Katie, you must put dress on before I can fix hair. And Corky! Snap, snap. Your hair is ready for me to start work? You run out of time quickly."

Corky slipped her dress over her head and Sophia helped her close the zipper in the back.

"Beautiful!" Sophia said. "Now I fix your hair and then you can put on lips. But not too much make-up, yes? You are still little girl."

Katie gently removed her dress from the hanger and held it close

99

to her face. She marveled at the cool softness of the fabric, and how it made her feel so elegant. As she slid the dress over her head, she was unaware that Sophia and Corky were watching.

"Oh, Katie, it's gorgeous!" Corky exclaimed. "It's really gorgeous!"

"You're lovely," Sophia said softly. "Now, sit while I make your braid." Sophia had pulled Corky's hair up into a pony tail and then twisted the pony tail into a shiny knot. Corky stood at the mirror admiring Sophia's work.

"How did you do that so fast?" she asked.

"Is trick I learned on daytime TV show," Sophia said. "I buy these little hooks and suddenly hair is beautiful style, not just pony tail."

"You sound like a commercial," Corky said. "But I have to say, it really does look neat."

Corky sat on the bed and watched Sophia wrestle with Katie's hair. She pulled, twisted, braided, pulled again, and suddenly, Katie's hair was up in a beautiful, thick braid. Several curls escaped from the braid, but they contributed to the overall impact of the braid and Katie's face, dominated by dark, mysterious eyes.

"Wow! Sophia, you're a genius!" Corky said.

Katie looked in the mirror, and could hardly believe that the girl staring back at her was real.

"You like your braid?" Sophia said.

"It's beautiful, Sophia. I can't believe it worked!"

"Okay, girls. No more wasting time. You have 10 minutes to finish up. Both are beautiful, and I must take picture, so make yourselves ready quickly."

The two girls stood next to each other, looking at themselves in Katie's mirror. They reached back for Sophia and pulled her close, both hugging her.

"Thank you, Sophia. Thank you." The three stood there for a moment, arms entwined.

"Finish now!" Sophia said. "I get your father, Katie, and take picture of the three of you." Sophia was getting emotional again, and turned to leave the room.

When the girls came into the living room, Katie's father whistled softly at them.

"Wow! You girls look absolutely beautiful! Like models!"

"Pictures now!" Sophia said, as she started arranging John, Tuffy and the girls. She snapped about five pictures, then the girls demanded that Sophia pose for some pictures with them. John focused the camera, set the timer and put the camera on a stack of books. He ran back to the group just in time. The camera flashed as he took his place in the group, holding Tuffy in his arms. They took several more pictures that way, and then it was time for the girls and John to leave.

The evening was cool, and the three were walking to the Dance, so Sophia insisted that everyone wear a coat. She waved at them as they headed off together, and checked her schedule. Chloe and Charlotte would be there soon. Sophia wanted to open a bottle of wine, so the two women could relax with a glass of wine while they changed for the dance. She had put a bottle in the refrigerator earlier, and had made some pate, which John had already sampled.

"Swear that we won't have to stay too long," Corky said in a mock pleading tone to Katie's father. "You must swear that we can leave quickly, and go someplace where we've no worry about being cool."

"Hey, I think both of you look very cool, extremely cool, as a matter of fact," Katie's father said.

"Sure, but have you seen the cool kids, then? You don't know what it's like."

"I know, I know. Cool is something you have to be born with, right Katie?"

The girls looked at each other and rolled their eyes. Sometimes grownups were so out of touch.

"I heard the food is supposed to be Chinese," Katie said. "Can you imagine? As if we didn't have that at least once a week. I hope they're getting it from 'Phooey Manchewy.' Do you think they'll get it from there, Dad? They have the best fried dumplings." Charlotte and John had brought Katie to 'Phooey Manchewy's' since she was old enough to walk.

"You don't think we'll be eating bugs, then, do you Mr. Farrell?" Corky was teasing again, but then remembered another school event, where the meal was a bit too exotic for Corky's taste. "Do ya think we might get lucky? Remember the thing they fed us at that party last year, before the main course? I hope to never meet another one of those again on my plate. Why would we eat an eel, in the first place?" Corky was getting so excited that her accent was getting stronger by the minute.

"Well, I *hope* there won't be any bugs on the menu," he said in a voice that suggested there might actually be some, "but I think it's a pretty safe bet that the food isn't coming from anyplace we've ever heard of. I'm sure they've got a caterer bringing in all the food."

"Maybe bugs in the food wouldn't be as bad as feeling like a total loser," Katie said, more to herself than to her father and Corky.

"You two are finding all sorts of things to worry about. How bad could it be? You'll be with your friends, and then before you know it, we'll be out of there."

They stood for a minute at the entrance to the school. John leaned down and kissed Katie on the head and gave her a quick hug. "Have a wonderful time, sweetheart!"

Once inside, Corky and Katie looked for Lily. Within minutes they spotted her and Tyler. Lily looked gorgeous! Her dress was a lavender silk print and she had very cool shoes to match. Lily's mom had done Lily's hair up on top of her head with little spit curls surrounding her face. She looked like something out of an old painting, the kind that Katie saw when she went to the Metropolitan Museum with her parents. It was no wonder that Tyler had asked her.

Feeling a little self-conscious, Katie and Corky walked over to the buffet table and picked at some of the strange dishes offered. They managed to find about three or four things they recognized, and took their plates to one of the tables scattered throughout the room and sat down. They felt less obvious sitting at the table and eating, and soon became engrossed in discovering who got dates and who didn't. They were shocked to see that Jordan didn't have a date.

"What do you think happened?" Corky whispered. "How could Jordan wind up like us?"

"I can't imagine. But look how pretty she looks. I love that dress." Katie said under her breath.

Jordan was walking toward them. The two girls were utterly shocked that one of the coolest girls in school didn't have a date.

"Hi, Katie. Corky. Um...can I sit with you guys?" Jordan was obviously uncomfortable.

"Sure...I guess...I mean, yes, of course, please," Katie said as she moved her purse off one of the empty chairs at the table.

"My dad was trying to guilt me into coming to this with Marco Lupini," Jordan said as the threesome watched their classmates pair off. Katie and Corky looked at Jordan as if she had just spit on the table. They couldn't imagine anyone saying no to someone as nice as Marco.

"Why did your father want you to go with him?" Katie couldn't stop herself from asking the obvious question. Corky's eyes were practically glued to Jordan's dress. *It really does look like a designer dress,* she thought to herself. *I wonder if she got it in Paris or something.*

"Mr. Lupini's construction company is some kind of big deal, and he won this award for being a...I don't know the word but it starts with an e...enter something...anyway, he's pretty rich and famous, so my dad's PR firm wants him as a client. My dad practically fell on the floor when I told him Marco had asked me to the dance and I said no."

"But Marco is so cute, and he's a really nice guy. How come you didn't want to go with him?" Katie was intrigued. Finally, she had the chance to learn firsthand how the cool kids thought about things.

"You think he's cute? I guess he is. But...you know...he's new here, and his father...his father is sort of ...You know...he's okay, I guess, but...you know...Brittany's father said he came to a meeting here at school in construction boots and working clothes..."

"But what does that matter? Mr. Lupini is a really nice man. He doesn't work at an office. And anyway, what does that have to do with Marco?" Katie was starting to get a little angry with Jordan. *Is this what it means to be cool?* Katie thought to herself.

"Yeah, Jordan. My mother would probably come to a meeting loaded down with a bag of hairbrushes. How uncool is that?" Corky had stopped gawking at Jordan's dress, and was suddenly on the verge of rage at Jordan's attitude.

"I...I guess I'm not explaining it very well. It's just that...well...you know...Mr. Morgan is this famous lawyer, and Rodney's father is a famous judge—and your mother is a famous actress, Katie! Some of my friends made fun of him, and I guess that's why...I know it sounds stupid...and mean." Jordan's voice trailed off to practically a whisper. She looked down at her hands, fidgeting in her lap.

"Well, then, I guess it's curtains for my ma in your book. She's not a famous anything. I'm shocked you've agreed to sit next to me." Corky was on the verge of one of her "episodes," and Katie was trying to figure out a way to quiet her down before everyone in the room stopped and stared at them.

"Jordan, do you really think your friends would dump you if you came to the dance with Marco?"

"No...I don't know. But Mackenzie really made fun of Mr. Lupini, and she said her father told her that he's very common. I'm not sure what that means, but it didn't sound good."

"Are you sorry you said no?" Katie asked.

"No...maybe...I don't know. But...you know...it's hard to...I don't know...to do something...you know...something that your friends aren't doing. You feel like an outsider, or something. You know?"

Katie and Corky looked at each other, amazed. Corky was still angry, but Katie was starting to feel sorry for Jordan.

"Wouldn't your friends be your friends no matter what you decided to do?" Katie asked.

"I guess I'm not sure," Jordan said, sadly.

"So, Jordan, where did you get your dress? Did you go to Paris for it?" Corky was determined to find out where the dress came from. "Is it a designer dress, then? Is that bracelet one of Mrs. Morgan's jewel things?"

Jordan laughed. "My mother made the dress for me. She learned to sew when she was my age. She even designed it. But Brittany and Mackenzie think it's a designer dress, too. I guess it is, actually, since my mom designed it." Jordan seemed genuinely proud of her mother's work, and Katie wondered if she ever talked this way with the cool kids.

"The bracelet was my grandmother's. She was from New Mexico, and had lots of friends who were artists. One of them made it for her."

"Wow! New Mexico? I heard it's gorgeous there," Corky said. "Ma said that Santa Fe is one of the prettiest places in the world. Was your grandmother from Santa Fe, now?"

"She lived in Santa Fe, but she came from Taos. My mom took me to Santa Fe once, while my grandmother was still alive. And we went to the Indian Markct and walked all over the place. It really is pretty. Almost all the buildings are adobe, even lots of the newer ones. And the food is really good!" The more she talked, the less nervous Jordan seemed. And Katie and Corky forgot that Jordan was one of the cool girls. They just enjoyed the conversation.

"Lily looks gorgeous!" Jordan said. "That dress is so pretty, and I love her hair!"

The girls watched Lily and Tyler dance. Suddenly it seemed so odd, seeing all their friends dressed up in such fancy clothes and dancing so formally.

"This is kind of weird, isn't it?" Jordan said. "I mean, it's like a prom, but it doesn't seem like we're old enough to be at a prom."

"Do you think they're having fun?" Katie asked, pointing at all the kids on the dance floor. The band was playing music that sounded like songs the girls knew, but they couldn't place the songs. Not everyone was dancing. Some of the kids with dates were lingering close to the dance floor, but not close enough to be mistaken for dancers. The kids who were dancing seemed awkward and shy. "I mean, it doesn't feel like I thought it would."

Brittany and Mackenzie were with two of the guys who were on the school's baseball team. Katie thought they were acting weird. *They seem to be ignoring Jordan, now. Is it because she's sitting with us?* Occasionally Jordan's two friends would glance over at them. They didn't smile. It was almost as if they were trying to send some sort of eye-to-eye message to Jordan.

"Did you see the pictures of Brittany's mother in *XC*? I think Brit is actually wearing one of those necklaces that Mrs. Morgan designed," Jordan said. The girls looked over at Brittany.

"Do they think you might be catching something deadly from us, then, Jordan? Is that why they're acting like this side of the room has the plague?" Corky, as usual, wasn't inclined to hold anything back. Her candor startled Jordan.

"I...I...what? What do you mean?"

"They seem to be givin' you the evil eye, or didn't you notice?" Corky gestured wildly with her hands, waving them in Jordan's face to emphasize her point.

"Corky!" Katie was impressed that her friend said out loud what she herself had only been thinking, but she felt sorry for Jordan and didn't want Corky to make it any worse.

"They're just...they have dates and I don't. You know, they want to be with their dates."

Jordan's heart sank just then, as Lily and Tyler sat down.

"Hey, guys! Did you like the food?" Lily asked. "This music is kind of weird, isn't it?"

Tyler looked uncomfortable, the only boy at what was now a table full of girls.

"I think they bought their music from a museum," he said, gesturing toward the small group of musicians crowded onto a makeshift stage.

"Would that be the Natural History Museum, then, Tyler? Maybe Mr. Needham thought rock music had something to do with real rocks!" Corky said, with a perfectly straight face. Her delivery made everyone at the table laugh out loud. Even Jordan was laughing.

Katie looked toward the band, and saw Mackenzie and Brittany glaring at Jordan, who suddenly became very nervous. She stopped laughing and began fidgeting with the bracelet that the girls had admired earlier.

"Are you okay, Jordan?"

"Huh? Oh…sure…I was just…" Jordan struggled to think of something to say to shift everyone's attention elsewhere. "Can you believe that dinner? What was that stuff in the pink sauce?"

"I think I saw something swimming in it," Tyler said. "Didn't the menu say something about seaweed soup? Maybe they caught some kind of fish when they dragged the seaweed in." He looked around the table and saw fake grimaces sprouting on every face. "Kidding!" He laughed out loud at their reactions, and actually seemed to be enjoying his status as the only boy at the table. His moment in the spotlight was brief. Lily had spotted one of their friends, standing in a crowd near the dance floor.

"Look at Ashley's dress! She looks gorgeous, doesn't she?"

The conversation at the table stopped as everyone turned to look at Ashley Sinclair.

"She looks so tall!" Katie marveled. "I love her shoes."

"That red would look good on you, Katie, with your dark hair. On me, it's sure the color would stop Big Ben himself," Corky said.

As Tyler sat by helplessly, the conversation turned to clothes, Mrs. Morgan's jewelry designs, hairstyles, lip gloss and other matters about which he knew next to nothing. He watched Lily's face and admired her pretty smile. He amused himself by listening to the sound of her voice and was so immersed in his thoughts that her voice speaking his name startled him.

"Tyler, would you like to dance again? Tyler?"

"Me? What? Yes….I mean…what did you say?"

"I asked if you wanted to dance again," Lily said, laughing.

"Earth to Tyler," Corky teased.

The girls all laughed as Lily and Tyler headed for the dance floor. The band had struck up another familiar-sounding song. The dancing couples seemed confused by the tempo of the music. Some of them were doing a fast slow-dance, while others struggled to slow down the fast-dance steps they knew.

"Look at how the guys are lurkin' about over there," Corky said. "How do we all manage to talk to each other at school but not here?"

I wonder why Jordan's friends are treating her this way, Katie thought. She looked at Jordan, who was looking at the line of boys. *Her face looks so sad. Is it because she doesn't have a date?*

Katie continued watching Jordan as she shifted her attention to

Brittany, who was holding court over near the table where the desserts had been served. She must have been telling some sort of joke, because everyone in the small crowd surrounding her was laughing. Suddenly, everyone in her audience turned to look at the table where Katie, Corky and Jordan sat. They had stopped laughing, and they only stared for a moment, but it was clear to Katie that Jordan was getting some kind of "treatment" from Brittany and Mackenzie.

"Hey, Jordan!" Katie tried to make her voice sound as if nothing was wrong. "Sophia found Smooches & Cream! Can you believe it? She got some for Corky and me. Would you like to try some?"

Jordan had not taken her eyes off Brittany. She hardly responded to Katie. "Um…no thanks…maybe later."

"You might think that Blondie over there would have better things to do than tormenting us with her tricks," Corky said, ignoring Katie's silent pleas for restraint. "I think we can all see that she's got the most expensive jewelry on earth, and that she's wearin' clothes that came all the way from some foreign country. Can someone tell me why she's wavin' her arms about as if she's swatting gnats?" Corky's voice was suddenly almost as loud as the band's music. "We can see that you've got flashy jewelry, Blondie. Maybe you should stop flappin' your arms before you take off!"

Several students nearby turned to look at Corky and snickered. Even Jordan was amused, and she was trying valiantly to stifle her laughter. Katie laughed out loud, and patted Jordan's arm as if she was in on the joke.

Although Brittany didn't hear Corky's remarks, the commotion that resulted from them attracted her attention. She glared at Jordan, who at that moment stood up, excused herself and left the table. Katie and Corky watched her as she walked out of the room.

"I don't think she's coming back," Katie said. "It's like Brittany and her crowd were trying to ruin her fun, without even coming near her."

"Katie, may I speak with you for a moment?" While Katie was watching Jordan leave the room, Mr. Murwata had stopped by the table.

"Mr. Murwata! Um…yes. Do you want to sit down?"

As he pulled a chair out, Katie told him how Corky and Lily knew about the locker incident. "I've told her everything that happened. And she was with me when some other things happened to Henry."

"Of course, Corky. Please, stay. You need to hear this too, since you have also been trying to help Henry."

"Katie, I've spoken to Mr. Needham about the incident at the locker, and, as you might guess, he's terribly upset. He is planning to do something, although he is not sure yet exactly what that will be. Henry chose to stay home tonight, as did his parents. They have said that Henry is fine, but feeling a bit anxious about coming here." He looked at Katie. "And you, are you feeling better tonight?"

"Yes! Yes. I'm fine. But thank you for telling us about Henry."

As Mr. Murwata walked away, Katie and Corky continued talking about what had been happening to Henry. They didn't notice the attention they were still getting from Brittany and her friends. They turned their attention to the fashions, and to the kids who stopped by the table to talk. Just before nine, Tyler and Lily stopped by the table with news that would make the evening even more interesting.

"Jordan was heading toward the bathroom, and Brittany got in front of her and started asking her what we were talking about, and why we were laughing. Jordan tried to go around her and Brittany pushed her—not hard, but she really did push her." Lily was talking so fast that she was nearly out of breath. Tyler helped out on some of the details.

"When she couldn't get past Brittany, Jordan just turned around and ran out of the building! She didn't even have a coat! And now her mother is looking for her."

"Do ya think she might be sick, now? Maybe she had to puke or something?" Corky was only mildly concerned.

"I don't think she's sick, Corky. I think it's something else. Didn't you see the way Brittany and Mackenzie and the others were looking at her?" Katie was really curious about so many things that had happened earlier, and Jordan's dramatic exit only intensified her eagerness to get to the bottom of the girl's mysterious behavior.

"Okay ladies, who's ready for ice cream?" Katie's father had come up behind Tyler and the girls while they were analyzing Jordan's situation. He had a couple of coats over his arm. "Hey, would you two like to join us?" he asked Lily. "We're going for ice cream."

"Thanks, Mr. Farrell. But I think my mom is waiting for us." She turned to Corky and Katie. "Call me tomorrow!" she whispered. "Bye, Mr. Farrell!" Lily and Tyler waved brightly as they walked toward the room where the parents' program was breaking up.

Chapter 20

Later that evening, at "Gelato's," the girls talked to Katie's parents and to Corky's mother, Chloe, about their encounter with Jordan.

"You should have seen her dress, Mom! Corky asked her if she went to Paris to buy it, but her mother had made it!"

"And the girl is one of the coolest in school!"

"And she could have gone to the dance with Marco Lupini but she didn't because Brittany said her father saw Mr. Lupini at a meeting in work clothes and he's very common, or something like that, and..." Katie was practically breathless as she tried to recall every detail of the conversation with Jordan.

"Whoa! What do you mean about Mr. Lupini?" John said. "Who said he's very common, and what is that supposed to mean?" He was struggling to control the annoyance he felt.

"It's her friends Mackenzie and Blondie that told her," Corky said. "They don't even want to know you if you're not famous or related to famous people." She looked at her mother. "So, ma, you can say 'good-bye' to your hopes of goin' to a fancy dinner at the Morgan place. Since you're not a famous person or rich, you'd be taken for the hired help."

The parents looked at each other, silently trying to decide which one would take the lead in this discussion.

"Girls," Charlotte said. "You know better than to make assumptions about people based on how they dress or what they do. Katie, haven't we talked about this many times? This is how all sorts of other bad things get started, when people believe that money and prestige are the same as integrity, or compassion, or the other things that are really important."

"I know, Mom. We told her that it was stupid to think that way. But how can we make her stop?"

"That's the dilemma," Chloe said. "You girls did the right thing. Maybe someday Jordan will think about what you said. Maybe not. But you showed moral courage. It's too bad that the cowardice of these so-called cool kids is a stronger force than your courage."

The Chinese food at the Dance hadn't been from 'Phooey Manchewy's' and the formal part of the program had been boring, but Katie's parents felt the evening had been a success because they had raised $10,000 for scholarships. Katie and Corky would spend days going over and over the conversation they had with Jordan—retelling every detail to Lily—in an attempt to uncover hidden meanings and clues to being really cool. Even though they didn't have dates for the Dance, they were intrigued by their chance meeting with Jordan. So the time they spent at the event would become a source of many hours of discussion and debate among Katie, Corky and Lily.

After John put Corky and her mother in a cab for home, he, Charlotte, and Katie walked the few blocks to their apartment. Katie was quiet on the walk home.

"Is anything the matter, honey?" Charlotte asked her daughter. Charlotte had noticed that Katie seemed a little sad. Katie hadn't said anything to her mother or father about finding Henry locked in his locker.

"I'm fine," Katie answered. "Just tired from a long week, I guess," and with that comment she gave her mother's hand a quick squeeze.

Charlotte knew that Katie had been disappointed not to have been asked to the Dance by a boy, and from her experience as a teenager, Charlotte knew how truly dumb boys could behave at that age. To Charlotte, Katie was a wonder—lovely, exotic and full of promise. It pained her to see how self-conscious Katie was about her looks. Even before she heard Katie and Corky talk about Jordan's fear of being different, she knew that the need to fit in was a powerful motivator for kids. Nobody wanted to break the code that required everyone to look the same, talk the same, dress the same.

Charlotte loved the way Katie's taste in clothing was eclectic and often unpredictable. She wanted to protect her daughter's emerging personality and the many intriguing ways that personality expressed itself. She wanted to make sure Katie never capitulated to the "rule of the cool," as John referred to the tyranny of the cool kids.

Charlotte sighed. Her daughter was growing up and frankly, Charlotte didn't know how to perpetually shield her from the reality of a society where it often seemed that an elite few made the rules for everyone. Sometimes Charlotte wondered if life at Manhattan Prep was too hard on Katie. She often thought about what Katie's life would have been like if she and John had never gone to Romania. How Katie would have grown up in a volatile country where the most basic needs of the babies in the orphanages were beyond the capacity of the system to deliver. She worried about how many ways life—even life with a loving family—

could crush a child's spirit.

"Your dress is beautiful, sweetie. Do you like it?"

"It makes me feel pretty, Mom. I really love it, even if Corky and I looked like a giant daffodil when we stood next to each other."

She put her arm around Katie's shoulder, and hugged her tightly. John put his arm over Charlotte's shoulder and kissed her lightly on her cheek.

"You're beautiful, too, darling," he whispered in her ear. "Little girls can be mean, but they can also be magical and wonderful." Then, to both of them he said, "You should have seen Katie and Corky tonight, getting ready for the dance. They're a couple of real comedians. And we've got pictures to prove it."

The threesome walked the rest of the way in silence, enjoying the early Spring evening and the rising moon.

Next week is the end of seventh grade. I can't believe I'll be an eighth-grader. This should be a happy time, but I'm so worried about Henry. I keep waiting for something else to happen to him. Lily, Corky, and I are watching Henry and watching Brittany and her crowd. It's horrible to think that Henry could be hurt. But Mr. Needham and Mr. Murwata are both watching everything, too. I want to believe that they can protect him. But I also know what they've already done to him. This is so scary, I'm even dreaming about it! Last night I dreamt that Lily, Corky, Henry and I were buried alive in coffins. We could hear each other, and we could hear people walking by. But we couldn't get anyone to help us. I was so scared! I couldn't breathe and I was crying, but when I tried to scream, no sound came out. Finally Mom and Dad woke me up. They had heard me crying, and Tuffy was jumping up and down and whimper-ing. I finally told them what happened to Henry the day of the Spring Dance. They were angry that something like this had happened at Manhattan Prep. I had to beg them not to call Mr. Needham. I just want to get through the rest of the school year.

Chapter 21

With final exams over and only four more days left of school, the students were looking forward to the school's traditional class trips.

Katie's seventh grade class had debated long and hard about

where to go. There were kids who wanted to explore caves, and others who wanted to go to a water park. Some wanted to go to the beach and others wanted to go to the mountains. It seemed as if a compromise would be impossible, until Mr. Needham found a place that had every-thing the kids seemed to be looking for.

Wallkill Valley Ranch, near the Mohonk Preserve, had swimming and tennis and horseback riding and hiking. They even had a spa, where, some of the students were thrilled to learn, manicures and pedicures and facials were available.

Katie was happy to go to a place so near her family's summer home in Hyde Park. The ranch was in the Shawangunk Mountains—known to locals as "the Gunks."

Katie and her parents hiked in the Gunks, exploring endless trails. Katie's father, a California native, fell in love with the Gunks immediate-ly, because the rugged terrain and spectacular views reminded him of home. Over time he found many other reasons to love these ancient mountains. He sometimes hated to admit it, but the East Coast was growing on him. It had crept into his heart when he wasn't paying atten-tion.

And suddenly, he could not get enough of the things that New York and Pennsylvania and the Atlantic Ocean had to offer. The frozen landscapes in winter, covered in snow, held secrets that would bloom flamboyantly every spring—his love of the outdoors and the mountains was contagious! Everyone caught it from him. Katie, Charlotte and Sophia—and even Tuffy—were as much in love with exploring the mountains as he was.

So Katie was looking forward to this trip—it was just the antidote she needed to counteract the sadness she had felt about not getting asked to the Spring Dance. Lily and Corky were looking forward to the trip, too. They had spent part of every summer in Hyde Park with Katie's family for several years. Although it was only a little more than a 90-minute ride from Manhattan, the Wallkill Valley Ranch might have been on another planet.

Sophia took Katie, Lily and Corky shopping for special outfits a couple of days before the trip. It was fun to go shopping with Sophia because she kept up a running commentary about teenage fashion that the girls found hilarious. Sometimes they weren't really sure what she was saying because she used Romanian words, but her facial expressions were so pointedly disapproving that it was all the girls could do to keep from howling with laughter.

"What kind of stuff should we look for?" Lily asked. "I mean, it's a ranch, but not like the ranches on television, right?"

"Are you thinking they won't even have lights, then? Is it supposed to be like an old fashioned place or what?"

"They've got to have lights, Corky! How else will Brittany and Mackenzie have their manicures and stuff?" Katie waved her fingers in the air for emphasis.

"Oh, yeah! I can see it now. Blondie and her crowd all fancied up with their spa treatments."

"And mud packs!"

"And maybe they'll have special ranch jewelry from Mrs. Morgan!"

The girls were starting to get silly—all three talking at once and laughing so hard they could barely walk straight.

Sophia put her hands over her ears. "In Romania, we not have these kinds of places. Horses very scarce and used only by lucky farmers who has enough money to affords them."

"In Romania, do kids celebrate the end of school?" Lily asked Sophia.

"Schools is such luxury, that students very unhappy when school over. Do not celebrate finishing school. Celebrate going back to school," Sophia said seriously.

"Oh, dear, Sophia," Lily said, "then today's shopping trip will be a new experience for you."

"Every day in America experience for me. There is no other country so great as America." She put her arm around Katie and hugged her. "We very lucky to be here, Ekaterina."

Katie knew that she was lucky to have been chosen by Charlotte and John. When Sophia told her stories about the orphanages in Romania, Katie felt the hair stand up at the base of her neck, it sounded so horrible.

Katie's and Lily's mothers had charge accounts at Becks, and so they brought plastic for the shopping trip. Corky's mom only shopped at Becks when there was a sale. Chloe had given Corky $75 for an outfit, and strict instructions to head for the sale rack. As the group stepped off the elevator onto the juniors floor, they were presented with a waterfall of summer colors, from yellow to turquoise to lavender to sea blue.

"I want to look at the swim suits first," Lily said, rushing toward a wall full of colorful suits.

Katie froze, realizing suddenly that the class trip might wind up being a source of embarrassment for her if her friends decided they wanted to spend a lot of time at the swimming pool.

"What is it, Katie? Don't you want to look at the swim suits, then?"

"Um...I...I don't really care about them, Corky." Katie tried to sound as if she really didn't care. But she could feel her face getting hot.

"What about the swimming pool, girls? Don't you like the swim?"

"No way, Sophia!" Katie said. "I'm not going to swim where the kids from school can see me."

"Ach, Katie. You such a good swimmer, like a fishie! What for thought you have about your look?"

"Sophia, I'd look like a whale compared to the other kids. It doesn't matter whether I can swim!" Katie was starting to get upset. Although she really loved shopping, she was always uncomfortable shopping for clothes. It seemed as though nothing ever fit precisely. If something fit around her waist, it usually didn't fit around her hips and if it fit around her hips, it was usually too big in the waist. The thought of wearing a swimsuit in front of her classmates horrified her. Sophia threw up her hands in mock exasperation and walked away, toward a rack of matching shorts and tops.

"Katie, you're gorgeous!" Corky grabbed Katie's arm. She pulled her friend around to face her, and looked into Katie's eyes as intently as she could. "Brittany and the others would die to have half of what you have, don't you see that?" Corky was mystified by Katie's attitude.

"I'd rather ride horses, and do some hiking, Corky. You remember last summer when my dad took us up into the hills? I'm sure the hiking trails around the ranch will be a lot like that."

"Don't horses scare you, though, as big as they are? What if they run away with you?"

"I think the horses they have at the ranch are pretty tame. Dad says that even if they do run away with you, they go right back to the barn. C'mon, you'll love it!"

"That will make the shopping much easier, won't it, then? I mean, we would wear jeans to ride horses, and also for hiking, wouldn't we?"

Katie didn't want to spoil the shopping trip, and she suddenly felt like she was acting like a brat. "I'm sorry, Corky. We should decide together what to do. It shouldn't be only my idea."

"Hey, it's fine. Anyway, like I said, it makes it much easier to figure out how to spend my fortune. I'm sure that once the salespeople hear that I've got $75 in my pocket they'll be all over me like ants at a picnic, so I'll just head for the Clearance Rack now."

"Hey, look at what I found! Don't you love the color?" Lily appeared with a jade-colored swim suit with bright yellow trim. "What do you think?" She was holding the suit against herself, as if her friends would be able to visualize what it would look like if she were actually wearing it.

"It's gorgeous!" Katie gasped, taking in the rich color of the swimsuit against Lily's delicate features.

"Lily! That's a find. Have you tried it on, then?"

"I'm getting ready to try it on now. What are you guys looking for?"

"We were just talking about the ranch, and how it might be fun to ride the horses. I'm thinkin' that the horses would be more agreeable to my budget."

"Horses? Oh! Um...well...what would we do after that? I mean...do you guys want to do other stuff, too?"

"We were just thinking about riding, Lily." Katie wanted to find a way to reverse the gears she had set in motion earlier. "I guess you want to swim?" She could feel her face getting hot, and she looked away from Lily momentarily. Out of the corner of her eye, she caught a glimpse of herself in a floor-length mirror. She looked at the mirror in disbelief. *Oh! My God! That can't be me...but it is me. I'm so fat!* She looked away from her reflection, and back at Lily. "Whatever you guys want to do...It's...it's really up to you."

Lily looked at Corky, then at Katie. She wondered what had gone on before she came back with the jade-colored swim suit. "Um...I guess maybe I'll...maybe I'll get the suit, anyway—even if we don't plan to swim." She stood before them, the swim suit now dangling from her hand, the air filling with tension.

Now I really feel terrible. I'm ruining everything. Katie was about to cry. She was upset after seeing herself in the store mirror, and now she had upset her best friends.

"I'm sorry. Really...I just...I don't know. What do you guys feel like doing? Maybe we could do both. I mean swim and ride horses?" Katie struggled to get the words out, even as she tried to imagine what sort of swim suit she could find that would hide all her flaws.

Lily looked at her, then at Corky. She looked down at the swim suit for a minute. "I know! We could ride horses and then see if we feel like swimming, or hiking or just hanging out."

"Now there's the diplomat, isn't it? I think we've got a solution, what do you think, Katie?" Corky clapped Katie on the back, and hugged her lightly.

"I guess so...I mean, sure...yes...it sounds great." In her heart, Katie was glad that they had reached a compromise. But she was really worried about what she would wear at the pool.

"You think we just need jeans if we're goin' to ride the horses?" Corky held up a pair of slim cut blue jeans with a turquoise sleeveless top. Lily went to the other side of the jeans rack, still clutching the beautiful swim suit she had found.

"Nice with your hair color," Katie said. "Honestly, Cork, you're so lucky to be so slim. You can really wear anything."

"It's not such a gift when I can afford so little. Sort of defeats the purpose of being able to wear anything, now, doesn't it?" Corky laughed.

Life is certainly strange, Katie thought. *Here's Corky, who looks cute in everything she wears, but she doesn't have any money. But I could buy anything I want, except that I look so horrible in everything.*

Corky grabbed a pair of denim overalls from the sale rack and took it, along with the jeans and the turquoise top to a fitting room. Sophia returned with a pair of chinos with a horizontally striped shirt.

"These cute," she said to Katie.

"Oh, Sophia, I can't wear those kinds of stripes! They make me look too fat," Katie said with a sigh. She took the chinos, but looked for a shirt in a solid color. "How do you like this color?" Katie asked Sophia, holding up a soft coral polo shirt.

"Color is beautiful for you," Sophia said nodding appreciatively.

"Good. I'll try it on and we'll see how the outfit looks together," Katie said as she followed Corky into the fitting rooms. The top was too tight and the bottom was too loose, so Katie had Sophia go back and forth fetching different size and color combinations until, finally, she found a pair of black denim pants, with a pretty top in a turquoise, green, and cobalt blue pattern.

Corky found an outfit with deep blue pants and a paisley patterned top that set off her hair and fair complexion perfectly. Lily found a pair of khaki pants, with a lavender top. She also bought the jade swim suit. "Okay, let's make a pact. We'll ride horses, then go hiking. And if there's still time, we'll go to the pool. Agreed?" Lily looked at her friends hopefully.

"Agreed!" Katie and Corky said in unison. They all shook hands and scaled the deal with a ritual they had created when they were in fourth grade. Katie placed her right hand on a table, then Lily and Corky would place their right hands on top of Katie's. Then each would place her left hand in the stack of hands. When all hands were stacked together, the girls would raise their hands and cheer. Afterward they laughed and hugged each other.

"You will ruin skins if you spend too much time in sun," Sophia cautioned. "To fight the sun, you must wear hat."

The group wandered over to the accessories, and the girls immediately began trying on hats. Straw hats. Western hats. Hats that looked like they belonged on gangsters. Their laughter and girl-talk filled the department. Katie pointed to a framed poster featuring a life-size version of a two-page ad that had appeared recently in *XC*. There were five stick-thin, leggy blond girls modeling western boots and hats. The models were wearing shorts that barely covered their bottoms, and shirts that were tied so their smooth, flat midriffs were exposed. One model was wearing a peasant-style shirt that was torn at the shoulder.

Sophia watched the girls as they stood in awe of the life-size versions of their ideal selves. The images confused her.

"They ride the horses in clothes that don't even cover bottoms? What for an outfit is this for farm wear?" She stopped speaking for a moment when the three girls turned to face her. "Is not logical!"

"Sophia! We like the hats!" Katie laughed as Sophia tried to imagine how anyone would see those images and gather that they were advertising hats.

"Hats? You want those hats?" She pointed at the pictures, then laughed with the girls.

The girls dragged Sophia over to the wall filled with hats just like those in the ad. Everyone tried them on.

"Sophia, you could wear that in Hyde Park, when you walk to the farmer's market! You look so cool! Let's get one for Mom too."

After a 15-minute exploration of the hats, everyone headed to the cashier, stylish hat in hand.

"Is beautiful even, yes?" Sophia inhaled the sweet spring air as the group emerged at last from Becks.

"A successful shoppings trip, yes?" She said as she hugged Katie.

"I love my stuff. Especially my hat!" Katie exclaimed. Everyone had a deep blue Becks shopping bag. It was 5:30 in the afternoon and the air was turning cooler as the group headed for home.

Chapter 22

The girls had enjoyed their shopping trip, although Henry's dilemma was never far from their thoughts. They had done some research on the Internet about bullying. From what they read, they knew this pattern of behavior at school would probably only get worse. All of Katie's anticipation about the class trip was tainted by the thought of how sad Henry looked.

Katie was torn. She was excited about the prospect of showing her friends one of the loveliest places on earth, and she really loved the new clothes she had bought for the trip. But she was also worried about Henry, and about what she had read about bullies. What was once just cool kids versus the uncool kids at school had mysteriously turned into cool kids versus Henry. And the game went far beyond snobbishness and snotty behavior.

Katie's uneasiness was contagious. Her parents and Sophia were worried as well. The adults tried to put a good face on the situation. They had spoken to Henry's parents, and had been reassured that they thought Henry was fine.

As his parents questioned him, Henry revealed the other things that had happened. The time he "tripped" coming down the steps, tumbling into a group of girls at the bottom of the stairwell. His glasses were broken and his hip was badly bruised. Less serious, but equally humiliating was his account of the day the kids dumped a large bottle of soda on him, soaking his hair, his clothes, his books and his lunch.

Henry's parents were furious, and they were hurt. They ached for their son, and the misery in which he had been living. They demanded some kind of action from the school's administrators, who knew only about the locker incident and were stunned to hear about all the other things that kids had done to Henry Rathbone.

"Why won't you tell us who did these things to you, Henry?" Mrs. Rathbone was practically in tears. She couldn't imagine why anyone would treat Henry so badly.

"I…I don't know who they are…anyway, it doesn't matter. I'm a geek. This is the way geeks are treated." Henry was ashamed and scared and angry and hurt. The emotions were too hard for him to separate. He felt as though he was drowning in confusion, and that only made him more anxious. *What if they do more?* He thought to himself. *What if they follow me home, or try to hurt me?* He felt alone and helpless and frightened. He was sure that if he revealed even one name, then the bullying would become worse than he could imagine. And now, everyone at the school would know about what happened, because of the emergency meeting Mr. Needham had called with the students' parents.

"I must say that I object to this proceeding," Mr. Morgan boomed after Mr. Needham had described the situation. He acted as if he were trying a case in court. "What do we pay these outrageous tuitions for, if not to ensure that our children are educated in an atmosphere of dignity and respect?"

Brittany's mother was a little more reserved, but still adamant that the school had no business reaching out to the parents for help unraveling this mess.

"We want our children to have an excellent education. That's why we enrolled them here." She was dressed in an elegant long purple vest and slender silk pants, and a white shirt made of some gauzy material. Around her neck she wore one of her massive jewelry designs.

"We're all very busy people, with high expectations for ourselves and our children," she continued. For emphasis, she made a sweeping motion with her right arm, and in so doing revealed yet another piece of extravagant jewelry, a gleaming gold and silver bracelet studded with glittering stones.

"Are we not agreed that the school should ensure that the students learn civility and decorum?"

She had obviously expected applause and shouts of approval. A few people said "She's right," or "I agree with Mrs. Morgan," or "She's got a good point." But mostly there was silence.

"My son was the victim of bullies, right in this school. I pay the same tuition you do, and I don't see this as an issue of 'decorum.' What I see are a bunch of spoiled brats who have decided that anyone who doesn't fit their narrow, superficial, brainless definition of cool should be victimized. I don't think it's the school's responsibility to teach these creeps to be civilized. They are what they are because their parents let them be bullies, and whatever else they've become." Mr. Rathbone's voice was cracking with emotion. His wife was standing next to him, clutching his arm and looking at the floor.

The other parents were silent. The room was suddenly as quiet as deep space. Mr. Needham, sensing that the meeting was veering off track, spoke up.

"Ladies and gentlemen, I understand your frustration. We called this meeting because you need to know that students in this school are engaging in behavior that none of us wants to see occur. We don't know who the perpetrators are. We cannot believe, however, that they have any intention of causing physical harm to anyone. Our hope is that each of you will discuss the issue with your children, and let them know that this behavior is not harmless and it will not be tolerated. This school has a sterling reputation. Nobody in the administration or in the ranks of teachers here is willing to see that reputation undermined."

He cleared his throat and sipped some water. Mr. Needham was not accustomed to confrontations, and was clearly uncomfortable discussing this issue and its implications. He did not want to alienate any of the parents, especially those parents whose social standing and political connections could be used as weapons against the school—or against him. Furthermore, he knew that, if they ever did identify the perpetrators (and Mr. Murwata had some pretty strong suspicions about who they were), the only viable choice of punishment would be to expel them from Manhattan Prep. Mr. Needham knew that there was no subtle or quiet way to accomplish expulsion—especially given the high profiles of so many of the families involved. He was pretty sure he knew some of the students involved, and he could imagine the fireworks that would accompany any disciplinary actions.

"I want to make it clear that if we find the individuals responsible for these acts, we cannot do anything less than suspend them. I'm sure nobody in this room wants to see that happen. And so we hope you will talk to your kids, and urge them to stop this behavior before the consequences become unpalatable to all of us."

John and Charlotte were relieved by the school's response to the situation. But still, they worried that the parents were not hearing the full story, and were not sufficiently informed about how dangerous the behavior had become. They were also concerned for Henry.

"Mr. Needham," John stood up to speak. "Does anyone know what is behind these pranks, as you call them? What precipitated them?"

Mr. Needham and Mr. Murwata glanced at each other briefly.

"No, Mr. Farrell. We don't have any idea what started it. Nor do we have any idea who is behind it." Mr. Needham's face was turning very red, and he had begun sweating profusely. "Paki, um, Mr. Murwata, and I, have been trying to get to the bottom of this. But we have virtually no suspects...er...no idea about who could be doing this."

Mr. Murwata was looking at his colleague with disbelief. The two had disagreed vehemently about how this meeting should proceed, and had argued about the seriousness of the situation. Mr. Needham wanted to let the situation blow over until Henry's parents called the school and demanded action. Mr. Needham's attitude was making it look as if they were dealing with pranks instead of bullies, and the Social Studies teacher thought that those parents most in need of getting the message were being let off the hook.

"I should explain," Mr. Murwata said, stepping out from behind Mr. Needham. "There have been some pranks. But these appear to have escalated into something greater. One student, Henry Rathbone, was forced into his locker and would have been there for several hours had a student not heard him calling for help."

Mr. Needham mopped his face with his handkerchief and sat on the edge of the table in the front of the room. Now he would be forced to act. Now he could no longer avoid angering some parents in order to do the right thing. *This is why I chose the private school route*, he thought to himself. *So I wouldn't have to deal with thugs and bullies. So I could be associated with a better class of people. How could this happen? How could these kids defile this institution so horribly? How could they not realize how profoundly fortunate they are to be here at all?*

Suddenly the parents were no longer silent. Now everyone wanted an explanation and action.

This is not going well, Mr. Needham thought as he stood up to address the parents.

"Young Henry Rathbone was subjected to a cruel prank," he said, hiding as much of himself as possible behind the podium. "We have discussed the situation at length with his parents, and have assured them that we will not tolerate bad…bad…er…incivility."

"Incivility?" Rodney Sabol's mother was incredulous. "You call it incivility? Mr. Needham, you have one responsibility that permits no negotiation. Your job is to protect our students from danger while they are in this building. What you call incivility is as remote from that concept as Mars is from the Earth. What actions have you taken or directed that would result in punishment for those responsible for this?"

Giles Needham felt his stature and prestige as headmaster slipping away from him. All his attempts to become a confidant to the students' wealthy parents, all the years he had spent coddling some of the most spoiled brats on the face of the earth, all his efforts to be Mr. Everything to the people he most admired were evaporating. It was as if his hopes and dreams were passengers on a runaway train that jumped the tracks over a 1500-foot gorge. He looked at Mr. Murwata, hoping the Social Studies teacher who brought this whole mess to his attention might be able to save him. Mr. Murwata stepped forward, as if on cue.

"Mrs. Sabol, you are correct. We have begun an investigation into the matter, and we have redoubled our efforts to watch the students carefully. We have installed video cameras around some of the more remote areas of the building, so at least there will be some record of any further incidents."

The parents were riveted to Mr. Murwata's every word. His quiet confidence and obvious concern for the students inspired trust.

"We are dealing with the angst of young people all wrestling with emotions and feelings they neither comprehend nor recognize. There are several unbreakable rules among these young people, and the first rule is that one does not, as they say 'rat out' a peer—even when a peer is doing bad things. We know that someone did something very cruel to Henry. Beyond that, there is very little else we know. Henry has been the brunt of several pranks. But this one, it is clear, is more than a prank. He says that he does not know who did this to him, that someone pushed him from behind. Our response, therefore, is to find ways to observe parts of the building that are remote, and to step up teacher presence in all common areas of the building before and between classes. Of course, we welcome any suggestions you might have."

The discussion was almost immediately calmed by Mr. Murwata's explanation. He had personally visited Henry at home and spoken at length to the Rathbones. He had also phoned Katie's parents, and discussed the situation with them. It was clear to everyone that Mr. Murwata was as concerned about the students and about what was happening at Manhattan Prep as they were.

"This trip to the ranch—Thursday, is it?—how are you going to make sure these kids don't get into any more serious trouble?" Lily's father, Dr. Hanover, had been silent through most of the discussion. He was shy, and clearly uncomfortable speaking in public.

"We've recruited several teachers, in addition to those already assigned to be chaperones, and we obviously would be pleased if any parents would like to go along on the trip," Mr. Murwata said.

A couple of parents stepped forward as volunteer chaperones before Mr. Needham stood up to speak again, his composure restored.

"I sincerely hope we've resolved all of your concerns, and that you're confident that we're doing everything possible to protect your children. There's coffee and dessert in the next room, and I hope you'll all stay and socialize for a while. In the meantime, if anyone has any other concerns, please feel free to discuss them with me this evening—or at any time."

After the meeting, Katie's father tried to talk to Mr. Morgan about the situation at the zoo. Ever since Katie had told them about the class visit to court, John Farrell could not get Henry's questions out of his mind. John's restless curiosity about events and people and how things happened had made his parents believe that he would one day become an investigative reporter like his father had been.

"Kyle, how are you?" John reached out to shake Mr. Morgan's hand.

"Oh, hello, John. Helluva thing, isn't it? What do you suppose is bothering these kids?"

"It's hard to say, Kyle. It seems kids have an awful lot on their plates these days, and they're struggling with too many grown-up things when they should be enjoying childhood."

Lydia Morgan was chatting with Charlotte about one of her

newest ventures.

"Have you seen the latest issue of *XC*?" Lydia asked. Charlotte was pretty sure Lydia wanted to talk about the feature about her and her new jewelry designs. Katie and Corky had been devouring that very issue the night of the Spring Dance, and afterward they had talked a lot about the jewelry. The girls seemed more excited about the clothes the models were wearing than the jewelry, but Charlotte didn't want to hurt Lydia's feelings and say that.

"Well, I know Katie has the magazine, and she was very excited to see you featured in it. I've been working pretty long hours lately and haven't had the chance to read the article very carefully yet."

"I'd love to hear what you think after you've read it," Lydia said giddily. "The story is about my new line of jewelry. Of course, we bought four pages of ads to promote it, but I figure it's a small price to pay for the kind of exposure a long feature in *XC* gives me."

Charlotte glanced at John and Kyle, and wished she could be in that conversation instead of this utterly ridiculous one. It was bad enough that the marketing people were trying so hard to take control of the show. But most recently, the crew was informed that *XC* had actually paid the producers of "Love's Labours" for what they called "placement." Suddenly, every other prop on the show included a copy of *XC,* and the scripts for the show included several references to the magazine every other day. The publisher of *XC* had actually bought the privilege of having her product referred to in the show's dialog 2.5 times every three hours of programming, and her product would also appear in at least one camera shot every day.

"We call the concept 'convergence,'" the oily network official explained at a cast meeting. "We display the product, and we get paid to display it. Then our partners at *XC* develop features about the show and its stars—particularly the youngsters. Within the next several months, we're going to green light a new partnership with *XC*, which will provide access to streaming video from '*LL*' several times a week through *XC*'s website. Oh, and get ready for lots of other products—we're creating value-added ops for some of *XC*'s premier advertisers by extending placement of their products on the show, too."

He sat back in his chair, proud of his accomplishment, waiting for Charlotte and her colleagues to praise him for his vision and marketing savvy. The praise never materialized, and the meeting broke up in the uncomfortable silence. Charlotte worried that the magazine had more influence over her daughter's self image than it deserved, and she struggled with the dilemma almost every day.

"So, how are sales of the new line, Lydia? The pieces are very pretty…and pricey," Charlotte said.

"Of course, it's a little early to tell, but the reports I have are pretty enthusiastic about the future of the line. By the way, I think Katie might be perfect for our 'Exotica' collection, which includes lots of unusual stones and metals."

"Lydia, Katie doesn't even have pierced ears. She has a watch and a bracelet from her grandmother. I'm trying to remember the last time she actually asked me for jewelry. Is there a big market for jewelry that expensive for kids? I guess I look at Katie and still see that she's just a child…"

"Children love to imitate their parents. Look at you, Charlotte. You've got stunning jewelry." Lydia gently slipped two of her fingers under the pearl necklace Charlotte was wearing. The necklace had been a wedding gift from John's mother. It had been in his family for three generations, and to Charlotte the pearls were as precious as five-carat diamonds. Lydia patted the pearls lightly against Charlotte's collar bone. The gesture seemed odd to Charlotte, almost as if Lydia was not-very-subtly trying to gauge the value of the pearls while complimenting Charlotte on her jewelry.

"My idea was to create a line of heirloom quality jewelry for youngsters that they could wear through their young adult years, and pass along to their own little girls. Don't you think Katie would love to have something, some lovely piece of jewelry that helps her define herself?"

Charlotte was mystified. She looked over at John, hoping he would find a way to rescue her. But it seemed as if the two men were engaged in a pretty spirited discussion of their own.

Charlotte looked back at Lydia, who pulled a slick, full-color brochure out of her purse. She opened it and drew Charlotte's attention to the photos of jewelry on the page.

"I almost forgot I had this with me. Look at this piece, Charlotte. Isn't it charming? Can't you just see this on Katie?"

She was pointing to a large brooch. It was three inter-connected stars, each covered in tiny grey, black and deep aqua stones. A slender gold wire wove through the piece, and there were tiny gold beads threaded along the wire, each held in place by knots so delicate-looking that Charlotte wondered how in the world they were made.

"Imagine how lovely this would look on a felt hat, or on the lapel of a black jacket." The brochure had multi-colored type proclaiming "Exotica, tomorrow's heirloom for today's girl." The model wearing the brooch looked to be Katie's age, but was wearing a lot of makeup. She was dressed in an outfit suggestive of Native American clothing—the kind made popular by old Western movies. The girl herself had long, straight black hair, and actually looked as if she were Native American. She was wearing a black ribbon tied across her forehead. The brooch was pinned to the ribbon.

Charlotte looked at the price, and blinked twice to make sure she saw it right.

"Lydia! The pin is stunning! It costs $850?" Charlotte couldn't conceal her astonishment, or her admiration for the piece.

"What's $850?" John had arrived, at last, and was looking over Charlotte's shoulder at Lydia's brochure.

"John, Lydia was just showing me some of her new jewelry designs. For children."

"Wow! That's a nice pin, Lydia. Kyle says you've been doing a lot of traveling overseas. Is that where you get your stones?"

"Well, I've been spending a lot of time in Asia and Africa, trying to cultivate some suppliers. Many of these stones are so unusual that there's not really a market for them yet. So they're relatively inexpensive. I've bought as many of them as the locals would let me have…you know…get them before they realize how valuable they are."

Charlotte and John just looked at Lydia in disbelief. The three of them stood there gawking silently at the brochure.

"Well, would you look at the time? Char, we've got to get home. You've got an early meeting tomorrow, don't you?"

"Oh! Yes. Yes. We're trying to shoot a couple of episodes every day so we can keep the summer work schedule down to a day or two every other week. Anyway, good luck with the new jewelry line, Lydia. It was nice speaking to you. I'm going to make sure I read the article in *XC*. Katie and her friends are thrilled that they actually know someone featured in the magazine. They just eat that magazine up, you know."

On their way home from the meeting, Katie's parents felt much more comfortable about the class trip, especially since a couple of the other parents would be with the students. Their conversation ranged from the ridiculous concept of heirloom jewelry for little girls, to the thoughtless actions of young people, to the curious case of the Greater New York City Zoo.

"Kyle clammed up when I asked him about the Zoo. He brushed off the question and changed the subject pretty quickly," John said. "He doesn't realize that he's just making me more curious than ever."

"It's hard to believe that they would actually hurt the animals, though. Just the thought of it makes me sick. Can you imagine what kind of people they must be if that's what happens there?"

"I know, I know. It stinks for so many reasons. But I just can't get it out of my head. The facts the zoo has presented just don't add up, and I think Katie might be right about that guy—what's his name, the zoo guy?—faking an illness to get out of testifying. It's like my father used to say when he was on the trail of some scandal. 'John, I can feel it in my gut. There's something rotten in Denmark.'"

Katie was still up when her parents returned from the school meeting. They told her all about it, and about how several parents would be going along on the trip to the Wallkill Valley Ranch.

"The school and all the parents don't want to suffocate you kids with too many chaperones, but we want you to look forward to this trip and stop worrying about Henry. Ashley's mother is going to be one of the chaperones. You know what a nice lady she is, and you and Ashley always get along really well together, don't you? Are you okay with this?" Charlotte had her arm around Katie's shoulders. She could feel Katie relax as they talked about the meeting.

"Honey, do you have any idea who did this to Henry?" John was trying to control the anger that had been lurking in his subconscious since Katie had first told him about the soda incident in the school cafeteria.

"I don't know, Dad. I just don't know." Katie was getting sleepy. She had been having so many nightmares lately that she was falling asleep practically right after dinner.

"Come on, honey. You're going to bed right now." John picked her up and carried her down the hall to her bedroom. Tuffy ran ahead of them and jumped onto Katie's bed. Charlotte turned the covers back and patted Tuffy on the head.

"Be a good dog, and watch over Katie," she whispered. Tuffy quickly snuggled up next to Katie, as if to demonstrate his readiness for guard duty.

John and Charlotte stood in the doorway, watching their daughter sleep. The outfit she was planning to wear to the ranch was draped over the chair near her desk, the bag from Becks nearby, surrounded by mounds of the department store's trademark gold tissue paper. In the semi-darkness, Katie's parents leaned into each other, quietly renewing the vow they made to Katie when she was an infant in Romania.

"We will protect and love you forever, and try to make every day of your life wonderful and happy."

Chapter 23

Tomorrow we're going to the Gunks. The whole class will be there. It's going to be our last day together as seventh-graders. I love the Gunks. I want all my friends to see how beautiful they are, but I can't stop worrying about Henry. Mom and Dad said that Mr. Needham and Mr. Murwata are going to make sure nothing bad happens. But they couldn't stop bad things before. In a couple of weeks, Mom and Dad and Sophia and Tuffy and I will be back in Hyde Park, and it will be summer again. I can't wait for that, and to see my cousins and aunts and uncles from California. I wish tomorrow could be over. I wish it was already next week. I wish I didn't feel so scared...

Thursday morning, resplendent in their new outfits, Katie, Corky and Lily excitedly waited to board the bus that would take them to Wallkill Valley Ranch. Katie spotted Henry standing by the door, alone, and motioned for him to join them. He reluctantly walked toward the trio looking as if he were truly dreading the day.

Henry hadn't wanted to go to the ranch, but his father had advised him that by not going, he was giving in to the whims of the juvenile bullies who had been tormenting him. He understood that argument intellectually, but in his heart he was uncomfortable and filled with a feeling of foreboding.

"Do you want us to go with you?" Henry's mother was struggling with her own fears for her son. She wanted to protect him, and had initially volunteered to go as a chaperone. But Henry was even more upset at the prospect of his mother going along on the class trip.

"Mom, please! I don't want you to go. They already think I'm a geek. If you go, I'll be the geek who had to bring his mother to protect him."

Mrs. Rathbone finally relented, and called the school to say that something had come up and she couldn't go on the trip after all.

On the bus to Wallkill Valley Ranch, Henry and Katie sat together and Lily and Corky sat right behind them. The chaperones were all gathered together in the front of the bus, sipping coffee and talking about the stock market, the day's news and the Yankees.

Katie and her friends talked quietly during the ride to the ranch. They sensed Henry's discomfort and tried to make him feel more at ease by talking about what they were doing during the coming summer months. Henry's father had been assigned a special project in England and the whole family would be spending two months in London. Henry told the girls about the apartment they had sublet—how it was called a "flat" in England, and how he and his sister and their mother were going to take in all the museums and shows in London. At the end of the project, Henry's family was taking a special train ride from London to Edinburgh, Scotland. For the brief time that he spoke of his upcoming summer trip, Henry seemed almost as relaxed and happy as he had before things started happening to him. Katie was glad to see him perk up a bit.

"Henry, go horseback riding with us, okay?" she said.

"I've never been on a horse before, but I guess it would be fun. Am I dressed okay for it?"

"Perfect!" Katie said. Then she turned to Lily and Corky, who had already decided on riding the horses.

"Let's all four of us ride together," Lily suggested. "That way we can watch out for each other and make a pact that, no matter how ridiculous we look, we won't laugh."

"It's a deal," Katie and Corky said looking at Henry to see if he wanted to be a part of their pact.

"I guess I'll give it a try if you girls promise not to laugh," he said smiling for the first time in weeks.

The day was bright, sunny, and the perfect blue sky looked gorgeous in contrast to the deep greens and browns of the mountains facing Wallkill Valley Ranch. As the bus pulled into the gravel drive, Katie and her friends could spot some horses peacefully grazing in the paddock.

Authentic looking cowboys, dressed in blue jeans, flannel shirts and cowboy boots with big spurs were dragging out saddles and blankets for the horses. Mr. Needham and Mr. Murwata stood as the bus came to a stop.

"Kids, we're going to initially gather right here in front of the restaurant for instructions and the day's timetable," Mr. Needham said. "There will be someone from the ranch staff in charge of each activity, and chaperones will also be with everyone all day. Please stay with your groups and do not wander off into the woods," he added. With that final warning, the door to the bus swung open and the class, laughing and talking, began to disembark.

Happy to be stretching their legs and finally at their destination, the kids milled about, settling into groups. Katie, Lily, Corky and Henry stayed together. A tall, thin man outfitted in cowboy gear spoke loudly to the group.

"My name is Ralph," he said with a slight southern accent. "Welcome to Wallkill Valley Ranch. We want all of you to have a good time today, but we also want you to have a safe day, so please listen carefully to these few rules.

First of all, stay with your group at all times. Do not wander off, not only because you'll give us all heart failure, but also because there are black bear that have been sighted in the woods and you'll be much happier not meeting up with those critters.

Second, listen to the ranch staff if they give you directions. We're only trying to keep you safe, so you enjoy your time with us. We'll have riding parties leaving the stables right now, then at 11:30 and again at 1:30. So that we can get the horses ready for you, we're going to ask you to sign up for a riding session.

Other than that, the pool is over here beside the restaurant, the tennis courts are on the far side of the hotel, and the nature walks depart from the lobby every hour on the hour. Now, please pick a time for riding," and with that, he moved to the side where several other ranch hands stood with clipboards.

"Would you guys like to ride first or later?" Katie asked her friends.

"Let's do it first before I lose my nerve," Henry said. Lily and Corky agreed. The four friends walked over and signed up with one of the cowboys.

"Git yourself over to the stable and git ready to saddle up," the cowboy drawled. "The first group rides out in 15 minutes," he added to no one in particular.

Katie, Henry, Lily and Corky walked over to the stable, where they saw Tyler talking to Mackenzie, Brittany and Jordan. When Tyler saw Lily, he finished his conversation and walked over to talk to her. "Are you going riding now?" Tyler asked Lily.

"Yes, we're all going now. What about you?"

"I hadn't made up my mind yet, but can I come with you?" Tyler stopped talking as if waiting for Lily to decide. She seemed to be tongue-tied, so Katie spoke.

"Tyler, we'd love for you to come with us," she said graciously.

"Thanks," Tyler replied, coloring slightly. "It looks like they've decided to go make out in the bushes," he said as he nodded in the direction of Mackenzie, Brittany, Jordan and the group of boys that were hovering around them.

The cool kids stared at Katie and her friends. She felt a momentary sense of dread as she looked back at them. During the last weeks of school—and especially since the dance—Katie had thought that Jordan had been less snobby. They had even talked to each other about the class trip, and Katie was surprised to find that Jordan and her mother had visited the Gunks, as the mountain range was called, many times.

After they had worked together on the project in Social Studies, they often found themselves talking about other issues that came up in the class. But now Jordan seemed uncomfortable as Katie looked at her across the paddock. For a split second, Katie had the sense that Jordan didn't want to be with the cool crowd any more. Something about the way she was standing made Katie think she was upset or frightened.

"Okay, young lady. Have you ever been on a horse before?"

The cowboy named Ralph had tapped Katie on her shoulder, startling her.

"What? Oh, no. Yes. Well, yes and no. I mean, I've been on the horses at the Dutchess County Fair, but not on a horse horse…I mean…not on a real trail ride…sorry."

The cowboy stepped back, amused at Katie's explanation.

"Well, then, we've got just the horse for you. How does Burt here look? He's friendly and smart, and he'll take good care of you."

Katie looked at Burt. He was shiny and dark reddish brown, with a white diamond in the middle of his forehead. He had a few pieces of hay sticking out of his mouth, and was sniffing the sleeve of Katie's shirt.

"Careful, miss. Burt here likes to chew on stuff. He'll start chewing on your shirt if you don't show him who's boss."

"Me?" Katie asked. "I'm the boss?"

"You are indeed. Just give him a little tap on the nose, and he'll mind his own business."

Katie laughed. She tapped her index finger on his nose, lightly, and was surprised by how soft his nose was. She was also surprised that he responded to that little tap.

As the cowboy helped her get settled on Burt, she wondered what Tyler had been discussing with Mackenzie, Brittany and Jordan. She wondered how Tyler could be so nice and still be friends with those three. *Oh well*, she thought. *I'd better keep my mind on not falling off this horse and making a spectacle of myself!*

"When you want your horse to move forward, just press your legs gently into their sides," Ralph said. "Remember, gently!" he continued, "these guys know what they're supposed to do. You don't need to beat them over the head with a stick to get their attention." The group laughed nervously.

"You kids listen to Ralph, now, and don't go doing anything silly. Horses are big animals, and you have to be sensitive to them, okay?" Ashley Sinclair's mother had decided to go out with this group of riders, and she was trying hard to cover her nervousness about being on a horse for the first time in her life.

Cowboy Ralph continued with his instructions. "Pulling back on the reins is a signal to the horse that you want him to stop." With that, the cowboy demonstrated tapping gently into the sides of the horse and reining in the horse to make it stop. "Any questions before we start our ride?" he asked.

"What if the horse starts going fast. What do we do?" Katie asked.

"These horses have mild dispositions. Unless they get spooked, they'll just stay right on the trail. But if, for some reason, they start to trot or gallop, pull on your reins, like this," the cowboy again demonstrated the position their hands should be in to rein in the horse. "And say 'whoa' real loud, like you mean it." Everyone said "whoa" and laughed. When he asked if there were any more questions, nobody spoke.

"Let's move out, then," and with that, the cowboy started leading the group on to the trail. There were two other cowboys riding with the group; one in the middle of the line and one bringing up the rear. Tyler was first in line, followed by Lily, Corky, Katie, Henry and Mrs. Sinclair. One cowboy was right behind Katie, so she felt fairly secure. She just prayed that she wouldn't do anything clumsy and make a total fool of herself in front of her friends, especially Tyler. The horses walked the trail in a quiet and orderly fashion, occasionally snorting and stopping to chew grass and dandelions along the way. Burt turned his head a couple of times to look at Katie.

After a few minutes, Katie relaxed and started to enjoy the scenery around her. The sky was such a brilliant blue and the air was so clear and fresh. *I love this time of year, before it gets hot and the humidity makes my hair all frizzy. I can't believe we got such a perfect day for our trip!* Katie was lost in thought when she heard an agonizing cry from behind her and the thumping sound of galloping hooves.

Before she could turn around to see what was going on, Henry's horse, with Henry holding on for dear life, shot out of the line and galloped at an absolutely furious pace into the woods! The cowboy in the middle and the one bringing up the rear broke out of line and galloped after Henry, trying to get ahead of Henry's horse so they could grab it.

Tree branches whipped Henry in the face, and everyone could hear him yelling and screaming in terror. He tried to stop his horse, but the reins had fallen out of his hands, and he couldn't gather them up. By this time, all the other students had stopped, their eyes glued to the scene unfolding before them.

Katie heard something in the brush along the trail. She thought she saw something moving among the trees. But she was so distracted by Henry's screaming that she looked back toward where Henry's horse was galloping across the hillside. Everyone was in quiet shock.

Suddenly, Henry's horse stopped dead in its tracks and Henry, surprised and caught off guard with such an abrupt stop, sailed over the horse's head onto the ground. The panicked horse had circled back and was galloping toward Katie and the rest of the group when it stopped. The spot where Henry fell was about fifty yards from where the drama had begun. The whole thing took less than a minute, but it was pretty clear that one tiny minute could hold immense tragedy. Katie struggled to dismount and rushed toward Henry.

"Young lady! Young lady!" Ralph shouted. "Stay back."

By the time the cowboy got these words out, Katie was already just a few yards from Henry. Mrs. Sinclair, momentarily forgetting her fear of horses, grabbed Burt's reins, and stared in disbelief at the scene. One of the cowboys grabbed Henry's horse; and another was crouched over Henry.

"C'mon, son, open your eyes. C'mon, son, please, wake up!"

Katie could see that Henry was unconscious. *Please be all right! Please don't be dead! Please, God, make Henry all right*, she prayed silently.

A cowboy named Curly was on his cell phone practically instantly, calling for help. He had dismounted and tied his horse loosely to a tree branch. Henry's face was cut and bleeding and his body lay limp and lifeless.

Lily and Corky ran over to join Katie and the three friends looked at each other without exchanging a word. They heard Curly questioning the cowboy who had been riding behind Katie.

"What happened, Joe?" he asked. "Smoky's never done that before. Did you see anything that coulda spooked him?"

"I dunno what happened, Curly, but I thought I saw something in the brush along the trail. It happened so quick, maybe I just thought I saw something...someone."

"Check Smoky. See if he's got any marks on him," Curly said.

Joe walked away, and it was clear that he was as shaken as the kids who now stood in shock, staring at their friend.

Curly motioned the other two cowboys to hurry over to where he knelt. "This kid is real bad. Is help coming?" he asked. After what seemed like an hour, but was actually less than three minutes, an ambulance roared up the trail.

Three paramedics jumped out of the vehicle and ran toward Henry. One paramedic opened the rear door of the ambulance and rolled a stretcher onto the trail. The paramedics gently lifted Henry onto the stretcher and, because the ground was so uneven, carried it to the waiting ambulance. In less than two minutes, the ambulance backed up, turned around, and raced back in the direction of the ranch.

Katie felt as if she were frozen. She could feel panic welling inside her, and her heart was thumping wildly. She could feel tears on her face, but couldn't hear her own sobs. She seemed to have taken root in the spot where Henry fell, and she couldn't take her eyes off the blood-stained dirt. She couldn't erase the image of Henry on the ground, bleeding and unconscious, and she was frightened that she might have been responsible, since she had persuaded him to try horseback riding.

Several of the chaperones and parents who were getting ready for nature hikes or pool duty had seen the ambulance. They came running up the trail toward the shocked group. Mrs. Sinclair had already gathered the students to her side and was trying to keep them calm.

Katie was gasping and sobbing hysterically, and choking on her tears. Mrs. Sinclair held her close, and Katie's panic and fear began to overtake her, too. She fought the waves of panic rising in her chest, and tried to focus on the children.

The other chaperones arrived, out of breath and full of questions.

"What happened?"

"Who's in the ambulance?"

"Was it a student that got hurt?"

Mrs. Sinclair, stunned and close to tears, looked at the other adults blankly.

"My God," she said. "My God. I...I...how? How could this happen?"

"What happened? Who got hurt?" The frantic questions evaporated unanswered into the air above them.

"We've got to get these kids and the horses back down to the stable." The cowboy named Ralph was addressing all the chaperones, and he started moving toward the group of horses. Tyler was holding the reins for three horses. He seemed calm, but there were tears streaming down his face.

"How ya doin, there, son?" Ralph gently took the reins from Tyler's hands and nudged the boy toward one of the chaperones. He gave the reins of one of the horses to another of the chaperones. "C'mon, folks. Please get ahead of the people walking the horses." The sad parade made their way down the trail, arriving at the stable within a few minutes. The word of Henry's accident had already begun to spread.

Mr. Murwata had begun working with the ranch staff to retrieve all the students from the trails, the pool and the tennis courts. He had a clipboard, and was checking off the names of every student gathered near the paddock.

"Students, there has been an accident," he said. "One of your classmates was seriously injured, and he has been taken to hospital. We will be returning to Manhattan as soon as possible. In the meantime, please do not leave this area. If you need to use the restrooms, please tell one of the chaperones where you are going."

Mr. Murwata had recruited a couple of the chaperones to help him keep track of where all the students were. Not that it would have been difficult. The students had begun gathering near the paddock as soon as they heard that there had been an accident. They huddled together, whispering about the accident, gossiping about what could have happened.

"Sir? Excuse me, sir. I need to talk to you. Privately." The manager of Wallkill Valley Ranch had tapped Mr. Needham on the shoulder, startling him. Mr. Needham was distraught, and terrified about the possibility that Henry might be critically injured.

"What? What is it? Has something else happened?"

"Sir. I'm sorry. We've called the police. This was apparently not an accident. It appears that someone did something to the horse the young man was riding, causing the horse to spook."

"Oh, God, no! No! No!" Mr. Needham buried his face in his hands and sank onto a nearby bench. "No! Please, no!"

The sound of sirens in the distance silenced the whole group. As three police cars sped up the dusty gravel driveway to the ranch, the students milled around in groups—some pressing close to the chaperones, some holding each others' hands—wondering what was coming next.

The ranch manager stood on a hay bale and explained the situation to the group.

"Folks, as you know, one of the students was seriously injured when his horse spooked. We called the police because we found evidence that someone did something to the horse, deliberately trying to scare him. It's getting a little warm out here in the sun, so why don't we just move into the lobby, where you can sit down and relax while we wait for the police to finish."

Several of the students gasped. The chaperones were stunned. The group moved slowly, silently toward the lobby. Outside it was still a beautiful spring day. The sky was still bright blue. But everything else in their world had changed forever. Katie, Lily and Corky stayed close to

Mr. Murwata, who was trying to console them. But even he could feel fear rising in his heart, at the thought that somebody in this group of children had the capacity for such thoughtless malice. Mrs. Sinclair had located her daughter, Ashley, in the crowd, and they joined the tiny group surrounding Mr. Murwata.

"Kathleen, do you have any idea what happened?"

"I wish I did, Paki. This is just horrible. I feel so helpless. Here I was trying to make sure nothing happened, and there was nothing I could do to help poor Henry. Has someone called his parents? Should one of us go to the hospital to be there in case...when...he wakes up, so he sees someone he knows?"

"I think the police probably wish to speak to you and the others who were there—even if you saw nothing. But I'll try to find out where they've taken Henry." He walked away, his head drooping in sorrow.

Mrs. Sinclair put her arm around Katie.

"I'll stay right here with you, okay sweetie? I won't leave."

Lily, Corky and Ashley cried, too, and Mrs. Sinclair pulled them all close to her. "Shhh. It's okay. Everything will be okay," she kept repeating, softly, gently. But she, too, was frightened and confused.

While one police officer questioned Katie and her group, other officers were questioning the rest of the students. Katie looked across the lobby and noticed that Jordan was sitting alone, and she seemed to be crying. Mackenzie, Brittany and the boys who had been with them earlier were fidgeting nervously near the front door.

Katie was starting to feel funny, as if she were in a dream. She felt like the trail ride was a movie, and it was replaying in her imagination. It was in slow motion, and Katie was looking right and left along the trail. She could smell the leather of the saddles, and feel the silky coat of the horse she had been riding. In her mind's movie, she watched the breeze catch the horse's black mane, tossing it gently back and forth. She saw the iridescent sheen of the horse's coat. It was like burnished copper, and such a lovely color Katie could hardly believe it was real. In a small grove of trees, Katie saw patches of sunlight. And something else. Something silvery and shiny. The shiny thing was moving toward the trail. She tried to see what it was. Was it a person? An animal? The shiny thing moved out of her field of vision, behind her. Then it happened! A scream. The horse out of control. Henry bleeding on the ground.

"Katie. Katie. Honey? What's the matter?" Mrs. Sinclair was worried about Katie. She seemed to be frozen, staring across the room. It was almost as if she were in some kind of trance. Physically she was right there; Mrs. Sinclair had her hands on her shoulders. But her eyes were blank. Something else was going on with her. Even though her body was right there, her mind was someplace far away.

This was not a new phenomenon. Katie's parents had seen it before when she was under stress. Her doctor always reassured the parents, saying that Katie was perfectly normal. She just felt things very deeply, he said. She has a very complicated emotional life, he said. But John and Charlotte thought something else was going on. The strange dreams she had, her stories about the dreams and the amount of detail she recalled about them were fascinating.

"Honey? What's wrong? Are you all right?"

"I saw something! Something shiny. It was moving and it went behind me and then Henry's horse ran away and Henry got hurt."

"Katie, did you see a person? Or what? What did you see?" Mr. Murwata, who had returned to the group, was stunned by what Katie was saying.

"Sir, excuse me. How about if I ask a couple of questions here." One of the police officers had been flipping through pages in his notebook, reviewing some of the other information he had gathered from other witnesses.

"I'm sorry. Of course. Please, go right ahead."

The officer asked Katie what she thought she saw, and she kept saying something about seeing a shiny, silvery thing moving through the trees, just before Henry's horse went crazy. The other cowboy had seen something, too. It was just a matter of finding out what they saw, where they saw it, how it affected the horse. By now the police were sure that something deliberate happened.

While the police questioned Katie and her friends, Mr. Murwata made several other calls on his cell phone. He was trying to stay close enough to the group to provide emotional support, but far enough away to ensure that his calls would not distract them or the police.

Mrs. Sinclair's heart went out to this teacher whom the kids respected so much. He had become such a role model for all the kids, but was an especially important role model for her daughter, Ashley. In fact, it was Mr. Murwata who had encouraged the Sinclairs to enroll

Ashley in Manhattan Prep. They had met him at a fund-raising dinner for the National Association for the Advancement of Colored People, where he spoke about his life in South Africa before the end of apartheid.

Mr. Murwata was finishing a call on his cell phone when Mrs. Sinclair approached him. She waited until she was sure he was not making another call.

"Paki...I...I'm sorry."

Mr. Murwata turned to face her. There were tears in his eyes, and it was obvious that he was struggling to regain his composure.

"Paki," she said gently. "Paki, you know there was nothing you could have done differently. Nobody could have predicted this." She put her hand on the teacher's shoulder comfortingly.

"I assured you and the other parents that the situation was under control...I failed."

Mr. Murwata was despondent, but struggling to maintain his professionalism in the face of tragedy.

"Henry has not regained consciousness. They arrived at Dutchess County Hospital just moments ago. His parents are on their way to the hospital. Can you imagine what they are feeling right now? We failed to protect their son...I think back to the meeting at the school. All the assurances we made to all the parents. Just days later, we're dealing with...with...attempted...an assault."

"We don't know yet what happened here." Mrs. Sinclair's voice was low and hushed. "Whatever it was, Paki, it was not your fault. The kids need you to lead right now...to be who you are...to be their teacher, someone they look up to and trust."

"And just what have I taught them? What have they learned today? What did Henry learn this day about adults who are here to protect and teach and lead them?"

"What matters is what we teach them now about justice and..."

"...and mercy?" he asked bitterly.

"Yes. And mercy and compassion. I still can't believe that there are kids in this school who would commit such an act of malice. I've got to believe that this was a prank that went wrong, not a deliberate attempt to seriously hurt someone."

"Nonetheless, Kathleen, we have a student for whom it matters very little whether the act was a prank or something far worse."

The police continued taking statements from the other students.

Within two hours they were ready to release the students and the chaperones.

The bus was nearly silent on the return trip. Katie was sitting next to Mr. Murwata, and she wondered if he wanted to talk about anything. She looked up at him. He was staring straight ahead, with a look of profound sadness in his eyes.

"Mr. Murwata?"

He blinked a couple of times, then looked down at her.

"Mr. Murwata, do you think someone tried to hurt Henry?"

"I don't know, Katie. I wonder how it could be possible. And yet...and yet..."

"Do you think they hate him?"

"Hate? I don't know. Hate is not something one would like to find in people so young. It is a poison that kills everyone."

"If someone did this to hurt Henry, will the police arrest them?"

Mr. Murwata tried to imagine the arrest of one of his young students. He tried to imagine what kind of punishment a court might order for this horrible act of...what?...stupidity? He was struggling with emotions that he knew could overpower him if he let them. He had seen hatred. He had seen violence. He had witnessed the deaths of young people, old people, people who had done nothing wrong.

"Do you think Henry is going to die?"

Katie's questions were so innocent. It was clear that she was struggling to understand how anyone could deliberately hurt one of her friends. He didn't know what to say to her. He knew that, as a teacher, he owed her more than evasive answers. But he, too, was struggling. He listened to the hushed murmuring of students and chaperones in the bus and recalled how, just hours ago, the cacophony of the excited students on their way to the ranch was nearly deafening.

"You remember when we spoke about justice, Katie? How complicated it is?"

"It is something that changes, and that maybe never fixes the person who gets hurt."

"That's right, Katie. But you know how we still must try to perfect it? How we cannot give up on it, just because it doesn't always work perfectly?"

"But how can this be fixed?"

"Ah, Katie, that is our challenge, is it not? There is the justice that happens in a courtroom. And then there is the justice that happens here…" he tapped his chest, near his heart.

"You mean, in our hearts?"

"I'll tell you a little story, about my home. There was a time when the government permitted horrible crimes against people like me. The government stood by while our homes were destroyed, our people were beaten and killed, our lives were made miserable. But then changes happened. The government and its institutions were destroyed. There were free elections, and people like me were permitted to vote, and to go to school and to get better jobs."

"Did they fix your house then?"

"No, Katie, they didn't fix everything. As you pointed out, justice doesn't always fix everything that was broken."

"Then did you get justice?"

"Technically, there has been justice. But the rest of what needs to happen is not something that a court can order. It must happen in peoples' hearts and in their attitudes."

Katie sat there, trying to absorb the horrible events of the day and the things Mr. Murwata was telling her. She was overwhelmed with sadness.

"Katie, you must care about what happens to Henry. But you must also care about how this happened to him, and why. I know you do, but as the days go on, and we find out more about this, it might become very difficult to still care about balancing justice in the court with mercy in your heart."

Katie looked at the back of the seat in front of her. She could feel tears welling in her eyes, and didn't want to cry in front of Mr. Murwata. She squeezed her eyes tight, and listened to the hum of other voices on the bus.

Mr. Needham broke the silence with an update on Henry's condition—although there was really nothing new to report. Still unconscious. Still in critical condition. The entire group of students and chaperones shuddered.

By the time the bus arrived at the school in Manhattan, everyone was emotionally exhausted. Parents had been called and were at the school to pick up their children. Mr. Murwata and Mr. Needham made brief but ominous announcements before everyone departed.

"The police have said they will be speaking with us again," Mr.

Murwata said. "They are treating this as a serious crime. For that we can be grateful. But many of you need to know that your children are likely to be questioned again."

"You should also know that the school will do everything possible to keep you all informed about Henry's progress and the progress of this investigation," Mr. Needham said.

"What, exactly do you mean, Mr. Murwata, when you say that some of these children will be questioned again? Nobody is going to question my daughter without my permission, and I would hope the rest of you would feel the same way." Mr. Morgan had once again lapsed into his court persona, and as he spoke, he waved his arms as if he were a conductor in front of an orchestra. This time, though, it was not playing well with the other parents.

Criticism of Mr. Morgan's arrogance erupted almost instantaneously.

"A child has a serious injury. Don you tink we should know all about it? What if your child is hurt?" Mr. Lupini was not accustomed to public speaking, and was trying very hard to control his emotions, and his accent. He was stunned that this trip had turned into such a tragedy.

"Do you have something to hide?" another parent called out.

"Is there any parent in this room who is not terrified for the Rathbone family? Is there anyone here who wouldn't do anything to find out how this happened? Wouldn't you want the same if your child were injured?"

"Quit being a hotshot attorney, Kyle, and think about being a parent for a few minutes. Don't you see what has happened here?"

Mackenzie and Brittany were standing close to Mr. Morgan, dodging his waving arms. To Katie, they did not look as cool and arrogant as they did earlier in the day. But, then, nobody looked the same anymore. Katie was surprised to see Jordan standing near Mrs. Hanover and Lily. She was struggling to keep from crying. Tyler was standing next to her, trying to console her.

"Ladies and gentlemen, please!" Mr. Murwata was practically shouting. "We will try to keep everyone informed of the progress of the investigation. The police have asked us for the names, addresses and phone numbers of all the students who were on the trip today, and we will provide that list for them within the hour. In the meantime, I think it would be best for you to take your children home. They have had a terrible experience today."

Katie, Corky and Lily embraced Mrs. Sinclair.

"You girls were very brave today. I'm proud of you, and I know that Henry will be just fine. It must be a great comfort for him to have such good, true friends," she said as she kissed each one goodbye.

"Corky, honey, you're coming home with Katie and me. Your mother is still working, and will pick you up at our apartment around 7 o'clock." Katie's father took both girls' hands and they walked home in silence.

This can't be happening. It must be a nightmare. I want to wake up, and
  Henry will be fine and we can all go back to the way it used to be. I
don't even care about being one of the cool kids. It doesn't matter. I just
want Henry to be all right. I want to go back to before, when no one was
  hurt, and Mom and Dad and Sophia and I were planning to move to
  Hyde Park for the summer with Tuffy. And Corky will come up and
spend a few weeks, and maybe Lily will come, too. And Dad will direct
the play about the Merchant and Mom and I will work on costumes or
help backstage. Most of all, I won't feel like it's my fault that Henry is
hurt. He's so sweet and kind, and he doesn't deserve to be hurt. I just
  want to wake up from this nightmare soon.

Chapter 24

Katie felt something wet on her face. She opened one eye to see a brilliant blue sky. The something wet on her face was Tuffy licking her. *Where am I? How could I fall asleep outside?* She sat halfway up, leaned on her elbow and looked around. There was nothing but trees and tall grass. *How can this be? Did I fall asleep in the Park? Why is the grass so tall?* When Tuffy saw her open her eyes, he started barking, and leaping for joy that now he would get some attention, and some food!

"Tuffy, where are we? Shh! Quiet, Tuffy, where are we? Where is our apartment?"

Tuffy would not stop his incessant barking. "Tuffy," Katie said, sitting up, "what's the matter with you?" She looked around, and saw nothing but tall grass and trees. "Whoa! What's going on?"

Fully awake now and in total shock, Katie stood up and surveyed her surroundings. She and Tuffy apparently had fallen asleep in Central Park. *How can that be,* Katie thought to herself. *I'm not allowed out of the house by myself, Mom and Dad and Sophia wouldn't let me sleep in the Park!*

This is too weird, Katie said to herself. "Tuffy, we've got to get out of here, and get home before they find out that we're not there. Come on boy."

Katie turned in all directions. Nothing looked familiar. It didn't look like the Park. At least not any part of the Park Katie had ever visited. There were no trails or paths, and the iron streetlights that lined the Park paths were missing from this section. Katie thought it odd that there were no streetlights. She shuddered, silently thanking God that it was daylight.

She checked her watch. *Nine o'clock? How can that be? Where are Mom and Dad? I never sleep this late.* She tapped the old watch, thinking it might be broken. *Maybe it stopped last night.* She put her wrist up to her ear, and heard the familiar tick-tick-tick of her grandmother's watch. *Maybe I just need to wind it...*

Katie took the watch off and started to wind it, but it was already wound tight. *What's going on? How could I fall asleep outside, in this place? How did I get here?*

She opened the back pocket of her backpack and pulled out her cell phone. *I better call Mom so she doesn't worry.* She pushed the power button, and the phone beeped twice. The light came on, but then nothing happened. The readout said there was no signal. She tried punching in the numbers for the apartment. Nothing. She shook the phone, then tapped it a couple of times. Nothing. *My battery must be dead,* she thought to herself. *But I just charged it yesterday, before we went to the Ranch. I haven't used it at all. Why does it even beep if the battery is dead?* She was confused and getting frightened. To stave off her fear, she stopped worrying about the phone, and turned her attention to positive steps she could take to get herself and Tuffy home safely.

"Tuffy, let's see if we can find a policeman to help us. Umm. Which way should we go?" Katie was speaking mostly to herself. Tuffy was busy sniffing the ground and running in circles. At least he'd stopped barking. "Nothing looks familiar to me."

Katie tried to see where the sun was, thinking that somehow she could navigate herself out of this place by relying on some of the lessons she learned in earth science. She thought that if she could figure out which direction was east and which was west, she might find her way home. But, then, she realized that she needed to know a lot more than the sun could tell her by its position.

"Tuffy, what good is it even if we do figure out what is east and what is west? We don't have a clue where we are. It's so quiet here. I don't even hear any cars, do you?" Katie looked at Tuffy in exasperation. He wasn't paying any attention to what she was saying.

Did we go to Hyde Park, and I just forgot? Katie wondered if she and Tuffy were somewhere near the family's country house. *Are we in the country? Is that why there aren't any streetlights, cars, or sounds?* The quiet was eerie and unsettling. Manhattan in the morning was usually bustling with activity. Car horns honked, and there was the constant whooshing sound of the subway whenever you walked near a grate or an entrance to the stations. And on busy weekday mornings, there was always the wheezing of the city buses starting and stopping. But there weren't even streets here in this meadow. There were no grates covering the caverns of the city Katie knew. There was nothing that even resembled Manhattan—or even Hyde Park for that matter. Katie tried to apply logic to her situation, as a way of staying calm.

"Maybe it's Saturday and that's why it's so quiet," Katie said to Tuffy. "That's right. It must be Saturday. That's the answer, Tuf," Katie said confidently.

"Well, we've got to start walking, or we'll never get home, Tuffy. Let's go." Tuffy barked and started trotting off in one direction, as if he knew where he was going. It seemed as good a start as any, and Katie was sure that they'd come upon some people in a few minutes so she followed Tuffy and started walking toward the sun.

After about 15 minutes or so, it became even clearer to Katie that she was really lost. There were no buildings, there was no familiar skyline filled with tall buildings, there were no airplanes flying overhead, there weren't even any people. The day seemed to be getting warmer and Katie was thirsty and hungry. She wished she could find a store where she could get something to drink. Then she remembered that she had a bottle of water in her backpack.

Tuffy looked thirsty, too. She opened the backpack and pulled out a plastic bottle of water. It was full! *Thank God, at least I remembered to get a bottle of water.* "Here, Tuffy, I've got some water for us." Tuffy ran back to Katie. He was panting and obviously thirsty. Katie took several gulps of water, then knelt down and poured some water into her hand. Tuffy eagerly slurped the water, and pleaded for more. "Okay, boy, don't worry. I'll give you more." She patted Tuffy on his head, then leaned down and kissed his ear. "We're going to be okay, boy. I promise."

She suddenly realized that her clothes were pretty rumpled, and her hair was probably a horrible mess. Her blue jeans were damp from the wet grass, and she had pieces of grass stuck to her shirt. She thought of how disapproving Sophia would be, seeing her and Tuffy in such disarray. She couldn't help herself. She started giggling as her imagination played the voice of Sophia admonishing her. "Young lady, what are you thinking? You look like goat."

The thought of Sophia reminded her that she was lost and alone and growing frightened. She looked at Tuffy, and felt fear rising inside her. She wanted to cry, but didn't want to upset Tuffy. For his part, he found their predicament fascinating.

Ummm! He thought to himself. *This place smells great! Why is she so upset? There's stuff here that I've never smelled before. I wonder where we are? Can't she smell all these new things?* Suddenly Katie heard a slight tinkling noise. She looked around but could see nothing. "Tuffy, did you hear that?" Katie asked. She stopped and listened quietly. "There it is again. What's going on? What is that noise?" She stood up and started walking toward where she thought the noise was coming from.

As she walked, Tuffy stuck by her side. Katie heard the tinkling sound again and Tuffy's ears perked up. He had heard the noise, too. He started running ahead and Katie knew that her little dog had a much better sense of hearing and smell than she did, so she chased after him. All of a sudden, Tuffy stopped dead in his tracks. Katie had been running to keep up and she stopped, too, and looked up. Before them stood a large cow with a bell around its neck.

"Moooooooooooo," the cow bellowed. The only cows Katie had ever seen had been behind fences. She wasn't sure, but she didn't think cows were vicious creatures. Tuffy was clearly in shock. At least Katie had seen pictures of cows. This was a totally new experience for Tuffy. And he reacted like a typical dog. He started to bark continuously so as to convince the cow that he was, somehow, in charge.

"Tuffy, hush," Katie said. "He's not going to hurt us. Or maybe I should say 'she.' I'm not sure whether this is a girl cow or a boy cow. And I have no idea how to find out. I wonder how a cow got loose in the park? This is all so strange. Maybe the cow escaped from a farmer's truck and it's lost." Katie was clearly puzzled by this odd turn of events.

"Wait a minute, Tuffy. Girl cows give milk!" Katie was so enthralled with the uniqueness of her situation, her fear subsided. She approached the cow gingerly. Speaking softly and gently, she tried to determine if it were safe to get closer.

"Mooooooooo," the cow bellowed. It seemed to be in some kind of pain. But Katie couldn't tell what was hurting it. She didn't see any blood, but she reasoned that its insistent mooing meant it was trying to tell her something. How she wished Dr. Hanover was here. He'd know what was wrong. As Katie approached the cow, she could see what looked like swollen fingers protruding from under its belly. "Oh my gosh, Tuffy. I'll bet she needs to be milked! That's why she's mooing!" Katie wondered what milking entailed. She had never done it. In fact, she had never even seen a cow being milked. But she wracked her brain to recall anything she had read about how people milked cows. She suddenly remembered a book Sophia used to read her when she was 4 or 5 years old. It was about an old farmer and his animals. She squeezed her eyes shut, trying to visualize the pictures of the old farmer milking the cows. She approached the cow, knelt down next to it and talked softly. "I'm not going to hurt you. I'm going to try and help you." Out of a combination of curiosity and instinct, Tuffy quieted down and sat next to Katie.

Eeuw! What are those things? How come they're all puffy? He thought to himself. *No! Don't touch them! What if they break?* He could hardly watch as Katie reached for one of the swollen "fingers."

Then the name of the equipment came to her—the cow's teats held the milk, and the farmers gently pulled them to make the milk come out. Katie gently pulled down. Nothing happened. "Mooooooooooo," the cow cried. Katie was so startled that she fell back on the grass. *I'm sure this is where the milk comes from,* Katie thought. *I'm just not doing it right.* She tried again. Nothing. "Well, Tuffy, so much for this being a spigot you can turn on when you want milk," Katie said laughing. *I'll bet Sophia knows how to milk a cow,* Katie thought to herself.

Determined to figure this mystery out, Katie grabbed one of the teats again. This time, she squeezed and pulled at the same time. She was rewarded with a squirt of white liquid streaming into the grass. "Tuffy, I did it! I did it!" Katie said laughing. "I figured out the secret to milking a cow!"

The next challenge Katie faced was figuring out what to put the milk into. She didn't want to waste the milk, and she thought the farmer would be mad if he found her milking his cow. Then she thought maybe the cow had wandered away from its pasture, and the farmer might be looking for it.

Cows probably don't walk far, she thought to herself. *There's probably a farmhouse nearby.* She decided to take the cow home, and let the farmer milk it. Bravely, she grabbed the cow by the tinkling bell around its neck and gently tugged to move it forward.

A cow doesn't end up in the middle of a field by accident, Katie thought to herself. *Where there's a cow, there must be some form of civilization nearby. At least, some people. Cows don't drop out of the sky.* And with determination, she led the cow toward a clearing she saw ahead.

After about 10 more minutes of walking, Katie, Tuffy and the cow came upon a dilapidated cottage. It looked very old, like some of the crumbling historical buildings Katie had seen on the History Channel. Another forlorn cow stood in front of the house and a girl about Katie's age was stooped over milking the cow. A small boy Katie guessed to be around two or three years old stood near the young girl. The children were dressed oddly, Katie thought. It was June and the young girl wore a long dress that looked worn. The little toddler wore short pants and an old fashioned shirt with puffy sleeves that tied shut in the front with what looked like rope. The whole setting was crude and very unusual for New York City. Tuffy started barking and Katie quickly bent down to pick him up. At the sound, the young girl turned her head to look up, genuinely surprised at the interruption. She stood and picked the little boy up in her arms and tentatively walked toward Katie and Tuffy.

"Hilp thee?" At least that's what it sounded like to Katie as the girl seemed to have some kind of foreign accent. Katie wondered if she had stumbled across some kind of Roma camp in the middle of Central Park. *Stop it,* she said to herself. *You've just heard too many stories about the Roma from Sophia.*

"I beg your pardon?" Katie said, tentatively.

"Hilp thee?" the little girl repeated. "Huh?" she added pointing to Tuffy.

"I wonder if I could use your phone? I'm lost, and I want to call my parents to have them come and pick me up."

"Huh?" the girl said, a frown creasing her forehead. "Phoone?" she repeated, struggling with the pronunciation. "Whot be that, huh?" she said.

Thinking that the young girl didn't, perhaps, understand English, Katie put Tuffy on the ground and pulled out her cell phone. Pointing to it, she asked again. "Your phone? Could I use your phone?"

The girl stared at the phone, then at Katie with a mixture of fear and fascination. She pointed at the phone and said something that sounded like "Yegod!"

Katie was beginning to think the girl was from another country and thoroughly confused. But she was taken aback by the way the girl looked at her cell phone. Feeling even more anxious about her situation, but believing that finding a phone was the first step toward getting help, she pressed on. She put the phone back in her pack and tried another approach. She gestured with her hands, pretending to dial a phone and then hold the receiver up to her ear. "Telephone, phone," Katie said. "Understand?"

"Tellyphone?" the girl repeated. She put the little boy down, and imitated Katie's hand gestures. "I can whot thou hast said, but I know not whot it is thou seek."

Puzzled, Katie decided to try another approach. She extended her hand out to the young girl and said, "My name is Katie Farrell and I live in Manhattan at the Shelbourne Apartments. This is my dog, Tuffy, and I think we're lost. I need to call my parents because they'll be worried about me when I'm not there for breakfast." The girl hopped backward, avoiding Katie's outstretched hand.

Looking down at her watch, Katie saw that it was now 9:30, and she was sure that her parents and Sophia were already in a panic.

Grabbing her hand, the young girl said, "Whot is't thou have there?"

"It's a wristwatch," Katie replied, slowly. "Haven't you ever seen one before?" As Alice in Wonderland would have said, this was getting "curiouser and curiouser."

"Ta' do whot?" the girl asked.

Katie thought the girl had said "to do what." "Why, to tell time, of course," she replied.

"Thou know'st the time with that wee thing?" the girl asked, incredulously.

"Really, it's no big deal. Everyone has one," Katie said. "Don't you have a clock in your house?"

"Maircy, no, art thou noddy?" the girl said laughing.

Not knowing what the girl was talking about, and wondering if she was slightly crazy, Katie said, "Are there other houses nearby where there might be a phone I could use?"

"Thar's Tom's house down the road a piece. Thou art lost, thou say'st?"

"Yes," Katie said, despairingly, "I'm lost. And I'm terribly thirsty and hungry. I don't suppose you could spare some water and some toast, could you? My dog and I just woke up," Katie said by way of an explanation. Even as she said the words, she felt how useless they were in describing her situation.

"Mum, comp'ny!" the girl bellowed. An old woman came out of the front door of the cottage, wiping her hands on her ragged, long dress. Her hair straggled down to the middle of her back and it was obvious it hadn't been washed in a while, for it glistened with oiliness.

"Whot is't, Sarah," she asked the girl, then looked across to Katie and Tuffy.

"This girl here wonts a drink and something called 'toast'. She's noddy, Mum," the girl explained.

"Git thee gone, little wench. We've not time ner money for rooks and dullards. Tarry not! Begone to thine own mum!" The old woman pointed toward a dusty road, and although Katie could not understand everything she said, she realized that the woman wanted her to leave.

With a backward glance at the young girl and little boy, Katie picked Tuffy up and started walking. When she reached the road, she looked back at the odd trio and the old woman shouted at her. "Begone! Git! Ch'ill swat thee, forsooth! Git!" And with that she turned and guided her two charges into the cottage.

"Tuffy, what is going on? I feel like I'm in the middle of some kind of play," Katie said, holding the dog close and comforting him. "Tuffy, is that possible? Have we stumbled into a movie set? That's it! I'll bet they're filming some kind of movie in the Park. Oh! Thank goodness, I thought I'd lost my mind," and putting Tuffy back on the ground and chuckling to herself, she set off down the road.

Chapter 25

After walking for what felt like hours, and wondering if indeed there were some sort of play going on in the Park, Katie came upon a slight incline, at the top of which was a large grouping of rocks. She sat on the rocks and looked over the edge. There, spread out at her feet—and at Tuffy's paws—was what looked like a rather large city. Not like New York City, but there were houses and people, and...horses! Horses in the streets instead of cars. Katie was torn. She wanted to go down the hill and into this strange city, but she couldn't understand what kind of city it was. A foul smell wafted up the hill, and Katie instinctively held her nose.

"Peeuw! Tuffy! What is that smell?" Tuffy was confused, too. He cocked his head and looked down at the city. *It smells so good!* He thought. *I wish she'd start moving! I want to see what's there!* He looked up at Katie and barked once.

"I guess we don't have much choice, Tuffy. If we're going to find a policeman, or someone to help us, we've got to go there, no matter how it smells."

Yes! Tuffy thought. *Finally! I get to see what this is all about!* He was practically leaping with anticipation.

"Now maybe we'll get someplace. The first thing we have to do is find a phone and a policeman, not necessarily in that order. Let's go,

Tuffy." And together, they sped down the hill toward the town.

The stench made Katie stop in her tracks, halfway down the hill. She gasped and put her hand over her mouth. Tuffy seemed thrilled by the smell. *Maybe they're having a garbage strike,* Katie thought. *This smells horrible.* Katie was afraid she was going to vomit. But Tuffy was as excited as if there were a truckload of steaks ahead, just waiting for him. Katie looked at him, looked at the city that lay before them and decided that—whatever the smell—they had to keep going.

Within minutes, they were on a slippery cobblestone street. The noise was deafening. The scene was almost overwhelming for Katie. Horses clip-clopping on the cobblestones, people shouting at one another, carriages clanking along, beggars sleeping in doorways, trash falling out of second and third-story windows and clattering as it hit the street—the sounds and the smells made Katie feel as if she were going to faint.

It all reminded Katie of the scenes in Oliver Twist. She and Tuffy stopped, stunned by what they saw, heard and smelled. They found themselves standing in front of a large wooden door with a crude sign over the top that simply said, 'Tavern,' and below the word there was a painting of what looked like a glass of beer with foam on top. Katie looked at Tuffy and the dog stared back at her.

"What do you think, Tuf? Should we go in?" As if understanding her every word, Tuffy barked once to indicate his approval of the plan.

Katie knocked softly on the door. There was no answer. She tried pressing down on the latch. The door opened easily. Stepping into the room, Katie could barely see a foot in front of her. The only light came from a few burning candles. The windows were small and let in very little sunlight, so Katie squinted, trying to see if she could make out any human figures.

"Hello!" she called. "Hello?" No answer. Katie stepped gingerly into the hallway and peeked into the room on the right. It looked to be a dining room with very old furniture. In fact, the furniture looked like it belonged in Old Williamsburg.

Stepping back into the hallway, Katie proceeded further down the hall toward what looked like a swinging door. Just as Katie was about to push the door, a woman pushed it from the other side and strode into the hallway, wiping her hands on a huge apron tied around her waist.

"Here, now, whot's this?" she asked.

Katie stared at the woman, surprised to see her mother's agent,

Sylvie Campion, in this dark place, and wearing such strange clothes.

"Sylvie, is that you? I'm so glad to see you!" She felt waves of relief at seeing a familiar face. "We thought we were lost and we were worried that Mom and Dad and Sophia would be looking for us and..." Katie was babbling questions faster than the woman could even begin to answer them. "...what are you doing here? Where are we? Can you call Mom? My cell phone doesn't work."

Even Tuffy was convinced the woman was indeed Sylvie. He barked excitedly, and began running in circles, searching for Sylvie's giant satchel which contained his treats.

"Me name's Starr, not Sylvie, we're in London, girl. Would'st Sylvie be thy mum? Com' on, whot's pestering thee?" the lady said.

It might have been that Katie was tired, thirsty, hungry, and confused. Or it might have been that she was scared out of her mind. She had no idea where she was and who these people were and she wanted to go home. Regardless of the reason, she had had enough and burst into tears. Embarrassed, she turned to leave, and the lady, Starr, gently put her hand on Katie's shoulder.

"Stay, me poppet, stop thy weeping. Thou art lost? Would'st thou have a morsel to eat? Art thou hungry?" Starr asked sympathetically.

This show of kindness just made Katie cry harder and louder and Tuffy joined in with barking. He couldn't stand to see his Katie upset or hurt.

Why is she crying? Didn't the lady say something about feeding us? How bad could it be? Tuffy thought. *I wonder if we're going home soon...I hope this lady knows how to make scrambled eggs the way Sophia does...*Tuffy nudged Katie to get her attention, but Katie was crying so hard she momentarily forgot about Tuffy.

"I don't know where I am. I woke up this morning thinking I fell asleep in the Park with my dog and now I feel like I'm in the Twilight Zone. Who are you? Where am I?" Katie said between sobs and gulps for air.

"There, now, me lovely," Starr said as she led Katie and Tuffy into a room at the back of the building. "Sit thee down, here, and banish thy tears and I'll make for thee and thy wee dog a bite to eat."

Katie looked around the room where Starr had taken her. It was some sort of kitchen, but not a kitchen in the true sense of the word...at least not a kitchen Katie had ever seen. There were wide wooden planks

157

for the floor and a table and chairs, but in Katie's mind that's where the resemblance to a kitchen stopped.

Over to one side of the room was a huge fireplace. It was so large, Katie and Tuffy could have camped out in it. The flames were low and what looked like chickens were on some kind of spit. It looked like the rotisserie Katie's father used when he barbecued in the country.

Katie and Tuffy were so hungry; and the smells wafting from the fireplace were so reminiscent of Sophia's roasted chicken that Katie momentarily forgot her confusion and gratefully took a chair.

"Could I please have some water, Starr?"

"Heavens! Water? Nay, me sweet. 'Tis poison. I'll fix for thee something good to drink—and for thy pup, too."

Starr bustled about the room gathering up plates and cups and bread. She dipped an iron spoon with a long handle into a pot simmering in the fireplace. It looked like she was spooning out vegetables. She then removed one of the roasted chickens from the spit and carved it, putting some chicken meat aside for Tuffy. Tuffy was so hungry and excited at the wonderful smells that he sat expectantly wagging his tail a mile a minute.

I really love this woman, he thought. *Even though I just met her. She's feeding us, and she made Katie stop crying. I wonder if she knows Sophia?*

"Now, thou must eat and drink, me lovely poppet. Eat hearty, dearie. And thou," Starr scratched Tuffy behind his ear, "wee thing, feast on me roasted chicken!"

Katie was ravenous and the food Starr gave her was absolutely delicious. The stew-like concoction turned out to be onions, peas and carrots and some other vegetable Katie had never eaten before. But she didn't stand on ceremony. She was wolfing down the food so fast that Starr came over to her and put her hand on Katie's arm.

"There, now, girl. Slow down or thou will'st sicken. There's plenty for thee. What's the name of thy wee friend?"

"Tuffy," Katie replied.

"Well, he's a sweet dog," Starr said. "Tuffy, eh? A funny name for such a mite."

Tuffy looked up from his plate, glancing at Katie and Starr. *She likes me! She really likes me!* He thought to himself. *She must know Sophia.*

After having eaten her fill and drunk what tasted like carbonated apple cider, Katie took the time to contemplate her situation.

Something was terribly wrong. She was not dreaming and she wasn't in New York. Only, she had no idea where she was, or how she got to this place. Katie was equally puzzled at the rudimentary life these people led. How could Starr cook in a kitchen with just a fireplace? Where was the sink? Where was the refrigerator? Goodness! Where was the microwave?

"Excuse me, Starr, but could you please tell me what's going on? I woke up this morning and since that moment, I've been terribly confused. I think I may be lost. Is this a back lot or a location shoot? Do you know my mother's agent, Sylvie Campion? You look so much like her, you could be her twin." Katie said.

"Thou speak nonsense, child. Thy tire and words, they be strange to mine eyes and ears. Perchance thou wandered off from some encampment? Didst thou tumble and knock thy head? Perchance thou suffer from some malady?"

"But where is this? What town is this?" Katie's confusion was mixing with a sense of fatigue that was creeping over her. She felt tingly and slightly dizzy.

"Why, we're nearby London, me little poppet. And this here," Starr waved her arms around the dim room, "would be me tavern. Perdy, 'tis all mine, debts and all, sith me husband went off and died. I don't know no Sylvie."

Stay calm, Katie said to herself. *There's got to be a reasonable explanation for this. I'm just too tired to figure it out.* Katie was getting so sleepy; it was hard for her to sit up straight. She leaned on her elbow, and stared into her empty plate.

Thoughts of Henry and home and her parents and the accident at the ranch were spinning in her head and confusing her even more. She could feel herself slipping into sleep, and she looked up at Starr, just as the woman lifted her out of her chair gently.

"Come on, love, we'll put thee and thy wee friend in the green room for a little sleep. Thou willst be right as rain as soon as thou wipe the cobwebs from thy head. Thou art a mite bestraught, that's for sure," Starr almost cooed to Katie. Her voice and gentleness calmed Katie and Tuffy.

Chapter 26

Starr put Katie onto a huge bed with a heavy brocade bedspread. Then she lifted Tuffy onto the bed, and he quickly snuggled up to Katie, who was already sound asleep. She dreamed about the accident, and the bus ride back to Manhattan. She saw the silvery shiny thing again, moving back and forth in the woods. This time it was coming toward her! She felt herself falling off her horse, and rolling across the hard dirt. *Help me! Please help me!* In the distance she could hear Tuffy barking and whining. She tried to scream, but no sound came out. She tried to see what or who was behind the silvery thing, which was now so close to her face that it was blinding her.

"Easy, love. Easy! Shh. It's all right. Thou art safe, love." Katie woke up to see Starr's face staring back at her, with a look of deep concern in her eyes.

"I…I'm still here? We didn't go home yet?" Katie patted the bed, searching for Tuffy. "Tuffy! Tuffy! Where are you?" She could feel panic gripping her again.

"Thou art still here, lovey. Though I wisht thee could fly to where thee want t'be, in this moment, thou art right here. Thy little friend is running his tail off outside, sniffing and howling."

Katie looked around the dimly-lit room. There was a burning candle on a small table next to the bed, and another one on a stand next to the door. The flickering lights made strange shadows everywhere. Katie was still confused, but glad that at least this time she woke up to see something familiar—even though Starr was a stranger, she was a nice stranger, who reminded Katie of someone she loved.

"Starr, could you tell me where the bathroom is?"

Starr looked at her quizzically.

"What's bathroom?" she asked. "Is't a town thou art lookin' for?"

Uh oh, Katie thought. *After seeing the kitchen, I should have known that there's no bathroom.*

Katie fumbled for an explanation of what she needed, and finally Starr understood.

"Ah! A privy! Thou art in need of a privy!"

"Privy?" Katie said, her voice a little shaken. "Yes, I think that's it."

Starr produced a large porcelain pot, from under the bed. "Goodness, lovey, where hast thou been living? Thou wanted…what was that word?…bath?"

Katie stared at the pot, wondering what on earth she was going to do, and how she would get home.

"Go on, now, whilst I get thee some water to wash up and maybe a brush for thy beautiful hair. Goodness! Methinks thy hair is too lovely for words. Thou art truly an enchanting child." Starr took one of the candles and started down the hall, leaving Katie with the porcelain pot. Her need to go finally overwhelmed her concerns about modesty and custom. She had just finished when Starr returned, carrying a bowl and a pitcher and a towel.

"Ah, good girl. I'll take this now, whilst thee scrubs that lovely face."

Starr picked up the porcelain pot and, without even flinching, left the room with it. When she returned, Starr was armed with a hair brush. She gently touched Katie's head and sighed.

"So beauteous and lovely! I swear by my troth, thou art like some fairy princess, here to bewitch me."

"A princess?" Katie laughed. "I'm fat and not pretty and my hair is all wrong."

"Wherefore dost thou say these things? Hast thou never seen thy visage? Dost thou never gaze upon thyself?"

Katie looked at Starr, and saw that she was serious. She looked down at her rumpled clothes and dirty sneakers. She didn't know what to say.

Suddenly she heard Tuffy barking downstairs, and there was a man shouting and laughing.

"Starr, me pet, prithee, where the devil art thou? I'm dry as Yorick's skull, and ravin for thy beauty and thy company! Let us convive upon thy wondrous roasted chicken, indeed the most acclaimed through-out England!"

Starr blushed, stood up and turned toward the door. She motioned for Katie to follow her. "Come hither, love."

When they entered the hallway, Tuffy came bounding up to Katie and leapt into her arms. He was quivering with excitement. *Dear heavens, had that voice said 'England,' Katie thought? London, England?* She squeezed Tuffy close to her and kissed him on the ear. She looked up and there in the doorway stood a tall, thin man in an elaborate costume. His sparse black hair was tufted on the sides and he looked like one of the actors in Shakespeare in the Park. Just last summer Katie, her parents and Sophia had seen *All's Well That Ends Well* in Central Park.

"Will Shakespeare, thou mayst smooth me with thy fine words. Prithee, where hast thou been hiding? Art thou plotting to shatter the very heart within me bosom?" Starr said with a hint of laughter in her voice.

Katie stared at the man. Then she looked at Starr. Whispering, she said half to herself and half to Tuffy, "Will Shakespeare? Tuffy, if we're not in a movie-of-the-week, we're in big trouble."

What has happened to us? Tuffy and I are lost!
I wish we could go back to worrying about the Spring Dance.
Are we in the middle of a dream or a nightmare? Or both?
I want Tuffy and me to wake up in New York, in our own bed.
I want to find out that Henry is okay.
I want it to be summer, and I want to hang out with Corky and Lily.
I want to see Mom and Dad and Sophia again.
Oh, God! What if Tuffy and I never see them again!
Please let us go home. Please let this be a dream!
I did <u>not</u> meet William Shakespeare.
Starr and the cow and the horrible smell and poison water
are just nightmares. Tuffy and I are not stuck in another century!
No way!

Chapter 27

"William, what in Halidom art thou doing here?" Starr asked. "Thou hast a play to perform on the morrow, dost thou not?"

"Starr, me lovely rose, I shall be back to the theatre by the time the curtain rises. Burbage, that wagtail, will carry on like a stuck pig, but he knows the audience doth worship me, and so he will hold his salty tongue and swallow his bile," William replied. "And who is this fair lass?" he added, pointing to Katie.

Katie had started to open her mouth to answer, but Starr grabbed her shoulders from behind. "Saints alive and dead. I never asked thy name, me poppet," she said chuckling. "I found her in me front hallway with this little mite of a dog, Will."

"Well, wee lass, who art thou?" William asked.

"My name is Katie Farrell and I'm from New York. That's in the United States of America. And this is my dog, Tuffy. I'm very confused. I went to sleep last night in my bedroom and I woke up in another century—and another country." She was half talking to herself, as if to try to reconcile the bizarre facts, and half explaining her situation to these two people. In her confusion, she forgot her manners, and blurted, "Are you *really* THE William Shakespeare?"

Starr furrowed her brow. She thought something else was going on with this child. She could feel it in her bones. "Express thy whole story, lass, not thy invention. How dost thou know of Will? We know him around here, by his plays. He hast performed them in Shoreditch and elsewhere, with Lord Chamberlain's Men. But if thou truly art from abroad, how could'st thou know him at all?"

"Everyone knows Shakespeare!" Katie said. "Are you really him?" She couldn't take her eyes off the man.

"Indeed I am, but then, how dost thou know me?" William asked, puffing out his chest. He obviously had an ego like the actors who worked with Katie's mother.

"My goodness, everyone knows you, sir. Are you kidding me? You're like worshipped by actors all over the world," Katie said seriously. "In fact, my father is directing one of your plays this summer in Hyde Park, where my family stays in the summer. It's near New York City…in America…Do you know anything about America?" Katie asked.

"America? Where is that?" William asked. "Thou would'st have me believe thou came from somewhere far away?"

"Oh, yes, sir!" Katie said emphatically. "I've come here from the other side of the ocean. The country is called America. It used to be part of the British Empire…the United States…maybe you call them the colonies?"

"The colonies, thou say'st? I seem to have heard of them. Starr, isn't that where that plant…tobacco?…came from? The colonies belong to England, child. How could thou come here without a ship? Hast thou dropped out of the welkin upon this place? Without thy parents? Hast thou run away from thy parents?"

"No! No! I love my parents and my home. I…I don't know how I got here. That's what I'm trying to explain." Katie was getting upset, and choking back tears.

"There, now, little poppet. Prithee, no tears! Tell me how is't that thou speak in such a strange tongue? 'Tis English…but not English. Where didst thou learn to speak? Didst thou say thy father is directing one of *my* plays? How has this come about?"

"To speak, sir?" Katie was confused.

"Thy language. Thy words seem strange, even though thou speak in English."

"My parents taught me to talk, and in school I learn new words. I go to Manhattan Prep, sir." Katie was trying to sound confident. She felt comforted saying the name of her school out loud. It made her believe there was a trail somewhere that would take her and Tuffy back home to her parents and friends.

"To school, thou say'st? How is't that a female hast the time and privilege to go to a school? Art thou of royal birth?" William was intrigued by Katie, even though he suspected she might be fabricating her situation. And yet…her clothes and her speech and everything about her screamed that she was indeed something—someone—unique and quite possibly brilliant.

"Why, everyone goes to school, sir. We learn to read and write and do math." Katie was trying to distill the American educational experience into evidence that would convince this man that she was telling the truth.

William was looking past Katie to Starr, who was staring intently at the child, as if she were some sort of apparition. Starr was experiencing incredible emotions and sensations. She had been mending some linens while the three of them talked, but had put her sewing down on the bar momentarily.

She was in awe of this child. She wanted to protect her, and to take care of her. Maybe she hoped some of Katie's magic would rub off on her. Maybe she was beginning to realize that the strange feelings she had experienced since Katie appeared at her door were turning into love for the children she knew she would never have. Maybe she was torn between helping Katie return to her real home and keeping her as one would keep a stray animal, always wondering if the real owners might suddenly arrive on the scene.

Starr was feeling things that she didn't understand. She felt something stirring at the core of her knowledge of herself—of who she was and what her own life was all about. She felt a deep connection with Katie, as if she and Katie were not strangers after all.

Her heart was confused and excited and hopeful and even a little frightened. But she knew one thing for sure: Katie was a remarkable creature who brought light and happiness into Starr's life.

"Thou can read?" William asked, challenging Katie for proof. Starr looked totally smitten by Katie. She tried to hide her feelings by returning to her mending. He decided to play the cynic…at least for awhile.

"Of course, sir. And write, too." Katie turned to look at Starr, then turned back to William Shakespeare. "I can prove it."

While Starr and William watched in fascination, Katie rummaged through her backpack, tossing her possessions onto a nearby table. Her half-empty water bottle and her wallet and a ballpoint pen were artifacts of such extraordinary design that neither Starr nor William uttered a word.

The zippers on the backpack's many compartments—some so tiny that they could barely hold loose change, others large enough to contain several books—opened and closed with a crisp *zzzipp!*, a sound that first startled, and then amused Katie's small audience. They hardly knew what to think of the wonders that tumbled forth from this magical sack. They were as fascinated by her casual attitude toward these inventions as by the wonders themselves.

"What else hast thou in that sack?" William asked in awe, as if what was already on the table were more than enough.

"I'm looking for my diary—I just had it a few minutes ago—and some other things, to prove to you that I've come here from the future."

"Thy diary?" Starr asked.

"It's my journal. I write in it every day."

"And thy father. What of him? And my play?"

"He's directing *The Merchant of Venice*, in Hyde Park, near our summer home. He's helping out a local theater group."

"What play is this?" William asked.

"*The Merchant of Venice*, about the guy who loans someone money and then wants to slice a pound of flesh off him and there's a trial and that lady, I think her name is Porcha?...she dresses up like a boy…"

"*The Venetian Comedy*! How can that be? How can thy father have my play in…where did thou say he is? A park? In the colonies? I have the play here, in my own possession. 'Tis not yet completed. How can'st thou say thy father will produce it?"

At this moment, this strange group was unified by one condition: confusion. Tuffy, however, stood alone. He was not confused. He was intrigued, his appetite whetted by the culinary wizardry of Starr, who seemed obsessed with devising new and tasty ways of making him happy.

Before him was a plate of the most savory meat he had ever tasted. *Hmmm…I wonder if Katie can find out how Starr made this. Starr should meet Sophia. They could work together on more treats for me,* he thought as he lapped at the delicious sauce covering the meat. He was half-heartedly listening to Katie and Starr and that guy with the funny clothes.

He tuned into the conversation only to make sure that Katie was happy and not scared. Listening for every nuance of her voice, he was ready to pounce like an enraged tiger on anyone who upset her.

William and Starr were pelting Katie with questions faster than she could answer even the simplest ones.

"Katie! What sort of a name is't?" William asked.

"What sort of glass is that, with many ripples? How is't that it seems no weightier than a feather?"

"Wherefore art thou clad in such strange tire?"

"What is't that makes that strange sound?"

"What is *that*?" William shouted in utter astonishment when he saw Katie's cell phone. His voice, a mixture of shock and awe, silenced everyone momentarily. The three humans and the lone canine all stared at the phone.

"It's my cell phone. With this, I can talk to people all over the country...everyone has one, or had one, when I left," Katie explained. As she held the small red, white and blue phone in her hand, it dawned on her that, even as she was struggling to understand how she wound up in this strange place, maybe her parents and her friends were also scattered into different times and places throughout the universe. Maybe this happened to everyone, not just to Katie and Tuffy. She looked at Starr and William. They seemed to sense her fear and confusion.

"There, now, thou must not take thought about thy predicament.

Haply thy quest will lead thee to the place thou wish't most to see. In a twink, little poppet, thou will be back whence thou hast come. In the nonce, thou must enjoy thy journey..." William was suddenly neither pompous nor bombastic. He touched her shoulder gently. "Might I have a look at this most strangest invention?"

He held the phone in both hands, as if it were some sacred object. He turned it around and around and shook it once or twice. Several minutes passed while William examined the cell phone from all angles. He touched the small numbered buttons and read the letters above each number. "Abc? What does this mean? What didst thou call this device?"

"It's called a cell phone," Katie said, and then wondered how in the world she could ever explain the concept to Starr and William.

Starr took the phone into her hands and ran her fingers over the buttons. "Let's see thee use it," she said, her curiosity mixing with fear of what this object could do.

"I've already tried. It doesn't work. I thought the battery was dead, but it's not. I think it doesn't work because it hasn't been invented yet...I mean, it doesn't exist in this century."

"Battery? How could'st thou have an entire battery within that thing?"

"It runs on a battery...do you know what a battery is?" Katie asked.

"A battery, child, is an artillery unit poised for battle. Thou cans't not have a battery in thy...what didst thou call it...thy cell?"

Katie thought for a moment, trying to separate the battery William talked about from the one she knew was in her cell phone. Although she could not call anyone on the phone, she could still show how the screen lit up, how the battery beeped, how the numbers showed up on the screen when she tried to call someone.

"I can turn it on for you! Look!" She pressed the power button, and was immediately comforted by the familiar beep that, in ordinary times, told Katie the phone was at her disposal, ready to work for her. At the sound of the beep, Starr gasped, and William gawked silently at the device.

Katie held the phone triumphantly for her audience to see the screen. It said "no signal." Katie punched the numbers that only hours ago would have summoned the familiar voice of her mother or father or Sophia. She was desperate for the phone to make a connection. But it

168

was not to be. The numbers appeared on the screen, and the phone beeped obediently when Katie punched the "send" button. The phone beeped several times as it searched for a signal. Nothing. She tried to retrieve her e-mail. "Mailbox empty."

She demonstrated how she could change the way the phone sounded when there was an incoming call. The phone beeped *The William Tell Overture.* William and Starr tapped their fingers lightly on the table in time with the beeps. Katie switched the phone to another musical pattern, then another, then another. Her friends were stunned by the musical notes coming out of the tiny instrument.

"Thou say'st everyone has one of these devices?" William asked. "Wherefore would'st everyone need such a thing?"

"Well..." Katie hesitated, and wondered to herself why all her friends, all her parents' friends, all her teachers—why everyone, it seemed—had one of these. She was too young even to remember a time when everyone didn't have a cell phone. "People like to keep in touch with each other. When I'm out with my friends, I like to call my parents to let them know where I am. Sometimes I call other friends to see what they're doing. When my friends and I are going to the movies, we call to find out what time the movie starts...it keeps us in touch with everyone."

"Ah," William said, wondering what a movie was, but intrigued by the device that seemed so important to everyone in Katie's life. "Thy friends require such a device in order to speak with people who are not there, because the people who are there are not interesting?"

"No, that's not it...at least that's not what it's supposed to do." Katie was trying to sort out the times when her cell phone was a critical link. "When my father's train is late coming into the city, he calls to let us know...and then...sometimes the cell phone helps people in emergencies, like when their car runs off the road, or when they need a doctor..."

"A car runs off the road?" William asked.

"It's...it's like a carriage, except without the horse!" Katie said, excitedly. "In the 1900s a man named Henry Ford invented a carriage that would take people places, and they wouldn't even need horses to pull the carriages."

"Ah," he replied.

"Aha," Starr said. Now they were trying to be polite. They didn't really understand, but then again, they wanted to see what other wonders were still inside Katie's magic sack. They had no idea what a train was, or a car was, but William figured they had something to do with transportation.

"See this?" Katie said. She was holding up the half-empty bottle of water. She realized that plastic was another concept that would be hard to explain. But she decided that, in this case, a demonstration would actually make the difference between plastic and glass abundantly clear. She shook the bottle, so Starr and William could see that it had water in it. Then she tossed it in the air and let it fall to the wood floor. Starr and William gasped in unison and leapt backward to avoid getting cut by flying shards of glass. Katie laughed.

"It's called plastic. It doesn't break. See?"

Starr picked up the bottle, shook it and then threw it on the floor. She retrieved it and examined it more closely.

"What is this liquid?"

"It's water."

"In a bottle?" William asked. "Where does it come from?" He had the bottle now, and was looking at the label. "From a pure spring deep in the woods? Thou hast a spring deep in the woods from whence thou fetch thy water?"

"I don't fill the bottles. We buy them at the store. There are hundreds of companies that sell bottles of water like this."

"So thy water is poison, too?" Starr asked.

"No! No! We have good water. The city purifies it and it comes into our houses through pipes. But people like to buy water in bottles, because..." She thought for a minute. The New York City water was certainly pure. It tasted good. She wondered for a minute why she insisted that Sophia buy this bottled water by the crate. She never left home without a bottle—and almost always came home with some left in the bottle.

"Because...?" William asked.

"I guess just because you can buy it. Everyone does it." She was still trying to think of why her bottle of water was so important to her.

Katie wondered if the others were as exhausted by this conversation as she was. It was hard work to explain every little thing. She noticed that Starr and William were looking at some of the other items on the table, and realized that, as hard as she was working to explain things that she never even questioned in her daily life, they were working even harder trying to fit these things into the world they occupied.

"Look, here are some breath mints," Katie said. "After I eat my lunch at school, I pop one of these in my mouth to freshen my breath because I can't brush my teeth at school." Starr took the small container of breath mints, and shook it.

"Plas-tick?" she asked. She threw the container on the floor and laughed when it didn't break. William took the container and examined the label.

"What does this mean?" he asked, somewhat annoyed by the words that made no sense to him. "I-see fresh. Min-tee?" He was laboring over every syllable of the strange words, trying to figure out what they meant.

"Icy," Katie said. "And minty. It's the way they tried to describe what the mints taste like." She showed him how to open the container, then tapped a couple of mints into his hand. She gave Starr a couple, too, and then took a couple for herself. She put the mints in her mouth. "You just let them melt on your tongue."

Her two friends put the mints on their tongues, all the time watching her for any sign that this was some sort of trick. Within seconds their eyes began to water, and they started gasping.

"Peppermint?" They said, in unison. They all laughed.

"Yes – it's peppermint, but they come in spearmint, bubblegum, and orange flavors, too," Katie said.

"If you liked the breath mints, you're going to love this," Katie said pulling a small, pink and red package out of the bag. "This is bubblegum," she announced.

"Ba-bull-gum?" Starr asked.

"Bubblegum," Katie said. "You put it in your mouth and you chew it and it gets stretchy, so you can actually blow bubbles with it. And," Katie added, "it tastes cool! Here, try a piece." *This is so much easier than explaining the cell phone,* Katie thought to herself. *And it's kind of fun, too.* She unwrapped a piece of the gum and stuck it in her mouth. She chewed for a few minutes and then drew her lips together and blew the biggest, pinkest, bubble.

William and Starr laughed in amazement when Katie blew the bubble. Starr unwrapped her piece of bubblegum almost reverently. She placed it on her tongue and started chewing. And chewing. And chewing. She was such a sight, that Katie started giggling, and then, when she tried to blow a bubble and instead, blew a wad of gum across the floor,

Katie thought she'd never be able to stop laughing. Soon the two of them were roaring with laughter, tears running down their faces.

"Will, thou must try this!" Starr said through her tears.

He was busy trying to identify the strange flavor of the gum, and he found it unnerving that the gum never got to a point that he could swallow it, despite his nearly frantic chewing.

"Wherefore dost thou chew this stuff?" he asked Katie. "Is it medicinal?"

"It's just fun," Katie said. "Everyone chews it…well, almost everyone. Some people think it's rude. And we're not allowed to chew it in school."

"Everyone has this! Everyone chews this! Everyone eats this! Everyone drinks this! Tell me, child, does anyone thou know'st do anything that he or she himself—and nobody else—does?" He was half-teasing Katie and half-serious.

He was thinking about what people must look like in Katie's world. They were busy talking into those strange cells, chewing on this rubbery stuff, drinking water from bottles that were not really bottles and dissolving tiny pieces of mint on their tongues. And in their spare time they made bubbles come out of their mouths.

But they know me, and they produce my plays! He thought to himself. *Is this child a sorceress? How did she come to this place? Wherefore?*

"Katie," he said. "What kind of a name is that?"

"Well, my real name is Ekaterina, but everyone calls me Katie. It's a nickname."

"Well, Katie is a simply dreadful name for such a charming lass. I won't have it. Thy name is Ekaterina. What is that? Katherine? Why would'st thou wish for another name?" He asked, raising his eyebrow to make his point.

"Of course…sir," Katie said. Giving in to William's demand certainly seemed harmless and Katie wanted to fit in with the times as best she could. The last thing she needed was to be viewed as an oddity. *Goodness knows! Maybe people who are different are burned at the stake or something*, she thought to herself, and shuddered. Tuffy barked as if to remind everyone that they were not paying attention to him and he wanted that situation remedied immediately.

"Quit that infernal yelping, dog!" Shakespeare roared. "For pity's sake, thou will give me a headache." He was confused, and not accustomed to being so confused by anyone, let alone a child. He was desperate to find more answers.

"Will, the dog is upset. He's as confounded as we are," Starr said.

Katie looked at them both, and tried to imagine what her parents would be like in this situation. She thought about them again. She couldn't squelch the thought that maybe they were spinning somewhere else in space, lost in someone else's world and time, and worrying about her, wondering how they would ever get home again. Maybe some catastrophic event had spilled everyone in her world into other worlds. Maybe there was no way to get home.

"Tuffy, sssh! It's okay boy. We're okay." She picked him up and held him close, so close that she could feel his heart beating against her chest. She took comfort from his familiar doggy aroma, the leathery scent of his collar, the soft fur of his coat against her cheek. She kissed him behind his ear and he looked up at her face, trying to find some clue about what was happening to them.

"Will, I told Katie ...Katherine...that thou art one of the smartest people in the land, and she has a story for thee that...well...let her tell it..." Starr was standing between Katie and William. It was clear that she wanted the conversation to head in a different direction. His tone softened immediately.

"Well, now...let's have thy story, wee lass," he said as he looked at Tuffy suspiciously. "And as for thee, my furry friend, thou had best stop yelping, lest thee find thyself on someone's plate for dinner!" He winked at Starr and gently scratched Tuffy behind his ear.

"I know Mr. Shakespeare's work because he's...you're...famous the world over," Katie began, not sure where she would finish this story.

"You see, where I come from, the year is 2002. You've...you...well, you've been dead for a long time—hundreds of years I think. I was born in Romania in 1990, and I have no idea how I got here or why I'm here. I just know I went to sleep in New York City in 2002 and now I'm here, in...in your century...what year *is* this?" Katie looked at them.

They looked back at her, their faces betraying shock, awe, confusion and dwindling skepticism.

"Whither is New York City?" William asked.

"It's in America," Katie said. "America came about after the colonies revolted against the King. They fought the British for independence. People came to America from all over the world, and we won our independence from the British and set up our own country in 1776," Katie recited proudly.

Suddenly United States history was no longer something that she read about in a book. It was now *her* history, *her* country, *her* revolution. She was searching her memory for more details, when she saw that her friends were looking skeptical. "Oh, I'm sorry, you lost the Revolutionary War," she added sheepishly. "I didn't mean to be boastful at your lack of success," she said.

"My dear, whatever art thou prating on about? Lose a war? Not possible! It's as impossible as Ireland rising up against the English!" William exclaimed. "Now really, from whence have thou come? And, prithee, explain thy tire."

Katie felt as if she was losing their confidence. She could understand their skepticism, because even she couldn't believe her situation. She struggled to find another way to bring them into her century. *If I haven't convinced them now, I don't know what else to tell them,* she thought to herself. Then she remembered Tuffy's rabies vaccination and license.

"Tuffy! Come!"

Are we going home? Boy, do I miss Sophia, and Katie's bed, and Corky, and Mom and Dad! Wow! I wonder what treat Sophia will fix for me first...I bet she missed me, too! Home! I can't wait! Tuffy leapt into Katie's arms, expecting to be transported instantly to Manhattan, where he understood life and all its smells.

As he joyously licked Katie's face, he realized that they hadn't left Starr's tavern. William was still sitting at the table, looking confused. *I'm really starting to hate that guy,* he thought. *At least Starr gives me treats. All he does is criticize...*

As Tuffy looked over Katie's shoulder at William, Katie tugged on his collar and slid it around so Starr and William could see his tags.

"New York City," William read. "Exp. Six, two, zero, zero three? What does this mean? How didst thou make this?" William tried to bend the tag. "What is this made from?"

"I think it's aluminum," Katie said. "He gets a new license every year."

"This doesn't mean anything," William said. Starr scratched Tuffy's ear gently.

"I can't read," she confessed solemnly to Katie. "Sorry, me poppet."

Katie knew there had to be a way to persuade them. She wondered if maybe they were afraid of getting too close to her situation. *Maybe they're afraid this could happen to them. Maybe they think time travel is contagious*, Katie thought.

"Romania, United States, New York," William cried. "This is just so incredible and unbelievable. I think of myself as a learned man, and yet, I have absolutely no idea what thou art talking about, Katherine. Thou may'st as well be from the moon," William said.

"Well…I'm not from the moon," Katie said. She thought for a minute, and decided to go for it. "Although in my world, we have people who have traveled to the moon. They're called astronauts, and Americans were the first ones to land on the moon over thirty years ago."

"Now, Katherine, thy tale is fantastic enough. Thou must not lead us astray with falsehoods." William was speaking so softly that Katie could barely hear him. He had picked up a quarter that had fallen out of her wallet, and was examining its engraving. The date on the coin was shocking enough. But the tableau featuring some sort of winged contraption flying above a man was almost too much.

"What is a North Carolina? What does this mean? First Flight?"

"North Carolina is a state—one of the United States. It's where Kitty Hawk is…" Katie remembered her history class about the Wright Brothers and their plane. "Kitty Hawk is the place where the Wright Brothers first flew their plane!"

Now Katie was searching through her backpack and wallet for more coins. "Look at this one!" she cried excitedly. "It's from Virginia. See the date on the settlement at Jamestown? It was in 1607! And look at this!" She was breathless as she handed William a quarter from Ohio. He turned it over and saw another of those winged contraptions and a creature that looked like a human being, but had no face. Where this creature's face should be there was nothing but a round blank space.

"What sort of creature is this?"

"It's an astronaut! It's one of the people who fly into outer space.

They wear suits that protect them from the…" Katie suddenly wasn't sure what the suits protected astronauts from. "The cold…and stuff…in space."

Starr was holding several of the coins, turning them over and over. She looked at William, hoping he would be able to explain away Katie's story. She hoped he would find a way to persuade Katie herself that she had only dreamed these strange stories about that other country. The whole thing confused and frightened her. Katie, meanwhile, was pulling one more thing out of her backpack.

"Here, here's the most recent copy of my favorite magazine, *XC*! You can see from the date that I'm telling you the truth."

William took the magazine from Katie and stared as if he were looking through a window that opened to a world even the most brilliant of men could not have imagined. The colors. The images. The type, with each letter so perfectly formed.

Some type was white on a black background. Some was red on a white background. Some was yellow on green or violet or red. There were images that seemed to replicate actual people, not drawings of people. He could hardly tear his eyes from the colorful pages. He carefully and methodically turned the pages. No words came from his lips. Katie and Starr sat silently and watched him.

He finally held the magazine up to Starr. He had opened it to one of the ads featuring Mrs. Morgan's jewelry designs. Starr touched the page lightly, as if she could actually feel the fabrics of the clothes, or the sharp edges of the jewelry. Then she looked at her fingers and pressed her hands together, fingertip-to-fingertip. She touched the page again.

"Oooh! Such grand jewels! Such colors! How didst thou make this?"

"I didn't make it. It's a magazine that gets printed and sold every month. There are hundreds of different magazines printed every week in America."

William had flipped some of the pages and he began reading from one of the ads. "Sex-ee lips?" He looked at Katie. "What does this mean?"

Katie looked at the page. It was an ad for "Smooches & Cream," the lip gloss that had seemed so important to her and her friends. Now it just looked silly.

"It's…it means…" she smiled and shrugged her shoulders. "I don't think I can really explain it. It's something we put on our lips to make them shiny. Silly, huh?"

Katie called the images on the pages photographs. For Starr, it was as if the images were frames around real live scenes.

"I don't believe mine own eyes, e'en though I haven't had a drop of ale to drink today!" William exclaimed, awestruck by what he was holding in his hands.

He ran his fingers down the pages, as if he could feel the images. *I wonder what they would do if they saw the scratch-and-sniff sample of 'Smooches & Cream' cologne,* Katie thought. *They'd have a cow!* She stifled a laugh when she realized that she was in enough trouble, without making more by laughing out loud while her friends were clearly dumfounded by *XC.*

"I'm speechless," William whispered. "I feel as if I could reach out and touch these flowers," he said pointing to an ad for a floral perfume. "Katherine, where did'st thou find this?"

"I get a new issue every month," Katie replied.

"An issue?" he asked.

"Every month a brand new magazine comes out with new pictures, new stories, and new advertisements. A new issue. That's what it's called. There are literally hundreds of magazines throughout the whole world," Katie explained.

"I wonder how they produce them so quickly," he said, half to himself.

"I'm not sure how it happens," Katie said, "but I know that there are huge printing presses and they have computers that set the type."

"Well, child, we have printing presses," William said. "But what is a computer?" William asked sounding out the word 'computer' in three separate syllables.

"It's a machine that…that…it does math—even the most complicated math—in seconds. You can play games on it, or write letters or…it's…everyone has one—almost everyone. They say that soon every single house will have one…" Katie never thought she would have to explain something so complicated to anyone. She realized that she knew very little about how computers worked, or even how her cell phone worked. Katie's voice trailed off as she realized that William and Starr had absolutely no clue as to what she was saying.

"Katherine, hast thou shown these things to anyone else since thy arrival here?" William asked, in a tone so serious that it startled Katie.

"Only to you and Starr…Oh, and the girl I saw at the farm outside of town. I found her cow wandering in the field and before I knew what had happened to me, I asked her if I could use her telephone. Why?" Katie asked.

"Katherine, I cannot explain why thou hast come into our life, but I believe a higher power does know. All these mystical things thou hast—thy clothing, with its shiny closures and thy footwear and thy sack...these powers, these..." William was stumped at what to say next. "Katherine," he began slowly, "There are some people in our world, Starr's and mine, who will not understand thy situation, not that Starr nor I possess even a shred of knowledge about it, but I know thou art not evil. I am acknown that thou art not a trickster or cutpurse. Mayhap some might see this...this...what didst thou call it?" He asked, pointing to the magazine.

"Magazine," Katie said, her face taking on a shadow of concern.

"This magazine, and this cell, and thy coins and thy tiny clock...some dullards might believe thee to be a witch," William said gravely.

"Ah, Will, would'st thou be exaggerating a bit?" Starr asked.

"No, Starr. Whereas I believe our beautiful Katherine is a sorceress, there are some dunces, thou know'st them, Starr, that will think she possesses evil powers. Perchance they'll seize her!"

"But I haven't done anything," Katie said, beginning to cry. Tuffy, bewildered by the sudden change in tone, and Katie's distress, began barking furiously. He stood before her, challenging anyone who would hurt her.

Starr put her arms around Katie and stroked her hair gently. "There, there, me lovely poppet. Thou will be fine. Will and I shall protect thee from all danger. Tuffy, dear, hush!" she said as she bent down and patted his head.

"Katherine, 'tis not safe for thee to stay here. Starr, thou must gather necessities for thyself and the child, and find some way to disguise her clothing. Surely someone can watch the tavern whilst thou art gone?" William said, taking charge of the situation.

"Will, what say'st thou? That Katie and I are taking a trip? I can't leave and I won't let thee take her," Starr said stamping her foot in anger. Starr had believed that once Katie had told William her story, he would figure out how to solve the problem. She had no intention of letting him take one of the best things that ever happened to her.

"Starr, listen to reason. Katherine showed the...the...what is it called again?" William said pointing to the cell phone.

"Phone," Katie replied miserably.

"Katherine showed the phone to the stupid Wiggins girl. In a twink, that ninny and her motley-minded mother will have the whole town riled up against Katherine, accusing her of witchcraft, and God knows what. We've got to get her out of here. We'll depart at daybreak, and stay away until things are safe here. Thou must agree this is the only plan that protects her." William said, pleading with Starr.

A tear slid down Katie's face. She sank into a chair and grabbed

Tuffy up into her lap. William looked from Starr to Katie. "My dearest Katherine. Starr and I know thou art not a witch. We know thee to be a sorceress, which is quite a magical thing to be, isn't it Starr?"

"Aye, a sorceress, if thou say'st, Will," Starr said sighing. "I guess I can get Maud to watch the tavern for me while I indulge thee, though God knows I'm not as worried about the Wiggins dolt as thee. Katie, gather up thy things, and put them in thy sack. I must find something for thee to wear that will not set thee apart from other children. Will, where will we go? Where will we stay?" Starr asked.

"We shall go to London, me lovelies. It will be easy for Katherine to get lost in the sea of people in London. Thou will stay in the small apartment behind the theatre. We shall be with actors and playwrights and all manner of people—people who will respect a sorceress!" William exclaimed triumphantly, and he swept Starr off her feet and danced her around the room.

Tuffy and I are going to London! Mr. Shakespeare and Starr are taking us, to protect us from people who think I'm a witch. He thinks my cell phone and all the things in my backpack are magic! One minute I'm ter-rified. The next minute I'm just scared. I can't stop wondering what's happening to Mom and Dad and Sophia. Are they lost, too? Will we ever find each other again? Mom promised me that we'll always be together, that we were destined to be together. But how will we find our way back to each other? What will happen to Tuffy and me if people think I'm a witch? Maybe in London there will be someone who will have the answers for us. Until then, Tuffy and I have to be brave and strong...

Chapter 28

"Here, pretty maid, buy a flower?"

Katie turned to her left to see a poor, toothless old woman with a bunch of bedraggled flowers clutched in gnarled fingers. *She looks like a character from 'Beetlejuice,'* Katie thought as she looked at Starr, won-dering how to respond. Starr grabbed Katie by the elbow and maneu-vered her out of the old woman's reach.

Katie didn't know where to look first. As they approached the border of Shoreditch, just outside of the city limits of London, Katie was struck by a noisy, smelly, crowded mass of humanity. Although it was not as populated as New York City, it looked like a cross between a set for "Survivor" and "Oliver Twist." There were few real cobbled roads, and piles of garbage were randomly tossed out of second story windows. Primitive buildings dotted the landscape; people were dressed in a wild range of fashions, from glamorous gowns to dowdy, raggedy, shapeless sacks.

The trio picked their way along the uneven, wet, smelly, littered streets. Katie felt like she was on a movie set. She half expected to see the Three Musketeers gallop through the streets with capes swirling in their noisy wake.

Tuffy was so overcome with the variety of scents—from unwashed bodies to raw and rancid garbage—that he didn't know where to start sniffing. When William, Starr, Katie and Tuffy first approached the city limits, they dropped off the carriage Will had rented as transportation from the tavern. He said they could easily walk the rest of the way to the theatre; and besides, he wanted to give Katie a sampling of the real London.

Starr rarely came this far south towards London. In fact, including this visit, she had only come to London twice, so the experience was nearly as overwhelming for her as it was for Katie and Tuffy.

"What'll thee take for thy cur?" Katie was startled by a man who suddenly materialized before her, cutting her off from her companions. He looked pathetic, and smelled terrible. His clothes were filthy, and he was wearing gloves with no fingers in them. His fingernails were long and ragged and crusted with dirt. His grin reminded Katie of a jack-o'-lantern. She wasn't exactly frightened by him, but William had instantly scooped Tuffy into his arms, and waved the man away from them.

It suddenly dawned on her that some of the citizens of London enjoyed eating dogs. She shuddered at the thought of her beloved Tuffy as someone's Sunday dinner.

William had acted so swiftly in rescuing Tuffy and getting between her and the stranger that Katie hardly had time to be afraid. She smiled up at William, who carried Tuffy protectively in his arms.

"Thou must be alert for lifters," he said to her. He tried to make his voice sound stern, but she could see the genuine affection in his eyes. "The streets of the city are awash with the facinorous and the sorriest of beggars. They're eager to pounce upon the innocent and gullible."

Starr put her arm around Katie, enclosing her in the deep blue shawl that nearly covered Starr from her head to her knees. The shawl had the smoky aroma of the tavern, and it comforted Katie. Before they left the tavern, Starr had dressed Katie in clothes more appropriate for the times. The dress didn't really fit, but Starr hitched it up with a cord and at least Katie wasn't tripping over it.

The fabric was a deep red color, and, like everything Katie had seen since her arrival, it had stains and holes and other evidence of extensive wear and tear. Katie's blue jeans and shirt were rolled up and hidden in her backpack, along with her cell phone, watch and other evidence that she had come from another century. The backpack was secured inside a large tapestry case, which William carried.

"Thy horologue," William had said, pointing at Katie's watch, "how didst thou capture time in such a tiny instrument? To some it would appear to be the work of fiends or witches...or..."

"But everyone has one!" Katie had protested, feebly. "And...and...the girl at the farm saw it...asked me about it..."

"And another good reason for us to be away from this place, until we understand more better the predicament of this wondered child!" he had said.

Katie wanted to believe that this trip would result in some answers for her. She hoped to discover a clue that would lead her home. But, now that she was in London, amid all the squalor and the wildness of the streets, she felt frightened and lost. She knew that she had to trust these two people, but it was a leap that she was afraid to make.

When her parents adopted her from a Romanian orphanage, she didn't have any understanding or awareness of the danger of her situation. She was incapable of reasoning through the process. But now it was different. She had to find it within herself to trust two strangers from another century, in a situation that had neither logic nor any relationship to reality.

She was lost in time. She had almost no guideposts. Her parents told her once that they understood how hard it was to make a leap into the unknown. They had each other, though, and a love that faced danger and grief and the unknown with courage and the realization that—even if they failed—they could never be defeated. She had Tuffy, and a growing sense of responsibility to protect him from the fear that gripped her.

"Sometimes," her mother had said, "you don't get to pick the time. Sometimes, the time picks you." *Time certainly picked me,* she thought to herself. *But for what? What am I supposed to be doing here?*

She was so thoroughly lost in her thoughts that she hardly noticed how far they had walked.

"Ladies, we are here," William said, startling Katie. True to his word, the walk to the theatre took only about 15 minutes and soon he gestured for them to enter the building where his colleagues, Lord Chamberlain's Men, performed.

"My fellow Thespians, I have returned to the fold," he shouted dramatically as they entered the back of the theatre. A chorus of what sounded to Katie like "Huzzah" echoed back from a group of men lounging around the stage. "And," William continued, "I have brought with me two very dear friends who are visiting from the countryside."

With a flourish that only he could achieve so effortlessly, William extended his arms and, with one hand grasped Katie's hand and with the other, Starr's hand. "By your leave, dear gentlemen, may I present Starr and Katherine," he shouted, twirling each as he introduced her.

Feeling neglected, Tuffy barked. "And, lest I forget, Katherine's constant and faithful companion, Sir Tuffy," William added, bowing to the barking dog. Amid cries of "Well met!" and "Good Morrow," one loud voice boomed over all the others.

"William, thou art tardy! Prithee, get thee backstage and into thy costume. The curtain rises in one hour. I beg thee not to drumble, Will!" The booming voice was attached to a rather portly body which emerged from behind a curtain.

"Ah, Master Burbage, thou hast noted that one of thy chicks was missing!" William exclaimed, smiling as he said it.

"Chicks indeed! We have a performance. Discipline, man, discipline," Burbage said, shaking his head in irritation.

"James – allow me to introduce my two guests. They need a place to stay for a few days and I assured them that the apartment behind the Theatre would be theirs. Since they are two such lovely ladies, and milady's little dog, I knew thou would'st take no issue with my invitation," William said gesturing to Starr and Katie.

Burbage approached Katie, Tuffy and Starr. As he came closer, Starr curtsied low and Katie imitated her, trying her best not to fall flat on her face. For once, Tuffy sat quietly. Perhaps he had been sobered by the fact that in London, dogs were delicacies. Burbage looked Starr and Katie up and down, as if he expected them to faint upon close inspection. Then he growled and mumbled something Katie couldn't make out.

Katie glanced over at Starr. Starr hadn't heard what he said, either, so she just shrugged her shoulders and gazed at William.

"Burbage, do not be a pumpion! Hark now, my good man, thou hast a simple decision. They stay, or I go." William lowered his voice, nearly to a whisper. "Prithee, do not be unrespective of these two, as they are in need of shelter." Seeing that Burbage was softening, and about to agree to let them stay, William resumed his more confident tone. "Now do be a good manager, and tell Cuthbert to get him to the market and fetch some bread and cheese for our guests." He thumped Burbage on the shoulder, as if they were the best of friends, then swept right past him. "Katherine, Starr, Master Tuffy, this way please." William led them to a small apartment behind the Theatre.

"William, what is this theatre's name?" Starr asked.

"Milady, this theatre is called, quite simply, the 'Theatre.' Not to be confused with that of our arch rival in Southwark, 'The Rose,' which is filled with candle-wasters and hacks and more rightly might be called 'The Thorn.'"

When the trio reached the apartment, William leaned over the rather ornate door handle and lock and opened the door, ushering them in. *This is really pretty*, Katie thought, admiring the antique tables and chairs—then reminding herself that the furniture didn't become antiques until many years later. There was a small parlor, with what Katie thought were the kitchen table and chairs, and a narrow hallway leading back to one large bedroom. In the center of that room sat a lumpy, rather disheveled-looking bed.

"Why, Will, 'tis perfect!" Starr said. "Isn't it Katie?" she asked turning towards Katie. Without waiting for Katie to reply, Starr said, "We shall be quite comfortable here, for the nonce, and quite safe, will we not, Katie?"

Katie was trying to keep up with all the things she was seeing and hearing. She couldn't get over how people talked, and how crowded and noisy everything was in the city. Questions were tumbling around in her brain, and she was desperate to start sorting them out.

"Mr. Shakespeare," Katie began hesitantly, "where are the actresses? The women in the play?"

Starr stopped what she was doing, and waited for William's response. She always found Katie's questions interesting, but her friend's reactions to this child were incredibly amusing.

"*Act-resses*?" William said it as if he had just eaten something that tasted foul. "Female actors? Thou would'st have females on the stage? What utter nonsense! Women are not allowed on the stage. Whatever art thou thinking?" William replied.

"No actresses?" Katie repeated. "Well then, who plays the girl parts?"

"Why, the young men," William said.

"Boys play girl parts?" Katie said giggling. Katie had visions of Tyler playing Juliet, and Rodney playing Buffy the Vampire Slayer.

"My mother is an actress," Katie began timidly. "She is the star of a show that is on television five days a week. A lot of times in the summer she performs in plays at the theatre near our summer house in Hyde Park. A couple of years ago she was in one of your plays, I think it was called 'The Comedy Errors,' or something like that."

William and Starr were looking at Katie with what she had begun to call *the look*. It was the way they looked when she had revealed things about her life in New York—things that were commonplace to Katie but astonishing to her new friends.

"You're doing it again, the look," she said, trying to understand what had caused their astonishment this time.

"Thy mother, she is a star on a telly-vizon?" Starr asked. She was struggling with the word, and the concept. "She is an actress? Prithee, are there men who appear with her in her dramas?"

"Comedy of Errors?" William asked. "How didst thou learn of this play? Where is this park of which thou speak so often?" William was overwhelmed once again by an odd sense that this child knew him better than he knew himself. He felt as if he were the one who had been transported to another time. He believed that Katie could teach him more than the most gifted professors of the world's greatest universities.

His own children were dear to him, of course, and the son he lost was still a memory so painful that the mere mention of the child's name made him weep uncontrollably. But he didn't view Katie as a child in the same way he viewed his children—or any children he had ever seen.

"It's called Hyde Park. It's a place near New York City. My parents have a small house there, where we go in the summer. And...and your play...I went to see it but I was too young to understand it. But my mother played someone called Adia...Adria..."

"Adriana. Her name is Adriana." William whispered.

"Yes! That's it. There were twins and boats and people getting confused…"

William stood there, transfixed. He wanted to learn more, to hide away with Katie and Starr for however long it took for Katie to teach him everything she knew—about him and about the world. The play had hardly been performed at all. It was one of his favorites, though, giving him the opportunity to dazzle audiences with language and his comic genius. *How does she know these things? What else can she teach me?*

"Will, what time is thy performance?" Starr asked.

"Ah, yes. My performance. I must depart for now and ready myself for today's performance. Thou and Katherine must come. I shall be honored to have thee in the audience." William said.

"Oh, can we Starr?" Katie cried.

"I do not see why not. T'will be a marvelous adventure. Too much time has passed since I've been to the theatre."

"Then, I shall look for thee in the audience, and see thee afterward. For now, I must be on my way, lest Burbage, that droning moldwarp, assail us once again with his pestering." With an exaggerated wave of his arms and a bow, he left them.

"What is a moldwarp?" Katie asked.

"My dear, it is like a geck…a fool…Will has quite an arsenal of arrows with which he punctures buffoons."

"Is he sad, though?" Katie asked. "He seems like there's something making him sad."

"There has been great sorrow in his life, Katie, and he holds his sadness within himself like a miser holds his money. But he covers o'er his sorrow with his clever barbs and jibes."

"You have had sadness, too, haven't you, Starr?"

"My love, it's impossible to travel through thy days on earth without meeting the grim face of sorrow. Mine own dear husband, Richard, died, leaving me nothing but the Tavern and a pile of debts. It is love that giveth us the greatest of joy and the deepest of sorrow. And it is that selfsame love that we cannot deny when it presents itself to us. It takes the greatest of courage to welcome love, and to do its bidding."

The talk of love and loss reminded Katie again that she had crossed some mysterious frontier. Two people who had their own sorrows and grief had stepped forward to help and protect her, without thinking about their own safety. She thought about Sophia, who had lost her husband. And her parents, who had discovered an empty space in their own lives—a space that became a haven for Katie and Sophia. A knock at the door startled her and brought her back to the moment. She and Starr looked at each other, then looked at the door, as Tuffy ran, barking toward it.

"Miladies, I've brought thee victuals."

It was Cuthbert, from the Theatre. Starr and Katie brushed some crumbs off the table and then spread a cloth under the basket Cuthbert brought them. As they enjoyed the chewy bread and the cheese, they talked about the play they would soon be seeing.

"Starr, what will I do with Tuffy while we're watching the play?" Katie asked. She was worried about leaving Tuffy alone in the apartment because she hadn't been apart from him since they got lost in time together, and she thought Tuffy would be afraid without her there to comfort him.

"Why, we'll bring him with us, love," Starr answered.

"Animals are allowed in theatres?" Katie asked.

"Of course, and why would they not be welcome?" Starr said.

"It's just that dogs aren't allowed in stores or theatres or movies, or in most public places where I come from," Katie replied. "People think they're pests and health hazards, I guess" she added.

"What motley-minded dolt would be gast of a sweet little tyke like Tuffy? He is no more dangerous than I am," she said bending down and picking Tuffy up. She rubbed her nose against Tuffy's nose.

Tuffy, of course, agreed with her and all of a sudden realized that he had, possibly, been born in the wrong century. *This is how life should be! Dogs should be allowed the same entertainments and privileges as people. Of course this is how life should be,* Tuffy thought to himself as he happily licked Starr's face.

Starr broke pieces of bread off the loaf and fed them to Tuffy. "Thou must not have the cheese, for it could sicken thee," she said to him, apologetically. "But thou art a lucky little one, for I have brought with us some cakes from the Tavern." She pulled a small meat tart from the basket she packed, and broke it into several pieces for him.

I was hoping she'd bring these, Tuffy thought to himself. *They are as good as those little pies Sophia makes. They must know each other!*

About an hour later, Starr, Katie and Tuffy made their way

through the crowded street to the front of the Theatre. Mr. Burbage was taking money from the unruly crowd, and he ceremoniously waved Katie, Starr, and Tuffy into the Theatre.

Katie could not stop staring at the people. While not downright dirty, most of them had smudges on their faces and their clothes looked and smelled as if they had slept in them for the past week. Some of them carried baskets of food and jugs of some smelly drink. Katie noticed a particularly shabby-looking group positioned in front of the stage, but there were no chairs for them.

"Are they just going to stand there, Starr?" Katie asked, pointing toward them shyly.

"Oh, whil'st I don't have a lot of knowledge of such things, dearie, Will has told me about these folks," Starr said. "He calls them groundlings, because they can't afford a seat during the show. They stand about the stage the entire time. William hast said that, when he writes his plays, he tries to show the life of these poor folks, bereft of position and rank. Indeed, 'tis a story not seen by many. These groundlings thus can see themselves upon the very stage where those of higher birth tread so proudly. He says it keeps the groundlings happy and coming back for more plays," Starr explained.

Starr and Katie took seats. Katie held Tuffy on her lap, and looked around her at the crush of people waiting anxiously for the play to begin. *Mom and Sophia should see these clothes, and the hairstyles,* Katie thought.

Although Katie listened intently to some of the conversations going on around her, it was very hard to make out what they were saying. They were talking in English. But it wasn't the English of 2002, or of America. She was beginning to understand what William had said to her. "Thou speak English, but it is not English."

Katie was somewhat intimidated by the throngs gathering around her. She leaned toward Starr, and looked up at her. Starr cocked her head slightly.

"Art thou frightened, little poppet?" she whispered.

"It's just so crowded and noisy."

Starr put her arm around Katie protectively, and kissed her lightly on her head.

"Thou art safe," she whispered.

Katie continued her surveillance of the crowd, secure in Starr's embrace. She tried to imagine herself—or her mother or Sophia—in some of the gowns she saw in the crowd—many of them low-cut at the neck but billowy in the sleeves.

On their heads, many of the women wore colorful hats with streamers. The men wore trousers that only reached to their knees. From their knees to their shoes it looked like they were wearing tights, although Katie was sure that's not what they were called. Their shoes were crudely made of wood or what looked to be leather, although it wasn't the shiny leather that Katie saw in the sophisticated and oh-so-modern displays at Becks Department Store.

The Theatre was open on several sides, and there seemed to be a breeze, but as the seats filled, the air got heavy and stagnant and the smell was overpowering.

Poor Tuffy! The people-smells overwhelmed even him—and his nose was designed for sniffing! Instead of investigating the smells, Tuffy buried his head under Katie's armpit to try and escape the malodorous fumes. *No wonder deodorant was so popular when it was invented,* Katie thought to herself. *What a stinky world it must have been before that!*

"Is this chair free?" Katie turned to her right, startled by the sound of a voice so close to her. She had been so engrossed in people-watching (and odor-avoiding) that she hadn't noticed a young man approach the row in which she and Starr sat.

"By your leave, milady," the voice continued, "the chair? Is't free?"

"Um…ah…yes, yes it's free." Katie was embarrassed at having been caught staring at the other patrons. "I'm sorry," she continued, "but my mind was somewhere else."

"Art thou from the city? Thy words, they are strange. Might thou have come to this place from Wales, or another distant place?"

"Wales?"

"Wales, yes," the young man said. "Though I've never in my life met up with anyone from Wales, I know that the language there is quite different. Me mum told me so."

"No, I'm not from Wales," Katie replied, and hesitated briefly. "I'm from New York."

"New York," the young man repeated. "Prithee, where is that? Would'st thou be speaking of the north or the south of London?"

Katie stammered. How was she to explain herself to this boy? She really didn't want to get too involved in blurting her story out to just anyone. Especially since William had said she was a sorceress, and brought her to London so she could blend in with the crowds.

Katie wasn't sure whether being a sorceress in the year 1596 in England was a good thing or a bad thing, but she didn't intend to push the issue now.

"To the west actually," Katie said. *Very far west*, she thought. *So far west that you probably wouldn't believe me if I told you.*

Katie looked away from the boy, who seemed to want to talk to her. *Why am I ignoring him? He doesn't look dangerous or mean.* Katie hugged Tuffy and kissed his ear. It was something she had done a thousand times since the first day Tuffy had come into her life.

But the gesture—so small and quiet—had taken on much greater significance since the two of them got lost in time. It comforted them, gave them each a sliver of normalcy to cling to and made the bond between them even stronger than either of them thought possible.

Katie thought about the people surrounding her in this theatre, and wondered why she felt threatened by them. Their clothes were shabby, and it was clear that bathing every day was not a high priority. The boy sitting next to her had an earnest and kind face. *Why am I acting like this? He doesn't know that I'm lost and afraid. He's living his life, and it's not his fault that I can't live mine right now. The people here don't have nice clothes, for that matter, neither do I.*

Katie looked at the skirt of the dress she was wearing. It was rough cloth, with holes here and there and a lot of dirt around the bottom. *Maybe I don't smell that great, either. I'm the outsider here. Maybe they think I'm strange. Maybe they'd be afraid of me if they knew what happened to me.*

The performance began suddenly, with little fanfare. Mercifully, it gave Katie a good reason to focus on something other than the boy next to her, and to pretend she was just another person waiting to be entertained by Lord Chamberlain's Men.

Since lighting hadn't been invented yet, plays and other performances took place during the daytime. The arrival of the actors, in costume, was the audience's signal to quiet down. A character dressed all in black appeared on the stage and began speaking softly.

Katie had a hard time following exactly what he was talking

about because it sounded like Old English to her. The whole theatrical operation was so different than backstage at "Love's Labours" and even at the Hudson Valley Players that it didn't matter to Katie that she really couldn't understand what they were talking about.

She couldn't wait for the "actresses" to appear. Ever since William had told Katie that there were no actresses, and that boys and men played the parts of girls and women, Katie had wondered how convincing it could possibly be to the audience.

They don't look at all like girls, Katie thought. *They look like men trying to look like women, but with the worst possible makeup, hair, and baggy clothes.* Katie looked around at the audience. For the most part, they were mesmerized by the action onstage. *I wonder what they'd think if they ever saw a play with actresses.*

She looked over at the groundlings, who presented another point of view. Some of them were leaning against each other, snoring. Katie guessed that they slept during the more complicated scenes, and didn't quite get into the play until the parts that Starr told her the playwrights wrote specifically for less literate Londoners.

It was an extraordinary experience for Katie. Although she understood little of the play (especially the parts that made the audience roar with laughter), it seemed to end quickly. Starr had understood much more than Katie and had thoroughly enjoyed herself.

When William had appeared on stage as a young suitor, Starr had nudged Katie. "Isn't he wonderful," Starr had whispered.

"What is he talking about?"

"I'll explain it to thee later!"

It reminded Katie of going to the movies with Lily and Corky.

I guess people in the 1500s are a lot like people in 2002, Katie thought to herself. Best of all, no one even gave Tuffy a second thought. In fact, Katie counted three or four other dogs—none as well-behaved as Tuffy—scattered throughout the audience. *I can imagine what they'd say at Lincoln Center if Tuffy arrived with Mom and Dad and me.*

The thought of it tore at Katie's heart. While the idea made her want to laugh out loud, it also made her remember how desperately she missed her family and friends.

"Milady, might I offer thee some refreshment?" the young man said to Katie, gesturing at a canteen he was holding. Katie had been so engrossed in the play that she had forgotten he was there.

"Who art thou, to speak to milady thus?" Starr admonished the boy. Tuffy perked up instantly at the sound of Starr's voice, planting himself in Katie's lap as if he were a wild animal that lived for the sole purpose of protecting this child.

"I beg thy pardon, ma'am. I didn't mean any harm."

Katie looked at the young man out of the corner of her eye. She didn't want to appear to be rude by staring, but, aside from William and Starr, he was the first person who had really spoken to her.

Suddenly William leapt off the stage, into the aisle and practically ran to the spot where Starr, Katie, Tuffy and the young stranger sat.

"Ah! Excellent!" he said. "I see thee have met my friends, Edward." His hand was resting on the young man's shoulder. "Did'st thou enjoy the play?"

"Oh sir, it was magnificent and thy acting was truly wonderful! Thy character, Proteus, was most entertaining," the young man named Edward replied reverently.

"Thou art too easy a critic, my fine lad. May I present my friends, Starr and Katherine...oh, and lest I forget, Master Tuffy, Katherine's companion."

Edward nodded shyly to Katie and Starr, and patted Tuffy on his head.

"Edward is one of the young men hoping for a part in our next enterprise," William explained. "He is very industrious and skilled in moving scenery, and even in coaxing the feeble memories of actors. In fact, young Edward is able to do most every job required of Lord Chamberlain's Men. Soon, young man, thou will be on the stage to act!"

Edward was blushing and staring at his feet. He shifted uncomfortably in his seat, his hands slipping off his lap to his sides. "Now, my good man, I pray thee, join us for supper. We can talk and thou can bring me news of thy family."

"I would love that, sir," Edward replied. He grinned and blushed again, especially when he looked at Katie.

"We're off, then. Come Katherine, Starr and little Tuffy. I'm famished and can't wait to have at a nice piece of mutton at Briarly's on the Square."

Arm in arm in arm the four of them left the Theatre, and made their way through the throngs of people down a cobbled street. Tuffy led the way, thrilled to be moving again and back on the street, where the smells of garbage, other animals and the ebb and flow of the city's daily life entertained him as much as the play had entertained his human companions.

Chapter 29

William led Starr, Katie, and Edward down a number of twisted, cobbled streets—streets so crowded that Katie finally picked Tuffy up and held him in her arms for fear of losing him. They walked quickly through the throngs of people. Not only were there people from the theatre, but there were also people on their daily errands.

Katie noticed that women carried baskets with bread and all sorts of fruits and vegetables. Some were carrying chickens or rabbits. She understood, on this day, what life was like without refrigeration or supermarkets or electricity or washing machines or clothes dryers or indoor plumbing. *It must take people forever just to get dinner ready*, she thought to herself. *No wonder people wear dirty clothes. These things would probably take days to dry!*

She looked up at Starr, whose eyes brimmed with excitement. The city, the play, the company of this brilliant playwright and a dinner she herself didn't have to cook—it seemed to be such a joyful day for her. Katie thought about what Starr had said when William was examining the contents of the magic backpack. "I can't read." *Why can't she read? Why can William read and write?*

Katie imagined the girl at the farm and her mother, and wondered if they could read or write. She thought about how Starr never seemed to sit still, except when they went to the play. She was always stoking a fire, cleaning something, washing something, cooking something or getting something ready to cook.

While meals were simmering in the giant fireplace, Starr was cleaning mugs, sweeping floors, bringing in water from the well down the block, taking garbage out, mending things or waging what seemed to Katie to be a futile war against the dust and dirt that blew into the Tavern every time the big wooden door opened.

If Starr had even a moment to sit and think about things, it was probably a very drowsy moment before she finally went to sleep at night. And she probably could only afford to think about what chores had to be done the next day.

Katie couldn't imagine what it would be like if she could not read or write. But she was starting to realize that, if she never made it back to her own century, these skills that seemed so basic to her would quickly become irrelevant. As she looked around her, it was clear to Katie that school and entertainment and lazy afternoons shopping with friends would be viewed as foolish wastes of time.

What will we do? How will Tuffy and I make it here? She hugged Tuffy close to her heart, losing herself in the familiar scent and feel of her only friend in this strange world. Sadness and intense grief crept over her. She was sad for Starr, and for the Wiggins girl and her mother. She was sad for all the people who dragged heavy baskets of vegetables and live chickens and wood to their dusty homes. She was sad for the beggars, waifs and mangy stray dogs she saw everywhere. And she grieved for the family and the life that she feared she would never have again.

Sophia had told her once about how she had wandered through Timisoara, grieving her husband's death and the horrors that confronted her country. But she had stumbled into the lives of two compassionate, generous people: Katie's parents. And Sophia had left her life and history in Romania behind, to go to America.

Maybe this is what life really is, Katie thought, as she swallowed back more tears. *Maybe we all get stopped in the middle of a regular day in our lives, and have to go someplace else. Henry was just having a fun day at the ranch when his life was changed. Did he expect to wind up in a coma? When Sophia married her husband, she was probably only thinking about how much she loved him, not about winding up in some strange city, hungry and cold and desperate to find him. Was Sophia this scared? Is this what it was like for her, when she met Mom and Dad?*

How did she manage to find a way to trust them with her life—and mine?

Katie felt as if she were in a cocoon, wrapped in the hum of Starr's and William's voices chattering in their strange language. Even Edward's shy silence engulfed her, with the weight of the things she suspected he wanted to say. She could feel him walking close to her—not close enough to touch her. She could feel him looking at her as if she were a painting instead of a person. She knew if she looked up at him he would blush and look away.

Finally, William stopped in front of a big heavy wooden door. There was a picture of meat cooking on a spit on a sign hanging over the door. Just like at Starr's tavern, the word "Tavern" appeared over the picture. No other name adorned the sign.

Katie tried to figure out how people would know one tavern from another. It was a question she didn't even ask her friends since they wouldn't understand why she was asking it. It seemed that stores, theatres, and taverns were identified by neighborhoods and most people probably didn't travel far so it didn't matter what the names were.

She was struck by the insular lives led by everyone. It seemed that this little piece of England was untouched by what was happening even a short distance away. Katie knew that at this time in history, the first settlements of colonists were taking shape in America, but the events across the ocean seemed to have no impact on people's lives in England. No one knew what was going on in the rest of the world.

I wonder what they would think about TV news, and satellites and instant pictures from around the world. Katie was imagining all the other pieces of her life that she had apparently lost when she crossed into William's world. From this dingy square in London, she wondered what people would think of Times Square in New York City, with its lights and giant television screens.

As the group entered the dark tavern, William ushered them to an empty table in the back. There were only four or five other tables, with families or groups of men and women huddled around flickering candles. Katie noticed that there were no female customers alone in the Tavern.

"Marry! Could'st mine eyes play the trick on me? 'Tis the bard himself, comes here to spread his grace upon our tavern most humble." It was more a shriek than a shout, and was followed by laughter so warm and compelling that it silenced everyone in the tavern.

The woman from whom this raucous greeting emerged was considerably smaller than Katie expected. It was clear that she knew William well, and she flirted shamelessly with him, before unleashing her considerable charms on his guests.

"Today is a wonderful rabbit stew on the menu," she said, with a smile. "For each one mayhap an ale?" The woman's accent was not the same as William's and Starr's. And her dark hair and eyes—and complexion much like Katie 's—further set her apart from the people Katie had seen in London.

Sophia! She reminds me of Sophia! Katie thought. She could feel her heart beating faster, as it dawned on her that this woman sounded and looked so much like her beloved Sophia. *Maybe I'm just imagining it, because I miss Sophia so much. Maybe I'm just making myself think that her accent is like Sophia's.*

"Katherine, wouldst thou try an ale?" William asked Katie .

"Ale?" Katie queried. "I'm not allowed to drink beer."

"Beer?" William asked.

"Never mind. You may not call it that. I'm just not sure. Could I have something else?"

"Mayhap thou would'st like some perry," Starr said. "Methinks it would suit thee."

Katie looked across the small crude table at Starr, and smiled. "Yes, please, ma'am. I'll have perry," she said to the waitress.

"Three ales, then, and a perry for thee, milady," the woman said, bowing slightly to Katie.

"Ah, Maria," William said. "In my dreams I see and taste thy sumptuous specialty, the mutton bursting with forcemeat. Prithee, say to me that thee have it on thy serving list today." William winked at Katie, who couldn't take her eyes off the woman.

"Thou hast the sugar of the tongue, dear Master William," Maria cooed, "but thy lovely parle will not smooth me this day. Alas, thy dream of mutton will not be true." She tapped his shoulder lightly, and winked at him. "Perchance the rabbit stew or cod will fill thy stomach and thy dream, and I make for thee a good and stout broth with fine veg-etives to start, yes?" Maria really was fond of him, and it showed in her smile and her eyes.

"Thou weave a trance around my heart, dear lady. The broth it shall be, along with the hare." He turned to his companions. "Starr? Katherine? Edward? Choose thy poisons!"

"I shall take the cod, please. Katie, would'st thou like some cod?" Starr patted Katie's hand gently.

"What is it?" Katie asked. After all the trips to the market with Sophia, Katie could never remember seeing even a sign for cod.

"Why it's a fish, milady," Edward replied softly. "Please try it. I shall take the stew, and if the cod does not please thee, I shall trade thee cod for rabbit," he finished gallantly.

"Why Edward, thou art a true gentleman," Starr said nodding approval at Edward's consideration for Katie.

With the orders taken, Maria disappeared into what Katie assumed was a kitchen. As soon as Maria was out of sight, Starr turned to William and asked, "Will, is Maria a stranger? She speaks in words that seem out of place."

"Maria and her husband, Petrov, come from Wallachia." He lowered his voice to a whisper. "They say they've come here from the same area as the legendary Vlad the Impaler, the man who called himself Draculya."

"Dracula? The vampire?" Katie was astounded. *I must have misunderstood. Could Dracula actually be a real creature? Were all those stories about the vampire true?*

"Vampire? Whatever art thou prating about, Katherine? Draculya was a prince of Wallachia, who killed his enemies and impaled their heads upon stakes in the woods around his castle."

"Will! Prithee, mind the young ones and their sensibilities. Thou should'st consider the dreams of evil thou will bring upon them." Starr was not angry. But she was worried about frightening Katie. She had been watching her become withdrawn and sad.

"Starr, I've actually heard about him! Dracula came from the same country I did—Romania. Except he was from another part, and, another century. There are movies and books about him...what did you call him?...Vlad the...?"

"The impaler. There's that word again. Prithee, child, what is a moo-vee?" William was looking around, wondering if people at other tables had heard Katie.

"Let's see. A movie is...well, it's...it's a play that is filmed— turned into pictures like the ones in the magazine. And the film can be shown to lots of people in different theatres all over the country. In movies, the pictures move, just like people do...I know it's hard to imagine what it's like, but if you ever saw one, you wouldn't be confused at all."

Edward was gawking at Katie now, so entranced by her that he didn't even look away when she looked right at him. He had thought she was beautiful and mysterious and exotic. He had thought she was as different from him as a deer was from a goat. He had imagined becoming her friend, and then he imagined that their friendship would grow and change over time—he thought time was one thing they had in abundance—the way the moon changed over time.

"But kids all dress up like Dracula on Halloween!"

"Katherine, art thou speaking of Hallowmas? Prithee, could it be that the people in thy century still harken to the ancient myths of the Celts?" William was perplexed, but also amused by this new revelation about life in another century.

"I…who are the Celts? We do it for fun! On Halloween, kids dress up in all sorts of costumes and go from house to house. People give out candy or treats. It's called 'trick or treat'. There are lots of different costumes, like scarecrows or witches or ghosts."

Talking about Halloween made Katie feel happy. It was as if her memories were crowded behind a closet door that had suddenly sprung open. All the contents came tumbling out. The memories quickly turned into words that mystified, enchanted and thoroughly entertained her companions.

"Last year I was the Tin Man, and Tuffy went as Toto. My friend Lily was Dorothy and Corky—she's from Ireland—was the Scarecrow. My dad was the lion. He had to go with us because we're too young to go out alone. They're characters from a movie called 'The Wizard of Oz.' It was about a tornado that picked up this little girl and her dog and they helped a Tin Man, a Scarecrow and a cowardly lion find Oz."

She suddenly realized that she was babbling, and wondered if they thought she was crazy. *How do they say crazy? What's that word they say?* She hesitated for a moment, thinking. Everyone was looking at her, waiting for her to finish.

"Do thous think I'm noddy?" she finally asked.

Starr and William burst out laughing—loud, joyous laughing—at Katie's first foray into the language of 16th Century England. Katie laughed, too, and Tuffy barked happily. Edward, though, was silent. William noticed the look on his face.

"Ah, Edward, our beautiful and bewitching Katherine, she is a sorceress, traveling a great distance in time. That she has seeming dropped out of the welkin upon this place is but one of the mysteries she brings with her. We must keep her secret among the four of us!" William whispered, leaning close to the boy.

Edward's eyes grew large. Since he had first seen Katie at the Theatre, he had been totally captivated by her beauty. Her hair, a tumbling mass of curls, framed her face and made her look as if she were wearing a halo. Her dark eyes shone and Edward thought he had never seen skin as soft and clear as Katherine's. Now it all made sense. He was drawn to her because she was a sorceress with incomprehensible powers. She seemed to have abundant knowledge and understanding of the world.

"But I am not a sorceress. I've simply gotten lost in time and my world is just different than your world."

Maria brought a plate of bread to the table, and set it down, with a sharp knife, in front of William. "We serve to our most revered guests our manchet today, along with our raveled bread, just now hot from the oven in back."

"Katherine, thou must have a piece of this manchet, one of the finest breads to be found in all of England," William said as he sliced the loaf, dividing it among the four of them. Although Edward was famished, he hesitated before biting into the bread. He was captivated by the way Katie broke her slice of bread into small pieces before eating it.

He set his piece of bread down and broke it apart, just as Katie had done. But he put several pieces in his mouth at once, his hunger suddenly overcoming his desire to mimic Katie's mannerisms.

"This is really good," Katie said. "What did you call it?"

"'Tis manchet," Starr said. "It is quite dear and beyond the purses of most. The other, called raveled bread, is what..."

She stopped suddenly, as Edward began gasping frantically for breath. His face was scarlet, and the panic in his eyes shocked Katie.

"What is't, lad?" William had grabbed Edward's shoulder and was shaking him.

"He's choking!" Starr screamed.

Everyone in the room stopped talking. All eyes were riveted to the scene at Katie's table. William was pounding Edward's back, screaming something that sounded like "come on, lad!"

I know what to do! Katie thought, then said the words out loud.

"I know what to do! Please, let me help him." As she said the words, she stood up and took a deep breath to calm herself. She walked around the table and stood behind Edward. William and Starr were momentarily stunned.

"Hello! What art thou…?"

Katie grabbed Edward around his stomach, just below his rib cage. She squeezed her hand into a fist, placed her fist under Edward's ribs and, with all the strength she had, pulled up as if she were trying to lift him out of his chair. A chunk of bread flew out of his mouth and landed in the middle of the table. Edward coughed once, then turned to look at Katie. He was breathing deep, panting breaths. There were tears in his eyes, and his face was streaky red.

"Thou...thou art a miracle! Thou hast saved my life!" His voice was raspy, but it was clear that Katie had indeed saved him.

The two of them grew silent, Katie amazed that the Heimlich Hug actually worked, and Edward overcome with emotions ranging from fear to adoration. Behind them, a steady hum of excited voices grew louder and the hum turned into words and phrases and shouts.

"By my troth, didst thou see that child?"

"Wondrous!"

"The boy was in the throes of death, yet is not scathed!"

Starr and William, momentarily stunned by what they had seen, quickly moved to quiet the room and protect Katie.

"All's well here, good friends!" William said, with a dismissive wave of his arm. The room grew silent as people returned to their own tables and resumed their own conversations. But they continued to sneak glances at Katie and murmur to one another about what they had seen. Some even recreated the scene at their own tables.

Edward, embarrassed and fearing a recurrence of his bout of choking, waited for the ale to arrive before attempting to eat more bread.

There was an uncomfortable silence at the table. The two adults were looking across the table at each other, unsure of what to say.

"Wherefore hast thou come to us? Didst thou truly drop from the welkin?" he whispered across the table to Katie. "How didst thou learn to do that?"

Katie looked around the room at the people stealing glances at her. She looked at Edward, wondering if he would be able to keep her secret.

"Trust Edward with thy life, Katherine. He is as honorable and true as Starr." William said. "He is an apprentice in our company and the son of a trusted friend. Whatever thou say'st to him he will keep within the very heart in his breast, 'till it stops beating and his soul flies toward heaven," he said, nodding encouragingly. The playwright for whom Katie had such profound admiration was overcome with the desire to learn the secret to the miracle she had just performed. He was astonished, once again, by the infinite range of her knowledge and her abilities, and by her modesty.

Is it possible she is truly unaware of her powers? What is the depth of the ocean that lies beneath her placid demeanor?

Katie faced Edward. She had noticed that Edward stared at her a lot. Oddly enough, it didn't make her feel uncomfortable at all. She thought about the way Henry had looked at her, and how her friends told her that Henry wanted to ask her to the Spring Dance. That day—it seemed ages ago—Katie was struggling with feelings she didn't understand. Now she saw it all so clearly.

Henry made her uncomfortable because he wasn't one of the cool kids she so admired. She worried that the cool kids would make fun of her if she went to the Dance with him. In a sense, she had betrayed Henry, even though he probably didn't know it. She worked so hard at being his friend, hoping that he didn't want her to be his girlfriend.

But now she was lost in time, and the landscape in which she found herself had been changed completely. There was no such thing as cool or not cool. There was a daily struggle to survive in, and to make sense of, a world about which people knew very little.

He's a lot like Henry, Katie thought. *He has that same look—like a kind, gentle soul who has been treated badly by the world. Why didn't I take the time to see Henry differently? Is this a chance for me to fix what I did wrong with Henry?*

Edward had picked Tuffy up and was stroking his back. Tuffy writhed contentedly in Edward's lap, reveling in the attention and the experience of actually going out to a restaurant to eat!

It makes me feel pretty, the way he looks at me, Katie thought. *It's the pretty I felt when I put the yellow dress on for the Spring Dance. Here I am, dressed in rags, and he's looking at me as if I were the Prom Queen.*

Katie took a deep breath and plunged into her story.

"A few days ago I woke up in a field with Tuffy. I thought I had fallen asleep in the park near where I live…" She hesitated for a minute, trying to think of a shortcut to get from Central Park to the Heimlich Hug.

"I know this is hard to believe, but I've come here from the future—from the year 2002. I don't know why I'm here, or how to get back. But here I am." Edward was silent. His eyes registered something more than surprise but less than shock. Katie reached over and patted Tuffy on the head, and smiled at him, pleased that he seemed so peaceful in Edward's lap.

"Anyway, in my world, in my school, we were required to take a course called 'First Aid.' We learned how to help someone if they stopped breathing or drowned, or if their heart stopped beating. And we learned what I just did to you. It's called 'the Heimlich Hug,' but I can't really remember why it's called that. We learned how to do it when one of the kids at school choked on a piece of candy. My favorite teacher, Mr. Murwata, saved him by doing that to him, and then he talked to the headmaster, Mr. Needham, about teaching everyone how to do it. So then some people from the Red Cross came in and taught us."

She stopped, waiting for Edward to say something. He was enthralled by her story, and lost in his own imagination, trying to fit himself into her century and her life where children learned to perform miracles. He knew he was supposed to say something, but he didn't know where to begin. There was so much he wanted to know.

"Thou hast performed a mere miracle, and yet thou art not puffed up." His voice was reverent, hushed. "Methinks thou art a metaphysical creature, I am but a servant of thy will."

"But don't you see? It wasn't a miracle. It was something that I learned to do in school. I'm just like you, except I know different things, things that you would know, too, if you lived in New York City in 2002."

Maria arrived with a tray filled with a large pitcher and four mugs.

"Prithee, William Shakespeare, what is that hurly all about in thy corner of my tavern?" Then turning serious she addressed Edward. "Art thou ill, young one?"

Edward shook his head, and William spoke for him. "My young friend choked upon a piece of thy fine manchet bread. The boy is baffled, but all is well."

Katie took a small sip of the perry she had ordered. It tasted bubbly, like the cider Starr had served her that first day in the Tavern. "What is this made of?" she asked Starr.

"Hast thou heard of a fruit called pear? 'Tis the juice of pears, love."

I'd give anything for a Coke, she thought, and then she remembered her manners. "It's sweet," she said. "And bubbly, like a drink in my world, called 'soda.'"

Edward sipped his ale in silence, thinking about what he had witnessed, and about Katie's dilemma.

"So, my young friend," William said to Edward, "art thou as enthralled by the tale Katherine tells as we are?"

"Sire, if this most beautiful creature could speak an untruth, then 'tis possible that the welkin and the sun and the moon are themselves mere figments. Methinks we are most fortunate that the tumult which tossed her about in time, delivered her to our time. But, sire, wherefore hast thou brought her from the country to London?"

"'Tis safer for her here. Whereas country folk are often kind, they do not suffer strangers kindly. In London, amidst the whoo-bub and the crowds, we can daub Katherine more better, whiles we conjure up a solution to her dilemma."

"And thou will stay, then, in the room behind the Theatre?" Edward's voice was hopeful, and his eyes so earnest that Katie thought for a moment she was looking into Henry's face. She was startled by the similarities between these two boys. She looked at Starr.

"Yes, we're staying there until…well, until we can figure out what to do. Tuffy and I …we belong in another time…I…I don't know how to get back there, but until we figure out what to do, I guess we'll be there."

"Thou art safe, Katherine. Thy safety will become my own fardel as long as thou art here among us." Edward then turned to William. "Sire, thou need'st fear nothing whiles thou art away from the Theatre. No one will draw near to these ladies, nor contrive ill will for them so long as my heart beats within my bosom, and breath fills my lungs."

"Edward, thou art our most trusted ally. I knew that from the start. But, hear now, some of the fantastical stories Katherine tells from her time. She hast said that I, William Shakespeare, am known the world over in her time. In fact, Katherine's father is directing my Venetian

Comedy, which they call *The Merchant of Venice*. Is that fantastical? I have yet to complete the play, and yet Katherine's father, what is his name, child?"

"John Farrell, sir," Katie replied.

"Master Farrell is directing my play this summer, where, child?" William asked.

"In the little town where we have a summer home. It's called Hyde Park. It's about an hour and a half from New York City," Katie replied. "My father is an English professor at Vassar College, nearby. He's always loved your work and he actually teaches a class about you," Katie said.

"I have yet to complete this play, and already know that it is a success! Fantastical!" William repeated. He seemed to say that word a lot, but the whole situation was simply indescribable and no other word seemed to properly stress the incredulity of it all.

"And thy mum?" Edward asked tentatively. Katherine had only mentioned a father, so Edward was afraid maybe her mother had died and he certainly didn't want to stir up any sad memories.

"Oh, my mother," Katie said smiling at the picture in her mind. "My mother is a beautiful actress. She stars on a soap opera called 'Love's Labours' where she plays a woman named Julia Devereaux."

"Thy mother acts? On a stage? Art thou jesting? Katherine, dost thou not realize that it is against the law for a female to appear on a stage? Is this some invention of thine? 'Tis simply not done, even among the lags and the most vulgar classes!" Edward was stunned, and frightened for Katie, who seemed so unaware of the dangers swirling about her.

"In my world, in my century, acting is a very prestigious profession for both men and women. How could there be a law against women appearing on stage? There have been actresses for two hundred years...at least...I think," Katie said.

"Ah, my dear Edward, as thou will'st soon discover, this is not the most unbelievable thing about the future...indeed, it seems that Katherine's world is one in which miracles are as common as the flies buzzing over the Thames in July. Thine eyes would'st blink in wonder if thou could'st gaze upon the contents of Katherine's magic sack." William said.

Katie was squirming. The people at other tables were still staring at her, and William was making her sound like some kind of freak from the future.

"William," Starr said, noticing Katie's discomfort. "Would'st thou care to speak of other things?" She gestured at Katie.

"Ah, of course, dear child. Prithee, could'st thou tell me about this opera of thy mother's, 'Love's Labours,' is she a singer? I myself have written a play called Love's Labour's Lost, yet there were no singers in the play. What is the play about?" he asked, truly curious.

Katie thought for a minute. *How could I possibly explain this concept? I never even questioned it, just like I never questioned how my computer works. It's so complicated. Who would have thought that I would ever have to explain this stuff to people who lived hundreds of years ago?*

"It's not a play, or an opera. They just call these programs soap operas, I...I'm not really sure why. But the program is on television five days a week—every day there is a new script! It's a serial...do you know what that is? The plot continues to develop and change all the time. I'm sorry. I wish I could explain it better."

"Why thou art making it perfectly clear to me, Katherine," Edward said. "What is the story about, though?"

Katie was given a reprieve because Maria arrived at their table with the food. Although it looked slightly strange to her, it smelled delicious. Best of all, Maria had put a little rabbit stew on a plate for Tuffy.

"Maria, would it be possible to have a little butter or margarine?" Katie asked tentatively.

"Butter! Hah!" Maria squealed. "Thou art playing with me, yes? Whither hast thou come from, that thou should'st want butter? We have none and have never had any. As for the other thing, what did'st thou name it?"

"Margarine. It's sort of like butter only it's...it..." Katie looked around at her companions, each of whom gawked at her with the same expression. "I'm sorry. This is just fine, thank you."

"Katherine, thou art one surprise after another," Edward said. "Hast thou truly tasted butter? In thy world, is't something everyone, the vulgar and the rich, eat?"

"I'm sorry. It sounds like I'm some sort of...what was that word you used once, Starr?...a cracker? It's just that I don't know when things were invented, so I don't always realize when I'm saying something weird."

"A cracker? Thou could'st not be a cracker if thou spent the rest of thy days practicing," Edward said.

Katie turned to him. He was so much like Henry—so serious and considerate. And he wasn't too cool to say what was on his mind.

"Edward, where are you from? Here in London?"

"…Um…yes, London, but me mum is very poor and me father, he died. He just took sick one day and by nightfall he was gone. I sought work and Mr. Shakespeare hired me to do odd jobs at the Theatre. Oh…I love it there. All the actors and the costumes and the words of the playwrights that weave a magical spell. I give what I earn to me mum, for I myself don't need much." Edward stopped and looked from Katie to Starr and William.

"I guess I'm prating like a ninny. Thou should'st hear about things vasty more interesting than my sad tale." He was blushing and seemed uncomfortable.

Katie had never met anyone who had left home so early in life to go to work. She had a new respect for the courage it must have taken for Edward to strike out on his own and get a job to help support his poor mother.

"Edward, I've never met anyone like you, who has had to struggle so much. You can't be more than a year or so older than me. I can't imagine what I would do if I were in your situation. I…I'm sorry that your father died."

"Well, 'twas not such a tragedy. He was a candle-waster and a violent man. He was not kind to me mum, and often beat her bloody. 'Tis not as though we truly miss his presence in our lives."

"Oh dear, I'm so sorry, Edward. How is your mother getting along?"

"Katherine, while Edward's tale is akin to one of Mr. Marlowe's sad plays, albeit a poorly written play, his experience is not unique in the grimy streets of London," William said. It seemed that this world was as eerily strange to Katherine as hers was to him and Starr.

Edward's story and the sadness it evoked made Katie think about poor Henry. She remembered the sadness in his eyes the morning of the trip to the courthouse. It almost seemed that Edward was an earlier version of Henry. *Could that possibly be? Could this be a world that is occurring at the same time as my world back in New York?* She thought.

Am I there now, too? Or is someone else in my place? This is too difficult to understand.

"Katherine, would'st thou care for more bread?" Starr asked.

"No, thank you, Starr, I've had enough. Tuffy, have you had enough?" Katie asked, patting him on his head. Tuffy barked once as if to assure her that he, too, was full. Maria brought a delicious cake that seemed to have been soaked in honey. *The food here is very plain, but it's good,* she thought. *But I'd give anything for a sundae from Gelato's. I'll bet ice cream hasn't even been invented yet!*

She smiled and turned her head slightly, catching a glimpse of Edward staring at her once again. This time he didn't look away. The look in his eyes made Katie wonder if this was how it felt to be Brittany or Mackenzie. *What a strange world,* she thought. *What a strange, strange world.*

Chapter 30

The day was still sunny and clear when Katie and her friends left the tavern and headed back to the apartment. Katie was listening to William and Starr talk about the play he was working on. He called it *The Venetian Comedy*. She knew it as *The Merchant of Venice*. Katie had begun to feel strange. It was almost as if she were walking in her sleep.

Starr's voice seemed to be coming from somewhere far away. She looked down at Tuffy, who was walking just ahead of her, and she called his name—she wanted to see what her own voice sounded like. It too sounded strange. Tuffy stopped and looked up at her. She picked him up, and hugged him. She kissed his ear, as she had done so often since they had gotten lost in time. His soft fur and his warmth comforted her and made her feel real again.

Starr had tied a ragged little bow onto his collar, and Katie cupped her hand around it, the rough fabric reminding her of her dilemma and of Starr's kindness.

"Tuffy!" she whispered softly into his ear. He looked up at her and licked her chin. "Tuffy." She felt as if gravity were letting go of her, and she was about to fly away. *What's happening to me? Why do I feel this way?* She thought. She wondered if she looked different to her companions. She glanced at Starr, who was lost in conversation with

William. She looked at Edward. He was staring at a couple of men who had stumbled out of a tavern. One man was picking the other man's pocket.

"Perchance I should seek counsel from the fair Katherine!" William said to Starr. His voice speaking her name jolted Katie. Through the fog that seemed to engulf her, she looked up at William.

"I'm sorry, sir. Were you talking to me?"

"I was speaking about thee, little poppet. Mayhap I should ask thee about my play, which is like a stone tied 'round my neck. The play—the very one thy father directs in the future from whence thou hast come to us—is not a play on this afternoon. 'Tis a fardel, weighing more than that horse and carriage yonder."

He pointed toward a horse pulling a carriage through a pile of refuse. The horse's hooves were slipping on the greasy cobblestones. The man driving the carriage was shouting at the horse and at people trying to cross the street in front of him.

"You want *me* to help you?" Katie was incredulous.

"Thou art a bounty of knowledge, and thy wit exceeds thy years. Methinks thou could'st inspire me and pull me over the stone wall that has grown between my invention and my play."

They had arrived at the apartment, and Katie was thankful to get inside. She was feeling nervous and unsettled. Her head felt as if it were stuffed with a pillow. *Maybe I'm getting a cold,* she thought.

"Art thou feeling queasy?" Starr gently touched Katie's shoulder. "Thy skin seems so rosy." She touched the back of her hand to Katie's forehead. "Art thou feverish?"

"I think I'm okay. Maybe all the excitement today just made me a little tired." Katie looked up at Starr, trying to reassure her. "Really. I'm okay."

"If thou art ill, mayhap we can talk on the morrow." William's voice betrayed enormous disappointment. He believed Katie could actually help him break through the wall that had arisen between his imagination and the end of this confounded play.

"I...I'd love to help you. It's just that I can't imagine how..."

"Child. Thou know'st things. Thou hast seen things in thy young life that I shall n'er see—e'en if I live to be as old as rock." William wasn't pleading. He was merely outlining the facts as he saw them.

"I know the things most people from my time know. But I

learned about your play from my Dad…" She hesitated, then whispered the name she longed to say again. "Dad." Katie felt a stab of loneliness for her other life, and wondered, for the millionth time, if her parents and Sophia and all her friends were also hurtling through time. She wondered if they were frightened and lonely and starving for the simple pleasure of waking up in familiar surroundings to the smells and sounds that meant home and love.

William sat down at the table, a candle lighting the mound of paper in front of him. Katie thought the scene was as picturesque and domestic as anything in the year 2002 except for the fact that candles lit the darkening room instead of electric lights.

William pulled another chair over to the small table and gestured for Katie to sit beside him. Along with the stack of rough paper he had a pen that looked like a feather. He watched her as she touched the paper.

"Tis not the fine stuff thou hast in thy sack. In thy table-book and that…what did thou call it a…a maga…?"

"It's called a magazine," Katie said. "I hadn't thought about the paper before. Is it expensive to buy paper?"

"Tis not cheap, little one. Mercifully paper is now made in England, but merely 10 years ago all our paper came from Germany. And, as thou can see, what we call paper would hardly be recognized as thus by thy friends."

Katie picked up a scrap of paper that William had crumpled up and tossed into the middle of the table. She looked at how the ink saturated it. William's writing was English, but Katie found it very hard to read. The paper itself felt thick and uneven.

"I never thought about it before," Katie said. "We use paper— lots of it—and we don't even think about whether it's expensive or scarce or even important. It's just everywhere."

"Methinks the people of thy real time must be as wealthy as King Midas himself, with maga-zeens and cells and all those sweets they melt on their tongues," William said.

Katie looked around the spare little room. Her three friends were looking at her warmly. She thought about all the good fortune she had in her life, and knew that there were millions of people in her world who would do anything just to have a roof over their heads or regular food.

"There are a lot of people who are rich. But there are millions more—in my country and in other countries—who are very, very poor. I

211

guess we have the same problems that people have in this century. We just have a lot of other inventions that get in the way of seeing those problems." She bit her lip and wondered if she was going to burst into tears thinking about her other life. She tried to change the subject. "But that's not important now. You asked me to help you…"

"Ah, yes, child. My play. I'm stuck like a carriage in mud. The more I fret and worry and try to escape, the deeper my wheels sink into the mire. My intentions are to tell the story about a bitter meazel, a Jew, whom I call Shylock. The play will show all that will beshrew this greedy, self-centered miscreant. For Shylock will be condemned in a court of law, and face death with the final realization that his greed cost him his life," William explained. He thought Katie looked confused, so he tried to explain further. "Shylock, the Jew, has struck a loathsome bargain and now he must pay the price. He desires a pound of flesh from his hapless victim in order to repay a debt. The cur should pay with his own life, dost thou agree?"

"What makes him evil?" Katie asked.

Starr and Edward had been preparing vegetables for soup, and they stopped to watch the unfolding drama between Katie and William.

"Shylock is a moneylender."

"A moneylender?" Katie asked, quizzically. "What's that?"

"A moneylender—one who lends another a sum for a price," William said.

"You mean a banker?" Katie offered.

"In thy world they are called bankers?" William asked curiously.

"I think so. I don't know a lot about it, but my mom and dad went to a banker to get a mortgage for our apartment in New York. The banker loaned them the money, but the money doesn't belong to the banker. It belongs to the customers of the bank who deposit it there for safekeeping," Katie answered.

"By my troth! People actually give their money to the banker? Wherefore would'st they do that? How do they get it back?" William was astonished. This child seemed to possess answers to questions he had never even thought to ask.

"In my world, people write checks or they go to an ATM machine. Let me show you," Katie said going into the next room to retrieve her backpack.

Katie rummaged through the backpack until she found her wallet and removed the plastic ATM card. She held it up triumphantly and explained, "You put this card into an ATM, that's what we call our money machines, and put in your secret code and the money pops out of the dispenser," she explained.

Although he had seen the rectangular card before in Starr's tavern, William again fingered the plastic thoughtfully.

"Might I see it, sir?" Edward asked.

Edward had not seen any of Katie's belongings, and he was fascinated by the array of strange objects that she had thrown onto the table while she searched for her wallet. While he surveyed these items—so commonplace to be almost invisible to Katie herself—he was aware of how his feelings about her were changing from infatuation to something more powerful.

He believed he was falling in love with her and wondered how in the world he would fulfill all the requirements of a prospective bridegroom. He knew that Katie was a flesh-and-blood human being who sat right in the same room with him. She had saved his life! She was beautiful and sweet and kind. And yet, there was that crazy story about her losing her way in time and waking up in a meadow in a country and a century that were totally alien to her.

He knew that he should ask her father for her hand, and even though her father was alive, he was apparently not available. Dilemmas piled onto dilemmas. Edward was confused and scared and fascinated and irresistibly drawn to this creature. Katie was surprised and a little confused by Edward's adulation. She wondered how Edward would respond to Jordan or Mackenzie.

William passed the card to Edward who weighed it in his hand. Katie wasn't sure whether Edward expected such a powerful tool to be heavy, and Edward looked surprised when the card practically floated in his hand.

"Thou place this device into some…kind of machine…and the machine…it gives thee money?" he asked flabbergasted. "And what magic dost thou possess to make that happen? What is the nature of this machine? From whence does the money come? Who gives it to thee?" Edward asked, one question tumbling out after another.

"I don't possess any magic," Katie answered. "I'm no different than you are…it's just that I was born in another time and place. If you lived in my time, these things wouldn't look so…so magical to you." She reached for the card and gently took it from Edward's hand. Her things were scattered on the table, and she looked at the pile of gadgets that had so fascinated William and Starr.

They're just things, she thought to herself. *When it comes right down to it, they didn't do anything to help Tuffy and me. It was Starr and William who saved us and helped us.*

"Edward, thou must try and fathom Katherine's world. 'Tis far different from our own, with divers inventions and marvels that we cannot comprehend. If she avows that such machines exist, then we must believe that to be sooth." William was trying to relieve Katie's anxiety, but he was also growing impatient to get back to his confounded play.

"Back to the story, Will," Starr said. "Just because Shylock is a moneylender, what is the answer to Katherine's question? What mean things does he do?"

"Shylock is facinorous and mean spirited. He's emulous of those with more than he has. He despises a generous spirit, and his misery is without boundary. One who this scurvy recreant would injure most is Antonio, who oft lends money without usance. Antonio is as kind as Shylock is cruel. The moral of the play will be that death will finally separate the avaricious from their money." William's voice rose dramatically to emphasize his point.

Katie suddenly recalled the conversation she had had with her parents. "What would you ask Shakespeare if you could talk to him?" her father had asked. *I can't believe that I'm actually sitting here with William Shakespeare. I can ask him every question Dad and I thought about!*

"Do you hate Jewish people?" Katie practically blurted the question, then felt badly for being so direct. "I'm sorry. What I meant to ask was...why do you...I mean...do you actually...I'm sorry. I guess the question is what I said. Do you?"

"What dost thou mean, child? What are we to think of the Jews?" William asked.

"My little one, everyone knows about the Jews and their practices," Starr said gently.

"But how do you know these things?" Katie asked.

"I only know what I have heard," Shakespeare replied defensively. He was really thrown off guard by this creature. She was a mere child but she made him feel like a dullard. In fact, Shakespeare *did* believe what he had heard…that all Jews were evil and greedy.

Is it possible that I'm wrong about this? He wondered to himself. *This child has taken but a few moments to turn my thoughts upside down.* The entire play revolved around the fact that Shylock was the evil character who would see the error of his ways in the ultimate punishment, death. *What if Katherine is correct?* He thought.

On the other hand, since there are no Jews in England of whom I am aware, how would my audience know that not all Jews are like this? Shakespeare reasoned through these new possibilities in silence, with his eyes half closed and his feather pen tapping softly on the paper. *Would these characters ring true? Perhaps I'm on the wrong course.*

"Sir?" Katie didn't want to disturb William, but felt there was more that needed to be said. He looked at her, tilting his head slightly. Then he cleared his throat.

"Very well, Katherine, thou hast again dazzled me. These things thou hast said…they hint at larger ideas that I shall be a mome if I ignore. Let us propose that thou art correct, whither must I go with this Shylock? What must I do to foil the forces that thwart my efforts to finish this play?"

"But that's just it. Do you hate Jews because your government says to hate them? My father said that it's against the law in your time in England to have a different religion from the Church of England, but that's not the way things are in my time. In my time there are lots of religions, and in my country the government isn't allowed to tell people what to believe."

Katie stopped for a moment, trying to keep her emotions in check. "I go to school with kids who are Jewish. My parents work with people who are Jewish. We have lots of friends who are Jewish…" Katie felt tears again, and wished she could contain her emotions better.

She stopped and looked at William. He was smiling at her. She had expected him to be angry, but the look on his face and in his eyes was almost…admiration! Starr and Edward were confused and a little surprised by Katie's outburst.

"Alas, dear child. Thou hast proved again that thy wisdom far exceeds my own. 'Tis true. I know no Jews. But I know the power of the monarchy can silence even the most brilliant words. So, what good is there in a pen that can ignite a fire if that fire is extinguished before anyone sees its flame? That is a reality my friends and I must abide. But tell me, what would'st thou have me do with this Shylock?"

Katie thought about Shylock, and about his cruelty. Her mind raced from there to Henry—a victim of mindless cruelty—and then to Mr. Murwata's conversation with her on the bus. She remembered the hours and hours her class discussed the issue of justice, and what justice actually achieved.

"I have a friend named Henry, who got hurt in an accident. Only it wasn't really an accident. Henry is a nice kid who is really, really smart. A lot of the kids in school don't like him. They make fun of him and play tricks on him, just to embarrass him. But my friends and I have tried to protect Henry and show him that we care about him.

We had a school trip to a ranch where some of us were riding horses, and someone did something to scare the horse Henry was riding. The horse ran away and Henry fell off and got hurt. He is in a coma in a hospital...I don't know if he's still alive." Katie was crying now, but she didn't want to stop her story. Starr was standing behind her, with her hands on Katie's shoulders.

William repeated the word he did not understand. "Coma? Pray, child, what is this coma?" His voice was gentle, and soothing.

"I...I'm not sure of the medical explanation, but a coma is basically when someone looks like they're dead, but they're really not."

"You mean it's possible for someone to exhibit all the signs of death, but not really be dead?" William asked.

"I think so," Katie answered, sniffling. "They're still alive, but when you talk to them, they can't answer."

"Can people in comas hear when others are talking to them?" William asked.

"I don't know for sure, but I've heard and read that people in comas *can* hear people talking to them. They just can't answer them," Katie said. She had finally gotten control of her emotions, and was using the corner of her apron to dry her tears.

"Go on with thy tale, dear," Starr said. Both she and Edward had pulled chairs close to the table, abandoning the soup.

"On the way home from the ranch, Mr. Murwata, my teacher, told me that the police were going to arrest someone for hurting Henry. The thing is, whoever hurt Henry will have some kind of trial and that's what we call justice. But justice doesn't make Henry better. Or it won't bring him back to life if...if..." Katie's eyes welled up with tears again, but she fought on. "Justice only makes people think that the right thing happened."

"And thy friend, Henry, had done nothing to inspire these pranks against him?" William asked.

"Nothing."

"These rogues, thy schoolmates, they have no reason to dislike this Henry so intensely?"

"None. Henry is smart and kind and friendly. He's never pushy or conceited or mean to anyone. It's almost as though he's being punished for being a nice boy."

"Whoever hath done this facinorous deed to thy friend, *does* deserve to be punished. And the punishment should be severe," William said.

"Yes, I think so, but…" Katie hesitated, and thought about Henry, wondering if time had swept past him or if he too was struggling through this fog.

"What would'st thou do, then, child?" William asked. "Should'st thou not venge thy friend's injury? Should'st not someone pay dearly for hurting young Henry?"

"Yes, they should pay. But what Mr. Murwata said is that justice without mercy doesn't work."

"Mercy?"

"I know this doesn't sound like it makes sense. But Mr. Murwata taught us about justice, and asked us to think about what made it different than revenge. It's hard to explain it, but he said that there is justice that happens in a courtroom, and then there is justice that happens here..." She tapped her chest, just as Mr. Murwata had done.

"In thy chest?"

"In your heart. Justice can't work unless people's hearts change, unless it is balanced with mercy. Mr. Murwata said that hatred is a poison that kills everyone—including the people who hate."

William began scribbling. He'd write, then stop, then crumple up the paper and start writing again.

"Justice balanced with mercy," William repeated with a faraway look in his eyes. "Justice tempered with mercy," he whispered to himself. Starr could tell he was absorbing all of this and trying to fit it into the context of his play. The playwright was clearly troubled by the way the play was flowing. Starr knew that Katherine had given William a lot to think about.

"So, child, in thy apprehension, if thy teacher…Mr. Murr…whatever, were advising me, would'st he influence me not to kill Shylock?" William said slowly.

"I'm not sure, but I think he might tell you not to kill him."

"Rather, the structure of the play would revolve around not only punishing but also redeeming," William let his words trickle to a stop because he was busy thinking about a new theme. *What if Shylock could go from being mean-spirited to humble? What would the vehicle be to so transform such a nasty character?*

William had been fiddling with the idea to introduce a strong female character. Perhaps she could be the catalyst. His head abuzz with new ideas, he began scribbling again. He said nothing. He muttered under his breath. Once in a while, he stopped writing and read aloud, stopped himself, made edits, and read it again, sometimes out loud, sometimes to himself.

"Don't stop. Keep talking, child." Shakespeare said, without taking his eyes off the paper on which he was writing.

The table top was nearly covered with scraps of paper with William's notes, and Katie didn't want her stuff to derail his train of thought, which seemed to be moving pretty fast. She grabbed her things and shoved them into the largest pocket of her backpack, thinking that she'd have time to organize everything later.

"My father and I talked about your play, and about standing up for what you believe in. I thought it was bad that you made Mr. Shylock so evil, but my father said he thought you tried to do the right thing by making Mr. Shylock someone who wasn't totally evil."

William stopped and looked at her again. Now the tears were in his eyes. "Thy father saw these things in my play? People speak about these ideas hundreds of years hence? Though I have died hundreds of years before thy birth, yet I live on in my plays."

"I think people believe you are one of the greatest writers in history. Your plays and your poems…everyone reads them and quotes you.

The room was suddenly silent. Katie felt tired and almost as if she were in a dream. She felt as if a fog were creeping over her. She could still see her friends, but they seemed to be moving away from her.

"Where are you going? Don't leave me…" They were receding into a golden mist, and Katie couldn't make them hear her. She reached for Tuffy and hugged him close to her chest. "Tuffy, what's happening to us?" she whispered into his velvety ear. She heard him whimper softly before they both fell sound asleep.

Chapter 31

What's that ringing? A phone? No! It can't be. Phones don't exist yet. Katie was confused and sleepy. The ringing was insistent, and getting louder. She buried her head deeper into the pillow to block the sound. Finally, mercifully, the ringing stopped. Silence once again surrounded and comforted Katie. She drifted back to that state of almost-awake-almost-asleep relaxation.

Abruptly and rudely, Katie was assaulted by a wet tongue licking her face. "Tuffy, go back to sleep. Starr will call us when breakfast is ready." And with that, she rolled over trying to avoid Tuffy's relentless nudging. When she did so, Tuffy started barking loudly. 'Get up, get up,' he seemed to be saying.

"Oh, all right. I'm up," Katie said somewhat crossly as she brushed the hair out of her eyes. Taking a deep breath, she opened her eyes. Looking wildly around, she recognized her familiar bedroom.

What's happened? Katie thought, panic stricken. *We're home? We're really home?* She leapt out of bed, Tuffy still barking, and rushed to the door. Flinging it open, she yelled, "Mom? Dad? Sophia? Are you here?"

Please, please, please be here! If you're not and I'm lost again, I don't think I could bear it, she thought frantically.

"We're here, sweetheart," Katie heard her mother say as she and

Katie's dad rushed down the hallway toward a seemingly terrified Katie. Breaking into sobs somewhere between joy at being home again and sorrow at losing touch with William, Starr and Edward, Katie stumbled into her mother's arms.

"Katie, what's wrong? Did you have a nightmare?" Charlotte asked. "How long have I been gone?" Katie asked, breathlessly.

"Katie, what are you talking about? You haven't been gone at all. You've been sleeping soundly for about the last ten hours, but we thought you were just exhausted from everything going on at school with Henry," Charlotte looked at John, her brow furrowed.

"Is my Ekaterina finally back from her dreams?"

"Sophia!" Katie was trying to stifle her sobs. "I can't believe you're here!" She bounced joyfully from her mother's arms into Sophia's and then into her father's embrace.

"Of course I'm here," Sophia replied slowly, confused by Katie's outburst. "I just go to supermarket."

Katie was struggling with her emotions. *Was I dreaming about Starr and William? Or am I dreaming now? Am I home? Was I really away?* She worried that waking up at home was another dream, or that waking up in 1596 was the dream. *But it seemed so real!* Katie fought to pull the pieces from her foggy brain. She walked back to her bed and sat on the edge. *It seemed so real! How could it have been a dream? How could I have dreamed the way it sounded and smelled? How could I have dreamed the way the food tasted?*

Charlotte and John looked at each other. They were starting to worry about Katie's confusion. She was obviously awake, but she seemed to be lost in a dream.

"Honey, what's wrong? Why do you think you were away?" John's voice was gentle, but it was clear he was worried.

"Katie, did you have a bad dream? You were sound asleep for so long, we didn't want to wake you. Sometimes dreams seem very real, but they're just dreams…do you understand, honey?" Charlotte brushed the hair out of Katie's eyes. "Do you want to talk about your dream? Was it scary?"

"It…it just seemed so real, Mom. I…we…Tuffy and I, we were in England and we met William Shakespeare and we stayed in a tavern and saw a play, and I met this lady who looked just like Sylvie and we saw horses and went to a restaurant where they even gave Tuffy his own plate…and then Mr. Shakespeare asked me to help him with his play…we were really there! But…but now we're here…I was scared that we would never see you again, or that maybe you were lost too…I…I thought Tuffy and I got lost in time."

John sat down next to Katie. "Honey, you know we've been talking about Shakespeare a lot lately. A lot of the stuff that goes on around you all day winds up in your dreams. Your brain tries to make sense of things, and to sort things out for you while you sleep." He kissed the top of her head. "With all that's been happening, it's not surprising that you had a pretty strange dream. But it was just a dream, honey…do you understand?"

"I guess so. But it seemed so real."

"Well, Katie, I've got some really good news for you, and it's not a dream." Charlotte still had the phone in her hand. "Mr. Murwata just called. Henry has regained consciousness. He's going to be all right," she said joyfully. "We're all so relieved. The call just came through. The ringing phone probably woke you up."

"Henry's okay? Really and truly okay?" Katie asked.

"Really and truly okay," Charlotte replied standing up and pulling Katie up, too. "Now let's get you something to eat and drink. Sophia's making French toast. Doesn't that sound terrific? You go brush your teeth and wash your face while I feed poor starving Tuffy. Then we can all sit down together and enjoy a nice breakfast." She nudged Katie toward the bathroom while scooping Tuffy up into her arms to take him to the kitchen for his breakfast.

I know I was there! It was so real, it couldn't have been a dream. But how can I prove it? If I was really there, then where are the clothes Starr gave me? Katie's mind raced as she brushed her teeth. She was confused and worried. She thought about the last few minutes she had spent in the apartment with Starr and William and Edward.

My backpack! I just grabbed everything off the table and stuffed them in it. If I was really there, then all my stuff would be jumbled together in that one pocket! She ran into her room and grabbed her backpack.

She hesitated a moment before unzipping the center pocket. *What if this proves I was there? What will I do?* She unzipped the pouch where her cell phone would normally be. It was gone! *I always put my phone in that pocket!*

She touched the center zipper, and as she slowly moved it backward along the track, she was nearly overcome with excitement. She closed her eyes and took a deep breath. With her eyes closed tightly, she pulled the zipper all the way open.

It's a mess in there! Katie looked into the backpack and saw her water bottle, her wallet, her diary and phone. She turned the backpack upside down on her bed and the contents spilled out in a disorganized heap.

Her ATM card was the last item to drop out of the bag, and she was shocked that it wasn't in her wallet. *Edward was looking at it!* Katie's heart was racing, and she felt as if every nerve in her body was throbbing with a mixture of fear and wonder.

She put her ATM card back in her wallet, and picked up a pen that had rolled off the bed onto the floor. She started putting everything back into its proper place in the backpack.

Bubble gum. Tic tacs. Water bottle. Each item was tied to a scene from her dream or her trip through time. She smiled as she remembered Starr and William tasting the mints and chewing the bubble gum. She picked up a wad of crumpled paper. Something stopped her from just tossing the paper into the trash can. She opened the paper and nearly fell over when she realized what it was.

"Mercy droppeth like the rain..

Mercy falls like gentle rain..

Mercy hath a quality like the rain..

The quality of mercy is not strained,

It droppeth as the gentle rain...from heaven?

From the sky?

It was the heavy rough paper she remembered, and it was covered with the strange handwriting she knew to be William's.

That ink! It wasn't a dream! I was there! We were talking about mercy and justice! He was writing this while I told him about Mr. Murwata and Henry and the accident. Katie sat on the edge of the bed, clutching the paper.

She looked around her room, a room she knew so well. As she focused on the map of Romania that hung above her desk, she remembered the waitress from the tavern, and William's story about Vlad the Impaler. She was deep in thought when Tuffy leapt onto her lap and startled her.

"Tuffy!" she whispered. "Tuffy, we were there, weren't we?"
Tuffy nudged her and she noticed he had something in his mouth.
"What's that, Tuf?"

He opened his mouth and a grimy piece of rough fabric dropped
onto the bed. She stood up, and took a step back from the bed as the
realization of what Tuffy was showing her sank in. "Tuffy! This was
your disguise!" It was the cloth that Starr had tied around Tuffy's neck to
cover his collar. "We went back in time!"

Tuffy stood in the middle of the bed, quivering with excitement.
It's true! He thought, joyfully. *Starr did make me all those yummy treats!
It wasn't a dream!* His tail was wagging at warp speed, and he leapt into
Katie's arms.

"It's true," she whispered to him as she kissed his ear. "It's true,
Tuffy. We were there with Starr and William. We traveled back in time."
She sat on the edge of the bed, feeling as if she were in a trance.

"Katie! What's keeping you, honey? Come on, we're ready for
breakfast!" Her mother's voice jolted her back to real time. *Now what?
Do I tell them? Do I show them these things?* She tried to imagine what
her parents would say if she brought them this evidence that she had
indeed met William Shakespeare.

*What would I say if Corky or Lily thought they had traveled back
in time? I'd call them crazy! What if everyone thinks I'm crazy?* Katie
was nearly overcome with a sense of loneliness. Apparently nobody else
was caught in the same time warp as she was.

All her fears that everyone else was spinning through time while
she was visiting with Starr and William were unfounded. Once again,
she felt like an outsider. Only now, she was an outsider with a secret that
was both frightening and exciting. *I need time to think, to figure out
what really happened.*

She stared at the evidence of her mysterious journey, and wondered how it had changed her. *Do I still look the same? I feel like I've
grown up, but I want to be the kid I was before. I want to be like everyone else.* She was nearly overcome with a familiar feeling of being different, more different than anyone she knew.

"Katie? What are you doing? Are you all right?"

"What? Mom! Oh! I'm sorry! I...I..." Katie practically jumped
over the bed, she was so startled. She gathered all the contents of her
backpack into a pile and stuffed them into the biggest pocket and closed

the zipper, all the while trying to appear nonchalant. "I guess I'm not totally awake yet."

"Are you still deep in your crazy dream? That must have been quite a drama." Charlotte put her arm around Katie's shoulders. "I know that sometimes dreams seem like the real thing. And it's hard to shake the feelings they leave you with, even when you're wide awake. But it was a dream, honey. A dream. Come on, let's go get some breakfast."

Katie and her mother drifted toward the sweet smell of cinnamon and the familiar sounds of Saturday mornings. Katie felt as though she left an unfinished sentence hanging in her room. It worried and fascinated her. She was torn between wanting to immerse herself in the cozy warmth of her family, and wanting to poke around in all the mysteries that seemed to be bursting at the seams of her backpack.

My journal! I know I wrote in it while I was with Starr. That will prove it once and for all. But if it proves I was there, then how did I get back here? What if I go away again? What's happening to me?

Katie looked around the kitchen and was overwhelmed with a sense of love for her family. Tuffy was licking his bowl eagerly, but— did Katie imagine it?—it almost looked as if he winked at her as she took her place at the table.

"I make the famous French toast for celebration," Sophia said as she handed Katie a plate.

"Celebration? Oh! Yes! Henry…yes," Katie was momentarily confused.

"What do you think, Katie? Should we go to the hospital to see Henry after breakfast?"

"Could we, Mom? I'd love to. And can Lily and Corky go with us?"

"Sure, honey. Why don't you finish your breakfast and call them. We can pick them up. Then after we visit Henry, your dad and I will take you all out to lunch at that new place over on Lexington. What's it called, John?"

"Burbage's. Odd name."

"You mean like the guy from Shakespeare's theater group?" Katie blurted out a question before she even realized what she had said. *Oh no! Now they're going to start with the questions. I can't believe I said that. How am I ever going to make this work? It's not easy to live in two different worlds.*

Katie's father looked over the top of the newspaper. He pushed his reading glasses up to his forehead. It was a gesture Katie knew well. She began picking at her French toast, hoping her father would go back to reading. No such luck.

"Katie, how did you know about Burbage? I mean, it's not like he's a household name."

"Who is Burbage, John? Katie?" Charlotte was confused. She looked at her husband, then at her daughter. "Anyone?"

"Katie, why don't you tell us who Burbage was."

"I...I just read his name in a book, Dad. He was with Shakespeare, in his theater group. Sort of like you and the Hudson Valley Players. Right, Dad?"

"Yes, yes, right, honey." Her father seemed distracted.

Why isn't he asking me more? What's he looking at in the newspaper?

"Well, well, well! Here it is, ladies! Henry was right about the zoo."

"What? What about the zoo?" Charlotte put her coffee mug down and tapped the back of the newspaper.

"Remember how Henry was asking that guy from the zoo...what's his name Katie?...the guy who faked a heart attack or something?"

"You mean Mr. Riverdale? Is he in the paper, Dad?"

"Honey, remember when I said I wanted to look into Henry's questions? Well, I did. I found out a lot of pretty strange things about zoos. I had lunch with a friend of mine from the newspaper, and we talked about Mr. Riverdale and the court case."

"Henry was right, then? Dad, that's amazing!" Katie slid her chair over toward her father's chair, and the two of them read the story.

"Come on, you guys, tell Sophia and me what it says."

"Mom! It says that the zoo was selling their grown-up animals to game parks and roadside zoos—what are they, Dad?—but the animals, nobody took care of them or protected them. The people who got the animals didn't know how to take care of them, or some of them let people come and hunt them, like on a ...what's that mean, Dad?"

"It means that the people at the zoo violated their charter, lied to the public and put these animals in terrible situations where they could be abused, or maimed or killed."

"The monkeys! They're the ones that Henry worried about. Look! It says a lot of them got starved to death!" Katie pointed to a photo of a group of monkeys that had been found living in a squalid fenced-in area behind a shack in New Jersey.

"John, how could this be? How could they get away with it? There must be hundreds of employees at the zoo! How could they not do anything, or say anything?"

"I can't believe this. Look, there's that Riverdale guy. Listen to this, Char. You're not going to believe this jerk's arrogance. 'While I'm sure there's a perfectly reasonable explanation for what seems to be a case of neglect, I must say that I have no day-to-day contact with the Zoo management. Thus, I regret that I cannot comment on these incidents.' How can he say that? I bet he's completely responsible for successful fund-raising campaigns."

"Doesn't he get paid to be president of the board of directors?"

"He sure does! Look at this chart showing the compensation for the board. Man, I'll bet people contributing to the Zoo's campaign didn't know that Riverdale and his cronies are being paid as if they really *are* running the operation." The chart showed that Mr. Riverdale was paid $100,000 annually as chair of the Zoo's Board of Directors.

"I wonder if Mr. Morgan knew this. Do you think he knew it, Dad?"

"Well, honey, I'm sure this story won't be a complete surprise to Mr. Morgan. I imagine he probably knew a lot about it the day you kids went to court."

"I wonder if we should tell Henry about it. Mom, what do you think? He was worried about one of the monkeys. That's why he was asking Mr. Riverdale all those questions. Do you think the monkey is dead?"

"Why don't we play it by ear when we go to see Henry? We might not get to spend a lot of time with him. We'll save the paper and give it to him when he gets out of the hospital. How does that sound?"

"Okay. I feel so bad for him, though. And what about Brittany? She must really be upset, if she saw this. She was really mad at Henry, but Henry was right all along."

"Well, we've got plenty of time to worry about Brittany and how she's feeling. Right now, we're going to focus on Henry. So, young lady, why don't you get yourself ready to go?"

"Okay, Mom. I'm going to call Corky and Lily."

"Tell Lily we'll pick her up at 9:30 and tell Corky we'll get to her place around 10, okay? And don't forget to invite them to lunch; and...honey, why don't you see if Lily's mom and Corky's mom can come, too?"

Katie took one last bite of French toast and left the table. *Before I do anything, I want to find my journal. I know I wrote in it while I was with Starr.* She was excited about seeing Henry, and talking to her friends about her adventure.

Tuffy and I have two pieces of evidence to show them. My journal will be even more proof. She rooted through the jumble of things she had stuffed into her backpack and found her journal. She opened it and thumbed through the pages. Nothing. Her last entry was the night that Henry had been hurt. *How can this be? I was sure I wrote in it. Now I don't know what to think.*

She sat down on the edge of her bed and fumbled around in the backpack for her cell phone. She was thoroughly confused. As she punched in Corky's phone number, she tried to conjure up more memories of her visit with Starr and William. *It was while we were still at Starr's tavern. I know I wrote about going to London...*

"Hey, Katie! What's up?" Corky's voice jolted Katie back to real time.

"Corky! Did you hear that Henry's awake, and that he's going to be okay?"

"Ma told me this morning, and I'm hoping to see him soon. D'ya want to go over there?"

"My mom and dad are going to take me today. Do you want to go with us? My parents want to take us to lunch afterward, and your mom, too. Can you come?"

"Hey, Ma! Katie wants to know if we want to go see Henry. Her parents are taking us to lunch after. Okay, Ma?"

Katie heard Corky's mother, Chloe, in the background, talking to Corky. Then Chloe got on the phone.

"Katie, are ya sure your parents want to take us both?"

"Oh, hi, Mrs. Nolan. Mom said I should call and ask you and Corky to go to the hospital with us, and to have lunch afterward."

"We'd love to go. I'm sure you're as thrilled as Corky about Henry. What time will you be by for us, then, darling?"

"Is 10:00 okay? We're picking up Lily at 9:30."

"That's fine, dear. D'ya want to talk with Corky again, then?"

"Um, no, that's okay. Just tell her I'll see her later. My mom thinks I've already finished getting ready, so I've got to go. Thanks, Mrs. Nolan. Bye!"

As she waited for Lily to answer her phone, Katie thought about how she was going to explain her adventure to her friends. *They'll think I'm crazy! Maybe they won't believe me at all. I wish I knew what happened with my journal. Maybe I wrote it somewhere else...no, I know I wrote in my journal.*

"Well, hello, Katie! I guess you're thrilled about Henry. Lily's out walking the dog, but she'll be back in just a few minutes, honey. Want me to have her call you?"

"Um...no, that's okay, Mrs. Hanover. I was calling to see if you and Lily want to go see Henry with us. My mom said we can pick you up at 9:30. And then, my parents want to take us all to lunch later."

"Why that sounds great, honey. I'm sure Lily will want to go. Count us both in, Katie, dear. We'll see you at 9:30."

"Okay, Mrs. Hanover. Bye!"

Katie sat on the edge of her bed, thinking about what had happened, and trying to relieve the confusion that was overtaking her again. *I need to talk to someone. Will Lily and Corky think I'm crazy? Will they believe me? How can I explain all this to them?*

"Katie, you've got 15 minutes! Come on, honey! Let's step on it. We've got lots to do this morning." Her father's voice brought Katie back to reality, or what she *thought* was reality. She got up and started moving around. She tried to focus on the details of her bedroom, looking for things that might be out of place, or for things that would help her understand what was happening.

She looked at the clock. *Oh, no! I've got to get ready!* She started rushing around, looking for clothes and putting all her stuff in her backpack. She held the shred of paper and the piece of cloth in the palm of her left hand, and stared at them. *I can't lose these. I've got to put them in a safe place, and protect them.*

She rummaged through her dresser drawer—the small one at the top, where she stored important things that didn't seem to belong in her desk, or her bathroom cabinet. There was an old watch she had found in Central Park. The watch band was broken, and the crystal was cracked.

The hands on the face of the watch were stopped—permanently, it seemed, since the crystal had caved in and was preventing the hands from moving anywhere—at 4:15.

Katie had been out with Sophia, walking Tuffy on a Saturday morning. They were talking about Romania and the countryside where Sophia remembered picnicking with her family when she was a child. Tuffy had stopped near a park bench, and was scratching around in the dirt.

"Come on, Tuffy! Stop digging. You know you're not supposed to do that." Katie was just about to pick him up and carry him away from the bench, when she saw the watch.

"Sophia! Look what Tuffy found."

"Watch don't work with face broken." Sophia turned the watch over and scraped some dirt off the back. "It say 10-9-90. Your birthday, Katie! This must be magic watch. It finds us in park, so we must takes it home with us."

Sophia put the watch in her pocket and it became a major conversation piece for Katie and her friends. Katie's parents put a lost and found ad in the newspaper, in case the owner of the watch was searching for it. After two weeks, and no phone calls from possible owners, Katie's parents told her she could keep the watch.

She clipped the ad out of the newspaper and stuck it in a red velvet pouch with the watch. Over time, as Katie showed the watch to her friends, the pouch—a frayed and fading little bag that came with a pair of earrings her mother had given Sophia as a gift—and watch were separated in the drawer, and the pouch soon found a permanent home at the very bottom of the drawer.

Katie looked at the watch, and fingered the engraving on the back. She pulled out other items by the handful—a barrette, a few scrunchies, a bead bracelet, a purple stone she had found along a creek near Hyde Park and a charm of the Eiffel Tower. Finally she reached the bottom of the drawer, and the pouch that once held the watch.

She put the piece of cloth and the scrap of paper into the pouch, and then put the pouch back in the drawer. She piled all the other items on top and closed the drawer.

As she finished getting ready to go see Henry, she thought about how she would tell her friends what had happened.

As if things aren't already complicated enough. Now I have to try and figure out what is going on. It couldn't have been just a dream. How could I get that paper with William's writing? And how could Tuffy get that piece of cloth? But Mom and Dad said it was a dream. They said I hadn't gone anywhere. Everything here is normal, and it wouldn't be normal if I was away...would it? Am I hallucinating or was it a dream? What's wrong with me? I feel like some kind of freak, except that William and Starr and Edward didn't think that. But were they just my imagination? They treated me like I was someone special, and pretty. And they were interested in what Mr. Murwata was teaching us. How could I imagine this? If I did imagine it, how could I know about Burbage? If it really happened, then it could happen again...Oh God! What if I go to sleep tonight and wake up someplace else?

Chapter 32

Katie snapped her journal closed and slipped it into her backpack. She was looking forward to seeing Henry and having lunch with her friends. She could hear her parents talking and knew that they were on the verge of calling her again. She rushed out of her room, down the hall and into the kitchen where they were waiting.

"Finally! I thought you might have gone back to London to find something to wear today." Katie knew her father was teasing her, and she tried to laugh it off. But in the back of her mind, she wondered if she would ever be able to persuade her parents that something truly earth-shattering had happened to her.

The three girls chatted excitedly as the group walked up the hospital steps. Katie was carrying a tin of Sophia's famous "power" cookies, baked especially for Henry.

"I make gift for Henry," Sophia had said. "To get well soon."

"Sophia, that's so sweet of you! I'm sure Henry will love them as much as I do." Katie sampled one of the cookies while Sophia tied a ribbon around the small gift box.

"You remember I invent 'power' cookies just for you, my Ekaterina?"

Sophia had been overwhelmed by all the wonderful nuts, flavoring, flours, spices, and raisins available in New York; she had whipped up a batch of cookies that included everything that she could squeeze into the batter. Katie's heroes then were the Power Rangers. The cookies seemed to embody all the magic that Sophia saw everywhere in America, and she told Katie that they were magic and powerful, just like the Power Rangers. They decided to call them "power" cookies, and they retained their special charm even after Katie outgrew the Power Rangers.

None of the girls had ever been to a hospital before, and they weren't sure what to expect. As the hospital door slid open, it was as if the girls stepped into another world, where peoples' voices were hushed and serious.

The three girls fell silent as they passed the reception desk and began to see patients and their loved ones walking through the halls. Some people were in wheel chairs. Some were dressed in robes, walking unsteadily, dragging contraptions with plastic bags of clear liquid hanging off them. In one room off the corridor leading to the elevators, there were five people huddled together. Some of the people were crying. Others drooped in postures that suggested profound grief and helplessness.

The halls didn't echo with laughter or happiness. The prevailing sounds were beeps and whooshes and voices that seemed to come out of everywhere asking Dr. So and So to pick up the phone.

The girls waited near the elevators for their parents, who had stopped at the reception desk to find out Henry's room number. In the silence, Katie turned her thoughts back to her strange trip. She thought about William and Starr, and wondered if they remembered her. *Do they think they imagined me? Did I leave a hole in their world when I left? They're dead now, so they wouldn't know anything...I wish I could understand what happened.*

"Katie! Are you okay? You seem like you're in another world." Lily was tapping Katie's shoulder insistently.

"Um...I...I'm sorry. What did you say?"

"I said I wonder if any other kids from school will come see him."

"If you think about the last couple of weeks of school, you might think he hadn't a friend in the world other than us and a couple of others," Corky said.

"I feel so bad for him. Do you think we could have done anything to make things different?" Lily asked.

Before anyone could even think of an answer, the elevator doors opened and the girls were stunned to see Jordan walk out and head straight for the hospital's front door. She was less than 10 feet from Katie and her friends, but didn't even acknowledge them. It was pretty obvious she didn't see them. She was walking quickly, looking at the floor and crying.

"What do you suppose she's crying over?" Corky whispered.

"Do you think she was visiting Henry? Maybe she got upset seeing him," Lily said.

"I didn't think she even cared about Henry," Katie said. "She must have been here visiting someone else. Maybe a relative got ill. Maybe someone in her family died."

The girls considered that possibility for a moment in silence.

"Well, when we get in to see Henry, then, I'm asking him," Corky said. "I'm still thinkin' Blondie and her crowd had something to do with the accident and all those nasty tricks played on Henry before the end of school."

"Let's wait and see how he is before we give him the third degree," Lily said. "After all, he's been through a lot. Maybe he doesn't want to think about all this right now."

"But doesn't it sicken you to think that they could have killed him?" As usual, Corky was reluctant to let go of an issue of injustice.

"Corky, we're all upset about it. But maybe we should wait until Henry is out of the hospital. We'll have plenty of time to talk about all

233

this stuff then." Katie had her hand on Corky's forearm. She tugged gently.

"Maybe you're right…but still…I'm thinkin' that Blondie is behind it all."

"Okay, girls. Henry is on the fifth floor, in room 5641. Let's go." Katie's parents and the other adults arrived just as Corky relented. As they waited for the elevator, the three girls stood silently, arm in arm. They were anxious, and unsure of what it would be like to see their friend.

The girls reached the door to room 5641 and tentatively knocked. "Henry? It's us!" Katie called, trying to make her voice sound cheerful, not nervous.

On the other side of the door, Henry also worked on sounding cheerful.

"Hey, come on in!"

They pushed open the door and nearly gasped at how their friend looked. His head was bandaged up and his glasses sat crookedly on his nose. His eyes were black and blue and there was a large cut on his chin. He fumbled self-consciously with his glasses, struggling to balance them. Finally he just threw the glasses down on his lap, and squinted at his friends.

"Henry, you're lookin' a bit like the guy from that old movie…what's his name, Rocky?" Corky said, with a nervous laugh. Lily and Katie cringed and gawked helplessly at Corky. Seeing Henry's injuries and his apparent frailty made everyone uncomfortable; and truthfully, nobody knew quite what to say. Corky always seemed to find a way to open up any conversation, although in the momentary silence that followed her remark, it seemed that she might have gone a little too close to the edge. Henry looked at Corky, then at Katie and Lily. Then he smiled, oddly distorting his battered face.

"But Rocky won, didn't he? I think I'm due for a win."

In the tiny room, filled with people who loved Henry, anxiety was suddenly replaced with happiness. And everyone seemed to begin talking at once.

"How do you feel?"

"Does that hurt?"

"What's in that tube sticking out of your arm?"

"Did you have dreams when you were unconscious?"

"How many stitches are in your chin?"

"Girls! Girls! Give the poor guy a chance to answer." Katie's father said, laughing.

"It's okay, Mr. Farrell. Actually I don't feel that bad, except for a big headache. I really don't remember much of anything."

"Henry, we're so glad to see that you're feeling better. Everyone was so worried about you." Lily's mother patted Henry's arm gently.

"Thank you, Mrs. Hanover. Really, I'm feeling fine."

"Maybe you kids would like to visit with Henry for a few minutes. We'll wait outside. But please, don't wear the poor boy out." Katie's mother leaned over and kissed Henry lightly on the forehead. "It's wonderful to see you, Henry. We'll see you again very soon."

"Good-bye, Mrs. Farrell, thanks again for coming. Bye, Mrs. Nolan...um...I think my parents just went out for some coffee a few minutes ago. They should be right back." Henry was embarrassed by all the attention from the adults. But once they were gone, he and the girls relaxed and fell into the familiar chatter that was as seamless and comfortable as an old t-shirt.

"So, Henry, what was up with Jordan? Did she have anything interesting to say?"

"Jordan? What do you mean, Corky?"

"Did you not see her, then? We saw her leaving the hospital, all weepy and sad. The girl ran right past us, lookin' straight at her feet and not seein' anything."

"No, no...I'm sure of it. She wasn't here. My parents were here just before you guys got here. She must have been here for someone else."

"Henry, did you have any dreams while you were, um...knocked out?"

"He was in a coma, Lily. I don't think you dream when you're in a coma, do you, Henry? Could you hear people talking to you, though?" Katie suddenly remembered her conversation with William about people who seemed to be dead, but who were really in comas.

"I don't think I had any dreams. But yesterday afternoon, I think, I did hear my mother talking. It was hard to figure out what she was saying, and I wanted to tell her to talk louder, but I couldn't. It was so strange, like I was stuck behind a wall."

Suddenly, Katie remembered the cookies Sophia had made. "Oh!

I almost forgot these," she said as she handed the tin to Henry. "Sophia made cookies for you. Do you remember her 'Power' cookies?"

"Wow! I love those cookies! I'm not sure if I'm allowed to eat anything yet, though. But thank her for me, will you?"

The girls all stared intently at the cookie tin, so intently that Henry finally untied the ribbon, pulled the lid off and invited everyone to dive in. As they munched the cookies they continued to pelt Henry with questions. Finally, they got to the one everyone wanted to ask. Naturally, Corky led the way.

"So Henry, d'ya know what happened out there...at the ranch? Have they told ya anything at all?"

Henry took a deep breath, and he closed his eyes for a moment. The girls wondered if he was in pain, or if he would cry.

"The police came and talked to me," he began, then hesitated.

It must be awful to think that someone would actually try to hurt you, Katie thought. *I hope it's not painful for him to talk about it.*

Henry shifted uncomfortably in the bed. "They said that someone shot something at the horse, or threw something. You guys probably know more about it than I do. Did you hear anything before it happened?"

"I thought I saw something in the trees, something moving around. I couldn't tell what it was, though, but it looked like something shiny. I don't think I heard anything, but...you know...the screaming." Katie looked at the floor, wishing she knew more.

Her thoughts drifted back again, to the conversation with William and Starr. "Whoever hath done this...to thy friend...*does* deserve to be punished. And the punishment should be severe," William had said. She shivered.

"What is it, Katie? Are you okay?" Lily's voice was loaded with concern, and it startled Katie.

"Oh! Um...yes...yes...I'm fine. I was just thinking...about it...the accident."

Lily and Corky looked at each other, wondering what was going on with Katie.

"Did you not hear anything, then?"

"No...No...I can't believe there was a gun. I didn't hear anything. Wouldn't there be a loud noise? I mean, if someone had a gun, wouldn't everyone hear it?"

"Apparently a BB gun wouldn't make much noise. That's what the police told my parents. But since they didn't find anything but a little mark on the horse, they can't really tell if that's what happened."

"Who would do something like that? It just seems so...so..." Lily struggled for a word that would sum up her feelings of sadness, betrayal and fear.

"So like some of the creeps we go to school with, you're probably thinking."

Everyone looked at Corky. As usual, she was willing to say out loud what others were thinking, even if they were thinking that it couldn't possibly be true.

"What! Isn't that what you're all thinking, then? Think about it. They've been doing nothing but torturing Henry for weeks, acting like street thugs. The thing I just can't get is, what's behind it all."

"My goodness! Are we having a party here?" The nurse had come into the room so quietly that nobody even noticed her until she spoke.

"Were we being loud?" Henry asked.

"No, you're not being loud. But you do need some rest, young man. Your friends can come back tomorrow, and maybe stay a little longer then. But for now, you need to say goodbye." The nurse was straightening the sheets and blankets on Henry's bed, and fussing with the gadgets on the stand next to his bed. She took the cookie tin and set it on a table.

"We'll be back tomorrow, then, Henry. And we'll solve this mystery, okay?" Corky patted Henry on the arm and smiled at the nurse.

"Bye, Henry. Get lots of rest." Lily said.

"Henry, I'm so glad you're feeling better. We'll all be back tomorrow. Do you want us to get anything for you? Books or magazines, or anything? Maybe Sophia will make more treats for you." Katie grasped Henry's hand shyly.

"No, I'm fine, really. But thank Sophia for the cookies, okay? I'll see you tomorrow."

In the hallway outside Henry's room, the girls' parents were talking with Henry's parents.

"Did you girls have a nice visit?" Mrs. Rathbone asked. "It was so sweet of you to visit him. I know he cares a lot about each of you, and is grateful for your friendship."

"He looks just like himself, Mrs. Rathbone, except for the black eyes and the chin and…I mean…I didn't think…oh, man! I can't believe what I've just said…" Corky was blushing and clearly at a loss for words. Her mother hugged her gently.

"It's fine, love," she whispered. "You've never even been to a hospital before. It's all pretty strange I know."

Corky stared at the floor, while the rest of the group said goodbye to Henry's parents.

There was silence in the elevator on the ride down to the lobby. Everyone seemed consumed with their own thoughts of the predicament Henry had found himself in. Katie, Corky and Lily were consumed with why Jordan had been at the hospital. As if by some secret pact, the three of them kept quiet. But they knew as soon as they were alone, they would again discuss why Jordan had been at the hospital.

Burbage's was just a few blocks from the hospital, so the group walked. Katie, Lily and Corky walked ahead of the parents.

"Well, I think it's suspicious," Corky said firmly.

"Corky, Jordan could have a relative like a grandmother or something in the hospital. Don't go jumping to conclusions. That's how rumors start," Lily cautioned.

"Lily, I agree with Corky. I think it's suspicious, too. Don't you think it's a coincidence that Jordan should show up at the same hospital as Henry, and crying like that? She knows something. I can just feel it."

"Well, how do we go about finding out? School's out, so it's not like we're going to run into her or see her to ask her. And she sure is not likely to run into us this summer. I mean you're going up to Hyde Park, and Corky and I are going to visit you there, but we probably won't run into her anywhere else."

"It's a mystery, and we've got to solve it. We need to figure out a way to get her to confess what she knows." Corky began to outline the suspicious behaviors the girls had witnessed recently.

"It started the night of the dance, when Jordan first sat with us and then ran out. Remember how Blondie and her gang were givin' us the evil eye? Then the day at the ranch, Jordan was starin' at us across the field. After the accident, she wasn't with the others, now was she? And now today here she is at the hospital. I'm sure she knows somethin' about all this."

"Corky's right. It does seem suspicious. But how can we get

Jordan to talk to us? Katie , do you think we should just call her?"

"I don't know. If it's true that she knows something, she might be really scared right now."

"What about calling Jordan up and asking her if we could get together and go shopping or something like that?"

"I'm not sure," Corky said. "But I'm thinkin' that maybe she would wonder why we would be callin' her. What would we be shoppin' for, then? School clothes? Shoes? Prom dresses?"

"But, Corky, she was nice to us at the dance. She talked to us a lot. Maybe she's scared and would want to talk to us. Maybe she got dumped by Brittany and the others. Remember how she ran out of the dance? Lily, you and Tyler saw it, remember?"

"Katie's right. She was really upset, Corky. I think something has happened with them."

"Why don't we just call her and ask her to lunch? Tell her we saw her at the hospital. Ask her if she's okay. Maybe she'll tell us what she knows."

"Katie, you always think the best about people, even when they're not deservin'. Are you really thinkin' she'll crack?"

"Corky! She's not on trial! We don't even know if she's done anything." Lily looked at Katie and both girls laughed at their friend's intensity. Corky pretended to be wounded at first, but then joined in the laughter.

"So when should we call her? Do you think she's around still?"

Katie's thoughts drifted back to Starr and William again. *William put himself in other peoples' shoes to figure out how they would react in different situations. That's what we need to do. We need to pretend that we are Jordan.*

"Katie! What's with you today? You keep wandering off." Lily gently poked her friend's shoulder.

"I...maybe we should talk about this...maybe we should do it after lunch." Katie thought for a minute. "No, wait! Wait! What about a sleepover tonight? Could you guys spend the night at my house? I'm sure it would be okay with my parents!" Katie actually had two reasons to want the sleepover. First, she wanted to get to the bottom of the ranch accident, and she thought questioning Jordan would be the key. Second—and this was the one she was really nervous about—she wanted to tell her friends about her trip through time.

By the time they arrived at Burbage's the girls had hatched a plan they were sure would help them solve the mystery of Henry's panicked horse.

During lunch, the parents sat two tables away from where the girls sat. They were close enough to watch, but not close enough to over-hear the girls' conversation.

The girls focused on how they would get Jordan to confide in them, or to "crack," as Corky liked to say.

"I think we have to put ourselves in Jordan's place," Katie said. "I mean, what do you think she's feeling right now? Is she scared? Is she feeling guilty?"

"If she feels guilty...I mean if she actually had something to do with the accident...would she even talk to us about it? You guys talked to her at the dance more than I did. Do you think she trusts us?"

The girls stopped talking when the waitress brought them menus. "Would you like something to drink while you think about lunch?" Katie was stunned by the waitress's appearance. She was dressed like the wait-ress in the restaurant where she went with Starr, William and Edward after the play. *Maria. That was her name, at the place where Edward choked on the bread! What's happening to me?*

Katie looked around the restaurant, trying not to panic. She saw her parents, engrossed in conversation with Lily's mother and Corky's mother. She looked back at Corky and Lily.

"Katie? What do you want to drink? Are you okay?" Lily was sitting across the table from Katie. "Are you sick?"

"No! No...I'm sorry. I was just looking at the costumes on the people who work here...um...I guess I'll have a diet soda, please."

"Do you think we should talk to our parents about the sleepover?" Lily looked over at her mother. "I'm pretty sure it will be okay with my mom."

"I'm thinking my ma would be happy to get me out of the house. She's been cleaning like a mad woman and I keep gettin' in her way."

"Why don't we ask them before we order. Then we can talk about how to talk to Jordan," Katie said, pulling her notebook out of her backpack.

The girls slid out of the booth and walked over to where their par-ents were sitting. Katie kept looking around at the restaurant's décor. The tables were all rough wood, and the floor was some sort of tile that was meant to look like cobblestones. Two walls were decorated with posters depicting scenes from Shakespeare's plays. Another wall had a mural of downtown London in Shakespeare's time.

I wish I knew what is happening to me. Why do I keep running into things that remind me of William and Starr? How am I going to explain this to Lily and Corky?

"Mom, is it okay if we have a sleepover tonight?" Katie leaned into her mother, half-whispering. Charlotte looked at the other girls, whispering to their mothers.

"Is this some kind of conspiracy?" she asked, laughing. "I think it would be wonderful. We'll make pizza for dinner, and you girls can get a movie if you like."

"Charlotte, are you sure this is okay?"

"It's fine. We didn't have any plans for tonight, and it will be fun to have the girls there, won't it honey?"

"Hey, girls, we can figure out what we should do about this zoo thing. Maybe we could write a letter to the editor or something. What do you think?"

"What zoo thing, Mr. Farrell? What kind of letter would we be writing?" Corky sensed that Katie's father was teasing her again.

"Ah, you girls didn't see the newspaper this morning. Henry was right about the zoo. There was a big article about how the zoo has been selling their adult animals to some pretty nasty characters."

"You should see the pictures of some of the monkeys," Katie said. "They were all skinny and sick looking."

"Can you imagine what Brittany's father must be thinking? He's Mr. Riverdale's friend. I bet he's really mad."

"Now, Lily, you don't really think Mr. Morgan was in the dark about all this, do you?" Corky asked, with just a hint of sarcasm.

"Girls," Charlotte said, "you'd better get back to your table. Your waitress is waiting for you. We can talk about all this later, over pizza."

I know Corky and Lily think something's wrong with me and ever since
we left Burbage's, I've been trying to figure out how to explain
this…this—whatever it was—to them. I've got to talk to someone about
it, before I explode. But on the other hand, it's so weird, I'm afraid
they'll think I'm crazy. When I was with William and Starr, I was afraid
people would think I was a witch or something. What if I am? What if
I'm some kind of witch? Would I even know it? Or would I suddenly
turn into something else, something that people would be afraid of or
hate or try to kill! I've heard about people who got possessed, and peo-
ple who can do magic. What if I'm possessed? What if everyone gets
afraid of me?

Chapter 33

Katie was sitting at her desk, lost in frightening thoughts about
what might be happening to her. Corky and Lily had been down the hall
talking to Sophia, and Katie was so engrossed in her journal that she did-
n't hear them come back into the room.

"Katie! Hey! There you go again, wandering off."

Corky's voice broke into Katie's thoughts and in an instant her
fears disappeared from her mind, although they still lived in the pages of
her journal.

"I'm sorry! I'm back!" She closed her journal and snapped the

little lock on it. Her friends looked at her, expecting some grand pro-
nouncement. "It's 6:00. Do you think we should call Jordan now? Mom
said we're going to eat around 6:30 or 7. If we call her now, we'll have
time to figure out what our next step should be, and to write down all the
facts we know."

"Katie, are you okay? I mean, it seems like you've been daydreaming a lot today. Is something bothering you?" Lily was sitting on
the edge of the bed, with a copy of *XC* in her lap.

"No…um…yes…I mean there's something I want to talk to you
both about…but…but I want to wait until later. Really, it's nothing
bad…really."

"Have you suddenly discovered that you're wildly and madly in
love with Henry?"

"Corky!" Katie didn't want to overreact, or to be too mysterious.
She just wasn't ready to talk about her "problem" before dinner. "Of
course not. Henry is my friend, the same as he's your friend and Lily's
friend."

*How am I ever going to explain this? It's so complicated and
scary and…and it makes me even more different. What if they don't want
to be friends after they hear this?*

"Look, let's write down what we want to ask Jordan, then we'll
call her before we have dinner." Katie took her notebook out and sat
with her pen poised above a blank page.

"Let's tell her we saw her wandering around the hospital and ask
her if she got a good look at the trouble she and her creepy friends
caused."

"Um…Corky…maybe we should try a different approach, like
asking her if something happened to someone in her family. Katie, what
do you think?"

"Well, we know she's upset about something. And something else
happened the night of the dance. If she *does* know something about
Henry's accident, she's probably very scared right now, right?"

"She should be scared, don't you think? After what they've
done?"

"But Corky, we don't even know if she had anything to do with it.
I think that if we were really scared about something, we'd be hoping for
someone to help us figure out what to do. Maybe she's afraid to talk to
her parents. Maybe we should act like we know something, and see what

she does." Katie scribbled some questions on the notepad.

"You mean we should try to fool her into telling us something?" Lily asked.

"Well, it's not like we're fooling her. We do know something. I mean, we have evidence. We just don't have all the stuff that makes the evidence stick together."

"But why would the girl tell us anything? She might just blow us off. It's not like that would be at all unusual for her to do." Corky looked over Katie's shoulder to see what she'd written so far.

"Wait a minute. You're really going to ask her if she knows what happened? Do you think she'll crack and just leak all the details out if we just ask her?"

"I don't know, Corky, but first I think we need to ask her if she's upset about something. We should tell her how we saw her at the hospital. We've got to think of something to say to her that will make her feel safe with us, you know, like she can tell us what she knows."

"I wonder if she's talked to Brittany and the others about it. Do you think they've talked about it at all? Do you think they're upset?"

"Lily, I can't believe those people get upset about anything, unless it's a chip in their stupid nail polish." Corky was exasperated. "Our friend was almost killed by their horrid prank. How can we even begin to be polite?"

Katie looked over at Lily. She suddenly felt helpless in the face of Corky's logic. *She's right. He almost died. What would have happened if he did die? But what if Jordan didn't have anything to do with it? Why was she acting so strange at the ranch after the accident? And at the hospital?*

"Corky, if we're going to solve this mystery, then we need to do what Katie says and put ourselves in Jordan's place. We know she's upset and probably pretty scared. I think if we call her and ask her about it, she'll..."

"Crack?" Corky was desperate for a dramatic confession.

"Okay...maybe she'll crack. Are you with us on this? You won't punch her or anything if we try to talk to her, will you?" Lily was nearly going to ask Corky to swear that she'd behave. But she didn't want to defeat her friend. And, truthfully, she believed that Corky's basic mistrust of Jordan and her crowd would be very helpful.

"So...you want to call her and just ask her about the accident, then?"

"I think maybe we should try to get her to meet with us. Maybe she'd agree to have lunch with us, or something. If she's really upset, she might be desperate enough to do it…you know?" Katie had a Manhattan Prep phone directory, and she was looking up Jordan's phone number.

"When? When would we try to meet her?" Lily asked.

"It would have to be soon…do you think tomorrow?" Katie was looking at a calendar on her desk. "We're going to be leaving soon…I think next week…for Hyde Park. We need to do it right away, before she…before something happens…before Brittany and the others get to her."

"Do you think she would meet us tomorrow?" Lily asked.

"Where should we go? She won't be confessing a thing if we're in a big crowd." Corky said.

"What about here? Maybe she could come here. Sophia might be able to make us lunch. We wouldn't have to worry about a public place. Jordan only lives a couple of subway stops from here."

"Do you really think the girl will actually come here…to meet us?"

"Corky, we won't know unless we ask her, will we?" Katie said as she punched Jordan's number into her cell phone.

Lily and Corky stared silently as Katie waited for someone to answer the phone.

"Jordan? Jordan…hi…um…this is Katie …" Suddenly Katie felt tongue-tied and stupid. *What was I thinking? She'll never talk to us…what am I going to say?*

Jordan didn't say anything. "Jordan…um, how are you? I…we…Lily and Corky and I…we saw you at the hospital this morning. Are you okay? You seemed upset." Katie looked helplessly at her friends, and grimaced.

"Katie …yes…yes, I'm fine." Jordan's voice sounded thick and exhausted. Katie's nervousness gave way to pity for Jordan, who had revealed so much insecurity at the dance.

"Jordan, do you think you might be able to come over tomorrow for lunch? With Corky and Lily? We can talk about…we can talk about whatever you want…about summer, or maybe school…whatever…." Katie was rolling her eyes, thinking she sounded really dumb. *She'll never do it...she'll tell her friends what a dork I am...*

"Katie ...um...this is pretty weird. I was actually going to call you. I guess it would be fine...lunch, I mean. You live at the Shelbourne, right?"

"Yes! I think it's just a couple of subway stops..."

Lily and Corky high-fived each other silently, then gave Katie thumbs up.

"What time? What time should I come?"

"Is noon okay with you?" Katie could feel her hands and face beginning to sweat. She was so nervous she could hardly speak.

"Um...noon...fine. I'll see you then."

"Okay. Good. Thanks, Jordan, we'll see you tomorrow."

Katie put her cell phone down and stared at her friends in amazement. "She said yes!" the three of them chanted in unison.

Chapter 34

During dinner, the three girls could hardly contain their excitement about their upcoming lunch with Jordan. They were distracted by what Katie's father was telling them about the Zoo's troubles, though.

"So, what do you think the District Attorney should do about this mess at the Zoo?" he asked the girls.

"I'm thinkin' they should put that creepy Mr. Riverdale in a cage and let everyone watch him pretend to be sick."

"Corky!" Lily was laughing, but trying to sound like she was serious.

"Dad, do you think they'll put Mr. Riverdale in jail?"

"Honey, I don't think he'll get much more than a slap on the wrist. It's the people who actually run the Zoo who will be in real trouble."

"But he's the one who is in charge, isn't he, Mr. Farrell? Why would they pay him that much money if he's not in charge?" Lily was outraged that there could possibly be a way out of the mess for Mr. Riverdale.

"Lily's right, John. Why shouldn't someone who is being paid $100,000 a year to be president of the Zoo's Board of Directors be held accountable? I know that you're right; nobody will go after him. But still it doesn't seem fair, does it?" Charlotte had been enjoying watching the girls struggle with such a complicated issue. They couldn't—or maybe they refused to—let Mr. Riverdale off the hook.

"Well, it will certainly make for interesting reading."

"Do you think Mr. Morgan will be their lawyer? I mean for the Zoo?"

"I don't know, Lily. It seems that he's a friend of Mr. Riverdale, and that's why he went to court with him the day you girls saw him. The Zoo might have somebody different represent them, if any legal action comes out of it."

"Do you think they'll ever find all the animals that got sold? I mean, how can they ever make this right? A lot of the lions probably got killed already, and nobody cared about them. Nobody will ever know that they died." Katie said, sadly. "Mr. Murwata told us that justice can't fix everything that gets broken. Even if they make Mr. Riverdale go to jail, it won't fix what happened to the animals that got killed or starved."

Katie poked her salad with her fork, as her father and the others talked about what could be done to help the animals that had been mistreated.

"Peoples what hurt animals die thousand times," Sophia said. "Is saying in Romania. No crimes can be worst than crimes to hurt little children or animals. Peoples that do…well…they get punished inside and outside. How do you call it? A conscience? It's the most terrible prison in the world."

"Do you really think Mr. Riverdale will be payin' for what he did? He seems like such a creep, I can't believe there's a conscience breathin' inside his miserable skull," Corky said. "Katie's right. They can't bring back all the poor creatures that were killed because of him. Who's lookin' out for their justice?"

Katie's parents looked at the three girls, and ached for the sense of outrage they shared. The adults knew that justice—or at least the settlement that would probably occur—would never satisfy the girls' sorrow for the lost animals.

"You girls need to remember that justice may take a lot of time to unfold. Even if there is some kind of trial, it may not result in what you think would be just." Charlotte's voice was so soft that everyone stopped talking and looked at her.

"Humans try to make events have beginnings and endings, even if they have to pretend that an ending has occurred by declaring that justice has been done. Sophia knows a lot about how governments try to give terrible events endings that people can live with, by holding trials and convicting people of murder or treason or other crimes.

But justice needs time to work its own way through history. In Romania, it didn't bring all the people who were murdered back to life. But it gave some of the people opportunities to change their lives and their futures."

There was silence in the room as everyone absorbed the meaning of what Charlotte had said. Katie's mind wandered back to 1596, and William's struggle to make this elusive concept into a story. *I wonder what William and Starr and Edward would think if they were here now? They would be shocked that more than 400 years later, people still haven't figured it out.*

She was lost in that other century, thinking about all the things she wished she had asked William and Starr. *I wonder if people in 1596 thought that William was brilliant. I wonder if he knew that some people would think he didn't really write his plays…*

"Katie! You're not traveling through time again, are you?" Katie's father was teasing her, but she was embarrassed that she had been daydreaming again.

"Huh? Dad! No, no…I'm right here." She looked at her father, who was smiling at her. She looked at her friends who were staring at her as if she had suddenly sprouted a pair of wings.

"I'm kidding, honey. What are you girls planning for this evening?"

"We're just hanging out…you know…talking and stuff like that." Katie suddenly realized that she had invited Jordan to lunch the next day. "Mom, is it okay if Jordan has lunch with us tomorrow? I mean with Lily and Corky and me?"

Charlotte looked surprised. "Jordan? I thought you girls didn't get along with her. Of course it's fine with me…Sophia, are you okay with another lunch to fix?"

"One more makes no problems for me. I make a nice salad, with the chicken, yes?"

"What's going on, girls? Something special? Are you recruiting another member to your exclusive club?"

"Dad! We don't have a club and you know it!"

"She's right, Mr. Farrell, we're just three para…what's that word, now, Lily? Parasites?"

"Um, I think Mr. Murwata said it was par-eye-something."

"Mr. Murwata said you girls are pariahs?"

"No! No! Mr. Farrell, he was telling us about people who were cast out by their communities because they stood up for the right thing. It was in history," Lily said, gravely.

"Dad!" Katie said it a little too loudly. "Dad, we've got some stuff to work on...um...could we be excused? Please?" She softened her voice considerably and sat primly in her chair waiting to be excused.

"Sure, honey. Um...you girls might want to consider hanging around a little longer for dessert. Sophia made a cake that almost— almost—looks too good to eat!"

The girls looked at each other and then at Sophia.

"I make room service. You go to work on stuffs, and I bring dessert later, yes?"

"Thank you, Sophia!" The girls all cried out as they dashed out of the dining room.

Chapter 35

"Okay, Katie, what's going on with you? One minute you're here, the next you seem to be at the other end of the universe. Are you sure you're not fallin' for Henry?" Corky had flopped onto Katie's bed, and was only half-kidding. But Lily quickly joined Corky's interrogation of their friend.

"She's right, Katie. What's happening? Ever since we met in Henry's room, you've been acting really weird."

"It's…it's something so strange…so…" Katie's thoughts seemed to be scattering in a hundred directions. *What if they think I'm crazy? What if they tell Mom and Dad? Will they still like me? What if I am crazy? What's going to happen to me?*

Corky and Lily looked at each other. Then Corky took the three-some straight to the heart of the matter. "Katie, you're scarin' us. What's going on with you, that's got you all tied in knots?"

Katie looked at them, as if she just realized they were in the room with her. She swallowed, then walked over to her dresser and opened the drawer that contained the evidence of her trip through time. She returned to the chair in front of her desk, holding the small pouch as if there were a live animal inside it. Tuffy had followed them back to the room and he sat at Katie's feet, expectantly.

"C'mon, Katie! What is it?" Lily's voice revealed more anxiety than impatience.

"You've got to swear that what I'm about to tell you will be our secret. You have to promise me you won't tell anyone. Do you promise?"

Lily and Corky looked at each other and nodded. "Yes! We swear!" they said in unison.

"Of course, Katie. If you don't want us to tell anyone, we won't. We're best friends and best friends keep their friends' secrets," Lily said gently.

"Okay." Katie cleared her throat and tried to clear her thoughts. "When was the last time you saw me?"

"What?" Corky asked, confused.

"Before today, when was the last time you saw me?"

"We saw you yesterday, Katie. Don't you remember?" Lily was looking at the pouch. "What's in there?"

"I've been away…only I don't know how long I was away. I know you won't understand. But it's true. I have proof." She waved the pouch at them.

The room was silent for a few seconds. When it was apparent that no one was going to speak, Corky said, "Where were you?"

"I know you're going to have a hard time believing what I'm about to tell you, but it really happened to Tuffy and me. It really did. And I can prove that it did," Katie said breathlessly.

"What are you saying? What happened?"

Lily interrupted. She was afraid impatient Corky would start shaking Katie by the shoulders. "Give her a chance to tell us," Lily said. "Go on, Katie."

"Somehow, I went to sleep last night, but when I woke up, I woke up in 1596 near London," Katie said. After she said it, she looked at her friends' faces, trying to gauge their reactions before continuing. Her friends were silent, and gawking at Katie.

"It was 1596? The year?" Corky said with incredulity.

"London, England?" Lily asked before Katie could speak.

"I know it sounds like I'm crazy, but I'm telling you it happened. I don't know why and I don't know how, but I woke up with Tuffy, lying in a meadow or something," Katie replied realizing, as the words came out of her mouth, how ridiculous she sounded.

"Katie, it was probably a dream," Lily said gently.

"Lily's got a point, Katie. You've got to know how fanciful this sounds. It was a dream, though it seemed as real as everyday life," Corky said.

"I was afraid you wouldn't believe me," Katie said glumly.

"Katie, what made you think you were actually there…in London in 1596, and not just dreaming?" Lily asked.

Katie hesitated. *If they don't believe me about waking up in 1596, they won't believe me about any of this. What should I do? Should I show them my evidence? Should I tell them everything?*

"When I first woke up in the meadow, I had no idea where I was or how I had gotten there. Tuffy and I started walking, but nothing looked familiar and I realized we weren't in New York City. I pulled out my cell phone and tried to call home and nothing happened when I turned the phone on. Absolutely nothing. All of a sudden, Tuffy and I saw a cow."

"A cow?" Corky said.

"Yes, a cow. I figured if there was a cow, there were probably people nearby. Maybe I was near a farm or something, but I still didn't know where I was or how I got there."

"But Katie, I don't doubt what you're telling us. Don't you think it could be a dream? I've had them, and they seem so real. What about you, Corky? You've had dreams like that, right?"

Katie didn't wait for Corky to answer. She felt the words tumbling out faster than she could control them. "After walking for what seemed like forever, Tuffy and I finally came to an old stone tavern."

"Wait a minute," Corky interrupted. "What happened to the cow?"

"Oh, we found a house with a lady and a little girl and it was their cow and the cow had run away, so I gave it back," Katie explained. "They were very unfriendly and told me to get out, though I must admit, I had a hard time understanding them," Katie said. "The whole thing was so odd, I figured that I had wandered onto a movie set, so I was sort of relieved and we kept walking, still thinking we were in Central Park."

Katie stopped, trying to recall exactly what had happened next. She remembered walking and walking until she had come upon the tavern. "That's when we found the tavern and met Starr," she said.

Lily and Corky sat utterly still. They looked at each other and mouthed the name. "Starr?" Neither knew what to think.

"It turned out that Starr owned the tavern and her husband had died, so she was running it alone. You know what was really weird?" Katie asked.

"You mean weirder than finding a cow?" Corky said.

"Starr looked exactly like Sylvie Campion, my mother's agent. I realized something was wrong when I saw Starr's kitchen and there was no sink or refrigerator, and when Starr had no idea what a bathroom was, I knew we were in trouble."

"Katie, I still don't know why you think this is anything but a dream," Lily said.

"Well, I haven't told you the best part yet," Katie replied.

"You mean, there's more?" Corky said.

"I was in the bedroom Starr had offered me so I could take a nap and I heard voices downstairs, so Tuffy and I went downstairs and that's when Starr introduced me to him," Katie said, thinking carefully about what she was about to reveal.

"Him? Him who?" Corky said, almost afraid of what she was about to hear.

"William Shakespeare," Katie said looking first at Lily's face, and then at Corky's to gauge how plausible it seemed to them.

"William Shakespeare," whispered Lily in a monotone.

"*The* William Shakespeare? The 'Romeo and Juliet' Shakespeare? You're kidding!" Corky said, in disbelief.

"You don't believe me, do you? I thought you, at least, would listen to the story and...I don't know...believe me." Katie was so frustrated. The two best friends she had in the world thought she had just been dreaming.

"Katie, please don't get upset. It's not that we don't believe you, but the story is a little fantastic. I...I just don't know what to think," Lily finished lamely.

"Well, I suppose it could happen," Corky said, slowly. "You know...parallel universes and all that kind of stuff. Maybe it did happen."

"It did! I'm telling you it did," Katie insisted. "And, I can prove it." She opened the pouch carefully and slid the scrap of fabric out.

Lily and Corky just stared at the dirty, disintegrating ribbon.

"Starr tied this on Tuffy's collar to disguise it when we went to London. Because dogs didn't wear collars and tags in those days. Oh, I forgot to tell you the part about William and Starr worrying that word would get around the little town where Starr's tavern was located that I was a witch. So they decided I'd be safer in the city, so we all went to the theatre where William was an actor and playwright and Starr, Tuffy and I stayed in an apartment in the back of the theatre. We went to see one of the performances—even Tuffy went!—and after the play, we went to dinner in a local tavern, and I saved Edward's life when he choked on a piece of bread." Katie stopped talking to take a breath.

Lily and Corky now appeared totally engrossed in the story, so Katie kept going. "When I woke up this morning, I thought I had been dreaming, too, but then I saw this piece of ribbon and I knew it wasn't a dream. It really happened to me," Katie paused.

"What did you talk to Mr. Shakespeare about?" Corky asked.

"Well, I told him that my mother was an actress and he was surprised about that."

"Why?" Corky asked.

"Because in 1596, women weren't allowed on the stage," Katie answered.

"Then who played the women's parts in his plays?" Corky asked.

Before Katie could answer, Lily gasped.

"Oh my gosh, that's right!" she cried. "Don't you remember? We learned that in Shakespeare's time, the men played the women's parts," Lily finished breathlessly.

"That's exactly what he said! But the most fantastic thing was that, while I was with him, he was just beginning to write 'The Merchant of Venice.' That's the show my father is directing this summer in Hyde Park. When I told William that, he flipped.

He had no idea that he had been famous all these years. In fact, he didn't even call the play 'The Merchant of Venice.' He called it 'The Venetian Comedy,' and I told him things my dad had told me about what people think about the play, and about mercy and justice.

Remember when we talked about that in Mr. Murwata's class? William seemed real interested in my ideas and I told him about the things that had been happening to Henry." Katie stopped talking. Her throat was dry and she realized that she had gotten so caught up in the story that she hadn't been paying attention to her friends' reactions.

"Katie, how did you explain where you came from to Mr. Shakespeare and Starr? Did they believe you?" Lily asked.

"I showed them my bottled water, my cell phone, and a copy of *XC*. They couldn't get over the magazine. William thought the people were going to step off the page," Katie said.

Then she started giggling. "But the funniest thing was showing them bubble gum. They couldn't get over that," and as the three friends laughed about how strange it would seem for people in 1596 to have chewing gum, Katie gently pulled the scrap of paper out of the pouch. No one moved. No one reached out to touch it. The girls could see the scratchy handwriting. They all looked at the paper and then at each other.

"It's his, isn't it?" Lily breathed.

"This is Shakespeare's handwriting?" Corky asked.

"That night, after dinner, William was in the kitchen working on his play and Edward and Starr were peeling vegetables to make soup. He was having a problem with a scene and he started over. I guess when I scooped up the stuff from my backpack, I must have picked up one of his papers," Katie explained.

"Who's Edward?" Corky asked.

"Edward was a young apprentice at the theatre. I think he liked me," Katie said. "He told me I was beautiful. Isn't that incredible?"

"No. You *are* beautiful," Lily said without hesitation.

"Yeah, but I don't look like Mackenzie or Jordan, and he still thought I was beautiful. It was weird. But actually, that part was kind of fun. Oh, I missed everyone and I was more than a little scared, but it was kind of cool to have a cute guy like me, and think that I could make miracles happen," Katie said.

"If this is a page from one of Shakespeare's plays, it's probably worth a small fortune, Katie," Corky said, ever the practical one.

"Doesn't matter, does it, because no one will ever believe my story and I don't intend telling anyone but the two of you. You swore you wouldn't tell anyone," Katie said.

"But we want to know more! What kind of food did you eat? How cute was this Edward guy?" Lily asked.

"He was really cute, but very sad, too. His father was very mean and beat his mother, but then he died. Edward didn't go to school, because he was too poor. In fact, they were all surprised that I was in school, and that I could read and write!"

"How come? Why would that be such a surprise? How did

Edward get out of going to school?" Corky was perplexed.

"Not everyone was allowed to go to school, especially girls. I didn't get to talk to them much about that, but I don't think I would want to be growing up in London in 1596. It just seemed that everything was too hard. There were no bathrooms, and it didn't seem like people took many baths. The lights were all lanterns and candles, and everybody just threw their trash in the street. It didn't smell very good."

"But did Edward kiss you? Or hold your hand? Do you think he could follow you back here?" The girls all laughed at Corky's idea about Edward following Katie through history.

"We didn't kiss. He was very shy and very proper. But...but...he kept looking at me—staring at me. I thought that must be what it felt like to be one of the cool girls."

Corky and Lily sighed.

"What do you think? Do you believe me? That Tuffy and I traveled back in time?" Katie looked at her friends, pleading for them to believe her story.

"Yes...yes. I believe you," Lily said softly.

Corky was silent. Lily and Katie looked at her. She looked at Tuffy, and the fabric that had disguised him in a city thousands of miles away, hundreds of years in the past. "But what does it mean? Why? Why did it happen? How did it happen?"

"I...I don't know. The whole time, I was afraid that something had happened to everyone, and we were all spinning through space in the wrong centuries. But that isn't what happened. It was only me."

"How did you do it? Did you wish for it? Did you get into a trance or something that made you find a way back in time?"

"I...I don't know, Corky. I just remember writing in my journal that I wanted to go back to the time before Henry was hurt, before things got so horrible and confused. And I wanted to wake up and find that Henry was alive and okay."

"So, you think it might have been a wish? But you wound up in a time that was hundreds of years before Henry got hurt!"

"And you got your other wish, too—that you'd wake up and Henry would be all right," Lily added, triumphantly.

"But how did it happen? Do you really think time travel is possible? I mean, I couldn't be the first person ever to do it! Right?" Katie looked into her friends' faces and found quizzical stares back at her.

"Right?" she said loudly.

"I can't believe you'd be the first—I mean, think about how long the world has been going on. Surely if it's possible someone else has done it too," Corky said.

"Katie! Have you tried to find out if time travel is even possible? Can we look it up somewhere?" Lily looked over at Katie's computer. "Let's check the Internet! If there's anything about time travel, it would be there, wouldn't it?"

They all leapt at the computer and waited while Katie turned it on and logged on to the Internet.

"What do we look for?" she asked.

"Just say 'time travel,' and see what comes up," Corky suggested.

As Katie tapped the words onto the screen, the girls waited impatiently for the search engine to find something exciting.

"What's taking so long?" Corky asked as she watched the little icon spin, indicating that a search was in progress.

"It hasn't been that long—less than a minute, Corky. Be patient," Lily said, tapping Corky's shoulder.

"Look!" Katie was pointing at the screen. "There's a website!"

"Click it! Click it!" Corky and Lily whispered.

Katie clicked the link to the website, and waited. The icon spun around and around, as www.timeandtimeagainandagain.com loaded. The girls stared at the screen as stories of time travel—and all the people who had attempted it—came up. There were graphics and links to other sites. They were immersed in the website when Sophia arrived with dessert.

"I bring room service to busy girls," Sophia called as she pushed the door open with her foot. She set the tray down on the edge of Katie's desk and handed each of the girls a plate. She looked at the picture of the melting clock that was on Katie's computer screen. "What for a clock is this? In museum I saw once a clock like this in a famous painting." She moved closer to the screen and tried to understand the strange words. "Timeandtimea...what for a name is this, Ekaterina?"

"It's just a weird website, Sophia. Don't worry—it's not bad stuff."

"Wow! Sophia, this cake is wonderful!" Lily said. Sophia turned away from the computer screen and patted Lily on the shoulder.

"Just plain scrumptious!" Corky said.

Everyone thanked Sophia with hugs and promised to bring all the dishes to the kitchen once they were finished. As she left the room, she acknowledged their thanks and warned them to behave. "You girls must be careful on Internet—is full of bad peoples who lure girls into trouble."

"Sophia, we're not doing any of that. I promise." Katie hugged Sophia, who still seemed a bit suspicious. "I promise!" Katie said emphatically.

As Sophia left the room, Katie scrolled down the list of hyper-links on the website. Lily and Corky watched silently.

"It's possible! It really is possible and Tuffy and I did it!"

The girls talked about time travel and the strange website until they were so sleepy they could barely speak. They managed to take the dessert plates into the kitchen and rinse them before dragging themselves into the living room to say goodnight to Katie's parents.

Corky and Lily stopped at the door of the guest bedroom adjoining Katie's room.

"We didn't even get a chance to plan what we're going to say to Jordan tomorrow," Lily whispered.

"After breakfast, we'll work it out," Katie said. "Remember. Don't time travel away from here tonight—we all have to be together to solve Henry's mystery tomorrow."

I don't know what I would have done if Lily and Corky didn't finally believe me about the time travel. That website we found was so strange, too! I wonder if I would have believed Lily or Corky if they had come up with a story like mine. The evidence Tuffy and I have convinced them both. I wonder if it is possible to time travel deliberately. Oh, well! I'm so sleepy, and tomorrow we're going to get some answers from Jordan. Maybe Corky is right. Maybe we can make her crack and tell us every-thing she knows...I'm just glad I'm back!

Chapter 36

"I need your help."

Jordan had arrived for lunch a few minutes early, but Corky, Lily and Katie had already spent a couple of hours planning what they'd say. Unfortunately, they hadn't planned on Jordan's plea for help. The four girls had barely sat down at the table in the kitchen when Jordan got right down to business.

"Help? What d'ya mean you need our help?" Corky asked.

"I need your help...because...I...I..." Jordan seemed exhausted. She looked down at her hands and began fidgeting with her bracelet. Katie remembered seeing the bracelet the night of the dance, and Jordan talking about how it had belonged to her grandmother.

"Why? Why do ya need us to help you?" Corky asked, somewhat belligerently. Lily shot Corky a look as if to say "cool it" and Corky retreated into silence. Jordan was quiet for a few more seconds before meeting their eyes. Katie could see that Jordan was frightened. Jordan seemed on the verge of tears.

"I...I know who did...who made the horse..." Jordan was practically in tears. She was twisting the bracelet further and further up her arm until it couldn't move any higher. "I know what happened to Henry's horse...who...did...it."

There was dead silence around the table. Corky, Lily and Katie looked at each other. When they had practiced their interrogation of Jordan, it never went like this. In their rehearsals, they took turns demanding information from Jordan. They were aggressive and combative.

Jordan sighed as if she were finally free of some terrible burden. She sat back in her chair and closed her eyes. And then she cried.

I'm glad everyone left us alone, Katie thought. Sophia had left a plate of sandwiches and a pitcher of lemonade in the kitchen for the girls and Katie had closed the kitchen door when Sophia left. She could hear her parents talking in the den, and Sophia had gone to the market. *I wish I knew what to do now. Should we call the police? Or should we make Jordan call them?*

"Jordan, how do you know? What do you know?" Katie asked as she handed Jordan a napkin.

"It was...oh, God! I can't believe they nearly killed him!" Jordan was now sobbing.

Katie, Lily and Corky fumbled with their own emotions. Finally Katie and Lily reached out and gently hugged Jordan, trying to get her to calm down. Corky glared across the table at Jordan.

When she finally stopped crying and looked up, her eyes met Corky's. "So, did you play a part in this prank? Or had you given up the torture of Henry before we went to the ranch?" Corky wasn't shouting, but her words were like stones pelting Jordan.

"I didn't have anything to do with what happened at the ranch, and I know you won't believe this, but it's true. I've been having a lot of trouble living with some of the things they say and do." She looked at Katie. "When we were in the study group, I...I started to understand...to think about a lot of things..."

"So what did happen, Jordan? Who hurt Henry?" Katie remembered some of the questions from the script they had prepared so carefully. She could feel her heart beating faster.

Jordan looked around the room. She took a sip of her lemonade and swallowed hard. "It was these boys. They worked in the barn, you know, cleaning up after the horses, feeding them and stuff like that. Brittany and Mackenzie decided that we should have some fun with them by flirting with them. They were sort of cute, and one of them was really nice, but I didn't want to be part of what they were doing."

"But why did they hurt Henry?" Lily whispered.

"Brit and Mackenzie had them all excited, thinking they would be out behind the barn making out once the trail ride left. Then Brit saw you guys getting ready to ride. She told the one guy, I think his name was Ron, that you were all...um..." Jordan hesitated and looked around, embarrassed.

"Dorks?" Corky said, sarcastically. "Or maybe nerds?"

"She was furious with Henry after the day we went to court. She said that he deliberately tried to make her father look bad."

"But what about all the things that you guys did to him before that?" Lily asked.

Jordan looked down at her hands. She started twisting her bracelet again, nervously. "I guess I don't really know why he got picked on. Or why I was...why I didn't stop them. It's...you probably don't understand what it's like. I wanted them to like me, to be my friends. I..."

"You can't be serious! What kind of friend would ask you to hurt someone that way?" Corky said, interrupting Jordan.

"Look, we're getting off the track. Jordan, what happened after Brittany pointed Henry out to the guy from the barn?" Katie had actually written a couple of new questions down, and was prepared to write Jordan's responses on her tablet.

"The barn guys were trying to impress Brittany—and she was telling them all about the bikini she was planning to wear later. You could see them just...just trying so hard to make her like them. Mackenzie was playing along with Brittany, telling the guys that she thought she had forgotten the top to her bikini."

Katie, Lily and Corky looked at each other, shocked.

"Then what?" Lily whispered.

"The one named Ron said he could play a really funny trick on

Henry. Brittany and Mackenzie asked how funny, and he asked them if they had ever seen a bucking horse."

"But didn't they worry that someone could really get hurt?" Katie asked.

"They said they wanted to embarrass Henry in front of you guys, and Ron said he could make something really embarrassing happen to Henry. I think Brittany and Mackenzie probably thought the horse would throw Henry into a mud puddle or something. I'm sure they never imagined what might happen. Brittany doesn't think ahead. She just wants things to happen—good things and bad things."

"So what did you do? Didn't you worry about what might happen?" Corky asked.

"Yes…yes, I worried. I made up my mind that I wasn't going to stick around with them at the ranch. They called me a chicken, and said that I was obviously not fit to run with the cool kids. The other guy, I think his name was Luke or something, he was pretty angry and didn't want any part of what they were planning. He said that he had broken his arm once when a horse bucked him off, and he thought that it was a bad idea to try to get one of the horses to do that. Ron yelled at him, though, and he left. That's when I left, too."

"Jordan, have you told anyone else about this? Have you talked to Brittany and Mackenzie since Henry got hurt?"

"Katie, I…I didn't know what to do. I know they hate me now, and I guess I'm not really feeling too good about them either. But…I…"

"You what? Jordan, don't ya see that if you say nothing you're no better than they are?" Corky's voice was no longer sarcastic.

"Jordan, are you afraid of them? Of what they'll do to you?" Lily asked.

"I…I can't believe they'd hurt me. But the night of the dance, Brittany got mad at me for talking to you guys. She thought I was going to snitch about what they had done to Henry that day—with the locker. Because I told them they had crossed the line and it wasn't a game anymore."

"Did you see them trap Henry in his locker?" Katie asked, astonished.

"No. They told me they were going to 'get' him, but they didn't say what they were going to do. I went to class, because I wanted to look up something in my notes before Mr. Murwata's class. I didn't find out until later what they had done."

The four girls were silent for a few minutes, each of them assessing the situation.

Katie finally spoke up. "Jordan, what are you going to do now? You know that you can't just keep quiet about it. Henry was almost killed."

"I know…I know…but what should I do? If I go to the police, they might not believe me—what if Brittany gets her father to take me to court or something?"

The girls thought about this for a minute.

"Jordan," Lily said. "What if we got the other guy at the ranch to talk to the police, too?"

"Wait! Maybe he's as upset as Jordan. Why don't we call the ranch and ask to speak to him—maybe we can get him to agree to talk to the cowboys or whoever is in charge at the ranch!" Katie was thrilled that they had figured out a way to solve the mystery. She went over to the small desk where the phone was, and started looking through a stack of papers.

"What are you looking for?" Lily asked.

"That folder we got about the ranch, remember? We were supposed to give it to our parents before we left for the class trip. Here it is!"

She brought the phone and the brochure over to the table, and they talked about how they would approach the barn guy.

"You're sure his name is Luke?" Corky asked.

"Yes…yes. I'm positive. I remember thinking that I had never met anyone named Luke—you know, it's sort of a different name."

"Okay, so we call the ranch and ask to speak to him, then Jordan takes over, right?" Corky said. "Then what? What does she say to him?"

"I think she needs to ask him if he knows what happened, and if he can help us get to the bottom of it." Lily said.

"But what if he won't talk to us? What if he's afraid, and clams up? Maybe that other guy will scare him," Jordan suggested.

"Jordan, you've got to make him talk to you—he's a kid, like us. If he didn't want to be part of what they were planning, he's probably feeling the way you are, don't you think?" Katie asked.

"All right. I'll try it. Let's call him."

Katie waited while the phone rang. When someone picked up at the ranch, she handed the phone to Jordan and nodded at her.

"Um…hello. Um…is Luke there?" She looked at Katie, and mouthed the word "yes."

"Um, Luke? This is Jordan…maybe you don't remember me, from the class trip last week? I was with the two girls who were talking to your friend, what's his name, Ron?" Suddenly Jordan's voice changed from soft and confident to nervous and excited. "Wait! Wait! Luke, I know you didn't do anything! Please! Don't hang up! Yes, yes, I know."

Katie, Lily and Corky sat forward, trying to figure out what the barn guy was saying to get Jordan so excited.

"Yes, you're right. Luke, I'll back you up, I promise. You've got to do this, okay?" Jordan's voice was now soothing. Finally she hung up.

"What?"

"What did he say?"

"What does he know?"

"He said that Ron isn't there anymore. He left the afternoon of the accident. But Luke found some stuff in the bunk room—stuff that belonged to Ron. He found a BB gun!"

"What did he do with it? Did he tell anyone?" Corky asked.

"He said that he didn't do anything wrong, but he knew that Ron had tried to impress Brittany and Mackenzie, and he did something really stupid."

"But *did he tell anyone*?" Corky was insisting on an answer, and it was clear that she would not relent until she had it.

Jordan looked at Corky. "No. He didn't tell anyone. He's scared. He said that Ron was not evil, but he was a little scared of him. He said he was going to go to the police."

"Jordan, you have to talk to the police, too. You know it's the right thing to do," Katie said.

"I…I know. I guess I was really glad you called, because I had to tell someone, but didn't know…you know. I actually opened Henry's door and looked in. I wanted to go in and tell him that I've been praying for him every day. But…"

"Jordan, you're going to do it, aren't you? Call the police?" Lily asked.

"I'm just so scared. What if they arrest me? What will I do?"

Jordan looked as if she were going to cry again. Katie reached out and took Jordan's hand. "I can ask my parents to call the police, or call your parents. We can do this together."

Jordan had begun twisting her bracelet again, and seemed to be trying to see how far up her arm she could force it.

"Jordan, don't you want to get this thing off your conscience? You're suffering from it and you need to come clean," Corky said, her voice suddenly soft and encouraging.

"Your parents…they'll hate me."

"No! No, they understand…honest. They'll help you." Katie was on the verge of standing up to go get her parents. But she didn't want to make Jordan more frightened. The room grew silent for what seemed like an hour. Finally, Jordan spoke.

"I can't stand to be afraid of this any more. I want to get rid of it. Are you sure your parents won't be mad?"

"I'll get them," Katie said, and left the room. Corky, Lily and Jordan sat in silence waiting for the next chapter in this strange drama to unfold.

Chapter 37

"Hi, Jordan. How are you, honey? Katie said you've got something on your mind." Charlotte pulled a chair up next to Jordan as she spoke. "Honey, would you like us to call your parents? Or the police? Or both?"

Jordan looked at Charlotte, then at Katie's father, then back again. She closed her eyes and leaned back. She took a deep breath. "What's going to happen to me?"

"Jordan, if you didn't do anything...if you knew they were planning some sort of prank...you're not guilty of anything but silence. Nobody could have predicted what happened to Henry. For all you knew, nobody would get hurt." Charlotte was trying to be supportive, without excusing Jordan of responsibility. "I think we should call your parents, and maybe together we can work this out. What do you think, honey?"

Jordan bit her lip. Tears rolled down her face and she wiped them with the back of her hand. "My mother is going to kill me. She was furious when she came home from that meeting at school with Mr. Needham. She said that if she even thought that I was involved, she would be very disappointed in me. I'm...I'm just so...sorry."

"I think Henry would like to hear that from you, don't you?" Charlotte said, hugging Jordan gently. She looked at Katie as if she were waiting for a response from her daughter instead of Jordan.

"Um…" Katie said, looking at Corky and Lily, "maybe we can go to see Henry with you, that is, if you want…um…okay?"

Jordan looked at Katie, then at Lily and Corky. "You would do that? Why?"

"Jordan, I…we…we care about Henry, and what happened to him. I guess we…maybe we can understand how bad you feel, I mean, because you didn't really have anything to do with what happened to him." Katie wasn't sure if Corky and Lily agreed with her, but she felt that she wanted to give Jordan a chance.

"I'll call your mother, okay?" Charlotte said.

Jordan looked helpless and defeated, not like one of the cool kids at all. The reality of this was not lost on Katie, who noticed that Jordan seemed so real and in such pain. It would have been impossible for her to not reach out to her.

While Charlotte called Jordan's mother, the girls sat around the table in silence. They listened to Charlotte explaining what had happened, and encouraging Jordan's mother to stay calm. Katie's father left the room, muttering something that sounded like "what were these punks thinking?"

"Yes, of course I understand why you're angry." Charlotte was saying into the phone. "But I do think Jordan has learned something. Um…yes. Yes, that's right. They called the boy and he's as frightened as Jordan. Okay, sure, we'll be here. See you then."

"Your mom is coming right over, Jordan."

"She's really mad, isn't she?" Jordan said, starting to cry again.

"Honey, she's upset, just as you're upset. But she's going to help you get through this, okay?"

Jordan's mother arrived within a half hour. She sat down next to Jordan, and put her arm around her daughter's shoulders. "Honey, I'm glad you walked away and didn't play a part in what those kids did to Henry. But…but why didn't you talk to someone about it before this? Why didn't you report those kids to someone before they did anything so…so unthinkable?"

Jordan started crying again, and Charlotte motioned for Corky, Lily and Katie to leave the kitchen so Jordan and her mother could be alone.

"What made you girls invite Jordan to lunch today?" John asked, once the girls had flopped on the living room sofa.

"We were conducting an investigation of her suspicious behavior, Mr. Farrell." Corky said. "We spotted her at the hospital yesterday, all weepy, runnin' out like she had done something really bad."

"You thought she had done something because you saw her at the hospital?" John asked. "I'm trying to understand how you made the connection between Jordan and Henry's accident. That's a pretty big leap, don't you think?"

"No, Dad. We had lots of evidence. We knew they hated Henry, and suspected they were the ones who had been doing mean things to him. Then something happened at the Dance—Brittany and Mackenzie said something to her that scared her. Then the day we went to the ranch, we saw her looking really miserable, like she wanted to get away from them."

"Did you guys ever think about becoming investigative reporters? I mean, you seem to have the instinct…" He was interrupted by Jordan and her mother, who came into the living room.

"We're going home now, and my parents are going to call the police," Jordan said. Her eyes were really red, and her face was splotchy. "Thank you for helping me," she said, beginning to cry again.

Jordan stood there, staring at the floor while her mother spoke briefly to Katie's parents. Katie mumbled something about hoping things worked out okay. It was a very somber end to what the girls thought would be a triumph.

What a curious day! Lily, Corky and I thought we were going to solve a big mystery. We were sure Jordan had something to do with the accident. But it turns out that she's just a sad, lonely person. I feel sorry for her, but Corky is still pretty mad about all the stuff she did before, when she was trying to be one of the cool kids. I wonder what the police will say to her. I wonder if someone will get arrested for what happened to Henry.

Chapter 38

"Quiet everyone, please. Nothing will get accomplished if we don't proceed in an orderly fashion." Giles Needham was sweating. He was looking at a lot of angry parents, who had come for a briefing about the accident that had nearly killed Henry Rathbone. Katie, Corky and Lily were there with their parents, and they spotted several of their classmates.

The crowd spilled out into the hallway. Katie looked around to see if Mackenzie or Brittany were there. She had heard that both girls and their families were out of town, but she thought that was just a rumor.

"Katie, there's Jordan!" Lily whispered. She had spotted Jordan and her parents in the back of the room. As Katie and Corky turned, Jordan saw them and seemed momentarily confused. She didn't wave.

She had a strange expression on her face, as if she wasn't sure whether to smile or not. After a few seconds, she looked down.

"She seems pretty upset," Katie whispered. "I wonder if she got in big trouble."

"Please, people! We can wrap this up in just a couple of minutes..." Mr. Needham's voice, coming through the speakers along the sides and back of the room, sounded whiny and frustrated. The insistent grumbling noises from 30 or 40 different conversations going on throughout the room and in the hallway finally gave way to silence.

"Thank you," Mr. Needham said as he wiped his forehead. He nodded at Mr. Murwata, who was standing with him in the front of the room. "Ladies and gentlemen, please quiet down so we can give you all the details as we now know them," he implored.

The room was hot and thick with tension. Although many of the students and parents had already left town for summer vacation, there was a pretty large crowd on hand to hear the latest news about Henry and the accident that nearly killed him.

The crowd began to settle down. Chairs scraped the floor as people adjusted their seats so they could see the podium. All eyes were trained to the front of the room.

"The other day one of our students came forward with information regarding Henry's accident," he said gravely. No one moved.

"Apparently, a young man—an employee of the ranch—attempting to impress a couple of our students, fired a BB gun at Henry's horse, leading the horse to panic and run away with Henry." Mr. Needham fumbled with some papers as the room started getting noisy again. "Please, people. Only another minute or two! The young man who fired the gun ran away from the ranch after he saw what happened. He has since been found, and the police are questioning him."

"Who was the delinquent trying to impress?" one of the parents shouted from the back of the room. His question riled up the audience and parents turned in their seats to talk to their neighbors. Soon the recently silent room erupted into a verbal free-for-all.

"Please, ladies and gentlemen," Mr. Needham pleaded. "Please quiet down so we can discuss this calmly. Mr. Murwata and I will try and answer any questions you might have, but please ask them in an orderly fashion."

"So answer my question," the man who asked the original question repeated. "Who was the hooligan trying to impress? More to the point, does this incident have anything to do with the bullying that had gone on here at the school?"

Mr. Needham wiped his face again and looked over at Mr. and Mrs. Rathbone. He looked at the papers in his hand, closed his eyes for a moment and then continued.

"Unfortunately...uh...regrettably...yes, this incident was related to what had happened here at the school in the days leading up to the Spring Dance. As many of you know, we addressed that situation, but at the time, we didn't know which students were directly involved. Now...now...we...uh...we know a lot more."

"What's going to happen to the students who were involved? Are you expelling them?"

"Yeah, who were they? Are you letting them come back here?"

The questions were coming at Mr. Needham in an angry torrent. He knew that this audience would not be happy with his answers—or the way the school had decided to handle the situation with the students. *If only they knew about Mr. Morgan's threats. He could shut down this school! I can't say anything, I can't do anything to his daughter. I can't satisfy these people, either. They'll never accept a compromise, but that's all I have to offer.*

"We're doing everything we can...everything we're allowed to do...by law...to discipline the students who were involved. You must understand, though, that we cannot discuss particulars, such as who they are." He looked over at Mr. Murwata, silently pleading for a rescue, as the angry voices in the room rose again demanding action.

"This has been a most difficult situation," Mr. Murwata had stepped up to the podium as Mr. Needham mopped his red face. While Mr. Needham appeared to be beside himself with the controversy, Mr. Murwata seemed calm. He held up his hands as if to quiet the crowd. It didn't work. The comments and accusations intensified.

Manhattan Prep parents, usually pillars of the community, had recognized how easily it could have been one of their children instead of Henry. The realization that all their social standing and wealth could not, in the end, protect their children, angered them, and they turned their anger on the representatives of the school.

"A great injustice was done to Henry Rathbone," Mr. Murwata said loudly, trying to make himself heard over the angry din. "We are trying to cope with that, and with what it means to our students and our school. Mr. Needham and I have struggled with this knowledge since the police called us. How could one of our Manhattan Prep students have allowed someone to put another student's life in danger?"

"You lost control of the class and you're talking about a great injustice?" one of the parents shouted incredulously.

"What are you teaching our kids?" someone else shouted from the back of the room.

"Yeah! What are you teaching our kids? To be thugs and bullies?"

Katie couldn't believe that people would attack Mr. Murwata and Mr. Needham. *It's so unfair! It wasn't their fault. I wish they could see that the school is good and that we're not learning to be bullies.* She thought about what William had said about revenge. And how she tried to explain some of the lessons Mr. Murwata had tried to teach about justice balanced with mercy.

When they were talking, she couldn't have imagined that she would actually be in a position to see how powerful the urge to take revenge could be. *This is exactly what Mr. Murwata was trying to teach us!* She thought. *I have to tell them!*

"I learned something at this school," Katie said, in a soft voice. She stood up and looked at her parents and her friends. Her voice got stronger. "I learned about justice…and something else. I learned about mercy…which…which is the only way to make justice work…I was angry, too, about what happened to Henry. But how will it help if we just hurt someone else?"

The room grew quiet. "In a Shakespeare play they talk about mercy, too. They said that the quality of mercy isn't strained, it drops out of heaven onto us…" She hesitated, wishing she had memorized the lines, and fearing she was going to make a mistake.

"The quality of mercy isn't strange—strained," she began again.
"What's that?"
"Shhh!"
"What's she saying?" People whispered and shushed each other, straining to hear what Katie was saying.

"It falls like rain from heaven and is…" Katie looked at her father, her mind a blank. *What are the next words? I can't believe I didn't memorize this!* She thought, feeling a sudden panic.

"Twice blessed." Her father said, gently. He remained seated, but took her hand and said the words with her. "It is twice blessed. It blesses him that gives and him that takes."

It seemed that a spell had been broken. Katie, suddenly embarrassed by all the attention, sat down next to her parents and leaned into her father's arm.

Henry's mother, Mrs. Rathbone stood up. "Katie is right…she's so right," she began, tears rolling down her cheeks. Her husband handed her a handkerchief and she dabbed at her face. "Nothing can change what happened to Henry. Thank heavens he's going to be okay, but trust that the young person who did this will be punished. And, he'll have to live with the knowledge of what he did for the rest of his life. Have mercy on his poor soul," she said, her voice breaking into a sob. She sat down and her husband embraced her and kissed her cheek.

In the silence that followed, it seemed that nobody knew quite what to say. Mr. Needham and Mr. Murwata looked at each other and finally Mr. Needham stepped forward.

"Please rest assured that we understand there are many conflicting feelings about this incident. We are grateful that Henry is nearly fully recovered from the physical injuries he suffered. We know we have work to do to ensure that all our students recognize that respect for one another is paramount. We asked you to come today so that you could hear an update on this situation. We shall keep you posted via e-mail and regular mail throughout the summer. And we look forward to welcoming our students back to Manhattan Prep this fall."

While Mr. Needham was speaking, Lily and Corky had been tugging at Katie's sleeve, anxious to be able to talk to her. Finally, the meeting was breaking up and several parents stopped to tell her what a wonderful thing she had done. Lily and Corky were giggling, practically uncontrollably.

"Katie, you said the words!" Lily whispered.

"I can't believe you used his words!" Corky whispered.

While the three girls stood in a small circle, giggling as if they were plotting something, Katie's parents looked on in stunned—but very proud—silence.

Lily's parents and Corky's mother gushed about Katie's maturity and eloquence and presence.

"I think she's destined to be an actress like you, Charlotte!"

Corky's mother said.

"Or an attorney or a politician," Lily's mother said.

Mr. Murwata patted Katie on the back. "That was a wonderful speech, Katie. It seems you've really grasped a concept many adults find too difficult to comprehend."

In this strange situation, where the formalities of student-teacher relationships are suspended for summer vacation, Corky decided it was time to put their teacher on the spot. "So, Mr. Murwata, was justice done?"

He looked at her with a mock frown. "I have great hope that it shall be," he said, and then laughed.

Mr. Murwata moved on to where Katie's parents were standing.

"Katie, what if your father asks you where you learned those words?" Lily asked.

"You know he'll be askin' you. Will you say you've sat with Shakespeare and he said those very words to you, now?"

"I...I don't know! What do you guys think? We *did* talk about all this in class, so that would be true. And...and maybe I started reading the play when Dad said he was going to direct it this summer!"

"Whatever you're plannin', you'd better be quick. Your parents are coming this way now." Corky said in a not-very-quiet stage whisper.

"Sweetheart, that was wonderful!" Katie's mother said. "Where did you find those words?"

"I...I...I'm not really sure. Maybe I read them? We were talking about mercy in class—maybe that's where I saw it."

"I don't think so, honey. I congratulated Mr. Murwata on choosing this play to teach the concepts of mercy and justice. He said he was as surprised as we were to hear you quote it." Katie's father said.

"Oh, well! I probably found it someplace else, then," Katie said, trying hard to sound like the whole thing was no big deal.

"First it's Burbage, now it's the *Merchant of Venice*...I don't know about you, young lady. You seem to be turning into a Shakespeare scholar. What are you reading these days that you'd find this stuff?"

"Nothing, Dad! I'm only reading regular stuff. Honest! You know. The Harry Potter stuff and all..." Katie knew that she sounded like she was trying too hard, but she couldn't help herself.

"Maybe she could be in your play this summer, Mr. Farrell, you know, did the Merchant guy have any kids?" Corky was usually able to distract most adults. But she knew Mr. Farrell was an especially tough customer.

"What about you, Corky? Play your cards right, and when you come up this summer, I could make sure to have a part for you. You, too, Lily"

"Is it too late to switch to a different play, now? I'm thinkin' that a more modern play might be more interesting." Corky didn't want to give up until Katie's father had been dragged completely away from the subject of Shakespeare.

"I think Corky wants to do a crime play, Mr. Farrell, so she can solve some mysteries."

"Well, I think you girls need to take a little time off from your sleuthing. You need to be kids and spend time hiking in the mountains and swimming."

"We know, Dad. Lily and Corky are coming up for a week in June, then two weeks in July and August, right?" Then she spotted Jordan and her parents standing near the doorway.

Katie grabbed her friends' hands and started pulling them toward Jordan. "We're going to go see Jordan, Mom, okay? We just want to see if she's all right."

"Okay, but don't take too long. We've got a lot of packing to do. We're leaving tomorrow morning, honey, and the last time I checked your room I didn't see much progress in getting ready."

As they rushed away toward Jordan, they were relieved that Corky had done such a good job distracting Katie's father, but nervous about what to say to Jordan.

"Do you think she'll still be in with the cool kids?" Lily whispered.

"D'ya think the cool kids will still be in this school, after what they did?" Corky said.

"I heard my parents talking last night," Katie said. "They heard that Mr. Morgan was fixing it so that Brittany wouldn't get in any trouble."

"What do you mean 'fixing it', like she broke a desk or something? How can that be right?" Corky practically screamed.

"Shhh! Corky! Let's talk about it later, okay?" Lily said.

Jordan saw them approaching, and seemed so unsure of herself that Katie was overcome with pity for her.

"Hi, Jordan," she said cheerfully. "How are you?"

"Hi guys…I…I'm…okay, I guess…you know, with what happened and all." She stood there, no longer one of the cool kids, but just a girl who seemed very sad and alone.

"What did the police say? Did you have to go to the station, or did they come to your house?" Corky was so curious that she hardly noticed the shocked looks on the faces of her friends. Katie gulped. Lily rolled her eyes. Jordan, though, didn't seem to mind talking about it.

"It wasn't too bad. They were actually pretty nice to me, but I think they want to charge that guy from the ranch with something really big." She sighed and smiled weakly. "I don't know what they're going to do about Brit and Mackenzie…I haven't talked to them since the…you know, since the day at the ranch."

"But you did the right thing, Jordan. You were brave to do it, too." Katie said.

The four girls stood nervously in a very awkward silence, everyone wanting to say something, but nobody knowing what to say. Jordan's parents, eager to get out of the room, rescued the girls from their dilemma by calling to Jordan, telling her it was time to leave.

Katie, Corky and Lily watched Jordan leave, walking between her parents. Her shoulders drooped and she was looking down, avoiding the stares of other classmates. Word had gotten out that she knew something about what had happened, and there were even rumors that she was one of the students directly involved.

"Did you ever think Jordan would seem so…um…"

"Uncool?" Corky asked, finishing Katie's thought.

"And sad, like she didn't have any friends," Lily said.

Tomorrow we leave for Hyde Park! I can't wait to get there and see the trees and the garden—and I can't wait to help Dad with his play. Lily and Corky and I made a pact that we're going to try to time travel together. When they come up to visit this summer, we're going to start planning. It's scary, but Tuffy and I found our way back once. We just don't know how we got back to 1596 in the first place! I'm sure we could all get back again…but what if we each wind up in a different place and time? We need to do more research, like the website said. Corky wants to travel back to April, when the cool kids started bullying Henry. She

277

thinks she could stop the accident from happening, but I don't think that's the way it works. Anyway, Henry is all better, and he's going to England next week with his family! We're all in eighth grade! I can't imagine what it will be like to be an eighth grader! Time will tell...

Want to know more?

Check out the website Katie and her friends found. The web address is www.timeandtimeagainandagain.com. You'll find:

- ▶ Links to websites where you can learn more about Shakespeare's England, Romania and important trials in American history;

- ▶ A bulletin board where you can post your thoughts and ideas about "Time Will Tell";

- ▶ Information about upcoming books featuring Katie Farrell and her friends.